A Bend in the Ganges

Also by Manohar Malgonkar

THE PRINCES

A Bend
in the Ganges

A NOVEL BY

MANOHAR MALGONKAR

At a bend in the Ganges, they paused to
take a look at the land they were leaving.

—RAMAYANA

New York · The Viking Press

Published in 1965 by The Viking Press, Inc.
625 Madison Avenue, New York, N.Y. 10022

Library of Congress catalog card number: 65-12031
Printed in U.S.A. by The Colonial Press Inc.

For Vibakar

This non-violence, therefore, seems to be due mainly to our helplessness. It almost appears as if we are nursing in our bosoms the desire to take revenge the first time we get the opportunity. Can true, voluntary non-violence come out of this seeming forced non-violence of the weak? Is it not a futile experiment I am conducting? What if, when the fury bursts, not a man, woman, or child is safe and every man's hand is raised against his neighbour?

—M. K. GANDHI

Author's Note

Only the violence in this story happens to be true; it came in the wake of freedom, to become a part of India's history. What was achieved through non-violence brought with it one of the bloodiest upheavals of history: seventeen million people had to flee, leaving their homes; nearly half a million were killed; over a hundred thousand women, young and old, were abducted, raped, mutilated.

Nothing else is drawn from life. The characters, even the ones shown as holding a particular office at a particular time, are fictitious: Patrick Mulligan is not intended to portray an official of the Cellular Jail, nor is Colonel Yamaki the wartime Japanese commander of the Andamans.

M. D. M.

A glossary of Hindustani words is provided at the end of this book.

Contents

A Bend in the Ganges

[1]

A Ceremony of Purification

THEY were burning British garments. The fire that raged in the market square was just one of hundreds of thousands of similar fires all over the country. On one side was the platform, the enormous tricolour flag with the spinning-wheel providing its backdrop. On the milk-white cloth spread on the platform, flanked by a dozen or so solemn-faced men in white caps, squatted the dark, frail man who was the leader of their struggle.

But the market-day crowd held back, suspicious, unwilling to be branded as followers of Gandhi—agitators and non-cooperators. The police stood in groups, guarding the outlets, swinging their studded lathis. Most of the group round the fire were young; students from schools and colleges. There seemed to be just as many girls as boys. It was they who shouted the slogans:

"Boycott British goods! Mahatma Gandhi-ki jai! Victory to Mahatma Gandhi!"

From the back of the crowd, Gian Talwar watched the fire and the men on the dais. So that was Mahatma Gandhi. For Gian this was a big moment. For years he had been hearing the name, Gandhi, the man who had come to represent true greatness to every Indian; the apostle of truth and non-violence.

Now at last he was seeing him.

The Mahatma was spinning, his right hand twirling a brass takli, the spinning-wheel, his left feeding it with little candles of cotton-wool, going up and down with the thread. He peered alternately at his takli and at the crowd, restlessly turning his head in small jerks. He did not look as solemn as the others on the platform. There was a twinkle in his eye, though it may have been the reflection from the fire.

Unfortunately it was a Monday, Gandhiji's day of silence; otherwise he would certainly have addressed a few words to them. It

3

was his lieutenant, the slim young man with the sad eyes in the refined, handsome face, who got up to speak. He spoke in English, with a cultured, public-school accent.

"Sisters and brothers, I should actually address you as soldiers—for we are all soldiers. Soldiers in the army of liberation. Our aim is to free our motherland, India, from the British, and we shall not rest till victory is won.

"But we are a new kind of soldier. Our weapons are truth and non-violence. Our war shall be fought only by peaceful means. Gandhiji has shown us the path. But make no mistake; our non-violence is the non-violence of the brave, arising not from cowardice but from courage, demanding greater sacrifices than ordinary fighting men are called upon to make. We are aware that there are in our country those who do not believe in our methods, those who aim to achieve freedom by resorting to violence. Such men have no place in our army, however patriotic they may be."

The thread lengthening on the spinning-wheel broke. The Mahatma wet his finger against his tongue and rejoined it expertly, almost without looking. Once again the wheel began to spin.

"And today we are gathered here," the earnest young man went on, "almost to administer a rebuke to some of our own brethren: those who, instead of opposing foreign rule, are content to remain under it—captives who hug the chain and vie with each other in imitating their masters. They wear clothes made of imported materials, cotton and wool and silk, helping the economy of the nation that rules us. It is only by renouncing all British-made goods, by wearing clothes made out of materials produced in this country—wearing them proudly and defiantly— that we shall foster the economy of our own country, defeat its poverty.

"Those of us who wear clothes of British materials help to pay the administrators who are sent to rule over us, to buy the rifles and bayonets for the soldiers who hold us in captivity, to arm the police who now surround us. But let us not be intimidated by the police or their lathis. Let us persuade our friends and our families to boycott British goods, to make bonfires of the garments that bear the taint of our shame. Let them come forward, bring their hats and coats and shirts and ties, to add fuel to this fire—the fire that has its counterpart in all our villages and towns, the fire that will purify us, will burn out all that is within us that does not conform with truth and non-violence. But remember:

there must be no coercion, no intimidation, used in carrying out this message.

"Boycott British goods! that is the message. I particularly ask those of you who are hovering behind, undecided, to come forward. Let us fling away our fear. Our fear of the police itself is a reflection on our national status. It brands us as a subject race. In a free land the police are only servants of the people, not instruments for imposing the law of a foreign land, whom the citizens have to fear. Let us come forward to make our offering. Let it not be said that while the trail to freedom was being blazed all over the country, we stood back through fear of the police.

"The path of ahimsa is not for cowards; in true non-violence, there is no room for timidity. Just as we are this day throwing away in this fire our garments made of imported materials, so should we be making an offering of everything within us which conflicts with our dedication to true non-violence—ahimsa.

"Mahatma Gandhi-ki jai."

He folded his hands to the crowd and sat down in his accustomed place on the right of the Mahatma, who stopped his spinning for a brief moment to place a hand on his shoulder.

Almost without knowing it, Gian Talwar found himself repeating the slogan. "Mahatma Gandhi-ki jai! Victory to non-violence!" He took off his dark-blue and yellow football blazer and began to push his way through the crowd towards the fire.

The blazer, made of imported English material, was his most elegant garment. Indeed, it was his most prized possession. As he clutched it to his chest, it felt soft and warm, like some furry animal. He felt a sudden desire to turn back, to fight down his irrational impulse, but it was already too late. The men crowding round the fire were making way for him, shouting encouragement. He stepped forward and flung the coat into the flames.

"Shabash!" the crowd yelled. "Well done!"

But the rank and file of the spectators were still hesitant; looking at each other for courage, casting furtive glances at the white police sergeants, muttering amongst themselves. And then a sudden silence swept over them as a woman broke through the line, tall and dark and elegantly dressed, her clothes making her stand out in the crowd like an exotic bird of fine plumage. Over a flame-coloured sari, she wore a knee-length coat of some expensive fur. She strode up to the fire without looking to right or left. For a moment she stood still, her head bowed, while her fur

coat, her sari, and her blue-black hair glinted with the light from
the fire. Then she took off her coat and hurled it into the fire.

For a moment the silence continued, and then, as though
some valve had been released, they broke into tumultuous cheers.
"Bharat-mata-ki jai! Victory to Mother India!" They surged forward, vying with each other to fling their coats and caps and
shirts into the fire. "Mahatma Gandhi-ki jai! Bharat-mata-ki jai!"

Gian trembled with emotion as he watched the woman standing by the fire, framed by its glow. Like the goddess of fire, he
thought, and then the bright patch of colour was lost in the
milling crowd, leaving him with the impression that she had
never been there, or that she had vanished into the flames.

But the reek of the burning fur was all around them. It was
still there when the meeting came to an end. Gandhiji put away
his takli and gave them a quick grin. He folded his hands in a
reverent namaskar. Then he rose to go.

"Mahatma Gandhi-ki jai!" Gian found himself muttering.
"Bharat-mata-ki jai! The path of ahimsa is not for cowards." The
words were almost like a private prayer.

[2]

The Green Flash at Sunset

THE floods were almost predictable. They came every year, late in June, soon after the colleges opened for the summer term.

The hot land of the Punjab waited for them, fissured and cracked with dryness. It quivered thirstily in the brassy glare of the summer sky, pinning its faith to the sudden affluence of the floods. The canals were like sunken lanes, the five rivers mean little trickles of brown liquid, the rains of the preceding monsoon a faint memory.

That was when the floods came like an answer to a prayer, flushing out the canals and the river-bed, overflowing the banks, ensuring yet another season of abundance.

Somewhere high up in the Himalayas, near the source of the rivers four hundred miles away, the fierceness of the sun had caused the vast piles of winter snow to melt. Millions of millions of snow crystals were transformed into drops of water. Natural dams stirred and shifted and collapsed. And three days later, the five rivers of the Punjab roared like monsters, glutted with water.

In Duriabad as elsewhere, men and women went to the river banks on bicycle and on foot, in tongas and rickshaws and bullock carts. They watched the swollen, hissing river that had humbled the summer and the sun, thankful and elated.

Some of them even went as far as Birchi-bagh, thirty miles to the north where, a hundred years earlier, the river Chenab had suddenly changed its course. There you could see the old river-bed, its deep, clean-cut white and pink banks gleaming with specks of mica, waiting for the largesse of the flood, for a momentary fulfilment, when some of the surplus water found its way into the old channel, making gorgeous blue pools in the sand. It was a favourite spot for swimming and picnicking. Barely half a mile away, you could see the main course of the Chenab, drunk,

7

angry, contemptuous, and vaguely frightening because it was believed that the river was once again ready to change course.

But a picnic in the sands of the old river-bed at Birchi-bagh was for those who had motor cars. Gian himself had never been there. He was sitting in the reading room, looking at the *Civil and Military Gazette*, when Debi-dayal came up to him.

"Some of us are going to Birchi-bagh this afternoon. Would you like to come?" he asked. And then he added, "If you have no other plans, that is."

No, he had no other plans; boys of his sort never had any other plans. They sat in their rooms, pretending to work because they had nowhere to go.

Gian thanked Debi-dayal, trying to sound offhand, wishing, for a moment, that he had thought of saying that he did have other plans.

"Bring your swimming things," said Debi. "It is quite safe to swim in the old river-bed."

"Thanks," Gian said again, and, as soon as the other had left, went round trying to borrow a pair of swimming trunks because his own pair, cheap, darned, and faded, would not do.

He wondered what had made Debi-dayal ask him. Debi was one of the important boys at college; he, Gian, just one of the students. Debi was the only son of Dewan-bahadur Tekchand Kerwad. His family had lived in Duriabad for over a hundred years. They owned large tracts of land along the canals, they owned the Kerwad Construction Company, and the Kerwad Housing Development, and God knows what else—even a street in the cantonment was named after them: Kerwad Avenue.

And there was Kerwad House, said to be the best residential building west of Lahore. Hitherto he had seen it only from a distance, standing red-roofed in the grove of trees bordering the river, secluded, opulent, forbidding. From the gate, you could get only a glimpse of the house, cream and green and red, through the foliage of the gul-mohor, casuarina, and eucalyptus trees bordering the drive; the high, pillared portico built for the days before American-made cars replaced two-horsed carriages as the status-symbol of Indian merchants; the garden tended by a dozen malis, prim as a chessboard.

That day he saw the house itself. They were driven into the porch and taken to the sitting room upstairs for tea, where white-coated servants carried in trays loaded with cakes and sandwiches and pakoras and jellebies. Gian had never tasted such food before, nor had he drunk his tea out of a cup as dainty and weightless and frail.

Debi-dayal's father and mother had gone to Lahore for the day, but his sister was there. It was Sundari who sat over the heavy silver tea service, self-possessed, cool, faintly perfumed, and breathtakingly lovely.

Gian did not know any of the other guests. There was Singh, a taciturn, bearded man with dark, hypnotic eyes; a Sikh who wore a turban and a steel bangle on his wrist and yet could not have been a Sikh because he smoked. There was another man, called Basu, who spoke with a pronounced Bengali accent. Neither of them were from the college.

There was another girl too, a friend of Sundari's, dressed in salwar and kamis, a typical Punjabi girl, lush, fair, and provocatively full-bodied, with her features slightly overemphasized; fiercely attractive even if you knew that she was going to be overweight at twenty-five and middle-aged at thirty.

But Gian had no eyes for the other girl, or for any of the others. Merely being close to Sundari made him feel sad and happy in turn. That the proverbial only daughter of wealthy parents should be so charming to him—a scholarship boy from her brother's college—made him wonder, was she being friendly or merely condescending?

"Why did you ask Debi to have the dog tied up?" she was asking Singh. "Spindle is such a little dog, and so friendly."

A minute or so earlier, Spindle, the dachshund, had been carried away, protesting, to Debi-dayal's room.

"Dogs make me feel nervous," Singh told her. "Once I was trailed by police dogs—for miles. It was the sort of thing one never forgets."

For a moment they were all silent, each trying to show that there was nothing out of the ordinary in his explanation, while Singh went on stirring his tea with concentration, his head turned away, as though his thoughts were still in the past.

"Do you think it would be possible to see the museum," Gian asked Debi-dayal, "since your father is away?"

It was Sundari who answered. 'Of course! But you could have seen it even if Abaji had been here. He would have loved to show you round, I am sure. Now you will have to put up with me as a guide, and I know nothing about bronzes."

They left the others still drinking tea, smoking and talking of the picnic to be held later in the evening, and went to the room at the end of the veranda to see the collection of brass, bronze, and copper antique statues which was said to have no equal outside the Prince of Wales's Museum in Bombay.

It was cool in the room, because of the high roof, and the light was dim, since the windows had been shuttered. At first Gian was aware only of being alone with the girl in the dimness, her bare arm touching his. Soft as the petals of a champak flower, he thought to himself, remembering a favourite simile of the Sanskrit poets.

And then, as his eyes grew accustomed to the dark, he saw the statues, all at the same time, and forgot about the girl. The gods and the goddesses and demons of the Hindu pantheon came crowding in on all sides, as though revealed to a disciple in one flash; dancing, laughing, caressing, fighting, killing, blessing, cursing, meditating, copulating, grotesque, frozen stiff in a moment of action, and yet with a compelling sense of motion, of living and breathing.

For a moment it was he who was the statue, lifeless, ageless, unbreathing, and the images that surrounded him were flowing with life, acting out a hymn of creation, the cycle of life and death, the drama of procreation and destruction. He stared, unblinking, abandoning himself to a higher consciousness as during a moment of prayer.

"Hi! What's wrong? Are you all right?"

The voice seemed to come from far away, from the depths of the earth, a part of the timelessness of the moment. But it had an urgency, an almost tearful trembling, which broke the spell. He shook himself. The girl was holding him by both shoulders, and her eyes were staring with alarm.

"Are you all right?" she was asking. "What happened?"

He blinked at her, a statue that had come to life, a face that was a mixture of irritation and anxiety, so beautiful, so near. He wanted to put his arms around her, to pull her close to him, smother her with kisses.

"Yes, of course," he said. "Of course, I am all right. It is just that . . . just that for a moment I seemed to black out."

"It's the heat," she said, releasing her grip on his shoulders. "Come on, let's go and join the others."

The relief in her face was so visible that he did not remind her that she had promised to show him round the museum. He followed her out of the door.

By the time they reached Birchi-bagh, Gian was his own self again, even though he could not bring himself to share the easy, lighthearted mood of the others. Debi-dayal stopped the car under a gnarled kikar tree on the bank of the old channel, and they carried their cushions and baskets of food and an icebox covered with felt to the pool in which they were going to bathe. Beyond the farther bank, no more than three hundred yards away, was the main river, now swollen and in full glory, flowing with speed as it emerged from the low hills in the north.

First the girls went and changed into their swimming costumes. When they came back and began to splash about in the shallow pool, the men went off with their towels and swimming trunks, each to a private spot in the bend of the river.

When Gian emerged in his dark green borrowed trunks, he found that all the others were staring at him. For a moment he wondered if there was a tear in his trunks, and then realized that they were staring at the sacred thread round his neck.

There was a moment of embarrassment. One or two of them tried to look as though nothing had happened. Debi-dayal got up to swim. And then Bhupinder, the other girl, began to giggle and came to their rescue.

"Oh, how sweet to be seeing a real sacred thread!" she squealed, and the ripples of fair flesh left out by her tight costume shook with her mirth. And the others all joined in her laughter, trying to surmount the awkwardness that had suddenly come over them.

But he did not understand. The laughter had stung. Their well-meaning gesture was outside the borders of his experience. He turned away from them, hot with shame, and went running towards the main river where the others would not dare to follow. He dived in, not surfacing till his lungs were ready to burst, and then struck out for the other bank, which could be seen only as a low line of trees against the water.

And there, far out in the rushing waters of the Chenab, out of sight of the others, he took off his janwa and allowed it to float away.

One thing about him at which no one could laugh was his swimming; all they were doing as they paddled about in the "safe" pools, wearing their flashy imported swimming trunks, was to show off their half-baked Weissmuller crawl to the girls. Not one of them would have ventured into the swollen current of the main river.

When, an hour or so later, he rejoined them on the sand, the spell of awkwardness was still there. Their glances kept straying towards his bare neck. But this time no one said anything about his janwa, even though they could not have failed to notice that he had removed it. Nor did they laugh at him.

But the day was ruined for Gian. He felt an inward resentment towards the others. He was the outsider, the poor college student asked out on the rich boys' outing, like something out of Sandford and Merton, he thought. He came from an orthodox Hindu background; in his world the sacred thread was still sacred. They, on the other hand, represented the forward generation, enlightened by Westernization. Admittedly, they were all scrupulously polite to him, careful not to appear condescending. But it was clear to him that they had nothing in common. He wondered why he had been asked.

And almost in answer to his question, they began to talk of politics.

The girls had gone off to change into their saris. The sun, now spent and shapeless, hung over the sand dunes in the west. The breeze which swept over the barren landscape had lost some of its fierceness. The stunted, dried-up palms along the river-bank and the lacy babool and kikar trees beyond completed the pattern of the Punjab landscape in hot weather.

"Why do you wear khaddar?" Singh asked.

Why did he wear khaddar, the rough homespun of the Indian peasant? Gian almost laughed. It was the uniform of the Indian National movement; it proclaimed you a soldier in the army that was dedicated to truth and non-violence.

"I am a follower of Gandhi," Gian said.

"Oh my God!" Singh said softly. "And what does that mean?"

"It means that I am one of those who believe that India should be freed from British rule—"

"Gandhi is the enemy of India's national aspirations," Singh pronounced, and after that no one said anything for a long time.

In the distance, a car was going along the road to Lahore, a brown beetle trailed by its own cloud of dust. Idly they watched it until it disappeared from view, until the dust cloud cleared.

Then, from the icebox, Debi took out bottles of beer, which he opened and poured into glasses.

Gian had never drunk beer in his life, but did not want the others to know it. "Would you like some lemonade in your beer?" Debi-dayal asked him.

He shook his head. "No, thank you."

They raised their glasses. "Here's to the Freedom Fighters!" Singh said.

"Freedom Fighters!" Debi-dayal and Basu repeated.

So that was what they were drinking to, the scion of the Kerward family and his friends, all dressed in fashionable swimming trunks and drinking iced beer imported from Germany. The dreaded name hung in the air, like a blob of oil on water. Gian drank his beer in slow sips, trying to get used to its bitterness, adjusting his mind to the mood of his companions, knowing now that they were revolutionaries.

"Look at the sun!" Basu said. "In a minute it will have set; then there will be the green flash."

They all turned their heads to see the sunset, the extravagant display of colour, the flamingo sky with the scarlet sun only half submerged and the pink-and-gold expanse of sand. And then they were aware that Singh had jumped to his feet and stood silhouetted in the sunset, that he was talking to them.

"The sun set for us a hundred and fifty years ago," he said in a dry whisper. "When the British took over the country, the sun died. For us the sun will rise again only on the day of our freedom. And to that sun I now ask you to drink. To the sunrise of our freedom!"

Solemnly, they all rose to their feet. "To the sunrise of our freedom," they repeated after him. "To the sunrise of our freedom!"

They sat down again and the warm sand shifted under them with soft crunching sounds. They did not see the green flash; it must have come and gone. For a time they watched the pink segment of sky where the sun had gone down, the sun that would rise for them only on the day of freedom.

A slight shiver ran over Gian's body. He realized that Singh was speaking to him again.

"Tell me, how did you happen to become a follower of Gandhi?"

How indeed? Was it merely a moment of weakness—the

heady glow brought on by an act of sacrifice, the reckless discarding of a much-valued blazer? Or the sight of a beautiful woman throwing away her fur coat into a fire?

"Any patriot, any man with any feelings for the liberation of the country is a follower of Mahatma Gandhi," he said.

"No, no!" Singh shook his head with scorn. "I certainly am not one of his followers, and yet I hope I qualify as a patriot."

"Have you ever met Gandhi?" Debi-dayal asked.

"Not actually met him. But I have seen him. He was like—like a god," Gian said, suddenly carried away. "He alone can lead us to victory. Even Nehru has become his disciple . . . the whole country. If there is any hope for us of achieving freedom, it is through his movement. Through non-violence."

Singh shook his head from side to side. "What harm the man has done with his hypnotic powers! Tell me of a single instance in history, of just one country which has been able to shake off foreign rule without resorting to war, to violence?"

Gian felt angry with himself as he groped for an answer. He looked at Singh, the Sikh who kept his beard and had laughed at his sacred thread and who was now trying to pin him down in argument. "Gandhiji is a god," he said in sudden defiance. "Only he can bring freedom to India."

"Just one single instance," Singh went on as though he had not heard. "Just one." He shook his head and answered his own question. "No, there isn't one. Freedom has to be won; it has to be won by sacrifice; by giving blood, not by giving up the good things of life and wearing white caps and going to jail. Look at America—the United States! They went to war. Turkey! Even our own Shivaji. Non-violence is the philosophy of sheep, a creed for cowards. It is the greatest danger to this country."

His voice was high-pitched, earnest as an angry preacher's. The faint glow of the sky falling on his heavy, bearded face made him look like a prophet—a prophet, or a man crazed with some inner hatred.

"No," Singh repeated. "It has happened nowhere; it can't happen here! Gandhi, by weakening the spirit of men, making us all into sheep and cattle, will only multiply the sacrifice. A million shall die, I tell you—a million! For each man who should have died in the cause of freedom, Gandhi will sacrifice ten. That is what non-violence will do to this country."

The wind and the sand and the glow of an already-dead sun

gave greater meaning to his words: he was like a prophet shouting a warning to an unheeding world. "A million shall die—a
million!"

It was the sort of thing they always talked about, and yet
today it was not the same. Gian felt a quite unreasoning sensation of revulsion, a creeping wave of hatred for this strange man
with the beard—or was it fear? It was the face of evil, the voice
of evil.

He shook himself, resentful of the other's hypnotic power over
him, searching for facts to counter his contorted arguments, angry at finding himself with no convincing answer.

"How seriously do you yourself believe in it?" Debi-dayal
asked.

"In non-violence? With all my being," Gian told him
defiantly. "Only the Mahatma can lead us to freedom, through
the path of non-violence, the creed of ahimsa!"

Singh slowly shook his head from side to side and clucked his
tongue. "It was a waste of time," he muttered to Debi-dayal.
"We should have known. College boys fall more easily for Gandhi's type of movement, it is much more face-saving. They shelter their cowardice behind the tenets of non-violence, and refuse
to rouse themselves to any form of positive action."

"Ahimsa is the noblest of creeds," Gian retorted, stung by
Singh's taunts. "There can be nothing more sacred. No man has
the right to raise his hand against another, whatever the provocation. I shall never do it. It takes greater courage; non-violence is
not for the weak."

"Ah," interrupted Basu, "there are the girls!"

It was good to see them rounding the corner of the bank.
They came back, laughing and quite unaware that, as far as the
men were concerned, the day had been ruined. They busied
themselves putting out the packets of kebab and rotis and achar
and tandoori chickens on the cotton khes spread between them.
Basu lit a fire to heat the water for the coffee. The moon came
out, lush and pale lemon, and Debi-dayal poured more beer into
the glasses. The big girl began to hum, weaving another kind of
spell round them, and they all began to clap their hands softly
and joined her song.

[3]

The Homecoming

THE train wound through the familiar hills, chuffing asthmatically over the climb, clanking and jolting at the turns. The rhythm of the engine changed. Now there would be the whistle for the Konshet level crossing. Pachwad station could not be more than five miles away.

The whistle came, two notes of remembered music. Gian had been saving the last cigarette in the pack; now he took it out and lit it, drawing in the smoke and filling his chest before letting it roll away slowly in the breeze.

This was to be his last cigarette for nearly three months. During the vacation he would have to give up smoking. Aji would be quite shocked if she were to find out that he smoked. But he wasn't really worried about that; it was so easy to shock one's grandmother. She would have been still more shocked had she known that he had quite given up wearing the janwa at college.

A frown shadowed his face as he thought of that day by the river nearly a year before, when he discarded his sacred thread. Now the janwa was back, because of his grandmother; and he must give up cigarettes during the holidays because of his brother, Hari.

Not that Hari would have minded; he was quite certain of that; Hari never seemed to mind what Gian did. He would only have laughed indulgently and tried to plead with Aji that any college boy in his senior year was bound to take to smoking because it helped concentration. He would even have suggested increasing his pocket-money to enable him to buy cigarettes without cutting down on something else. Somehow he would have found the money, too.

Oddly enough, that was why it was so important that Hari

16

should never find out, Hari who had had to give up schooling when their father died and whose respect for learning was so exaggerated. Hari had made do with three dhotis a year, wore patched chaplis, and had not bought a warm coat for himself as long as he could remember, so that Gian should be able to go to college and live there as the other boys did.

Not that Hari could ever have any idea of how some of the other boys did live at college—at least not those who really mattered. They played tennis, they spoke familiarly of dance bands and of expensive restaurants, and of shopping at Whiteways and the Army and Navy Stores; they wore flannels and silk and shark-skin, they went out with girls; they were rich, flashy, self-assured, some even had their own cars, like Debi-dayal.

Being at college was not just a matter of studying for your degree; learning was only part of what college had to offer, and not a very important part at that. Somehow, to absorb all that college had to offer, it was important to be a part of that glittering inner circle, the rich, sporting set. Most of the time you looked at the circle only from outside, as if gazing into the windows of Whiteways.

And yet, under the surface, they were all rather nice people, not at all unfriendly or snooty. If they kept themselves to themselves, it was because they were self-sufficient, conscious that they constituted the higher order; when they spoke to you, they did so with a heartwarming lightness and lack of condescension. They were brittle, gay, impulsive; and if, once in a while, they asked you to join them, it was with unaffected casualness, as though speaking to one of their own set. Like that afternoon when Debi-dayal had invited him to come and see the flood. They even took you to their homes and introduced you to their sisters.

And then you did something silly, like being discovered wearing the sacred thread, brown with use, and not being able to join in the laughter of the others because in your shame you did not realize that it was just their way of putting you at your ease. So you went and did something even more childish, like diving into the flooded river and striking out, fighting against the current, showing off your fast, flashy, fisherman's glide against their clumsy paddling in the shallow channel that had been discarded by the river, and shaming them in return.

In return for what? Their hospitality and kindness?

No, not shaming them, really, but somehow accentuating your own sense of not belonging. He would never behave like that if they ever asked him again.

If.

And yet, deep within oneself, one knew perfectly well that it was wrong to hanker to belong to Debi-dayal's and his sister's set —with their enormous radiogramophones, carpeted staircases, and servants gorging on the remains of elaborate teas. They did not have to spend their Sundays in the dim hostel rooms, waiting for the dal and rice and vegetables of the evening meals which only filled your stomach but did not assuage your hunger. And they did not have to "sign out" once every week from even those meals to be able to save money for cigarettes, and for yet another meal whenever they went to see a film, queuing up for the cheapest seats.

And they did not have to wear the cheapest khaddar clothes, to be thankful that khaddar had now become synonymous with nationalism.

The frown on Gian's face deepened. The gap between the world he secretly longed for and the world he fitted into was wide enough, but, by the standards of his particular background, it was a rare achievement for him to be at college at all. For the likes of him, it was enough that they were at college—it cost every bit of a hundred rupees a month to keep him there, and it would have been impossible unless his brother Hari had given up the most elementary comforts of middle-class life.

All these years, he had taken everything that was done for him for granted. Now the thought of his brother's sacrifices was vaguely uncomfortable. Somewhere under the surface, there was an insult in it too, that one should have to owe so much in life to the kindness and self-denial of another.

The train was already slowing down. Just before it took the last turn into the platform, Gian flicked away his cigarette and leaned out of the window to see if the bullock cart had arrived. It was there, as he knew it would be, in the usual place under the jack-fruit tree at the back of the station yard, the two matched, rust-coloured bullocks, Raja and Sarja, unyoked but not lying down. As always, they looked well-fed and sleek, their coats glistening, the rows of brass bells on their collars gleaming dully. And there was Tukaram, the cartman, in his faded red turban, perched on his seat and screwing his body to peer at the train, his hands shading his eyes against the sun, his brown legs dangling, shining like molasses.

Tukaram had been with the family ever since Gian could remember. As a young man, he had dandled Gian on his knees and carried him on his shoulders to school when it rained and taught him all that he knew about swimming and climbing the coconut palms and had dosed him with bitter chiraita juice every Sunday morning "to keep your stomach from going sour."

Now he was grown up and gnarled and grey, the trusted family servant; simple, unlettered, devoted, domineering, and quite indispensable. He still addressed Gian with the familiar "tu" of equality instead of the "aap" that was customary from a servant, and generally acted as if Gian were still a small boy who must be made to drink his chiraita juice every now and then for his own good. At times it was difficult not to be annoyed by Tukaram's familiarity, even his air of condescension. But of course there was no question of telling the old man where he got off.

On the platform, Gian could see his brother, standing close to the wall, holding himself back, the picture of rusticity; like a farmer in his going-to-town clothes, thought Gian, or like the man in the "Grow More Food" poster: brown and sturdy, his face hard, handsome, weathered but not wrinkled, earthy, anxious, wholly out of place in the bustle of a railway-station platform.

There was still time for one last, lingering moment of objectivity, the pause before going over a barrier, of making last-minute adjustments for the transformation from college to home: from lectures and cinemas and professors in long black coats and tasselled pugris to bullock carts and rice fields; from the honk of American-made cars and neon lights to the coo-ees of the cattlemen and the sombre loneliness of the forest; from the giggles and glances of willowy girls to the withered grandmother in the prayer room.

He took another look at his brother, who was still craning to locate him: the man in the short, homespun jacket done up with laces, the cheap white turban, the home-washed dhoti reaching just below the knees, the sturdy farmhand's legs, the heavy, studded chaplis caked with dust, the gnarled, horny feet. Hari looked so much more like the cartman perched on the yoke-seat than like the home-coming college boy in the milk-white clothes and the sunglasses. Was that how other people saw him?

The thought, fleeting as it was, left its own smear of guilt. That was no way in which to think of Hari. Gian waved his hand to him and answered his quick smile of recognition. He pushed open the door and jumped out of the still-running train. He ran forward to meet his brother.

Hari carried the bedroll; Gian carried the fabric suitcase and the reed bag containing his college books. By the time they came to the cart, Tukaram was already holding up the yoke and trying to coax the bullocks to come under it. He turned his head and gave Gian a sharp, searching look.

"What's the matter with your eyes, Chote-baba?" he asked.

Gian did not like being addressed as Chote-baba, the little boy. "Why, nothing," he told him.

"Then why the glasses?"

"They are for the sun," Hari explained.

"Glasses at your age . . . not even married yet! Your grandmother can still thread a needle."

"Oh, you leave Chote-baba alone," Hari told him. "You don't have to study in college, read all the books he has to read—look at all those books, a whole bagful!"

"And the white clothes," Tukaram went on. "Have you become a Congress-wallah?—joined the cranks who want to send away the sahibs? What will we do without the sahibs? They don't take bribes, like our people." He clucked his tongue in mock-disgust and turned to his bullocks. "Come on, you fatted tiger-baits!" he shouted. "Can't you see I am waiting? Or do you too need black glasses to see? Ho, ho, Sarja, hoa-hup . . . that's better. Still, still now. Why are you holding back, Raja, son of a black shaitan—hoa-hup!"

There were no milestones along the road, but their village, Konshet, could not have been more than ten miles away from the station. Normally, Raja and Sarja covered the distance in well under three hours, cantering most of the way at their going-home clip, their bells jangling merrily, and once they had accomplished it in exactly two hours. But today they were being held in check. Hari explained that the bullocks were overdue for a reshoeing and he did not want to risk injuring their feet. He sat at the back of the cart, his legs folded under him, having given Gian the more comfortable seat near the cartman. After fidgeting for a time, he jumped out and began to walk behind the cart.

"I was sitting all the time, on the way to the station," he told Gian. "Just want to stretch my legs. I don't seem to get much exercise these days." And he slapped his belly hard with his right hand.

His stomach was flat and hard and all muscle, and the slap made a sound like a mallet on wood. Gian laughed. He knew that Hari had got out of the cart only because he wanted to make the going a little easier for the bullocks. Without a word, he too jumped out and joined his brother.

The road was striped with shade; the thick jungle on both sides was like a wall; the ribbon of sky overhead lost itself in the curve just ahead of them; the culverts arched over the rock-strewn nullahs. Occasionally, there was a minute clearing, a patch where man had pushed the wilderness back and made a rice field. But the fields were now brown and bare because of the summer. The jungle reigned supreme.

That was what one always came back to: the emptiness and the brooding silence of the jungle, just as one always remembered it, unfriendly and ominous. It was home, even though one had begun to feel an outsider in it.

And this silent, thick-set man lost in his own thoughts, walking with the easy, swinging gait of a man used to long distances, was your brother; now bareheaded and coatless because he had put away his turban and coat in the cart, the coat carefully folded for future use, walking because he did not want to risk injuring his bullocks' feet, walking as he must have walked all the way to the station that morning, otherwise there would not have been all that dust on his feet. Your brother, and also your father and mother and uncle and aunt—all kinds of relatives except, of course, your grandmother, who was very much there. . . .

Gian shot a quick glance at his brother; at the man who had given him everything he ever had. He looked older than his twenty-five years, more serious and sullen too. Why didn't he say something, anything at all? Was there something on his mind—something worrying him?

Once again he was conscious of the new feeling within himself, the hard seed of resentment digging beneath the surface, so unaccountable, for how could one bear any sort of grievance towards someone who had done you only good; someone so basically incapable of unkindness—viceless, god-fearing, self-denying; the man who had vowed to remain unmarried until he had put his younger brother through college, the man who wore his janwa all the time, took no food without first doing his pooja, and fasted every Saturday and did not smoke?

The awareness of what Hari had done for him, given up for him, was curiously humbling but did not lessen his bitterness. What right had anyone to burden another with so much that could not be repaid, making him powerless, breaking down his defences with unwavering kindness, saddling him with lifelong self-denial?

He was so lost in thought that he gave a start when his brother turned and spoke to him.

"We won the case," Hari was saying.

For a moment, it did not make sense. "The case" was something they never talked about. It carried the rancid smell of a family feud, recalled past humiliations, defeat, privation. It was always there, a rock in the path to be carefully skirted around. It had gone on for years, like some malignant disease, eating into their resources voraciously, imposing its own hardships. Gian had always thought it so hopeless, he had implored his brother not to appeal when they had lost it in the lower court. But Hari had not listened: with him it was a matter of family honour, almost of life and death.

"Won the . . . Oh, not really! Oh God, how wonderful!" He was thrilled. "How wonderful for you! When did it happen?"

"The judgment was given two days ago—in our favour, by the grace of Shiva. We're having a pooja next week. Both of us will have to sit down for the pooja."

"Everyone in the Big House must be furious."

"Drowned in shame. They cannot show their faces in the streets."

"What about Vishnu-dutt?"

Hari threw his head back and laughed. "Vishnu-dutt, oh, Vishnu-dutt! Like a bull after castration—wild! All sound and fury."

They both laughed again. The cloud had passed away. Gian felt close to his brother now, sharing his triumph. "Remember how he taunted me when we lost in the magistrate's court and you decided to appeal? Vishnu-dutt standing on the banyan-tree platform, twirling his moustache and shouting at me so that everyone could hear. 'Go and tell your brother that your bones will be coals but we will not let Piploda go out of our hands!' "

Gian remembered how he had slunk past with his head lowered, gulping down the taste of defeat, conscious that the whole village was witnessing his humiliation. The taunting, mocking words, the sound of arrogant laughter followed him long after he had turned the corner.

"You should have seen his face when the judgment was given —at the things the judge said about the lower court decision," Hari said, chortling. "Black as in mourning—both father and son, humbled before everyone; they were certainly not twirling their moustaches."

"And to think I had begged you not to appeal," Gian said.

"We were lucky there was a British judge—no question of bribing him, though the Big House must have done their best. Remember that. We in India can get justice only at British hands—never from our own people. They are clean—clean as grains of washed rice."

Was this a reproach to his white garb? Gian wondered.

"How many acres is it?" he asked.

"Ninety-six and a bit, thirty-three under rice. Irrigated land too; oh, yes, plenty of water. Good for two crops a year. The rest is jungle."

"How much—how much would it be worth in money?" Even as he asked the question, he felt he had struck the wrong note. To Hari it had always been a matter of prestige rather than money, of family pride; his was the sort of emotional involvement that could not be reduced to terms of profit and loss.

"Money!" Hari said. "Oh, anything from seven hundred to a thousand a year."

Impulsively Gian grabbed his brother by the hand and thumped his shoulder. "What a wonderful feeling it must be for you, after all you have gone through. Now it won't seem so much of a burden, keeping me at college."

"The new field alone will pay for your studies—I mean, the income from it. We don't have to penny-pinch any more. Besides, there is a good deal of timber too, always good for three thousand rupees, at least."

The scene of the picnic at Birchi-bagh flashed through his

mind; a copper-haired girl in a white sari, her hair blowing in the breeze; the same girl in a flowered swim-suit with drops of water trailing down from her golden limbs. All at once he felt more akin to the others at the picnic, not the last man in the group. A new world was opening at his feet, and it was all made possible by winning the legendary case.

"Three thousand just for the timber?" he asked.

"At least, but that will have to be set aside for paying off the old debts. . . ."

"You mean for my college?"

Hari smiled indulgently. "No, not your college. It was the case; the lawyers' fees and other expenses. But we need not worry about that any longer. I can pay it off just as soon as I have sold the timber."

"I am dying to see Vishnu-dutt's face," Gian said.

"That is not going to be easy. No one has seen him for the last two days. They say his old man has taken to his bed. They cannot be feeling very big in the Big House just now."

The bells of the bullocks must have brought Aji to the doorstep. There she stood, in her skimpy cooking sari, tiny, wrinkled, rigid, one hand gripping the jamb of the door but not for support, the other holding up the heavy brass tray containing the sandalwood paste with which to "purify" her grandson before he entered the house and the popped rice to be showered over his head in fistfuls to propitiate all the evil spirits that might be lurking around.

She looked thinner than ever, Gian thought, as he bent low to let her put a daub of the paste on his forehead. Her skin, clean as if scrubbed with a stone, was almost transparent, like parchment. The two thick gold bangles she always wore looked more out of place than ever on her frail wrists, oddly like a pair of handcuffs. They were smooth with the erosion of lifelong use, as though they had never borne a pattern, and dull from fifty years of bodily contact. She was a wonderful woman, Aji, who had never stepped out of the premises since her husband had died, a remnant from a world which had already perished before he was born, and who seemed to keep going by sheer hard work. How old could she be?—sixty?—sixty-five?

She smeared her finger with the pink paste and made a precise horizontal line on his forehead with it. She showered the popped rice in the four directions, muttering a prayer, beseeching the house gods to keep away the evil spirits. Then she handed the tray to Gian and solemnly cracked the fingers of both hands against her temples.

But it was not easy to laugh at the superstitions of a person like Aji. This was home, and somehow she was the spirit of home, having lived in it from the day it was built, this house that was called the Little House.

"Remove your shoes and wash your feet," Aji reminded him, her voice, as always, strong and resonant, like some stringed instrument. "And then go and do your namaskar to Shiva."

Gian took the tray indoors. He removed his shoes and washed his feet on the stone slab at the back of the house. Then, wearing the wooden khadavs on his feet, he entered the small prayer room to seek the blessings of the family deity: Shiva.

Shiva stood behind a bank of flowers and a burning oil lamp, the nanda-deep or eternal lamp which was always kept lit. He stood in his own circle of flames, his face calm in celestial repose, his pose, caught up in a moment of the tandav dance, angry, threatening, malevolent: the god of destruction dancing the dance of destruction—destruction of what? Of evil, they said. Did that mean the world itself, the human race?

It was foolish, primitive, almost a relic of some barbaric ritual, something like wearing a piece of string round your neck as a badge of purity of caste, this going into a dark prayer room to seek the blessings of Shiva: Shiva, the grotesque image of a dancing devil with four arms sprouting fanwise from his naked shoulders, parading an abnormality like the Siamese twins in a circus, and yet dancing the dance of destruction with such exquisite, quite celestial detachment. Shiva, whom you had to approach with bowed head and folded hands even though you knew that he was nothing but a statue fashioned of an alloy of five metals by some craftsman who had died centuries ago, and sold for money; immune, they said, to corrosion, and indestructible, because of the secret mixture of metals; encrusted with sandalwood paste and red ochre from many generations of prayer, and, on his back, bearing the nick of grandfather Dada's pickaxe.

Not that he, Gian, had ever seen Shiva's back.

And yet, here in Konshet, in the depths of the dark, solid family house, it was easy enough to think of him as a god, to endow the five-metal creation of some mercenary craftsman of long ago with divinity, the power to do good and evil; for had he not brought prosperity to grandfather Dada, seen them through the years of endurance since his father and mother had died in the plague epidemic; had he not, above all, done the impossible and wrested the Piploda field from the stranglehold of the Big House after all these years, triumphed over all the money and the influence and the cunning of Vishnu-dutt and his father?

And yet, if he were a god, might he not have prevented Gian's mother and father from dying so young instead of saving his blessings for their sons; could he not have arranged for the Big House to have surrendered Piploda from a sense of fairness rather than as the result of a bitterly fought-out court action— they who already possessed so much?

But this was not the time to entertain doubts about the godliness of the family god, Shiva, who had worked the miracle and brought them triumph; Shiva, who, in his wrath could burn down the whole world and the worlds above and below it. Gian bowed his head and folded his hands. He lit a piece of camphor from the eternal lamp and with it lit a small bunch of joss-sticks. He stuck the joss-sticks, now exuding their smothering, perfumed smoke, into a bowl of rice. He daubed the sandalwood paste on the pedestal, conscious that he had not had a bath and thus was not pure enough to anoint Shiva's forehead. He gazed directly into Shiva's eyes and folded his hands again.

"O-om, namah-Shivay," he began, mouthing the words of the Sanskrit prayer. "God Shiva, I bow down to thee. . . ."

The dissimilar, almost opposite qualities of the face and the pose troubled him: the face was calm, serene, lost in the enjoyment of the dance; the pose, caught up in the throes of anger, frozen in a particularly violent gesture of the death dance.

Then he found Shiva's face replaced by another, a bearded face equally capable of composure while pronouncing words charged with malevolence: "A million shall die, a million!"

[4]

The Little House

THE pandit had a clean, luminous face, the colour of a polished lime, a short, beaky nose, a razor-slit for a mouth, and pale, rounded eyes. He sat cross-legged on a wooden board, prim and erect and slightly condescending, exuding the importance of a specialist at a consultation. He was reading out from a list. His head and shoulders were draped in a brown shawl, but his legs were bare to the knees.

Aji stood by the door, leaning against the wall. Hari was making the list, with Gian looking over his shoulder; Gian, wholly at home now, caught up in the excitement of preparing for a religious orgy, this thanksgiving pooja to Shiva.

". . . semolina, fifteen seers—medium grain, don't buy the fine variety. Butter, fifteen seers. Sugar, now sugar; you always have to put in more than they say—make it twenty seers. Milk: I don't know where you are going to get all the milk that will be needed . . . at least fifteen seers . . . better to have twenty." The pandit paused and shook his head doubtfully.

"We will find the milk," Aji told him confidently.

"Twenty seers, then. Bananas, twenty-five. Saffron, a rupee's weight; get the Spanish saffron. Cardamoms, double that weight —two rupees. Almonds, one seer, shelled, the Kabuli variety. . . ."

The priest droned on. The list grew longer. Poor Hari, Gian though; this pooja is going to cost at least a hundred rupees. But Hari could afford it now; what was a hundred rupees?

The pandit pecked away, an owl in his dark brown hood, dignified, elderly, sanctified; his voice low-pitched, sonorous, unctuous: betel nuts, coconuts, betel leaves, red ochre, camphor, joss-sticks, cuts of doob grass, tulsi leaves, spinning cotton, til oil —all the requirements of a full scale pooja ending with a gold-bordered dhoti for himself and a silk choli-piece for his wife.

"What date?" Aji inquired.

The priest aimed his nose at Hari and removed his glasses. "About when do you want it?"

"Any time after Tuesday. On Monday we will go over and take possession—get the men to start the ploughing. After that, any day that is auspicious."

The priest took out his religious calendar and put on his glasses. He ran his finger up and down a column of writing, his thin, dry lips moving noiselessly. Dramatically his finger stopped. He stabbed at the page.

"Thursday is best," he pronounced. "After that, Saturday too is good. But Thursday is all gold."

"Then let's have it on Thursday," Aji said. "Are you free?"

He cleared his throat and blinked at her. "I actually had a naming ceremony in Kodli, but I can manage. Finish it off in the morning . . . oh, yes, Thursday will be all right."

He snapped his book shut and stood up. He flapped his shawl and pulled it more tightly around him—the brood-owl fluffing out her wings and drawing them in—and sallied forth on his thin, bare stork legs.

"Now he will go to the Big House and tell them all about it," Gian said. "After all, they are his biggest clients."

"Do them good to know," Hari said. "Do them good to know that we are having a pooja on this scale to celebrate—celebrate their rout. The crooks!"

Hari had every reason to feel bitter towards the inmates of the Big House.

Until their grandfather was a young man, there had been only one house, the Big House—even in those days it was called the Big House. The Talwars of Konshet had always lived as a joint family, all under one roof, a banyan tree taking its strength from the subsidiary roots; and every day, so they said, as many as sixty people would sit down to the afternoon meal in the long central room of the house, glistening rows of friends, relatives, hangers-on, and visitors. The Talwars were hereditary landlords, established, influential, solid, orthodox, and full of prestige.

It was their grandfather, Dada Talwar, who had quarrelled with his father and had separated from the family. He was the younger of two brothers. The cause of the quarrel had been Aji.

He had fallen in love with Aji, who came from the Koshti

caste, and had refused to marry the girl they had chosen for him. The fact that the girl he loved was not even a Brahmin made his lapse really serious. And when his father, Tulsidas, had rebuked him and, in spite of his protests, had gone on with the marriage preparations, he had shocked everyone by running away with the girl he loved.

It was difficult to think of Aji, now in her sixties, as the girl who had made her husband renounce his family; of Aji, steeped in religious ritual, her fine, sharp-featured face shining with character, as the girl who had lived with a man out of wedlock.

As soon as they had got over the initial shock, the family rallied to smother the scandal. The fabric of a united Hindu family had to be preserved at all cost. The erring son was pardoned and received back into the Big House; after a decent interval, his marriage to Aji was solemnized at a quiet ceremony and Aji too came to live in the Big House. She was even given the customary bridal ornaments. The two heavy bracelets of gold that she still wore were relics of her bridal jewellery.

But the crack had been mended only on the surface. Inside the house, in the darkness behind the mardaan or male portion of the house, the rift went on widening. The women of the house had their own methods of ostracism, subtle but effective, and Dada found that his wife was not permitted to enter the family prayer room.

For nearly a year they had lived with the humiliation, Aji smouldering at the sniggers and whispers of the numerous women of the household flaunting their acceptability in the shrine. And when one day Aji found that even the cotton wicks she had prepared for the oil-flame lamp in the prayer room had been rejected by her sister-in-law, there had been an explosion in the dark, all-female world behind the central room; she had rebelled.

Angrily Dada had faced his father. If his wife was not permitted to use the prayer room, he was not willing to remain in the house any longer, he told Tulsidas.

"If you break up the family, you will cause its ruin," his father had pleaded. And yet there was no question of his overruling the women; the family shrine could not be desecrated by a girl from the weavers' caste, a girl who had left her home to live with his son in sin.

It was Brahmin orthodoxy against a woman's vanity; stone

against stone. There was no room for compromise. Dada's father agreed to his leaving the Big House.

Dada had hoped for at least three hundred acres of the family land, but all they gave him as his share was a hundred and fifty acres and twenty thousand rupees in cash. The Big House, his brother Damodar told him, had numerous dependents, whereas Dada had only himself to think of.

Only himself, as though his wife did not count as a member of the family.

Dada had been shocked by their meanness. "It is not fair," he argued. "I must have at least another hundred acres. Do you want me to live as a pauper?"

"Let him have Piploda, then," Damodar jeered. "Give him Piploda, Father, that will give him his extra hundred acres."

Dada's eyes smouldered. It was a challenge, that laughter, for Piploda had been a barren tract, almost a liability, and they had been on the point of surrendering it to the government to save paying taxes on it. "Is that the measure of your generosity?" he asked very quietly.

His brother and father avoided his eyes, but they did not increase their offer.

"All right, I will take Piploda," Dada said. "I will take it, and I will make it pay, if it is the last thing I do."

And with that, Dada Talwar, the stormy petrel, turned his back on the Big House. He went off with his bride, and with the twenty thousand rupees he built on his property what came to be called the Little House.

Almost perversely, he even built in his new house an exact replica of the prayer room in the Big House; perversely because a division of assets in a Hindu family certainly did not involve sharing out the household gods, perversely because only the main branch of the family had a right to its own shrine. The younger sons could offer their prayers only in the temple of the head of the family.

Piploda was only a piece of scrub and jungle and marsh in those days, untidy as a bearskin, with a sluggish, weed-choked nullah running uselessly through one corner. It was so far from the village that no farmhands could be persuaded to live there, out in the wilderness, pestered by wild dogs and pigs and an occasional panther.

Dada accepted the challenge. He dug up and burned down all

the soapnut and lantana bushes that infested the land, and levelled it for paddy cultivation, doing his full share of work with
the three farmhands he had taken out with him, all living together in a tiny straw and bamboo hut he had built there. One
of the men who went out with him was Tukaram, but of course
he was hardly a man then, more like a boy.

After the first rice had been harvested, they set about putting
a bund against the nullah to form a tank and divert its water
through the field. It was when they were digging up the earth for
the foundation of the dam that they unearthed the statue of
Shiva.

Dada's four-seer pickaxe made a hard, ringing sound against
the metal, something between a sudden cry of pain and the
sound of a temple bell, they said, and Tukaram and the two
other farmhands came running up to see what he had discovered.

Dada cleared the earth with his bare hands. There lay Shiva,
covered with the sludge of unknown decades, lying on his face,
the mark of the pick gleaming on his back like a diamond.

Dada lifted the image tenderly and washed it in the brook.
And then and there he knelt down and folded his hands to the
god he had discovered. They had stopped work and gone back in
triumph to the new house on the far side of the village, Dada,
strong as an ox, carrying the image on his shoulder. The very
next morning he sent for the priest and installed Shiva in the
prayer room with due ceremony. The Little House had been
given its own god.

Without a single qualm, Dada, who all his life had been a
staunch worshipper of Vishnu, now defected to his new-found
god, Shiva, and began to wear his caste-mark in a horizontal
line. His family had always worn it as a perpendicular line. But it
was more than a question of wearing a different caste-mark.
Vishnu was the god of creation, Shiva of destruction. The
difference was as wide as that.

After that Dada went back to Piploda and resumed work with
renewed zeal. He built a small brick hut on the land and began
to spend most of his time there.

Shiva with the mark of the pick on his shoulder brought prosperity to the Little House, even though Dada's own determination
and relentless labour must have helped. In no time at all the
dam was complete. Its water was guided into a three-foot-deep
channel that ran all along one side of the field. The entire field

was soon under cultivation, with the rice paddies clean and square and level, and the slopes thick with coconut and betel-nut palms.

This was the hour of the Little House. His new-found god blessed Dada with everything he wanted. Shiva even gave him a son to carry on the line of the Little House. The break with the past was complete.

The Big House had gone on its own way, ponderous, elephantine, earthbound, its stride unaffected by the emergence of the Little House, its wealth not visibly diminished by the portion made over to the younger son, its prestige enhanced by the grant of a British-Indian title to the head of the house. At the time of King Edward's coronation, Dada's father, Tulsidas, was created a Raisahib.

In one respect, however, the Big House had lagged behind. Dada's elder brother, Damodar, had fathered a succession of daughters, one after the other, but he had no son. After five girls had been born in twelve years, his wife, the one who had rejected Aji's cotton wicks for the lamp in the prayer room, acquired some wasting disease. The British doctor from the civil hospital at Sonarwadi was called in to examine her and gave a warning that it would be inadvisable for her to bear another child.

This was a crisis indeed. Lack of a son is a major catastrophe for any Hindu household, regarded as a retribution for the sins of an earlier incarnation. Without a son to light his funeral pyre, no Hindu can go to heaven. Above all, without a son there would be no one to carry on the line of the Big House—unless it was to be Dada's son Shankar.

Almost inevitably the Raisahib had turned to the family god. He had ordered a mahapooja, a ceaseless chanting of the prayer of Vishnu for ten days and nights, with ten Brahmins working in relays, and at the end he had given away ten blemishless cows, one to each priest.

The gods had relented. Damodar's sixth child was a boy. They named him Vishnu-dutt, the gift of Vishnu.

The boy's mother died on the day of the naming ceremony, but they had almost expected this to happen and no one particularly minded. After all, she must have died a happy woman, everyone said, for had she not been forgiven by the gods and redeemed herself by giving birth to a son?

Even though he was brought up as what they called a "boon-child," Vishnu-dutt grew up into a fine, strapping boy. They sent him to school at Sonarwadi, the first among the Talwars to be educated outside the house. He had passed his matriculation before the old Raisahib, his grandfather, died. He too must have died happy, his affairs all neatly arranged according to the best tenets of Brahminism. And on his deathbed he sent for Dada and made his peace with his erring son, a good Brahmin preparing himself for the dark journey ahead.

Dada took his own son, Shankar, to the cremation, both bearing flowers and sandalwood faggots for the pyre, repentant, humble, the long years of feuding momentarily forgotten in the presence of death.

But the new master of the Big House was not in a forgiving mood. He did not permit either Dada or his son to approach the bier. A staunch devotee of Vishnu, he did not want his father's funeral pyre to be polluted by the offerings of those who had defected to other gods. Dada and his son hung back in the outer circle of mourners, well behind the hordes of in-laws and dependents and hangers-on with false tears and red roses, watching the priests pour clarified butter into the raging fire. When they returned to the Little House, they were still carrying their offerings.

For five years more the feud lay dormant, an indestructible spore burrowed in the soil, a hooded cobra coiled in the depths of its hole, while both sides went their ways, through lean years and fat, carefully skirting the hole, marrying, begetting, dying.

So long as grandfather Dada was living, it had not come into the open. But the Big House had been planning, jealous of Dada's success, smarting at the rise of the Little House, waiting to prod the snake when the time came.

Dada died in 1926. No one from the Big House came to his funeral. Instead, when his body was taken to the burning ground, they quietly went to Piploda and took possession of the property.

The snake had uncoiled and struck; the evil spore had multiplied underground and erupted; the feud was out in the open, the talk of the village: the Big House against the Little House, the Big House represented by Damodar, Dada's brother, himself now made a Raisahib as a reward for the help rendered to the government during the World War, and assisted by his son, Vishnu-dutt, educated, cunning, daring; the Little House represented by Gian's and Hari's father, Shankar, unlettered, hot-headed, ineffectual.

The quarrel had raged as only a family quarrel in a remote, isolated village can rage, sweeping the landscape. From then on it was the most dominant topic of conversation in the village, transcending Mahatma Gandhi's movement for the oppressed cultivators of Champaran, and, later, the salt march to Dandi, and even the activities of the terrorists in the Punjab and Bengal.

Shankar Talwar, the new master of the Little House, had not much time for farming. He spent the rest of his days in grappling with the Big House. Even before the period of mourning was over, he dashed off to Sonarwadi, the district headquarters, to consult a lawyer. He found he had to engage two. On their advice, he filed a police complaint against the Big House, charging conspiracy, trespass, and wrongful possession. The case dragged on for nearly two years, being subjected to endless adjournments, a boon to the lawyers of both sides, who came accompanied by their articled clerks and juniors. Although everyone knew that the property at Piploda had been Dada's share, there were no papers to prove his title, only the fact of actual possession. But facts, it turned out, were pitiful substitutes for the resources of the Big House, the prestige of a title, the wiles of Vishnu-dutt. It was not easy to find witnesses to testify against the Raisahib and his son. In fact, the other side was able to produce an impressive array of witnesses to swear that the land had never been sequestered from the family estate and that Dada had tilled it only as a member of the family.

The case failed for want of evidence, but the lawyers were hopeful of winning it in a higher court and advised Shankar to appeal. The litigation went on, first in one court and then in another, branching off into intricate legal quibbles, over the question of jurisdiction, of what was called "adverse possession," of what constituted an agent, of the rights of inheritance according to Hindu law, all involving staggering consultation fees to the lawyers of Lahore and Allahabad. Shankar Talwar's resources dwindled; his expenses rose steeply. He had to mortgage a whole hundred acres of his remaining land, and then, in a desperate effort to raise money for removing an injunction, to sell it.

It was only after the deed of sale was completed that Shankar discovered that the buyer of the land was none other than Vishnu-dutt, astutely acting through a third party.

At this time came the great plague epidemic, sweeping the country like a great prairie fire. Shankar and his wife died within three days of each other.

But Shankar Talwar had really died long before the disease took him away, a broken and disillusioned man, leaving his two sons a bare fifty acres of land and the Little House, to say nothing of a great mound of legal papers.

Automatically the litigation had come to a halt. The lawyers ceased their visits, wrote letters of encouragement to Hari, and waited expectantly. Then they sent what they called their final bills, and, when these remained unpaid, letters threatening litigation of their own. Then came terse telegrams beginning "unless."

Aji surrendered her ornaments, keeping only the bangles, which she had never removed from her wrists since they were first put on by Dada. The debts of the dead had to be paid. They were paid.

One thing of which Hari was convinced was that if only their father had received the sort of education that the Big House had given to Vishnu-dutt, he would not have made such a hash of his life. Hari himself had had to give up school when he was fifteen, his father's strained finances making it impossible for him to go on. Gian was the privileged one and was permitted to continue his studies. He was in the high school at Sonarwadi when their father died. Hari was determined that nothing should be allowed to interfere with his brother's schooling. He had made up his mind, whatever the cost, to give him the best education in India.

The cost had been high, but Hari did not waver. He had now become the Karta, the head man of the family, and he was not the sort of man who would shirk the responsibilities of a Karta. He sent Gian back to school and set about putting their neglected land in order. Within two years Gian had matriculated. By then, what remained of the family land was producing as much as it ever had in grandfather Dada's days, and at that point Hari turned his mind to Piploda. He took time off to go to Sonarwadi.

The old lawyers who had conducted his father's cases approached him, smiling, slavering, scenting meat, guaranteeing success. But Hari paid no heed to them. He went to the law courts every day for a whole week, listening carefully while the business of the court went on, looking over the practising lawyers as though he were choosing cattle at a fair, for their looks, performance, and zeal, trusting to his own judgement. And on the last day he had approached a dark South Indian with cold hooded eyes who argued his cases in a soft, confidential voice. The lawyer's name was Ramunni Sarma, but Hari had not even bothered to ascertain it.

Sarma did not jump at the offer. He asked Hari to leave the papers with him and to see him three days later.

"Who had been paying the land revenue on the field?" he had asked Hari at the next meeting.

"My grandfather," Hari told him.

"Are you quite sure of that?"

"Every November, as long as Dada was alive, he personally went to the Taluka office to remit the money."

"I will take your case," Sarma said. "We have a very good chance."

They agreed about fees, and once again litigation began. But this time there was none of the old confusion and panic. Sarma had told Hari that the only conclusive proof would be the entries in the official records. "If it is true that your grandfather paid the government assessment on the land, it is clear that he owned it."

"It was he who paid, not the Big House," Hari assured him.

"Then we have nothing to fear."

But when, after the usual number of objections and adjournments put in their way by the Big House lawyers, the records were finally produced in court, Hari was in for a shock; the entries clearly stipulated that, while Dada had been paying the government dues, he had only been acting as an agent for and on behalf of the owner. They lost their case.

That was the time when Vishnu-dutt stood in the village square and hurled insults at Gian, who happened to be passing: "Go and tell your brother that your bones will be coals before we let Piploda out of our hands!"

Gian implored his brother to refrain from further litigation. The Big House was too powerful for them. It had money, influence, cunning. Even Sarma, the new lawyer, had advised against an appeal.

Hari turned to the family god. Humbly he went into the prayer room, a single marigold flower in his hand, to seek the verdict of Shiva. He would appeal only if Shiva gave his kaul.

Reverently Hari placed the flower on Shiva's head. "If the flower falls to the right, we should appeal; if it falls to the left, we should give up," he told himself.

The yellow flower lay poised on Shiva's head for a second or two, a crown of gold on the upraised, serene face of Shiva. Then it fell. It fell to the right.

Hari came out, his eyes bright with gratitude. "We will go ahead with the case," he announced. "Shiva had given an unmistakable kaul: the flower fell on the right side."

Whose right side? Gian could not help asking himself: Shiva's or the worshipper's? Could it not have an opposite meaning? But Hari's eager exultant face restrained him from giving expression to his doubts.

The lawyer had no faith in the god's kaul, in the chance dropping of a flower. He hemmed and hawed and held back, until, only one day before the time for lodging an appeal had lapsed, he went and filed it. Three days before the hearing he sent for Hari.

"How long do your revenue collectors at Konshet stay there?" he asked Hari. "I mean, how frequently are they transferred?"

"Usually they are there for only two years, never more than three. Sometimes the transfers are much quicker. One or two have gone away within a few months."

Sarma gave him a sly, meaningful smile, and his drooping lids fell lower and lower till they covered his eyes completely. "It just occurred to me," he said with his eyes still closed, "that all those entries to the effect that the taxes were paid on behalf of the Big House were made in the same handwriting—in the same handwriting and in the same ink."

"What does it mean?"

"It means they were written afterwards. Forgeries! We could . . . we could get whoever was responsible sent to jail. When we demanded that the records should be produced, they must have realized the case was lost. So they bribed some clerk in the records office . . . it could even have happened here, in the court itself. Such things are not unknown in our subdivisional offices."

"But how will that affect our case?"

"The judge is an Englishman, Mr. Stewart—a real fire-eater, but just. If forgery is established, I would hate to be in the defendants' shoes."

"And *can* forgery be established?" Hari asked.

Sarma opened his eyes and gave him a long look. "I think we can take it that we have won our case," he said.

"Shiva's kaul was right," said Hari and reverently folded his hands.

So, with Shiva's blessings, they won the case, and the fire-eating Mr. Stewart passed strictures against the revenue officials and ordered an investigation into who had tampered with the records.

Jubilantly they prepared for the pooja to Shiva. The prayer room was littered with bundles of groceries and the whole house bore an air of festivity. As he lay in bed on his first night back from college, Gian heard his brother singing in his room at the other end of the house, singing in his hard, resonant voice, a bhajan to the greatness of Shiva.

Gian turned on his side and raised his head. He had not heard his brother sing for a long time. It was spontaneous, like a bird bursting into song at a moment of inner peace.

When Gian fell asleep, his brother was still singing.

[5]

Figures in a Sunlit Field

BUT in India land disputes are seldom resolved by decisions of the courts. When, on Monday, they went to take possession of the field, they discovered that a large tree had been neatly felled across the track at the entrance, blocking their path. Tukaram had to halt the bullock cart. Even from where they were, at the edge of the field, they could see the lean brown farmhands busily preparing the field for the monsoon sowing, breaking the sod, shaping the edges of the paddies, diverting the water channel.

Hari jumped out of the cart and ran up to the fallen tree. "Oh, the misbegotten son of a churail!" he cursed. "The nerve!"

The noonday sun shone brightly over the jungle and the rectangles of the rice paddies. There was a stillness in the air—a pregnant, electric stillness as before a storm. An unknown fear nicked Gian's heart as he watched his brother scrambling over the fallen tree. He ran after him and held him by the hand.

"I don't think we should go into the field," he whispered.

Hari turned back on him almost viciously and flung away his hand. "Not go into the field! This is my field!—our field, yours and mine!"

"Let's go back and inform the police—show them the court order," Gian entreated. "We should consult a lawyer . . ."

"Haven't you had enough of the law?" Hari snapped at him. "I am going to do this myself, clear them out with my own hands, if necessary."

The nick of fear had widened and come to the surface. The sun-drenched clearing in the jungle was more silent than ever; even the sound of the bells from the bullocks had stopped. Gian swallowed hard to overcome the dryness of his tongue and followed his brother mechanically. Side by side they stepped over the branches of the fallen tree; side by side they approached the

39

centre of the field, aware that the men working there had seen them but were going on with their jobs with exaggerated concentration, pretending not to have noticed them.

"Stop work at once!" Hari yelled at them, his voice like the challenge of an enraged bull. "Get out! . . . Get out! Get out, this minute!"

The men turned their heads to look at the two brothers, hesitated, and stopped working. Slowly they straightened themselves, dark brown figures standing like scarecrows in the boiling sun, each in a little dark pool of his own shadow.

And then, out of the long, low hut at the edge of the jungle, the hut that grandfather Dada had built, emerged the stocky, full-blown figure of Vishnu-dutt, dark and forbidding, like a boar coming out of its lair. He stood framed in the doorway, crouching, his head bent, his stomach swelling out on both sides of the canvas belt he wore, his thick, stumpy legs wide apart.

"Get off my property!" cried Vishnu-dutt. "You are trespassing!"

"It is our property! . . . our house! . . . our field! . . . and I have come to take it back," Hari shouted back. "You are the trespassers, you and your men—jackals who stole from the dead! Jackals and sons of jackals! Unless you clear out this minute, I am going to throw you out!"

Vishnu-dutt lifted his head high and laughed hoarsely, making a staccato guttural sound like a dry, throaty cough, short and abrupt. Then he said, "Throw us out, then! Come and throw us out, if you dare!"

Gian could see his brother's face taut with rage, with the blood drained away from it, his eyes black slits of hatred, his fists half clenched, his neck pink as a flame, but within himself there was only the cold hard pebble of fear, making him shiver in spite of the summer sun beating down upon them—in spite of the sweat running from his limbs.

He forced himself to speak. "But surely you know we won the case? And the judge ordered that the land should be given back to us." Even to himself, his voice sounded meek and pathetic—a child pleading for mercy, he thought.

Once again there was that guttural laughter, but this time it was much longer. "Don't you know anything about appeals, you college prick?" Vishnu-dutt scoffed. "Your brother knows all about them; why don't you ask him?"

"Appeals! Appeals to whom? It was the district judge who has ordered—"

"————the district judge!" Vishnu-dutt retorted and followed it by an obscene gesture with his fist. "Don't you know there is such a thing as the High Court at Lahore and after that, if necessary, the Privy Council in London, where it costs a lakh of rupees to defend a case? You will have to put up the Little House for sale, even for the High Court. How much are you asking? I don't mind buying—"

"Are you going to clear out or not?" Hari yelled.

"No!" Vishnu-dutt told him. "Get on with your work, men!" he ordered the farmhands. "Don't take any notice of these trespassing scavengers!"

None of them moved. They stood as if transfixed, their feet ankle-deep in the dust, circled by their own shadows, watching the drama develop.

"Then I am going to make you get out," Hari thundered, striding forward towards the cottage.

Once again Gian attempted to restrain him, but this time Hari flung his hand away in anger, without even looking back. Gian felt weak and was trembling, but he followed his brother over the narrow path leading up to the hut. The sweat was running down his armpits, and his lips were gumming up for lack of moisture.

For a moment Vishnu-dutt stood his ground, defying them to come closer, and then he turned and made a dart into the hut. When he came out again he was holding a long-handled timber axe in his hands, the blade blue-black, broad, and shining. He stood, a bloated dark figure barring the doorway, crouching, ready to spring. "I forbid you to take another step!" he yelled. "Stop where you are! I am warning you—warning you for the last time."

But this time the ring of assurance was gone. There was a slight tremor in his voice, betraying a streak of fear, of uncertainty.

Only Hari was wholly himself, grim-faced but deliberate, his walk an easy stride, his arms swinging naturally. Suddenly he stopped. He turned and gripped Gian by the shoulders. "You stay right here, Chote-baba," he whispered. "I want to sort this out on my own.'"

There was a quick, unwanted moment of relief, but he tried to thrust it away. "But I want to be with you . . . be with you whatever happens," he pleaded, his words almost choking in his throat.

But he did not want to go on. He wished to hang back, to run away, to leave this evil place and never to see it again. This was not his fight; it was Hari's, their father's, grandfather Dada's. His was the path of non-violence—the non-violence of the strong, he reminded himself, arising from courage, not cowardice.

But he did not feel courageous. "Let's both go back," he blurted out, almost in spite of himself. "Please, please, let's go away."

"Oh, stop being so silly!" Hari admonished him quite gently. "I don't want you to be involved in this. You stay right here; I'll go and tackle the fat bastard. Don't you see he is frightened? We can't back out now. Have we started wearing bangles, are we emasculated that he can turn us away from what is ours?"

With that Hari turned on his heel and went up the slope towards the hut where his adversary stood clutching the timberman's gleaming axe. Gian wanted to run after him and face whatever lay ahead together, but he stood rooted to the ground, unable to move.

"I forbid you to come closer!" Vishnu-dutt yelled. "I warn you! Stop! Stop!" But this time the fear in his voice showed clear through the bluster; his words were almost like a croak, trailing off into a whine.

Hari went on unheeding, confidently, easily, relaxed, almost as though he were enjoying this moment of showdown, the end of the long fight. Confidence against bluster, good confronting evil.

When he was still a few paces away, Vishnu-dutt suddenly turned and fled into the hut, slamming the door behind him. But Hari darted after him and flung his shoulder against the door. For what seemed a long time the door resisted, thudding against the frame. Then, all of a sudden, it flew open, and Hari ran into the shed.

From where they were standing, they all heard Vishnu-dutt yelling defiance at Hari. "You son of a churail, daring me to—" And there was the abrupt, faintly crunchy sound of an axe plunging into soft, pulpy wood, followed by silence.

Gian felt faint with weakness; the fear inside him bloated like a balloon, choking him, bringing out his breath in short gasps, blinding his eyes. His knees trembled.

All round him, there was the pounding of feet scuffing into the dust, and, far away, the sound of the bells round the necks of Raja and Sarja. He shook himself and ran forward, saying, "Oh, God, please don't let it have happened; oh, please, please, Shiva, lord of the universe!"

His prayer was too late. It had happened. Hari lay just inside the doorway, his face downwards, his arms stretched over his head. And on his shoulder-blade there was a deep gaping wound from which the blood had already stopped gurgling out.

There was no one else in the hut. The door at the back was wide open.

[6]

Red and Blue Triangles

THE mantle of death lay over the Little House, blanketing the new flame of revenge that was kindled within. The materials for Shiva's pooja lay neatly stacked in the prayer room. Gian brooded, sick with guilt. "Coward! . . . coward!" he kept accusing himself, fanning the flame. Was that why he had embraced the philosophy of non-violence without question—from physical cowardice, not from courage? Was his non-violence merely that of the rabbit refusing to confront the hound?

Vishnu-dutt was arrested for the murder of Hari. Within the week the subdivisional magistrate at Pachwad, himself invested with what were called "second-class" powers, held a preliminary trial and committed the case to the sessions court at Sonarwadi. The charge was first-degree murder.

Even for the preliminary trial at Pachwad, the Big House had brought over a barrister from Lahore; black-robed, saturnine, dignified, he walked into the dingy up-country courtroom trailed by three assistants—an elephant heading a procession—and sat down only after he had delicately wiped the chair with his handkerchief. And when he rose to speak, it was with the air of a prima donna participating in a village charity show. He made a plea for the accused to be allowed bail while the trial was pending, quoting at length from numerous High Court rulings in support, cunningly slipping in a "m'lord" every now and then while addressing the magistrate, who was only entitled to be addressed as "your honour." The little magistrate listened, his head cocked to one side, almost as though he too were enjoying the performance. Then he turned down the request for bail.

"May it please your lordship," the barrister said, bowing low, barely concealing a sneer at so unreasonable a ruling.

The trial was fixed for the third of June, almost exactly a

44

month from the day of the murder. For Damodar and the members of the Big House it was a period of feverish activity. They flung themselves desperately into the fray; no holds were barred —influence, blackmail, flattery, bribes, prayers, everything was tried, and money was spent like water. A ten-day mahapooja was performed in the family shrine and another, still more elaborate, was promised Vishnu if he secured the acquittal of his boon-child.

Lawyers and their touts, relatives, common friends not seen for years, even strangers calling themselves "well-wishers" began to make furtive visits to the Little House, carrying offers of bribes and threats of reprisals. Gian was equally firm with all of them. "Go and do what you like," he told them. "I want to see Vishnu-dutt hanged, nothing less." Once he actually had to use force to throw out Kakaji, one of the Raisahib's numerous sons-in-law, who had come with an offer of mediation.

After that the visits stopped, but not for long. The date of the trial was drawing closer every day; the Big House had no time to waste.

Late one evening appeared the pandit, the village priest. He came to the back of the house, so as to avoid running into Gian, and demanded to see Aji. When she came out, he told her that he carried a message from the Big House. Could he speak to her alone?

Aji brought out a wooden board for him, and the priest sat down, crossing his legs under him, the man of God on an errand of good. He spoke earnestly, his soft, unctuous voice trained by countless poojas, his jargon enriched by quotations from the scriptures.

"They are prepared to give back Piploda—if only he will be sensible," he told Aji.

"Who is to trust Damodar's word?" Aji said. "He will promise anything now, to save his son."

"I shall stand guarantee for that . . . swear on Shiva's feet."

Aji shook her head. "He won't listen to me; Gian will not listen to anyone."

"He must listen, must come to his senses. It is madness to go on in this way! You must explain it properly; tell him where his interests lie. He is only a boy, and hotheaded like his father. He will only invite destruction if he persists. The way he talks—he wants to see Vishnu-dutt hanged. It is ridiculous! I can tell you nothing will happen to Vishnu-dutt. Even the police darogah is on our side—the Big House's side. Why not take whatever you can get? Now is your chance. Bathe your feet while the Ganges still flows."

Aji gave a sigh. "The boy will not listen to me. He is the Karta now, the man of the house. Who am I to tell him?"

"Kshama virasy bhushanam," the pandit quoted. "Forgiveness only enhances bravery, as the scriptures say. Besides, what is gone is gone—become one with the Ganges. Now one must dig only where the ground is soft. How can he go to college now, if he has to live here and manage everything? Where is the money coming from, tell me?"

"Who gave the beak to the bird will also provide it with food," Aji quoted. "It is in Shiva's hands, whether he goes back to college or not. I cannot tell Gian what he should do."

"It is your duty. Do you want to see him ruined and living in penury? Do you want to see your husband's line perish?"

Little drops of spittle flew from his mouth, his finger travelled up and down with the beat of the words, his eyes puckered into little black spots. Aji shook her head once again and gestured helplessly with her hands. The pandit clucked his tongue in desperation. Haughtily he pulled his brown silk shawl more tightly round him and rose to go. "You're only pulling the stone on your own feet," he warned. "I have done my best."

He put on his chaplis and walked to the door, his nose in the air, his hands held rigidly at the sides. In the doorway he paused. He turned, came back, and sat down again, his voice now dropped to a confidential whisper.

"They are moving heaven and earth, I can tell you. In the end, they'll get their way. It is you who will be ruined—your house. You will be failing in your duty if you cannot convince Gian that he should not persist in his madness."

"I will tell him what you said," Aji promised. "That is all I can do."

"The Raisahib is absolutely sure of getting his son set free. Gian will not get anywhere by his obstinacy. Tell him that. And listen; just before I came, Damodar told me that he is even prepared to return the hundred acres that your son sold to raise money. Think of that! Gian will be rich, don't you understand? He will get Piploda back, and also all the fields that once be-

longed to Dada and you. Your grandson can continue his studies;
he can marry and bring a daughter-in-law to help you in your last
years; he can carry on the line."

"I can only tell him all you have said," Aji promised in a
resigned voice. "It is up to him. Why not send for him and tell
him now? He must be—"

At that the priest had drawn back. "No, no, don't do that," he
said, shaking his head, gesticulating with his hands. "He is very
hotheaded. But he should realize where his own interests lie. I
hear he nearly broke Kakaji's arm—such rudeness!"

"The boy is not himself," Aji explained. "After what has happened. He rarely talks to anyone now. He does not even do his
pooja."

"Unpardonable!" the pandit pronounced. "It is up to you to
bring him to his senses. You tell him when I have gone; explain
where his interests lie. And mind you, make him swear on Shiva's
head."

When, later that evening, Aji told Gian what the pandit had
been saying, he listened in silence. Then he left the room and
went to bed, still without saying a word to her. At night he went
out. He pulled one of the window panels from his bedroom
window out of its socket and slipped out without Aji's knowing
anything about it. For most of the night he wandered aimlessly
through the fields and for an hour or so sat down under the
peepul tree in the village square. The cocks were already crowing
when he slipped back into the house through the window. Later
in the morning he caught a bus to Sonarwadi. He wanted to
consult Ramunni Sarma, the lawyer who had befriended Hari.

Sarma listened to him with bent head, doodling on the blotting pad on his desk with a red and blue pencil.

"You are quite right not to have had anything to do with
those people," he said after Gian had finished what he had to
say. "But surely it was not necessary to be rude to them?"

"I could not help myself," Gian explained. "I want to see
Vishnu-dutt hanged, and here they come trying to make me say
that I did not see him in the field. Just as well I wasn't there
when the priest came with his offer. . . ."

The lawyer raised his head. "Have they found the axe?" he
asked.

"The axe? They are bound to find it."

"Bound to! I don't know. Where could Vishnu-dutt have hidden it, do you think?"

"Oh, anywhere in the jungle—it's quite thick there. He might even have thrown it into the water, while going past the dam."

"Have they made a search there?"

"I hear they sent a diver in, soon after the—the murder."

"And they still haven't found it."

"No."

Sarma began to doodle on his blotting paper once more, drawing precise blue triangles, one within the other. "You don't think the police are—are deliberately not discovering the weapon, do you?" He looked at Gian, level-eyed. "It is not unknown. Anything is possible. Remember, they even got the kanungo to make false entries in the revenue records. . . ."

"But the police! In a murder case!"

"The police!" Sarma stabbed the point of the pencil at the centre of his triangle, almost viciously, so that the point broke. He turned the pencil upside down and began doodling again, making red triangles instead of blue. "It only means that the stakes are bigger. The Big House can afford to play for big stakes."

"But what about the evidence? I saw him myself, brandishing the axe, threatening . . ."

The lawyer held up his pencil in a gesture of impatience; his heavy lids drooped. "You did not actually see him kill your brother," he said. "Bear that in mind. In law, that is important; vital, almost. Besides, by itself, what you say in the court won't really count for much. You are an interested party, with the background of a long family dispute. The lawyers will tie you up in knots—impute all sorts of motives."

"But there are at least six other people who saw all that happened!" Gian pointed out. "All the farmhands . . . Tukaram."

"Not *all* that happened—no one saw the murder being committed; they will keep harping on that. At best they only saw what you saw, heard what you heard. But can they be made to testify? They all belong to the other side. They will do their best to discredit your evidence."

"Thank God there is an English judge," Gian said. "We can expect complete fairness." He was aware that he was trying to reassure himself, clutching at all the straws.

"Even the fairest judge cannot go against facts that come out in evidence."

"Do you mean he is going to be acquitted?" Gian asked. His mouth suddenly felt dry.

The lawyer made a fresh triangle and began to fill it up with smaller ones. "Much depends on how the cartman, Tukaram, fares in the witness box. He is the most important witness. Don't let any of their people get at him."

"Tukaram is even more determined than I am," Gian said. "He has always been like an uncle to us—to both Hari and me."

"I am glad to hear that," the lawyer said. "They are bound to make efforts to turn him against you."

He could breathe easily once more. It was good to know that the case rested on what Tukaram would have to say; Tukaram, dependable, fiercely loyal, proud of the Little House. "He is absolutely reliable," he told Sarma confidently. "Nothing will make him go against us—nothing! Not all the money in the world!"

The triangle was now all red. The lawyer placed the point of his pencil in the exact centre and pressed. It broke.

"There are other kinds of pressures besides bribes," he said, his eyes almost fully closed.

The sun had already gone down when Gian returned that evening. He found the sub-inspector of police, the darogah, waiting on the veranda, sprawled in a canvas chair. On the bench along the wall sat two constables.

Aji had obviously given them tea. The empty cups and the plates with small piles of blackening banana skins were still on the bamboo table.

The darogah did not move, he gave a slow, oily smile as Gian entered. "Been waiting for over an hour," he said complainingly.

"I had gone . . . er, gone out," Gian told him.

"To Sonarwadi?"

"Yes."

"To consult some lawyer, perhaps."

"Umm, yes."

"You don't need your own lawyer for this kind of case; it is conducted by the state, by the public prosecutor. And Ramunni Sarma . . ." He stopped in mid-sentence and made a vague, dep-

recatory gesture with his thumbs. "Crooked as they come. But
that is up to you. I just wanted to check a few things, purely routine." The inspector tapped his pockets perfunctorily. "I seem to
have run out of cigarettes," he explained.

Gian took out his wallet. "I will send for some," he offered.
He looked for a one-rupee note but found he had only fives and
tens. He took out a five-rupee note.

"No need to send your man," the darogah offered. "Here,
Harnam and Kasim." He turned to his two constables. "Run to
the bazaar and bring some cigarettes, will you. Gold Flake. Both
of you can go."

"Jee-sahib." Both the constables rose with alacrity. One of
them took the note that Gian was holding out.

"Bring two packets of Gold Flake," the darogah ordered as
they made for the door. "And some matches."

"Jee-sahib," they said.

"And you'd better have something to eat while you are there,"
he yelled after them. "And bring me a masala-paan. But don't be
long!"

By now Gian was inured to the petty graft of the darogah and
his men. He cursed his luck for not having had a one-rupee note
in his pocket.

"The poor devils have been out since the morning, working
hard," the darogah explained. "Haven't eaten a thing—only bananas."

"What did you want to ask me?" Gian asked.

"Oh, just some routine questions."

"Anything you want to know," Gian offered. "Anything at
all."

The man leaned forward in his chair. "This is rather awkward
for me as a police officer in charge of the investigation, but are
you really going to say all that you said in your original
complaint?"

"Absolutely. Why?"

The darogah shook his head doubtfully. "Very awkward; very
awkward for me. We are unable to find the weapon. The case
becomes weak in the absence of the murder weapon. You realize
that, don't you?"

The dry, sick feeling was back in his mouth. "You mean you
are going to give up your search for it? There are still—"

"We have already called off the search. What is one to do? So much work everywhere; so few hands. That is why I was anxious to know if you are pressing the original charge—murder."

"Oh, yes, I am," Gian told him. "I know he killed my brother. I as good as saw him."

"As good as." The darogah shook his head slowly. "Not actually, but as good as."

"Other people saw him too. His own farmhands."

The loose, flabby lips drooped in a travesty of a smile, but the dull marble eyes were lifeless as ever. "The others did not see Vishnu-dutt," he said. "At least that is what they say, the lying ————s! What can we do, poor policemen, in the face of such dishonesty, if people will not cooperate with us in the cause of justice? We tried our best to elicit the truth. Gave them—how do you say it?—yes, the third degree; even gave them the third degree. No luck." He shook his head sadly.

This is not true, Gian kept telling himself. This was not happening. There was an emptiness in the pit of his stomach and a prickly feeling all along his spine, as though a hairy spider had crawled up his back.

"So I was wondering," the voice from the opposite chair went on, syrupy, low-key, confidential, "wondering if there was any point in going on. I was even told that you had decided to curb your original, somewhat—well, your original impetuousness and thought better of it."

"Never!" Gian said vehemently. "Never!"

The smile vanished from the darogah's face. In its place there was a slight frown. The voice suddenly became slightly edgy. "In that case, there is no use in our—our continuing this discussion."

"Not if you came to persuade me to retract my statement," Gian told him. "The man is a murderer and must be punished. And it is your duty to see him brought to justice."

The darogah drew himself up. "We always do our duty," he said with acerbity. "But we are handicapped. How can we secure conviction only on your evidence?"

"Mine and Tukaram's. That should be enough. He was there too, in full view. He will tell you no lies. He is . . ."

Something in the way the darogah was looking at him made him stop. He stared at his eyes, opaque and unrevealing, convinced that there was no point in going on.

It was a long time before the other spoke. "We shall have to see what he has to say, your Tikkaram—"

"Tukaram," Gian corrected him.

"Yes, Tukaram. We shall have to see whether he too is going to be—as adamant. I am taking him to the thana, for questioning. Just routine."

The fear deep within him was ballooning, and there was a steady flicker before his eyes. "Can't you—won't it be all right for you to question him here? Now?" he asked in a voice that even to himself sounded dry and rasping.

The darogah shook his head, ever so slowly, sadly, as though regretting that he was unable to grant so reasonable a request. "No. It is much better to do it at the thana; away from—from other influences. Besides, there we have—er, we have much better facilities there."

"I really cannot . . ." Gian began. He had to stop to clear his throat. "I mean he is our cartman here; the only servant in the house, in fact. He has to be here all the time. Without him we are really stuck. The bullocks too; they have to be fed, watered." He attempted a weak smile.

The darogah seemed oddly distressed by that. "I am sorry he is so indispensable," he said. "But what can I do? There is a procedure laid down for such things. When we record a statement, a witness has to be free to say what he likes, away from those who might have some influence over him. We all have to undergo these inconveniences in the cause of justice, Mr. Talwar. Justice makes such harsh demands on one sometimes."

He smiled, baring his teeth and gums. Gian had to clench his fists to keep his hands from trembling.

"Ah, here are the cigarettes," the darogah said. "At last! Arre, why did you bring two tins? I told you two packets."

"The man did not have packets," Harnam said. "Only fifties."

"And did you remember the paan, the masala-paan?" the darogah asked.

It was three days before Tukaram came back. He came slinking in through the back yard. There were no visible marks on his body, but he could barely walk. His face looked haunted and his eyes stared as though frozen. He must have been sitting for quite some time before Aji noticed him, a hunched up, stooping man, the picture of shame. She went and brought him a cup of tea and then called out to Gian.

His hands shook as he drank the tea. Gian watched him with a mixture of contempt and rage. "What did they do to you?" he asked after Aji had gone back to the kitchen.

Tukaram merely stared at his master, but he did not say anything.

"Was it ice? Did they make you sit on a slab of ice—without clothes?"

Tukaram shook his head. Tears welled up in his eyes and rolled down. "No . . . a stick of ice in my . . . oh, it was torture—I could not bear it." The tears continued to flow.

"What else?"

"They—they also put chili powder. Oh, don't ask me what they did, Chote-baba. It was obscene, shameful. . . ."

"Yes? Go on."

"The pain—the pain when they kept beating the soles of my feet with rope, shooting right up to my neck every time, like stabs . . ."

"But why didn't you cry out—you fool! Shout at the top of your voice that they were beating you up, so that any passer-by could have heard you?"

"Cry out! How could I, with a thick police chapli thrust deep into my mouth. The pain and the shame—the shame was worse, but the pain I could not bear. I should have died. I must go away; I cannot show my face here, in this house, after what has happened. Not in this village . . ."

A black rage swept over Gian. He had to prevent himself from lashing out at the old man gasping before him. "And did you do what they wanted you to do—change your statement?"

Turkaram hung his head; his shoulders shook with unrestrained sobbing.

"Speak, Tukaram! Speak the truth!"

Instead of saying anything, Tukaram crawled forward and fell at Gian's feet. "Forgive me, Chote-baba, forgive me. I am an old man, but I have never touched another man's feet. Now I seek your forgiveness. I have eaten your salt but I have not been true to it. I could not bear it; it was too much—the shame and the pain."

Gian thrust away the crouching, sobbing man with his bare foot. "That's all I wanted to know," he said. "You can leave the house now. You have no right to show your face in this house."

The old man stared uncomprehendingly at his master and wept silently; the young man stared back with no forgiveness in his heart. From the courtyard came the faint clang of brass bells. Painfully, Tukaram rose to his feet and sat down again with a groan.

"I have nowhere to go. Where shall I go?" he asked.

"You have no place in this house any longer.'"

Tukaram wiped his tears with the end of his shirt, cocking his head as he listened to the clang of the bells from the cattle shed. He rose to his feet, holding the wall for support. "It is time to water Raja and Sarja," he muttered.

"No, you will not water the bullocks," Gian told him sharply. "All you can do for us now is to leave us."

The old man gave him a long, beseeching look, like a hunted animal looking at the hunter. He took a step, leaning against the wall, and then another. His face was contorted with pain and sorrow. The young man watched him as he went out of the house, until he was out of sight.

[7]

Bullocks and Bangles

THE day of Vishnu-dutt's acquittal was a black day for the
Little House. It even made a crack in Aji's equanimity. For the
first time, the eternal lamp in Shiva's room remained unlit.

At the trial no one except Gian said that he actually saw
Vishnu-dutt in the field. The farmhands working in Piploda
steadfastly swore that they had not seen him for days. Tukaram
gamely admitted that his eyesight was weak and that he saw
anything beyond a few yards only as a blur, and that even if his
sight had been perfect, he could not have seen what was happening at the other end of the field because his vision had been cut
off by the fallen tree. Under cross-examination he said that his
earlier statement to the contrary had been motivated by his loyalty to the Little House.

"Coward! . . . coward! . . . coward!" Gian kept muttering to
himself as Tukaram gave his evidence, without faltering, mouthing his phrases as though they had been carefully rehearsed. At
the moment he hated Tukaram even more than Vishnu-dutt.
And then out of nowhere had come the memory of his own
cowardice, back in the sunlit field, when he had hung back at a
safe distance instead of going forward with his brother. Tukaram
at least had the justification of being subjected to the dreaded
torture-chamber of the Indian police. What was his justification
—his lighthearted acceptance of the creed of non-violence? But
that was merely a political expedient, a weapon specially forged
to serve the struggle against the British; how could it ever serve
as a philosophy of life itself?

The darogah had bought a new motorcycle. The Big House
had announced a major pooja to the family god. The priest
bustled about his tasks importantly. In the Little House, Gian
grimly applied himself to the tasks of the Karta, despising himself.

Three days after the trial was over, as Aji was serving the midday meal, she asked, "When do you have to go back to college?"

For a moment he had blinked at her uncomprehendingly. He had not thought of college since Hari's death. "College! Oh, no; I'm not going back," he told her.

"You have to go; there is only another year left."

He shook his head. That part of his life had already ended. "Aji, my work is here, taking care of the fields, looking after you."

"I don't need looking after," his grandmother had said very evenly. "You must go and finish your studies; become a big man —a district collector. Your father wished it. Hari too—you owe it to him."

"What I owe to Hari can never be paid," Gian said very gravely. "He would not have died if I had done what I should."

But Aji went on with her own theme. "He would not even buy a new coat for himself, nor chaplis, so that you should be given everything you needed. He would not even get married, although there were many offers. Now you are not even prepared to finish what he gave up so much for."

Was she mad, the old woman? Where was the money coming from? They had only about fifty acres of land left. Enough to live on but certainly not enough for him to go to college; not unless you had an elder brother looking after things without taking anything for himself. How could she imagine that he would leave everything and go away?

"The fields will be cultivated by the tenants," Aji said, almost in answer to his thoughts. "Even if we do not get the full yield for the year, it won't matter. The bullocks, we shall have to sell."

"Sell Raja and Sarja? They were like children to Hari."

"A man cannot have bullocks as his children."

"And who is going to buy them? No one will buy ten-year-old bullocks."

"We can sell them to the Vaccine Institute at Sonarwadi. They are always ready to buy cattle; we can arrange for them to come and take them away."

"Yes, and do you know what they do with the animals they buy—the Vaccine Institute?" Gian snapped in sudden anger. "They make long razor-cuts all over their bodies and inject them with smallpox serum so that they go sick. Then they take out the serum and—and sell them to butchers. By that time, they are just skin and bone."

Aji nodded her head. "Yes, I know what they do there."

"And yet you are willing to sell Raja and Sarja—to have their skin taken off in little strips and then be sold for meat!"

"Cattle cannot be allowed to come in the way of human beings," she told him in a flat voice.

It was quite unbelievable. Aji, who had pampered the bullocks since they were calves, as family pets who would come and nibble at the cabbage-stalks from her hand whenever she called out to them. Raja and Sarja, whose bodies were always hand-rubbed by Tukaram, their brass bells polished with tamarind juice every week. He remembered their ride from the station, when Hari and he had walked behind the cart to spare their feet.

Aji was talking nonsense, of course, and at any other time he would have laughed at her ignorance. Now all he said was "But we won't even get much money for them. The vaccine people pay by weight; two annas a pound. We will hardly get a hundred and fifty rupees for them."

"We cannot turn up our noses at a hundred and fifty rupees," Aji said.

"But, don't you understand, it will cost at least seven hundred for me to go back to college?"

"I know," Aji said. "This should bring you the rest—at least five hundred."

Even as he glared at her, speechless, she removed the two gold bangles from her hands. "They are five tolas each," she was saying. "At least they were, when they were made."

When they were made, almost fifty years ago now, when she was a little girl, rebellious, unbending. Now she was surrendering them, when she was grey and wrinkled and silver-haired; still rebellious in her own way, still unbending. It almost brought tears to his eyes to see her bare wrists.

She had risen, leaving the bangles before his thali. "You have not taken your second helping of rice," she was saying. "Wait, I have set some curds. You have always liked curds."

"And if I do go," Gian asked, "what happens to you?"

"Me? I can look after myself. We can have a woman come in to do the washing. . . . I don't need anyone to look after me."

"Are you really sure you will be able to manage—without anyone looking after you?"

"Don't you give it a thought. Go back to college and study hard."

It was good to know that his grandmother was confident about being able to manage without him. He had been worrying about that. It simplified so many things.

"I am really glad to know that," he told her. "And of course, that fifty acres will still provide enough for one person to live comfortably."

"Yes," Aji said, putting the katori of curds on his thali. "Why should you give up your studies—in the last year, too. Surely not on account of me, an old woman, a leaf about to fall any day." She shook her head. "When do you have to go back?"

She had brought it to a head and he had to tell her. But somehow it was much easier than he had feared, particularly now that he knew that she could manage without him.

"Aji, I am not going back to college," Gian told her very evenly.

Aji stared long and hard at her grandson, and for a moment he wondered whether she had fathomed his innermost thoughts. But it did not bother him. For the first time since the death of his brother, he was suddenly aware of hunger. He began to mix the curds with the rice.

The people from the Vaccine Institute came and took Raja and Sarja away. They went away willingly, almost jubilantly, clanging their bells, having gorged themselves on their last big meal of cottonseed and munched their last titbits of cabbage stalks at Aji's hands.

After that, Gian began his search for the axe. Every morning he would leave the house before sunrise, carrying his midday meal with him, tied up in a bundle. He would not return till long after dark, tired and footsore, his eyes red, his clothes covered with dust, his arms full of new scratches. For a while, Aji must have taken it for granted that he was working in the fields, just as Hari had done—just as her husband Dada had done all those years ago. He even bore the same look—the look of a man working to redeem himself, setting himself a gruelling pace to overcome some inner enemy. But when, a few days after the bullocks had gone, one of the tenants came to the house to ask for paddy-seed, she discovered that Gian had never once been to the fields. That evening she tackled him about it.

"Sohansingh was here today, from the lower field," she said, "to ask for seed. He was saying that you have not been there even once."

"I will go tomorrow," Gian told her.

"Where did you go today?"

"Oh, I was just—just working; working elsewhere. I cannot be expected to go to the fields every day," he said irritably.

Aji had left it at that. "You will go tomorrow, won't you?" she had asked.

"Yes, of course," he promised.

But the next morning too he did not go to his own field. He went where he had been going every day for the past week: to Piploda.

There was no one there any more, in the field or in the hut. A murder had been committed there, everyone knew that; and no farmhand would have dared to set foot on the field so long as the evil spirits that haunted the place had not been propitiated. Until then, Piploda would be under a curse.

The propitiation would be duly attended to. The pandit would see to it that it was performed with the fullest ritual so that no one should have any doubts that the evil spirits had been exorcised, the curse lifted. For the time, however, the field was deserted.

Gian worked undisturbed. He had gone about it systematically, beginning his search at the back of the hut. He had already combed both sides of the path to a distance of thirty paces, because that was how far a strong man might be able to hurl a timber axe. He had dug ant-hills and poked about into ant-eater holes; he had looked behind every bush, climbed some of the bigger trees. . . . It had seemed hopeless.

That afternoon, as he lay on the grass, exhausted and unaccountably hungry, he once again tried to work out in his mind where Vishnu-dutt could have secreted the axe as he was running away. He tried to put himself in Vishnu-dutt's place—the place of a man who had just committed a murder. He could not have carried it very far, nor could he have thought out any really elaborate hiding place. How could anything as big as an axe—a five-pound blade on a four-foot-long handle—be hidden so successfully that the police could not discover it?

And, as always, his thoughts brought him back to the tank, the tank that grandfather Dada had built by putting a bund across the brook. The footpath from the hut led to the tank and past it, and that was the path Vishnu-dutt must have taken. He was a strong, agile man. If he threw away the axe with all his strength while passing the tank, it would almost certainly fall in the deepest part. How deep was it there—thirty feet?—more? And what was the bottom like? It was bound to be mud—soft black mud.

Overhead, the clouds were like heaps of enormous grey cabbages. They were the advance guard of the monsoons which would break within a week or ten days. After that, because of the way things sprouted in the jungle, it would be quite impossible to look for an axe. And the longer he concentrated on the jungle itself, the longer he was putting off the most obvious place, the tank.

Gian shuddered. It had to be faced. The slime, the eerie green light under water, the prolonged holding of breath, the tangle of dead bamboos and underwater creepers lining the floor of the tank, the black remains of decomposing vegetation, the treacherous, sucking mud.

He sat up and looked about him. The jungle was picked clean by the summer. It trembled under the fierce sun, and yet the trees bore new leaves, tender and flesh-pink. The pebbles underfoot were hot to the touch.

He opened the bundle containing his lunch, but his hunger had already vanished. It was just as well, he reminded himself; it was always better not to have had a full meal before entering water. He munched the dry rotis and pickles mechanically and threw away the mixture of rice and curds. He washed his fingers and lay back for a time, his eyes closed. Then he took off his clothes and walked to the bund.

He began a systematic series of dives. He was going to search the floor of the tank as he had searched the jungle along the path, foot by foot, right from the embankment to a distance of thirty feet. When he finished work that afternoon, he felt limp with exhaustion and had barely covered a tenth of the dam's length.

Three days later he had still not covered even a third of the length. But on the fourth morning he found it, on the sixth or seventh dive of the day. He saw it because it was lying on a layer of clean white mud which looked grey-green in the water. It was clearly visible from some distance away, the blade shining dully like a black pearl-shell, the shaft standing awkwardly aslant.

It was surprising that a professional police diver should have missed it, Gian thought, and then began to wonder if he really had missed it.

Later the same evening Gian walked into the police station and demanded to see the darogah. They made him wait outside for a few minutes, and then a constable came and told him that the darogah-sahib would see him.

"What is it?" the darogah asked crossly.

"I have just killed Vishnu-dutt," Gian told him. "Killed him with the same axe with which he murdered my brother."

And then the darogah noticed the blood that was spattered on his shirt in a diagonal streak.

"I had to find the axe," Gian was telling him. "You see, it was important that he should be killed with the same axe."

[8]

Angry Young Men

DEBI-DAYAL had always wanted to be a strong man; not muscle-bound or broad-chested, but quick and wiry and able to hit hard, an adept at judo, that ancient art of the Samurai which was said to be so much superior to the wrestling of India and the boxing of the West. It taught you to conquer by yielding. You did not have to possess strength; you made use of your adversary's strength. What you needed was agility and a knowledge of where to aim. He was determined to be the equal of any man, however tall or muscular, the man versed in the art of hand-to-hand fighting whom no British soldier would dare to challenge.

Debi hated the British, as they all hated the British; that was what brought them together, Hindus and Moslems and Sikhs, men of differing religions united in the cause of freedom as blood-brothers: the Freedom Fighters.

He was that man now, at nineteen; his muscles were supple, springy, his reflexes conditioned for quick retaliation, his action catlike in its deliberation; confident that he could cripple an assailant by lashing at his windpipe with the edge of his palm, the palm which was made hard as wood by constant hammering against wood, or by ramming his knee into his opponent's groin. He ached to prove himself, to match his precious skill against a real-life adversary, so that he could maim with a spine-breaking guillotine-chop, or break an arm with the hold known as the elbow-twist, or emasculate a man for life by administering a scrotum-kick.

It had taken him six years, but it had been worth it. Six years of relentless training, of rigid discipline, to say nothing of cultivating reverence towards the art of judo itself. Every day he had knelt before the black-belt shrine, recited his prayers, and made solemn promises never to use his skill except in self-defence. He himself had never believed in all that mumbo-jumbo at the shrine, but the Japanese instructor, Tomonaga, had always insisted upon it; Tomonaga, obese, repulsive, deceptively soft. Tomonaga who resembled nothing so much as a pale yellow, mangy gorilla who looked at the world out of rheumy eyes and hissed like a reptile through blackened teeth, but who was a fourth-degree initiate in the hierarchy of judoists and was entitled to wear the black belt.

"No-evah use pressa for sprine-break," Tomonaga used to warn his pupils. "And no-evah use sclotum-kick—no-evah!" It was all very well for the professional judoist to be concerned about the rules of the game. He, Debi-dayal, would use all the pressure he could for the spine-break, or for busting the Adam's apple in a white man's neck; and he would use all the force of which he was capable for the scrotum-kick. That was the whole point of learning the thing: to maim, to disable, to kill—and to hell with Tomonaga and his shrine and his trade union of judo devotees.

If only he had possessed this skill six years earlier!

He could never help squirming at that image of himself, weedy, pampered, overdressed, a typical rich man's son being lifted bodily by that enormous bull-necked soldier from the Scottish Borderers.

That was in the summer of 1933, when his father had gone on his first trip to Europe and Sundari was at a summer camp with her school friends. He had cycled back from the cinema late in the evening and was going in by the back gate because he had gone to see a Norma Shearer film when he was supposed to be playing hockey, and did not want his mother to find out.

As he entered the narrow, one-man opening in the back wall he had perceived a movement to his right, in the grove of casuarina trees, and then in the bright summer moonlight he saw the enormous dark figure of the soldier leaning over the woman who stood rigid and silent against the wall. The woman was his mother. He had stared, numb with shock and fear, and saw the soldier fumble at the knot of her choli and the two white breasts leap out in their nakedness. And then the man had given a vicious tug at the waist-band of her sari, and there stood his mother, against the wall, her body bathed in moonlight, rigid and silent as though paralysed, and then he saw the man bend down to thrust his loutish white-necked head into her chest.

A blind rage had swept over him. He jumped off his bicycle

and hurled himself at the man and began pounding his back with his fists. With a foul oath, the soldier turned and behind him he saw his mother's face, white with terror. She struggled free and fled towards the house, crouching, gathering her sari around her as she ran, her head hung low.

After that the big man had turned on him, slowly, almost lazily, like a dog noticing a puppy, and reached out and caught both his flailing hands into his own, locking him against his enormous sweat-reeking body. For a long time he had held him like that, breathing out heavy fumes of drink, and then lifted him with a jerk and perched him up on the wall.

"You damned little squirt!" he had said drunkenly, shaking him by the shoulders. "Don't you know better than to come bashing in? Just when I was about to get her too, ——— you!"

Then he had released his hold and turned away, walking jauntily, his shoulders rolling, his hands thrust deep into his trouser pockets, whistling "You Are My Sunshine" and not looking back. In the bright moonlight, the tartan of his trousers could be seen distinctly until he had vaulted lightly over the wall.

Debi-dayal remained on the wall, paralysed with anger and shame, unable to move, his head bursting with thoughts of revenge, hot tears running down his cheeks, listening to the sound of the whistle growing fainter and fainter. "Little squirt!" he had called him. That was what had hurt even more than the final obscene swearword. "Damned little squirt!"

He was no longer a little squirt. He was the most skilled judoist among the Freedom Fighters.

He had stayed on the wall for a long time, just where the soldier had perched him, not daring to go inside the house and wishing that his sister were not away, because when Sundari was not there, he had no one to confide in. The tears had dried on his cheeks by the time his mother came looking for him. She had been standing near the entrance, she explained as she led him in, waiting for him because he was so late, when the soldier jumped over the wall and attacked her.

"I was so terrified," she gasped. "I couldn't even cry out for help—like in a dream. It was God's mercy that you came when you did."

He shuddered at the thought. Rape, a word often heard, only

half understood, came to his mind; that was what would have happened, with all its accompanying scandal and humiliation.

And yet he was acutely conscious that he had failed to do what he should have done.

He would have liked to meet that man now, now that he was in a position to do something that would stop him from ever molesting a woman again.

He had wanted to report the man to the authorities, but his mother dissuaded him. It would have meant going to an identification parade, and who could tell one white soldier from another? And, still more important, it would never have done to have that sort of inquiry associated with people in their position, when the commanding officer of the regiment himself was an occasional guest at their house.

Even before he went to sleep that night, he had seen the sense of her arguments. This was something that was never to be mentioned, a humiliation that only multiplied itself by the number of people who knew about it. No one must know, not even his sister or his father.

He had lain awake, staring into the darkness, his clothes wet with sweat, cuddling the thoughts of revenge.

The Freedom Fighters prided themselves on being the most successful band of terrorists outside Bengal. Although less than three years old, they had an impressive record of achievement. They also prided themselves on the fact that their leader, Shafi Usman, was the most wanted man in the state; the British police had proclaimed a reward of a thousand rupees to anyone giving information leading to his capture "dead or alive," as the official phrase put it.

So far, none of them had been caught. That was because their number was small, their discipline was strict, and their leader never permitted them to take foolhardy risks. But above all it was due to the fact that their leader had friends in the police department; they all knew that.

They were all fervent patriots, dedicated to the overthrow of British rule in India. Anyone who represented that rule, British or Indian, was their enemy; anything that represented that rule was their legitimate target. "Jai-ram!" answered by "Jai-rahim!" was their secret mode of greeting. The name of Rama, sacred to all Hindus, and that of Rahim, equally sacred to the Moslems.

In the context of the sharp differences that had now arisen between the Hindus and the Moslems heading the nationalist struggle against British rule, the terrorist movement was the last gasp of those who wanted to carry on the struggle united. They were all willing, almost eager, to die for their motherland, and it needed a leader of Shafi's calibre to keep them from making thoughtless sacrifices. Shafi Usman was wholly unaffected by the new wave of religious fanaticism which was sweeping the country. Hindus, Moslems, and Sikhs had banded themselves under his leadership, convinced that it was they and their counterparts in the other states who would finally oust the British from their country. They had nothing but contempt for the non-violent agitation of Mr. Gandhi and his followers; the white man, they were convinced, would never respect such abject passivity. To them, the apostles of non-violence were the enemies of the nation, bent on emasculating the population. They even suspected that it was a movement secretly supported by the British to strengthen their hold on the country: was not the Indian National Congress itself started by an Englishman?

"They will end up by making us a nation of sheep," Shafi used to tell them. "That is what Gandhi and his Congressmen want. That is exactly what the British too want us to be—three hundred million sheep!"

Their members were required to renounce vegetarianism and the taboos of religion. Their oath of initiation was signed in blood, blood drawn from the little finger of the left hand. Their meetings always ended with their partaking of a curry made of equal parts of beef and pork, symbolising the flouting of the sacred impositions of all the religions of India: Hinduism, Sikhism, Islam. The Hindus and Sikhs venerated the cow; she was the go-mata, the universal mother; the Moslems abhorred the pig as an unclean, unholy animal. After eating a dish made of pork and beef no Hindu, Moslem, or Sikh could practise his religion.

That had been a major ordeal for Debi-dayal. On that first day he had nearly brought up his food. Countless years of penance in earlier incarnations that had made him a Brahmin in this one had been thrown away by the single act of sacrilege, the eating of beef. But it had to be done. You could not have both orthodoxy and freedom. Religious differences among the races of India were the root cause of the country's slavery, and the British had learnt to take the fullest advantage of these differences, playing the Hindus against the Moslems and the Sikhs against both.

"The nationalists have just played into their hands—Gandhi and Jinnah both," Shafi would pronounce. "The only saving grace of the nationalist movement has gone; it is no longer united, no longer secular. The Hindus and Moslems are both going their own ways, both trying to propagate non-violence."

They themselves were the elite, having smashed down the barriers of religion that held other Indians divided; blood-brothers in the service of the motherland.

Outwardly they were the members of the Hanuman Physical Culture Club. Their headquarters was a low mud-walled house behind the Hanuman temple. Inside were the authentic gloom of a gymnasium, the smell of stale sweat, rubbing oil, and embrocation, the sounds of the thuds and bumps of human bodies in the process of hardening, and of heavy, controlled breathing. On the walls were framed photographs of wrestlers and boxers: Charles Atlas, Gama and Gunga, Ibrahim, Muller, Jack Johnson, Primo Carnera, and several others. In the centre of the room was the akhada, the sunken wrestling-pit filled with soft red sand. Beyond the akhada was the roped-off arena for judo with a special corner devoted to the shrine—a black belt draped over an arrangement of five photographs of the ranking judoists in Japan. Stacked along one wall were the bar-bells, the dumbbells, the graduated wooden clubs, and the chest-expanders. Out in the walled-off back yard were horizontal bars, single and double, and the oiled malkhamb, the climbing-pole of the Deccan. They even had a padded vaulting horse for developing initiative and daring, just as they were supposed to do in the British army.

Every evening there were at least a dozen of them present, which usually meant that the others were on some sort of an assignment. On Saturdays all thirty-seven of them turned up. On Saturdays they did no physical exercises, and neither Tomonaga nor the wrestling master was present. They bolted the doors and windows and talked, talked late into the night and made plans. Before dispersing, they ate their simple meal of coarse bread and the beef-and-pork curry, washed down with water.

They sat around the sand-pit in a horseshoe, leaving the fourth side free, their legs resting on the sandbags that lined the stone coping of the pit. At the head, on the fourth side, sat Shafi Usman.

He now called himself Singh and had grown a beard and wore a turban because his photograph without the beard had been circulated to all the police stations in the Punjab. A figure of romance, he was said to be a favourite of the prostitutes of Delhi's Chandni Chowk and Lahore's Anarkali, but his associates knew nothing about that part of his life. The beard went well with his face and figure; it lent tone to his over-all air of virility and latent power, and even helped to set him apart as their leader. He spoke in a soft, earnest voice, his large hairy hands held limp in his lap, his accent sounding slightly outlandish to the others because of his prolonged sojourn in foreign lands. He had been to Germany and Russia, and it was a treat to listen to him talking about the wonderful achievements of Hitler and Stalin.

They accepted his position as leader without question: he belonged to that select coterie of the first batch of terrorists, the associates of Jitin Das and Hafiz Khan. Jitin Das had died in jail in the Andamans, and Hafiz Khan was said to be living in Bombay, directing the entire movement; he was the acknowledged chief of the terrorists in India, just as Gandhi was the chief of the National Congress.

But Jitin Das and Hafiz Khan were just names to the members of the Freedom Fighters. Their leader was Shafi; Shafi who came to talk to them every Saturday evening and allotted to them their tasks, Shafi who shared their risks and hardships.

They knew his history. Shafi had a good deal to avenge. As a boy of seven he had been taken to identify the body of his father, flung obscenely on a heap of other bodies, in the enclosure of the Jallianwala bagh. It was a hot April day in the year 1919, and the dead of Jallianwala had already begun to smell. There were three hundred and seventy-nine bodies in the enclosure—the authorities knew the exact number because they had been counted—and it had taken him a long time to discover his father's body.

"The poor man had nothing to do with Mr. Gandhi's non-cooperation movement," Shafi had told them. "If anything, he was in the opposite camp, a staunch supporter of British rule in India. He had merely strayed into the bagh to see what was happening and could not have been there for more than a few minutes when General Dyer ordered his machine guns to open fire.Within minutes, there were three hundred and seventy-nine dead and over a thousand wounded."

That same evening, returning from the funeral, Shafi Usman and his wailing mother had found that while going down Kucha Kaurianwala alley they had to crawl on their bellies because General Dyer had promulgated what was called the crawling order.

"Everyone had to go on all fours," Shafi had told them. "Like dogs!—all of us, men, women, children, no one was exempt. That is the sort of insult we have to avenge. And then we talk of non-violence! The creed of non-violence is a naked insult to the land of Shivaji and Akbar and Ranjeet."

They had begun under his guidance, modestly enough. At first they had merely painted Hindu numbers on milestones and on road signs, and written anti-British slogans on walls. After that they went about tarring the statues of British generals and administrators. Then they went on to cutting telephone and telegraph wires, setting fire to postboxes by putting burning oil-soaked rags into them, and playing havoc with unattended motor cars by dropping fistfuls of sand into their oil tanks.

Now they had graduated to bigger tasks: burning remote government buildings, burning wooden sleepers on railway tracks, and removing the fishplates which joined the rails. They possessed several sets of German-made pliers for cutting wire, and heavy spanners which exactly fitted the fishplate bolts, all neatly stored behind the sandbags on which their feet now rested. During the two previous weeks, they had managed to remove no less than seven fishplates from the railway track. So far, their most spectacular achievements had been to burn down a forest rest-house in the jungle and to derail a goods train.

But just as they were beginning to feel pleased with themselves, Bengal had gone ahead. A college girl had fired a revolver at the British Governor while he was addressing a university convocation.

"A mere girl has shamed us," Debi-dayal said.

The leader shot a quick glance at him. He was not like the others, Debi-dayal, with his cream silk shirt, sports jacket, and Rolex watch on his wrist. Neither poverty nor frustration had brought him into their ranks. What was at the back of all that fervour? he wondered. For him, the other members' motives were easy to fathom; Debi-dayal had always been secretive about his.

At times Shafi even felt a little uneasy about him. He was aware that all the other members had come to accept Debi-dayal as a sort of deputy leader. They knew Debi's father's generosity had helped to build up the front of their athletic club; that the few sticks of dynamite which Debi-dayal had managed to steal from his father's store had enabled them to derail the goods train.

"When are we going to start using our revolvers?" Imam Din asked. "In Bengal, even girls . . ."

"And what was the use?" Shafi demanded coldly. "Cranwell did not die. They all wear steel jackets under their shirts when they go out to these functions. The girl was caught red-handed. Now she will squeal. The police will make her tell—you know their methods. The whole group will be uncovered and sent to jail, and our entire movement endangered. For what? For a girl's impetuousness. That is no way to do our work. We want to kill; we don't want to be caught. Not because we are afraid to die, but because we want to go on doing our work until the job is finished."

The others watched him, spellbound, the leader who was a Moslem and now looked like a Sikh. His transformation gave added significance to their movement. A man's religion meant nothing. Here was a man who had been born a Moslem but had now become a Sikh; he even wore a kada, the steel bangle of the Sikh religion.

Nor had he any words of sympathy for the girl, only anxiety about how she had endangered the movement. That too was a measure of his dedication. She had made a mistake. The torture to which she would now be subjected was just an accepted risk of their calling—in her case, perhaps, what she almost deserved.

"Can't we devise some absolutely foolproof method of wrecking a train?" Imam Din asked.

Shafi shook his head. "There again, we must calculate the risk against the results. If we want to do it without fuss and make a clean getaway, the only thing is to remove the fishplates and hope that the train is heavy enough or fast enough to displace a rail. We would only get another freight train, most likely. It is the weight—something like a thousand tons as against the five hundred tons of a passenger train. We can't afford to waste explosives or fuses—these we must save for emergencies."

His face was expressionless, calm, his voice sonorous, his eyes almost hypnotic with the big dark pupils half concealed by the thick, drooping lashes. As the light now fell on his face, he looked like the statue of Buddha in repose, Debi-dayal thought; a bearded Buddha in deep contemplation, radiating inner peace— a Moslem who had become a Sikh and looked like Buddha, transcending the religious insularity of ageless Indias.

"At the Begwad turning I and Debi-dayal removed three fishplates," Basu said. "Nothing happened."

"The ties hold the rails clamped to the sleepers," Shafi explained. "It is often a matter of luck."

"Is there no way of removing the ties?" Debi-dayal asked.

"They are nine inches long, hammered deep into the wood, four to each sleeper. It would take hours to loosen a dozen ties— but then, that would make things certain."

"Surely we can do that," Debi-dayal said, leaning forward in his eagerness. In the harsh glare of the hissing petromax lamp which hung from the rafter, his pale, refined, almost ascetic face, with sleek black hair falling over one eye, glowed with fervour. He was strikingly handsome, Shafi thought, this boy who was their chief financial prop and who had been practising the holds of judo as if his life depended on it. His eyes were large and lustrous, his lips parted. He typified the general mood of the council of war—the lust for spectacular action. Shafi felt a surge of pride for his men.

But he had to be practical; it was up to him as their leader to curb their rashness, to prevent them from wasting themselves. "If we remove the plates, and at the same time pull out at least a dozen ties, and then saw off or burn, say, four of the end sleepers, then we can be absolutely certain of an accident," he told them. "But with us doing the job, it would take at least two hours. The experts do it in much less time. Near Madras they managed it in forty-three minutes. Absolutely split-second timing, but they were railway workers themselves."

"But surely we are capable of all that," Debi-dayal said. "We will rehearse for days, and then go to it, all of us working at the same time."

"No." Shafi shook his head, running his tongue over his thick bright pink lips. "No. There is never enough time for all that between trains. We can do it much more simply, of course, and more quickly, with explosives. But not unless the rewards are proportionately higher. If we can blow up a British troop-train, for instance, we will do it, or if the governor's 'special' is going. But then we will need much larger quantities of explosives, dynamite, than we now possess. An electric fuse too, operated by a battery, not the sort of wick affair we have to light and run away. It's not very easy." He looked pointedly at Debi-dayal.

Debi-dayal shifted his eyes, stabbed by an inner guilt—a two-pronged guilt. He had already raided his father's store and stolen a bundle of gelignite sticks and a box of detonators, the loss of which had caused a good deal of commotion in the office. At the same time, he was aware that he had contributed less fully than the others had expected. Explosives were the lifeblood of any terrorist movement, and he was the only one of their group with access to them, all neatly stacked in the Kerwad Construction Company's store.

The thought of destroying a British troop-train held them together, settled over them like a savoury smell, reducing them to silence. One by one, they all began to look at him.

"Any suggestions, Debi-dayal?"

Debi felt weak and defenceless. They were as good as asking him to rob his father's godown again. There was no way out, if he was to prove himself a dedicated Freedom Fighter. "I was thinking," he said lamely, trying to play for time, "I was thinking . . . there is a statue of Queen Victoria in the park at Jamboti. It is made of marble. After six, the gates of the park are closed. All it needs is a crack with a hammer."

He could feel the contempt in their gaze. This, he was aware, was kids' stuff. They must do something that would match the activities of their group in Bengal.

It seemed a long time before Shafi came to his rescue, almost as though he too wanted to make him feel that he was not really pulling his weight. "Very good," Shafi said. "It is a one-man job. Would you like to take it on, Basu?"

"Yes, of course," Basu said with alacrity. "Thank you."

"Good. Has anyone got anything—er—more ambitious to suggest?" Shafi asked. "Something that will give our friends a real jolt?"

For a few seconds they all looked blankly at one another. There was an uncomfortable silence, and then a member made as if to speak.

"Yes, Ahmad?" Shafi asked.

"Three planes landed on the military aerodrome this morning. Two of them went away. One is still there."

The leader shook his head doubtfully. "We cannot strike so close to this town. We have always avoided drawing attention to Duriabad."

He had been careful about keeping their activities cleverly dispersed. He had explained to them how the police pinned little flags on maps to mark down terrorist activities. Once they got a clear pattern, it was easy to locate the centre of the activities. It was vital to avoid the vicinity of Duriabad.

"I think we go in for far too much caution and very little action," Debi-dayal said. "What is to connect us with Duriabad? We've never struck within twenty miles of this place. They will only think we have come from outside. And if we can destroy a military plane, I think we should take the risk."

"Hear, hear!" Basu applauded. "That's the way to talk."

The murmur of assent that followed disturbed Shafi. Almost in spite of himself, he experienced a feeling of resentment. Was his leadership slipping? Was it Debi-dayal whom they now looked up to?

He gave them a reassuring smile—the first time he had smiled that evening. This was the moment to play along with his followers and to respect their mood. Targets for sabotage were not easy to come by.

"There is something in what you say, of course," he said, turning his smile on Debi-dayal. "Does anyone know why the plane is here, how long it will remain?"

"The planes were on their way from Peshawar to Hyderabad and landed here to refuel. There was trouble of some kind with one of them. The others went on, but this one is waiting for parts to be brought," Ahmad told them eagerly.

"How do you know?"

"One of the bearers from the officers' mess was heard talking about it."

"I take it the pilot is living in the officers' mess?"

"Yes," Ahmad said.

After that there was silence in the room for a full minute. Shafi sat staring into the distance. The others sat staring at his face.

"It is too tempting to turn down," Shafi said. "An absolute gift, in fact. I have frequently walked along that airstrip. There was never anybody there. It's only an emergency landing ground for Air Force planes. They have a watchman's hut and a storeroom for petrol cans. I was thinking that we might burn down the storeroom, too, with all that petrol. But I think we'd better concentrate on the plane. So far as I know, there is only the watchman, no other guards or anything. Am I right, Ahmad?"

"They have put on an extra police sentry, because of the plane. But he too stands at the entrance of the field. The river side is quite unguarded."

"What about . . . whatever it takes to destroy a plane?" Basu asked.

Shafi gave him a level stare. "Yes, we've got whatever it takes," he said with another faint smile, and then paused. "The main requirement is, of course, human courage and resourcefulness. And that we've got, in great abundance, in all of you." He waved a hand at the circle around him. The moment of doubt had passed. Once again he experienced the warm glow of their confidence.

"In Germany, there is a school for teaching sabotage," Shafi went on. "Everything from bridges and railway engines to telephone receivers. Aeroplanes are about the easiest targets of all. An unguarded plane is an absolute gift. It's a two-man job. I shall be one. I want another. Volunteers?"

Every one of his listeners raised his hand.

Shafi's glance swept over their faces; this time it was a cold, professional going-over, the captain assessing his men according to the special requirements of the assignment.

It was wonderful to see their eagerness. Shafi experienced a surge of pride as he scanned their faces, rigid, expectant, aglow with fervour, and for the first time that evening he wondered how long it could be maintained. The Congress and the Moslem League had come to a final parting of ways, with Hindus and Moslems separated into opposite camps, learning to hate each other with the bitterness of ages. Even their own leaders had begun to take sides. Hafiz had already written to him from Bombay complaining about the callousness of the Hindus towards the Moslems, suggesting that they should reorientate their activities. How long would it be before the flames of communal hatred caught up with them?

He looked at Debi-dayal and once again felt that quick, unreasoning pang of jealousy. He reminded him of a more youthful

Nehru: the theatrical good looks, the background of wealth and learning, the refinement of manner, the awareness of built-in leadership.

"You!" he snapped, pointing a finger at Debi-dayal.

In the black night, the two men lay side by side; the elder, bearded, dark and muscular, proud in achievement yet calm and deliberate; the other, fair and lissom, sick with nervousness, trying desperately to control the trembling of his body.

From where they lay, watching from behind the trunk of a kikar tree, their chins cupped in their hands, they could clearly see the plane, barely three hundred yards away, and could hear the crackle of twisting metal and smell the burning oil and rubber and fabric.

The flames rose, swallowing the outline of the plane, and casting a faint pink mist over the surroundings. They saw a lorry drive up and stop near the watchman's hut, its lights still on. Five or six men ran up to the circle made by the glow and then came to an abrupt halt and instantly fell back as if thrown off by an invisible barrier. They stood by, gesticulating, puny figures in a shadow drama, their words drowned by the roar of the fire.

As he watched them, the older man grinned and stroked his beard with his fingers. He turned briefly to look at his companion. There was just enough flickering light for him to see that Debi-dayal's face had assumed an almost frightening malevolence, as though he were gripped by the joy of some secret fulfilment much greater than the mere burning of a plane. His staring eyes reflected the speck of fire, his lips were pressed together in a hard black line. Shafi went on staring at the face, almost in spite of himself, observing the weird play of light on it —like someone looking on at a cremation, Shafi thought: the face of the god of vengeance, gloating. With conscious effort he turned his gaze back to the burning plane.

For a long time the two continued to watch the scene. They saw a car drive up along the airstrip; three men, all of them white men, jumped out of the car and joined the others.

"Officers!" the older man whispered. "Colonel Dreyford and his adjutant. Still in mess-kit, so they must have been having a guest night. The third man will be the pilot." He grinned and looked to the other for response. But the face was still in a trance, frozen in a bloodless mask of triumph.

Silence and darkness returned, though the smell of the burnt-out plane lingered on. For a few minutes longer the two men surrendered to their separate thoughts; then Shafi put out a hand and shook Debi-dayal's shoulder. He had to prod quite forcibly before the younger man looked at him, with a start. "Time to be off!" he whispered.

They slid away on all fours, their bellies to the ground, crawling all the way through the shrubbery beyond the trees until they reached the river-bank, both of them conscious that this crawling itself was some kind of an answer on behalf of the men and women who had been made to crawl in the streets of Amritsar twenty years earlier.

[9]

The Strands of the Net

SUPERINTENDENT Bristow of the C.I.D. walked into the map room for what he referred to as his Friday morning prayer meeting, a lean greyhound of a man in khaki gabardine jacket and grey flannel trousers, smoking a pipe. With his close-cropped iron-grey hair, his short moustache, and his iron-grey eyes, he typified the warm, easy-going colonial officer. And yet, under the casual exterior, he combined a knife-edge sharpness with bull-headed determination which made him the sort of man who would either die by the assassin's bullet or rise to be an inspector general of police and receive a knighthood at the hands of a grateful sovereign.

The others were already there, grouped around a table on which there was a map of the Northern Punjab province. The traditional little blue, red, and green pins marked the incidence of terrorist activities, the blue ones marking the previous week's incidents.

Bristow gave a quick smile to acknowledge the greetings of his subordinates, and walked up to the map. For a minute or so he studied it in silence. "Humm, eight this week—no, nine," he muttered. "We certainly are doing well, aren't we?"

The others grinned sheepishly at the implied rebuke. "Six are only the usual tarring of milestones, sir," Manzoor, the chief inspector, told him.

"Oh, six—one less than last week. Not all in one place, I take it?"

"No, sir; well spread out, as usual."

"And the other three?"

"The Air Force plane at Duriabad airstrip, the postbox burning at Kurandi village, and breaking up Queen Victoria's statue in the park at Jamboti."

"Poor Vicky . . . what a lot of statues they used to put up in those days." His eyes wandered over the map. "What's the red one? That makes two in Duriabad."

"Pearce was there, sir," Manzoor said.

"That red one is the complaint from the Kerwad Construction Company . . ." Sergeant Pearce began.

"The one about missing sticks of dynamite?"

"Yes, sir, and the box of fuses."

"Anything?"

Pearce shook his head. "Nothing, sir. The company uses a lot of explosives and fuses every day; they are building the Nashi bridge. It may only have been a mistake in accounting. This sort of thing happens all the time, and frankly some other people wouldn't even have thought of reporting it. It just happens that Dewan-bahadur Tekchand is very finicky so he told the commissioner that we weren't investigating his complaint with sufficient zeal—"

"Oh, yes, I remember. Everything has to be just so, or I'll speak to the commissioner."

"That's right, sir."

"Anything else?"

"I also took a look at the Hanuman Physical Culture Club, since I happened to be there. You may remember that last week we decided to keep it under observation for a few days."

"That's right; one of those routine checks of institutions where young men gather together."

"Yes, sir."

Bristow raised his eyebrows. "Anything?"

"Well, nothing to speak of, sir," Pearce said. "I kept a watch for three days, Wednesday to Friday. Nothing there. Just some boys doing weight-lifting and wrestling and that kind of thing. I sneaked in once, after they had closed. Single-catch padlock. Nothing but gymnasium equipment inside. Only—only I thought I might just mention it, sir: the chest-expanders and bar-bells and things are all German-made."

Bristow gave a short guffaw. "That's because they are cheaper, and very well made too. Even my son has acquired a pair of German-made spring dumbbells."

Pearce grinned sheepishly. "I thought I might just mention it . . ."

"And quite right too, well done. Who paid for it—the dumb-bells and things?"

"It is all done on donations, but the principal donor seems to be Dewan-bahadur Tekchand, sir. He gave them a thousand rupees for equipment."

"Our own Dewan-bahadur-sahib, of the explosives?"

"Yes, sir."

"Oh, then there can't be anything in it. We can't go suspecting someone like Tekchand of supporting a terrorist gang and then sending in a complaint about missing explosives! He gives just as generously to police welfare. A thousand, you said?"

"Sir."

"Rather a lot. What is his interest in the Hanuman Club?"

"His son is a member, Debi-dayal."

"Ah, that explains it. Tell me about the son," Bristow said.

"College boy; very keen on Japanese wrestling."

"Judo? Who takes them in it? Tomonaga?"

"Yes. Twice a week."

"He is very good, Tomonaga. He gives classes at the university too." Bristow shook his head. "Tell me about the plane. How did they manage to set fire to it?"

"It was difficult to reconstruct, sir. Nothing left on the spot— all gutted. But it is pretty certain they piled a lot of cotton waste soaked in petrol under the belly of the plane, then set a match to it and bolted."

"Just a match? It couldn't be a fuse?"

"Can't say, sir."

"How many of them?"

"Two sets of footprints."

Bristow perched himself on the table and began to light his pipe. "What about the footprints?" he asked.

"Tennis shoes, soles quite smooth."

"Humm, doesn't help much, does it?"

"No, sir."

"And yet it means that they must have had a pretty good idea of the layout—that there was no guard on the river side. They must have known that the plane would be there overnight. Who could have seen it land?"

"Hundreds of people, even though the strip's nearly ten miles from the town. Aeroplanes are rare in that part of the world."

"So they had only a few hours to get a message sent to wherever they are located and bring down a burning squad. Seem to be a damn sight more efficient than we are. What was it?"

"I beg your pardon, sir?"

"The plane. What make was it?"

"A Wapiti, of the Thirteenth Reconnaissance Squadron."

"And no other clue?"

Sergeant Pearce shuffled his feet and squirmed in his seat, sensing the displeasure in the superintendent's voice. "Well, sir," he began, "it may be just a red herring but . . . I questioned all the mess servants. Just a routine questioning because that was where the pilot had been put up—in the Greyforths' mess. And I thought I ought to check whether any of them had heard the pilot talking to the officers and then gone and broadcast it in the bazaar."

"Much more likely that the officers themselves talked, after a couple of drinks at the club," Bristow commented, but there was a slight grin on his face as he said it.

Encouraged by the grin, Pearce went on. "All the mess servants denied that they knew anything about the plane, of course —pretended that they did not understand English. Most of them do understand it a little."

"Of course they do," Bristow said. "But you'll never get them to admit it."

"One of them looked a little familiar to me. For a time I could not think where I could have seen him, and then it suddenly came to me that two days earlier I had seen him in a teahouse with a young man called Ahmad Khan. I had just gone in for a cup of tea when these two walked in, quite matey."

"This Ahmad, have we got anything on him, Manzoor?" Bristow asked the chief inspector.

"No, sir," Manzoor said. "There doesn't seem to be any use following that up."

"That's why I was reluctant to mention all this," Sergeant Pearce explained. "It just happens that Ahmad is a member of the Hanuman Club, and I had seen him going in."

Bristow shook his head uncertainly. "I am inclined to agree with you, Manzoor, and yet, I don't know; it might lead to something. What had you in mind, Pearce?"

"Well, sir, with your permission, I was going to remove this waiter to the thana, for a thorough questioning."

Superintendent Bristow grinned at the sergeant. "Yes, do that," he said. "But mind you, don't overdo the—er, the questioning. The army officers don't realize the difficulties we are up against in this country or appreciate that these things are sometimes unavoidable. And if they find one of their servants showing up with bruises or anything, they are capable of creating no end of trouble. Some of them have a lot of pull too, right up to the governor. But do go ahead. I can trust you not—not to overstep the mark."

Sergeant Pearce grinned. His bulldog face glowed with pride at the unaccustomed expression of confidence, his snub nose quivered. "No, sir," he assured Bristow. "I will see that there is no cause for fuss—no bruises."

"And you, Manzoor." Bristow turned to the chief inspector. "You had better arrange for the local chaps to keep a night-and-day guard on the Hanuman Physical Culture Club. Just in case something comes out of all this."

"Yes, sir," Manzoor said.

[10]

Two Leaders

HAFIZ KHAN's letters had been quite explicit, and yet they had not prepared Shafi for the change that had come over him. Shafi had never really cared much for Hafiz as a man, but of course there was no question of showing his indifference openly. Hafiz had always been somewhat unbalanced; everyone knew that. During his last term of imprisonment, they had actually placed him in the psychopathic ward at Yerawada.

At the same time, he was one of the top men in the movement, one of those who had inaugurated the Freedom Fighters, and he was exceptionally touchy; it was important to give him no cause to take offence. Shafi invited him to attend their Saturday evening meeting and address his men, but Hafiz declined. It seemed he wanted to speak to Shafi alone.

He received him in his room high up in the first lane behind Peshawar Gate, pigeon-loft of a room with a view of the back yards of the bazaar, and there Hafiz and he talked earnestly for nearly two hours. The night was breathless with the oppressive pre-monsoon heat. The kerosene lamp in the window was dark with soot, but neither of them had cared to lower its flame. The food that Shafi had offered, specially cooked in pure ghee because of his guest's finicky appetite, still lay under the covering plates on the window sill, exuding odours of spices, but the bottle of Dewar's whisky was nearly empty.

Now they were not talking. Hafiz, a little runt of a man, his face narrowing to a pointed mouth, his ears sticking out of his head, leaned forward and watched Shafi anxiously as he read the cuttings from the *Dawn* and *Trident* and the *Awaz* and the *Sulah* and the *Subah* which he had brought with him, all heavily underlined and boxed in red and blue pencil. For a long time there was silence in the room, silence except for the papers rus tling in Shafi's hands. The scowl on Shafi's face deepened as he read. It was only after he had put away the last clipping that Hafiz spoke.

"Now do you agree with me?"

Shafi shifted his eyes from the other's face. "I don't know," he said. "All that is hardly conclusive." He pointed at the stack of paper clippings that had been shown to him. "Everything twisted to suit a line of thought—"

"I am surprised at you!" Hafiz said with passion, his beady, tormented eyes looking straight into Shafi's. "We who once ruled this country as conquerors shall be living here as inferior citizens, as the slaves of Hindus! Unless we heed the warnings and stand up for ourselves."

"Whose warnings? Jinnah's? Have you become a Leaguer?"

"I am not a Leaguer only because the League does not believe in our methods. But there is no denying that Jinnah is a great man. He has pointed out the way. We must now turn our back on the Hindus, otherwise we shall become their slaves!" His fists were clenched; his nose quivered with passion; drops of spittle flew out of his mouth.

This was bad, very bad. Shafi's eyes were bloodshot; his frown betrayed his annoyance. "I still don't see it as you do," he protested. "It means putting the clock back, undoing all we have done!"

"Hai-hai!" his visitor exclaimed. "You have been living in the past—in the Jallianwala days, concentrating on your own work. You don't know what's happening in the rest of the country. The time has come to take a second look—to reorientate ourselves. The enemies of the moment are not the British; they are the Hindus. That's what we must recognize!"

Shafi shook his head. "It goes against the grain. The whole movement, what we have striven hard to build in the past, becomes meaningless. It was *your* teaching—you and the others—the pioneers. We worked under your guidance, your inspiration. You were equally ardent."

"And you have done excellent work," Hafiz interrupted. "But we must move with the times. If new dangers threaten, we must change our stance to meet them. In our hatred of the British, we had altogether lost sight of a far greater menace: the Hindus!" His voice crackled with emotion.

"The Hindus can never constitute a danger to the Moslems—

not here in the Punjab. Never! Only fanatics can believe such nonsense."

Hafiz sprang up. Angular and bony, his narrow face close to the other's, he stood over Shafi's chair like a hungry hawk eying its prey. He pointed a finger at Shafi, and the finger shook as though electrified. "Fanatics! We have to turn fanatic in sheer self-defence. You talk of the Punjab, but even the Punjab will not escape the fate of Bombay and Madras, where already we are second-rate citizens, working ants in a society of ants."

"But even there they have taken one or two Moslems into the government," Shafi pointed out.

"One or two! Are we to be satisfied with crumbs? We who ruled the whole country? Have we now become dogs? And who are the one or two? Who—I ask you? Stooges—their own men. Moslems who are members of the Congress, renegades. Don't you know that the Congress will not have anyone who is not a member? That is what will happen here too. You will find a Congress ministry—a Hindu ministry with a couple of Moslems who are obedient servants of the Congress. Even today, there are Congress administrations in eight of the eleven provinces. What is happening? They will not take any Moslems who will not join them. Jinnah has exposed them: 'The Hindus have shown that Hindustan is for the Hindus.' Now we Moslems have to look after ourselves. Organize yourselves before it's too late. Carve out our own country—"

"A new country? Apart from India?"

"Yes, a new nation. Not apart from India, but a part carved out of India that will be wholly Moslem; pure, uncontaminated."

"But how are we to drive out the British? Are not we forgetting that? You can never achieve freedom by driving a wedge between the two communities!"

Hafiz threw up his arms in a gesture of despair and turned away. He picked up his glass and drained it. Then he flung himself in his chair, limp and exhausted. When he spoke again, his voice sounded tired, like the rustle of paper on tin.

"That is outmoded thinking. We don't want freedom if it means our living here as slaves of the Hindus. If we succeed in driving out the British, it is the Hindus who will inherit power. Then what happens to us? We are heading for a slavery far more degrading—struggling for it. That's what Jinnah is worried about. That's what all of us are worried about."

"It doesn't bear thinking about," Shafi said. "To break up with one's own hands what we have striven so hard to build up: communal solidarity."

"It has to be done. We have to organize ourselves—Moslems against the rest of India—if we are to survive. Organize, not so much to win freedom, but to protect ourselves from being swamped by the Hindus, emasculated, to become a race of serfs in a country ruled by idolators."

"But this is just playing into the hands of the British. They want to keep the Hindus and the Moslems divided, so that they can go on ruling. Our only salvation lies in solidarity—that is the only way to oust the British."

Hafiz shook his head and clucked his tongue. "I am surprised," he said, "surprised and sad that someone with your background should not heed the signs." He shook his head again and a strand of silver hair fell on his forehead. "Don't you realize we must change our tactics to suit the nature of the danger?" His voice rose and quivered with passion. "The Congress has contested elections and won them. And in their triumph what did they do? They made it clear that there is no place for anyone in this country except on their terms. For them the great Moslem League does not exist; according to them, they alone represent India—all of us, the Moslems and the Christians and the Parsees. In short, either you accept Hindu overlordship or you have no place in this country. Who wants a freedom like that? Would you not rather have the British?"

"Never!" Shafi exclaimed with passion. "Never—so long as I remember Jallianwala!"

"Yes, you only remember Jallianwala—something that happened twenty years ago. Do you know what happened in Bombay three months ago, in the Dassara riots? The police actually sided with the Hindus. I saw policemen shooting down Moslems, picking them out. At least they did not do that at Jallianwala. That is what is happening everywhere today, and you harp on Jallianwala!"

"What you are telling us is to stop all activities, in short, to dissolve the Freedom Fighters. Is that what you have done in Bombay?"

Hafiz shook his head in slow motion. His eyes were narrowed, his nostrils flared, his lips were retracted. He looks more like an angry rat than ever, Shafi thought contemptuously. "The

Fighters must go on," Hafiz pronounced. "Go on with ever greater vigour—but only as a purely Moslem organization. The Hindu element must be eliminated. Our methods remain as they are; only our targets have changed. We have to be ready to use the same methods against the Hindus."

"I don't understand what you are saying," Shafi confessed. "Then the Hindus too will use terrorist methods against us—the Moslems. It would mean—it can only mean—civil war."

The other laughed. It was an arrogant, assured laugh. "That is exactly what we have to prepare ourselves for: a civil war. We have to think ahead, a year, two years from now, to a time when the British will leave this country, leaving our fate in the hands of the Hindus. Are we to sit back and take whatever indignities they have in store for us? We must hit back tenfold. It is to that end that we must all work, must all recognize the new enemies: the Hindus!"

"I don't like it," Shafi said weakly. "I don't like it at all that we, who have always striven for communal solidarity, should now prepare for civil war. Our only solution was to keep together so as to fight the British. In fact, if Gandhi's movement had not been so irreconcilable with my own thinking—all that nonsense about non-violence—that is the movement I would join, not a communal organization."

"That is what has brought us to this pass," Hafiz said, rising to his feet again. "We who ruled this country and had enslaved the Hindus, are now being enslaved in our turn. The Hindus are winning. They have laid traps for us. As soon as the British are made to leave—made to leave with our fullest cooperation, mind you—the Hindus will take over. They are clever, cleverer than ourselves in their trickery. Take Gandhi's own words: 'In the midst of darkness, light persists; in the midst of death, life persists.' Is it nonsense? No, it is not. It is the peculiar escapism of Hinduism, the utter meaninglessness of words. Light in darkness, life in death; why not violence in the midst of non-violence? That is what I say. In the midst of Gandhi's non-violence, violence persists. Violence such as no one has ever seen. That is what awaits this country: the violence bottled up in those who pay lip-service to non-violence. The Hindus are preparing for it— to kill us, to swamp us."

Far in the distance a train whistled. Shafi got up and poured the remaining whisky into their glasses. For a few moments they waited, looking at each other, like spent wrestlers in an arena, reluctant to go on with the bout.

"Here's to our movement," Hafiz said. "To our survival, to our victory!"

Both men drank in silence, not aware that anything had been decided, agreed upon. Hafiz put down his glass with a bang and said, "I am leaving the papers here. It will do you a lot of good to read them at your leisure; it'll open your eyes. Remember that in the Muharram riots, seven people were injured in the rioting itself, eighteen men died by police fire—all Moslems! The police killed more than the rioters—doesn't that mean anything to you?"

"What does it mean?"

"They shoot to kill—they pick out the Moslems and shoot to kill."

Long after Hafiz Khan had gone, Shafi sat slumped in his chair, looking vacantly at the lamp, which was now thickly layered with soot. He was still fully dressed, still staring vacantly at the lamp, nearly an hour later, when there was a faint knock on the door. He sat up with a sudden catlike motion and listened. Then he got up and opened the door.

A man stood in the darkness outside, a tall man in a Pathan turban. Shafi's heart began to pound as he recognized Manzoor, the chief inspector from the Criminal Department. He crept close to his visitor, walking on tiptoe.

"It is bad news I bring," Manzoor whispered. "They are going to carry out a raid today: the Hanuman Club first, and then arrest the others in their houses."

"Hai-toba!" Shafi exclaimed. His body was suddenly bathed in a cold sweat, as though at the end of a fever. "When?" he asked.

"About seven this evening, but the place is being watched even now. You had better clear right out of town. Lie low for a time."

"Thanks," Shafi mumbled. "How did they find out? We had been so careful."

"The missing explosives. Tekchand complained to us. That haram-zada Pearce was on it. That led to other things."

Shafi cursed under his breath.

"Pearce happened to be in Duriabad, looking into the complaint, when the plane was burned."

So that was how things ended. A timid, pernickety man report-ing the loss of some sticks of dynamite, a police sergeant stum-bling on some incongruity, and all that preparation, all that care, went up in smoke. His knees felt weak.

"And don't warn too many people," Manzoor cautioned. "Otherwise they'll suspect you've been tipped off; who knows, they might even suspect me; that —— Bristow is as cunning as they come. Those who habitually go there should be there . . . when it happens."

"All right," Shafi promised.

When he came back into the room the feeling of headache and nausea had already left him, and he no longer felt weak. There was work to do. He had to think, make up his mind about whom to save, whom to sacrifice.

For a time he sat staring vacantly at the heap of papers left behind by Hafiz. Then he picked them up and began to read, peering at the lines in the smoky light. When he finished reading, the cocks in the streets below had already started crow-ing. He put out the lamp and walked out of the room without a single glance behind.

It was later that morning, as he sat in a crowded third-class compartment of the Sind Mail, that Shafi had time to think of the events of the past twelve hours. He was satisfied with what he had been able to accomplish. He had warned as many of the Freedom Fighters as he could. The others would have to be sacrificed. Seven of his best men—no, eight. But that could not be helped.

And then he suddenly realized that all those who would be in the club at the time of the raid would be Hindus; there would not be a single Moslem among them. It was the sort of coinci-dence that worried Shafi for a long time, but even to himself he refused to admit that it had anything to do with the visit of Hafiz, or with the clippings he had left behind him.

[11]

The Canoe Song

"NA-JANE kidhar aaj meri nao chali-re," Sundari was humming to herself as she sat embroidering Debi's initials on his handkerchief in black silk.

The "Canoe Song" fitted her mood. "Today I know not where my canoe is headed for," was what the song said; nor did she. Her mother had told her that a young man to whom they had offered her hand in marriage was coming to tea in the afternoon.

"Chali-re, chali-re meri nao chali-re," she went on repeating the chorus, picturing herself in a canoe on a wide, sunlit river, drifting, not knowing where she was going.

The young man who was coming to see her was Gopal Chandidar. She had, of course, heard of the Chandidar family; her parents had often talked about them. The Chandidars belonged to one of the thirty-seven premier families, and Gopal was the nephew of the Maharani of Begwad. He was said to have been educated in England and had a well-paid job with a British firm.

In the photograph which her mother had shown her, he looked handsome, in a somewhat big-boned, heavy-jowled, wavy-haired way, but that, she told herself, was because she was used to associating good looks in men only with the sensitive, eager, sharply chiselled face of her brother.

"They are a very old family," said her mother. "Established. The old Majaraja of Begwad is said to have given twenty lakhs of rupees when one of the daughters married his son—that is the present maharani; she is a Chandidar girl. And of course, Gopal will come into quite a bit of money even though he is the third son. You are a lucky girl. He's already turned down dozens of offers—some from the most prominent families too. Even the Yadav girl was offered to him."

"The Yadav girl was born under Mars," Sundari said. "Everyone knows that. She had been turned down by at least three other families."

"Who worries about horoscopes these days?" her mother scoffed. "You'd better put on one of my pearl necklaces. What sari will you be wearing?"

"I don't know," Sundari had told her.

She still did not know which sari she would wear. All she knew was that she was said to be a lucky girl. She felt light and gay, almost weightless. It was difficult to think coherently, to concentrate. She ached to talk to someone about it, someone close to her. She never thought it odd that her parents should be arranging her marriage. At school and college they had often talked of "love-marriages." But these were only for the most daring. For the rest of them, there was only the conventional kind of marriage, arranged by parents.

Was it going to be a success? Would she ever come to love her husband?

She had to talk to someone. She almost felt angry with Debidayal for not being in the house. He hardly ever was in the house these days, Sundari reflected. He seemed to spend all his spare time at that ridiculous gymnasium. And even at home, he was forever doing exercises and practising judo holds before a mirror. And how often she had seen him, sitting on the balcony reading a book, and at the same time banging the edge of his right hand against the sill.

At the thought of Debi's efforts to harden his hands, Sundari had experienced a pang of sisterly affection. To her, even now, he looked so small and in need of help, the baby with spaniel eyes and soft, chubby hands. He had grown much taller than herself, now, and his hands were hard as teak planks. The thin-limbed body now rippled with muscles, and the round, wide-eyed face had become sharp, insolent, and yet somehow eager—like that of a Spanish film star, she had always thought, or a bullfighter's; his movements were no longer gawky but graceful; even the way he walked was oddly like a panther's prowling.

Thinking of Debi like that, Sundari felt a little disloyal to the man whose photograph her mother had shown her. He was handsome too, she conceded, but in a different way; darker and more earthy, somehow more virile and sensuous. She finished the last handkerchief and bit off the thread. That would be a nice surprise for Debi, to find six new handkerchiefs, all neatly initialled in black silk. Now she had nothing to do except dream—dream of the young man who was coming to see her. How prosaic it sounded, someone just coming to *see* one; but of course they never went to see a girl unless they had already made up their minds.

Marriage? What did it mean? Did it invariably mean happiness—did it always lead to romance, to love? How could one tell? The thought momentarily darkened her mind.

But her Hindu upbringing reasserted itself. A girl had to trust her parents blindly, realizing that they alone knew what was good for her, they alone could find the right young man for her.

She felt too excited just to go on sitting in her room, doing nothing. To go and offer to help her mother with the arrangements for the evening would have seemed too forward. She picked up the stack of handkerchiefs and got up. Spindle, Debi's dachshund, which had been lying, fast asleep, at the foot of the bed, suddenly came to life, knowing that she was going out. Sundari walked across to Debi's room, at the other end of the house, past the slim bronze posturing figures standing at intervals on pedestals on both sides, Spindle scampering ahead of her. She deposited the handkerchiefs on Debi's dressing table, just in front of the mirror, where he could not help noticing them. Then she turned, as she always did, to take a look at the room.

Both windows were wide open. She knew that they were open day and night, and that sometimes at night Debi slipped out by dropping from the window down onto the badminton court. It was extraordinary that no one had found out about this, and she herself knew only because Debi himself had told her. Now sunlight came flooding through the windows and fell in long parallelograms on the grey cotton carpet, somehow accentuating the unrelieved masculinity of this room with its black and white striped handloomed curtains, heavy chairs of unpolished rosewood, an enormous leather club chair on the balcony, a bronze head-and-shoulders statue of Shivaji, and pictures on the walls of athletes, wrestlers, and judoists. There was not a single picture of a woman in the room, Sundari reflected, except, of course, the snapshot of herself and their mother on the dressing table. It was odd, but even their father's picture was not there.

And the books on their tall unvarnished shelves. It was almost queer, the sort of books Debi read. She walked across to one of the shelves: lives of Garibaldi, Terence MacSwiney, Tippu Sultan, Shivaji, Savarkar, Napoleon, Washington, Lincoln, and Booth. The next lot of books seemed even worse, for they were all on physical culture: *The Four-Minute Mile, The Art of Judo, Gung-ho* by Ishikawa, Zybsco on wrestling, and Muller on unarmed combat. It was quite puzzling, all this dull reading and preoccupation with masculinity in anyone as handsome as Debi.

Idly she looked for something to take to her room to read, passing her eyes over the books she had seen before: Nomad, Selous, Leveson, Sanderson, Dunbar-Brander and other books on big-game hunting. Then there was a life of Alfred Nobel and beside it a stack of hunting yearbooks and catalogues of guns and rifles and pistols.

Then she saw something familiar: a copy of *Gone with the Wind.* She had already read it, but it was the sort of book she would not mind reading again. She pulled out the volume, thinking that it was the ideal book for her present mood.

In the empty space behind where *Gone with the Wind* had been, she could see a flat, square box with a shining blue label. Contraceptives? she thought at once, with a sudden vicarious feeling of guilt, behind all that façade of clean living? And yet, why not? He was a man, after all, virile and good-looking; he had to learn sometime. Or were they erotic photographs? Some kind of potency pills? Her mind probed all the possibilities. And yet— sex and Debi? Women? It did not fit in.

The dog watched her movements, cocking its head, adding to her feeling of guilt. But she had to take a second look, knowing that it was wrong to pry into her brother's secrets; knowing how angry she herself would have been if he had come rummaging in her room in her absence and seen the letters from a boy at college which had made her angry when she received them but which she had kept, and read.

She took out the box. The label just said "Nobel." It meant nothing to her. She opened the box. Inside were little tubes of white metal, slightly thinner than cigarettes, each about two inches long, with one end open.

She looked at the lid again. Under the word "Nobel" was written in smaller print: "Thistle Brand Detonators."

And suddenly it hit her. Her hand shook, her knees felt weak, and her face was hot. She deposited the box on the floor very gently and pulled out the other books where *Gone with the Wind* had been. She found two thick yellow cartridges of waxed paper, each about eight inches long and as thick as her wrist. "Submarine Blasting Gelatine" read the inscription on the label. "Strength 90%."

Sundari sat limply on Debi's hard bachelor bed. She had heard her father complaining about detonators and gelatine disappearing from the store. So this was where they were: Debi had been helping himself to them.

She kept thinking of her father's anguished words. "I'm only worried because this material may find its way into the hands of terrorists—those people who go about blowing up bridges and railway tracks."

Was that what he had got himself mixed up with? Debi, her little brother with the once-soft hands and the eager, trusting look? Was that what he was up to when he slipped out of his room at night?

They had always been so close to each other, and yet he had guarded his secret well. This was something he had done on his own, without consulting her. When they were young, it had always been she who led; he had followed, looking up to her for guidance. He used to creep into her bed, complaining that he had seen strange figures in the shadows at night. She had bandaged his finger when he had cut it and had nearly fainted at the sight of blood. He had made a scene when Mr. Muller was going to drown a puppy and had shrunk from breaking up the white-ant hill that had sprung up on the badminton court overnight.

And now he was playing about with detonators and explosives and blowing up bridges!

Below the stairs, the clock in the hall chimed the hour. It was ten o'clock. Sundari put the sticks of gelatine and the detonators back where she had found them and carefully replaced the books in their original positions.

She picked up the handkerchiefs and slunk out of the room; now she did not want him to find out that she had been there at all. She had even forgotten what she had been thinking about when she came into Debi's room. Gopal Chandidar, of course, the young man who was going to be her husband. It seemed of so little importance now. She must find out in what her brother had got himself involved. She had a right to know, after taking the blame for so many of his childhood misdemeanours. Could she still help him and shield him from the blame?

She was not singing as she came out, nor did she care what sari she would wear for the afternoon.

[12]

Only in Pearls

STANDING at the window of their bedroom, Dewan-bahadur Tekchand looked nervously at his watch and then down at the waiting car where the chauffeur, tall and bearded and dressed in a fresh white uniform, was running a dust cloth over the bonnet of the Buick. His wife sat at the dressing table, wearing a gold-bordered white sari and her pearls, putting the final touches to her make-up.

"Sundar is wearing the other necklace," she said.

He grunted absent-mindedly and again looked at his watch.

"I don't think you were so nervous even when you came to see me the first time," she taunted him.

Tekchand gave her a fond look. "Somehow this seems much more important," he said, and then, as though to make up for his lack of grace, added, "It was different with you. I knew I was going to marry you long before I ever came to see you—after seeing your photograph."

"You certainly took a long time making up your mind." She pouted.

She was putting a chain of white mogra flowers in her hair. The palla of her sari had dropped off and her choli was still unbuttoned, its silk stretching tightly across the back. In the mirror of the dressing table, he watched her breasts straining against their narrow strip of gauze. Like fruit showing through a net, he reflected, some wheat-coloured fruit, lush and ripe. She was an attractive woman, mature but well preserved, with a glowing skin and a firm, vibrant body, and today she looked breathtakingly lovely, he thought, all primped up and flushed with excitement. "He is coming to see your daughter, not you," he chided. "Otherwise I would not have been nervous at all."

In the mirror, he saw his wife blush at the compliment and

95

reward him with a hard, level, low-lidded look, a look that, in the secret language that had evolved between them over the years of intimacy, held a special message for him. Who would have thought a woman in her thirty-ninth year could make you tremble all over like that, just with a look? Tekchand mused. "Just as well she looks a little like you," he said. "A lot like you."

"She is much more like you, really," his wife said. "Everyone says so. It is Debi who takes after me."

The mention of his son's name caused Tekchand to frown, shadowing his thoughts with a vague sense of uneasiness which he could not explain. "He should have been here now, to—to help with things," he complained, looking once again at his watch. "Surely he could have given his gymnasium a miss today."

"He will be here all right, before you get back from the hotel—he promised," his wife assured him. "I am rather glad that he does go to the gymnasium so regularly. He is looking so fit these days; much more colour in his cheeks."

"It is most odd, all this interest in physical culture. And it has lasted six years almost. I should have thought it would have passed off by now. I mean it just isn't normal! I don't like it at all. And staying out late every now and then." He shook his head. "You don't think it's a woman, do you?"

"A woman! Oh, go on! Debi isn't twenty yet. He is with boys all the time, wrestling and doing dands. I don't think he's even given a thought to women. How old were you?"

"What d'you mean, how old was I?"

"You know perfectly well what I mean," his wife said, narrowing her eyes. "How old were you when you began to think of women—I mean, seriously."

"Not till I married you. But then no woman had made eyes at me like that."

"Liar!" his wife said, but she was not looking at him any more. She was rubbing the stopper of the perfume bottle behind her ears and in the centre of her palms and in the cleft of her breasts and finally under her nostrils.

He had always adored these gestures, the routine finishing touches to his wife's toilet. She caught his eyes in the mirror but said nothing. She put back the stopper on the Chanel bottle and tucked away her breasts in the choli. Then she got up and stood before the mirror for a final look at herself. A well-to-do high-born Hindu woman dressed up for a formal occasion, poised, self-assured, exuding the aura of housewifeliness extolled in the myths of gods and goddesses, disturbingly beautiful but, dressed up like that, vaguely sanctified and unsexed. Like Ravi Varma's picture of Lakshmi, the goddess of prosperity, her husband thought. One could not think of making a pass at someone who stood on a pedestal, waiting to be worshipped.

Satisfied with what she saw, she came and sat down once more.

"What does Sundar feel about—about today?" he asked.

"Excited, excited and happy too, I think. At twenty a girl understands these things. I told her about the young man, and I think she's really thrilled—what girl wouldn't be? Will he be bringing any friends with him, do you think?"

"Oh God—I hope not!"

"I have told them to lay tea for eight, just in case. But he shouldn't really bring more than a couple of friends. It's wrong to bring more, just as it is wrong to come alone."

"I expect he will be sensible about it," Tekchand said. "He's a very modern young man, from all accounts."

This was a great moment in their lives, the culmination of months of planning and manœuvring. The young man who was now on his way to the formal ceremony of a bridegroom coming to "seek" his bride was something of a catch by any standards. Admittedly, he was seven years older than Sundari, but that hardly constituted a major drawback. How many parents of marriageable daughters must have written to him since he was nineteen or so, sent photographs, made overtures through common friends, dangled handsome dowries before him—as indeed Tekchand and his wife had. He had turned down all offers so far; and now he was coming to their house to see their daughter. There was not a more eligible bridegroom in the whole of India. But there could not be many girls like Sundari, either: looks, upbringing, a certain amount of money, a college education; someone who would fit in with the Westernized life that most well-to-do Indians had become accustomed to.

"You had better take out a bottle of sherry," his wife said.

"Sherry! At teatime?"

"Yes, of course. These days, all young men have a drink now and then. And he is said to be so modern. We don't want him to think that we are old-fashioned."

"Of course we don't. And yet, sherry at teatime . . ." he trailed off and glanced at his watch again. "I wish Debi had thought of staying in today."

"If you look at your watch once more, I shall scream!" his wife said in sudden exasperation. Her voice was slightly edgy, showing that, under the flush and the rouge, she too was feeling the strain. Or was it something else? The lash of some other kind of tension? Something to do with Debi-dayal? He wondered.

He came and perched on a corner of the cane stool and took her hand in his. Then, encouraged by her response, because she had edged away a little to make room for him, he put his arms around her and drew her close. He began caressing her throat, now smelling of perfume, at first gently, and then with a suddenly aroused hunger.

She freed her arms and pushed him away, gently but firmly. "There is not much time." She laughed. "I still have to see to a number of things. Perhaps it would be just as well if you were to go and bring Prince Charming, the way you're behaving!"

"Yes, of course," Tekchand said, rising with alacrity.

"You had better put out some whisky too," his wife told him. "In a decanter—just in case."

Her husband gave her a hard stare and then went downstairs to take out the sherry and the whisky.

Once again they were in the bedroom. Tekchand could see that the tension of the afternoon had left his wife. Now she was relaxed and elated at the success of the day. She looked slightly drunk and ready to grant reckless favours, eager to engulf him in her private glow of ecstasy.

Tekchand was already in bed, slightly angry with himself over his preoccupation with affairs of business, thoughts which held him back from savouring the full glow of their triumph. The way the police had handled his complaint had been most slipshod. A mistake in accounting, they had tried to tell him. Such mistakes did not occur in his company, not with explosives. He had complained to the commissioner of the C.I.D. that they were not taking his complaint seriously and had been fobbed off with the same sort of reply. . . .

His thoughts were deflected by the sudden tinkle of bangles, almost deliberate in its insistence. He looked at his wife but failed to catch her eye. She was undressing, giving the process the sort of concentration that only a woman could be capable of, he reflected. She took off her sari and folded it neatly before putting it in the cupboard. Then she peeled off her choli and brassière and put them away in the wicker basket for washing. After that she stood in front of the dressing table and wriggled her hips until her petticoat slipped off with a swish and dropped around her in a pool of shimmering silk. For a time she stood, studying herself in the mirror, and then sat down on the low stool in front of it.

It was hot in the room, and the ceiling fan revolved in slow circles over their beds, kept separated as she had always insisted, with the reading-lamp table between them. He lit a cigarette and turned to look at his wife, suddenly remembering the promise of the afternoon.

She was removing the flowers from her hair, putting them away in a saucer of water to keep them fresh for the morning. Then she began to remove the jewellery she wore.

In the harsh glow of the cluster of lights overhead, he looked at his wife's arching back, and then at the reflection in the mirror, his mouth, in spite of all the years of intimacy, feeling slightly dry. She was unscrewing her diamond ear-clips. Her lips were pressing on the slightly protruding tongue and her face held the suggestion of a wince as though turning the screws was causing her pain.

Few women close to forty could sit stark naked in front of a mirror in that kind of light with so much assurance, he mused, with a purely possessive glow of pride, and then he found himself trying to determine exactly where the process of ageing had begun to show: two minute furrows on her forehead, accentuated now in her preoccupation over the removal of the ear-clips, the slight coarsening of the skin around the nostrils, the fullness under the jaw that had not been there before, the slack of the breasts, the darkening patches around the nipples, the almost unnoticeable heaviness of the abdomen with its suggestion of a fold, the mottling of the flesh over the hips and inside the thighs. And yet, the over-all effect was one of ripeness and bloom, he told himself, like a mango at its juiciest, not of decay and age. She had been careful about her figure, and lucky with the bone-structure of her face . . . where had he read that a woman was at her loveliest at thirty-eight, or was it something that he had made up himself? In softer light . . . He ran his tongue over his lips.

"Don't take off the pearls," he told her. "I like you in pearls—just pearls."

She said nothing in reply, but she did not take off her necklace. She soaked a pad of cotton wool in some kind of toilet water and began to remove her make-up, and after that daubed some of the lotion under her arms. Then she turned the stool and sat facing him.

"I like him," she said. "Sundari is very lucky."

"Did Sundari say anything?" he asked.

"She didn't have to say anything—girls don't, unless they have objections."

"I am glad that Mr. Chandidar said 'no' when I asked him to have a whisky—and thank heavens he didn't bring anyone else with him."

"He was just being on his best behaviour. And you had better learn to call him Gopal now; he is going to be your son-in-law."

"Is that what you call him?"

"I call him Gopi—he told me to call him Gopi. That's what his friends call him."

"He certainly seems to have made a hit with you. He was all over you."

She smiled. "It is customary for a prospective groom to make himself agreeable to the girl's mother."

"I don't know. I should have expected him to be a little more reserved—you know what I mean, shy. . . ."

"Oh, but he was so delightfully spontaneous. So natural."

"And yet I could hardly get a word out of the man," he grumbled.

"And who is to blame? The way you kept glaring at the poor thing; as though he were someone who had come to kidnap your daughter . . ."

"I! I thought I was most courteous, I even tried to press a drink on him."

"Darling, if you could only have seen yourself—as though merely being civil was an effort. And the whisky—why, I knew you were dying for a drink yourself. I noticed the way you poured it. It looked quite fierce."

He wondered if he had ever had a drink in her presence without her noticing its colour. "And I'm not so sure about his being on his best behaviour," he said. "The way he jumped at it when you suggested that he should take Sundar for a drive!"

She laughed and made a face at him. "But darling, they've got to get to know each other; they have to be given all opportunities. And don't you remember how you yourself wanted me to go out for a walk with you in the garden after my parents had left us alone on the veranda?"

"But you never came," he complained. "Didn't you want to?"

"You know I wanted to, but my mother had not said anything about it. These days, a mother just can't afford to miss out on any of these things."

"Do you mean to say that you had told Sundari she should go for a drive in the car with him after tea?"

She nodded. "Naturally. But don't you—don't you like him?"

"Oh, I suppose he's all right. And yet I can't help feeling that they should not have gone for a drive all by themselves. It—it seems so forward. Why couldn't Dhansingh have taken them?"

"No, Dhansingh could not have taken them; oh, no. And remember, Gopi is not a—not a bachha, like our Debi. He has been abroad, been around with girls. . . ."

"You mean he has—that he has had sex experience?"

She went on smiling, but did not answer his question.

He sat up in bed. "Do you really think so?" he asked.

She still ignored his question. Instead she said, "I did not like the way Debi seemed to react to him. They had hardly anything to say to each other."

The thought of the way his son had behaved towards their guest brought a frown to Tekchand's face. He stretched back on his pillows. "I don't know what has come over the boy; Mr. Chandidar, on the other hand, was so courteous. He even asked Debi to go and stay with him in Bombay during his holidays. It would do him a lot of good, instead of his being always tied up with wrestling friends. So—so common."

"I thought it most sensible of Gopi not to bring anyone else with him. I wonder what sort of ring he will give her."

"I hope he will go."

"Who?"

"Debi. I want him to go and stay with Chandidar—Gopal— for a while. Do you think he will?"

"Of course he will," his wife assured him. "I shall make him go. Then perhaps we could even send Sundari for a few days, without causing comment." She rose and picked up the petticoat lying at her feet and folded it and put it away. Then she went into the bathroom. When she came out, a few minutes later, she was still naked. She switched off the overhead lights and went and lay down on her own bed.

He turned and leaned on his elbow to look at her. Now, with the shaded bedside light casting only a soft glow over the bed, she looked just as he had always wanted her to look, the imperfections that had not been there when he had first seen her naked suddenly touched away by an artist's brush.

"I like him," she said. "So handsome, so well-mannered."

In spite of himself, a sudden prick of jealousy flashed through his mind for the youth and good looks of the man who was going to be his son-in-law. Why was she going on about him like that? It was curious, how their minds worked.

"I thought he was so much—oh, so much like you when you came to my father's house to see me," she was saying. "So refined and a little shy at first; and then, when you got to know him, so friendly."

He did not say anything. His thoughts flew back into the past, to the day when he had first seen his wife; the slender, demure girl in the pale-green sari who at first would not raise her head to look at him, and then, when her parents left them together for a few minutes, reached out and touched his hand. It was difficult to think that the woman lying on the bed without a stitch of clothing, wearing only the pearls he had given her because he wanted her to wear them, was the same girl.

"How you keep staring at me," she complained, "after twenty-one years of marriage!"

"I don't feel we've been married all that long, and in any case, you look exactly as you did then."

She closed her eyes and covered her breasts with her hands. "And I don't feel married at all," she said, very flatly, not addressing the remark to him, but just speaking out. "Not to you or anyone."

"What are you, then? What are you doing on that bed with nothing on? Nothing except the pearls."

"I am your mistress; a kept woman, and you have just bought me by giving me the pearl necklace, and I am a little frightened

of what you are going to do to me, because this is the first time
—just shows what a woman will do for a string of pearls, wait to
be ravished by a complete stranger."

He was slightly shocked by her mood; and yet, in some way, he
was prepared for it, since, however inadequately, it matched his
own mood. Twenty-one years, he remembered. How often, in
those years, he had stilled the raging fires of that body? Two
thousand one hundred times at least. And yet, whenever she
wished, she could still evoke within him the wildest longing for
her. Even though her body had lost its girlish slenderness and
hardness, it was more than ever capable of responding to a caress;
he thought of the way her breasts swelled under his hand's gentle
stroking, the way her legs shivered at the touch of his lips; matur-
ity had only given it a fiercer, wilder appetite. Like a musical
instrument, he thought, seasoned by use, a taut string tuned for
its best performance.

Two thousand and one hundred times? Three thousand? But
for him it was like the first time, always. What did that mean?
That theirs was the perfect marriage, the perfect love? And yet,
God knew that in those twenty-one years he himself had not
always been faithful to her.

And yet, with the others it had never been the same. It was an
act of lust, an almost purely physical experience, something that
a healthy and hard-working man needed for toning up his
system, like exercise; toning up his system and clearing his brain.
It did not mean anything at all, did not stir something deep
within you.

But what about her? What happened when he himself was
away and she felt like this, during all his business trips, those
three months in Europe in 1933? Did she then lie like that, a
wanton brown goddess stretched out on the white sheets, desirable, desiring, for someone else—mad with desire, not caring
who it was as he himself had not cared? Who? Some lover with
whom she had made an assignation? It was difficult for a woman
situated as she was. A casual tumble in the bedroom with some
lusty servant called up on an errand? The chauffeur Dhansingh—
built like a dark Apollo; virile, young, earthy; the perfect counterpart of the sort of woman he himself would choose; someone who
could give her all that her body longed for.

Suddenly he was ashamed of his thoughts. What did it matter?

Love such as theirs could not be polluted by lapses of the body, lapses he himself had succumbed to. If ever a marriage had been blessed by the gods, it was theirs.

She turned her back to him and settled herself more comfortably, drawing up her knees and wriggling her toes, spelling out another unmistakable signal for him. The way their marital relationship had developed, he was usually the one who responded, even though it was for him to show that he was making the initial advance, exercising the prerogative of the male. For a moment longer he went on looking: the black hair falling on both sides of the neck; the square, well-set shoulders; the straight, narrowing back; the sudden voluptuousness of the buttocks; the inner whiteness of the silk-soft thighs; the long, slender legs.

She turned and lay on her stomach, lazily stretching out her legs. Obeying a private signal, he shed his muslin kurta and pyjamas and walked across to her bed. He gave a slight pat on her seat and she turned on her back, swiftly as a fish in water. As he crouched over her, he found her feet planted on his chest, resisting him, pushing him away.

"From the beginning, darling," she whispered. "Remember we are not married. You are a bad man who has bought me with the pearls. This is the first time. You are my lover."

Obediently, eagerly, he joined in, beginning at the beginning, following a method in the chapter of Anangaranga which bore the heading "How to seduce a virgin" and which he had long ago read to her in bed.

On that occasion they had laughed rather a lot about the elaborate ritual prescribed. Today neither of them laughed. He kissed her insteps and then the palms of her hands and then thrust his face between the breasts where the scent of Chanel No. 5 was mixed with the scent of her body. It had a distinctive scent of its own, heady and delicate. He remembered reading somewhere that the odour of perspiration under sexual stimulation was quite different from that of normal sweat.

"You are a wild man from the jungle; a soldier who has killed his adversary and abducted his wife, me; a big, red-faced soldier smelling of drink," she was whispering.

Her mood had already changed, from the subtleties of Anangaranga to the brutal, gluttonous love of soldiers and wild men, but now they were too close to each other for him to feel shocked by what she was saying.

Fate did not deny them that particular favour that night, the last time they would ever make love to each other like that; the coiling together, the surrender and the rapture of two human bodies made for each other, tuned to each other's demands by long years of practice, like two musical instruments playing in perfect harmony, a last loud pæan to the act of procreation.

It was later that night, as they lay spent and contented and sleepy but unwilling to surrender to sleep because they wanted to relive the triumph of the day, that they heard the crunch of wheels of the car in the driveway below, and after that of the car stopping and of doors being opened by the night watchman and the sound of conversation in the hall below the stairs.

"I can't imagine who it can be," Tekchand said as he slipped on a dressing gown, "at this time of night. I'll go down and see."

A white sergeant and two constables were waiting for him in the hall, and behind them he could see the blue-black police car with wire-gauze windows.

"My name is Pearce," the sergeant introduced himself, touching his cap. "Sergeant Pearce. I have a warrant for the arrest of your son, Debi-dayal."

This was not true. There must be some mistake. Things like this did not happen to people like him. Not in the India of the British. "What—what is my son supposed to have done?" Tekchand stammered.

"Revolutionary activities," Sergeant Pearce said. "Burning up an aeroplane. Stealing explosives and detonators—stealing them and using them too, to blow up trains." And then, seeing the expression of shock on Tekchand's face, Sergeant Pearce said, "I'm sorry about this, sir."

[13]

The Seashore near Bombay

NOT many of them belonged to the Cricket Club, but they made a point of addressing the barman as "Eddie," and fewer still belonged to the Willingdon, but they spoke familiarly of the special facilities of its dressing room. They travelled between Bombay and Poona according to the racing season, and every three years they made trips to Europe, just to keep in touch, as they said, and to buy some suits and shoes in London; and of course they always took the Italian Line because they didn't want to be mixed up with all the koi-hais who travelled by the P & O, so that by now they had come to know all the pursers and stewards on both the *Contes*. Most of them had their own shacks at Juhu or Marve, or at least shacks belonging to friends which they had been allowed to use, and in these shacks they gave the most delightful pyjama parties by moonlight and played poker and rummy and vingt-et-un every night for no-limit stakes.

On racing days they dressed conventionally, the men in pearl-grey suits made in London, with matching English-made felt hats, and carrying outsize binoculars, and the women in gorgeous gold-bordered saris, and carrying race-cards and elegant little pencils. They all found their way into the members' enclosure even though it was known that few of them would have qualified for membership, and they placed heavy bets on all the races and spoke casually of their losses and even more casually of their winnings.

The rest of the week, both the men and the women wore white linen bush-shirts, coloured slacks, and Bombay chaplis. Most of them possessed, or had friends who possessed, red sports cars equipped with superchargers, in which they invariably beat the Deccan Queen to Poona by several minutes.

They were the fast set of a metropolis, the high-living men and women who were almost a natural growth on the life of a big city, like mushrooms growing on a dry log; and if you made allowances for climate and upbringing and religious inhibitions and eating habits, they might just as easily have belonged to Shanghai or San Francisco or Buenos Aires, as to Bombay.

The core of the set was formed by the more sporting princes; the inner circle comprised young Indians from Oxford or Cambridge who now could not fit themselves into any truly Indian backgrounds, also the sons of rich marwaris feeling their oats. The rank and file were the men and women who lived off them: racing sharks, card sharpers, society prostitutes, bootleggers, and pimps. There was the usual leavening of foreigners: a couple of White Russians with grandiose titles and unpronounceable names, diamond-wearing refugees who had fled from Hitler's Germany, and a dozen or so Middle European women of indeterminate ages and easy morals who spoke no language known to any of them but who seemed to get along just as well without. There was, too, the inevitable sprinkling of Eurasians pretending to be Italian counts, Arabian horse-dealers who were actually gold smugglers, and Chinese shipowners who were actually opium smugglers.

It was almost by a natural process of gravitation that Gopal Chandidar had found his way into this set, for, without being aware of it, he provided just the cementing influence to hold its disparate elements together. They needed him for the prestige of his family name, and even more so for his money. And he too needed them. After three years at a college in England, he had become too Westernized to fit smoothly into his own kind of society. He represented the modern generation, staunchly opposed to the structure of the joint Hindu family with its rule by the elders, its clinical segregation of the male and the female. In his own family it was considered sinful to drink a glass of beer, and ballroom dancing was a shockingly immoral Western innovation. He had cut himself away from it without regret, and the nearest substitute for what he—and other Westernized young Indians like himself—hankered for, was the linen-bush-shirt-and-sunglasses set of Bombay.

A young Parsee journalist who was a few years his senior at Oxford had taken him to a game of poker at one of the prince's parties, and now, barely six months later, he was a part of the circle himself, though he had not yet taken to wearing dark glasses. He fitted neatly into the pattern. He had joined the Race Club, bought a half-interest in a horse, and begun to enjoy playing cards for high stakes. His secluded double-storied bungalow on the far side of Juhu was ideal for parties.

And yet at times he could not help feeling an outsider, the man who did not quite belong. It was all very well playing cards for high stakes for an hour or two after dinner, but it was not his idea of fun to spend an entire night playing chemin-de-fer in a smoke-filled room.

Tonight was one of those nights. They had gathered at the house of Prince Amjid and had far too much to eat and drink. He felt a headache coming on. He had slipped out of the little air-conditioned room where they were playing, and lay back on one of the enormous stuffed chairs on the veranda overlooking the sea. From the inner room he could hear the murmur of their voices, interspersed by sudden sharp exclamations.

What did he have in common with a myopic prince with fat legs and diamonds in his ears? he found himself wondering. The prince who slept throughout the hours of daylight and came to life only at night. He was said to receive ten thousand rupees a day for his pocket money—about three times as much as Gopal himself made in a whole month. And yet he was in debt to some of the marwaris. He even owed Gopal over two thousand rupees since their last poker game three weeks earlier. He had made no move to settle up.

For a moment Gopal wondered if he could slip away without telling anyone. Or would that look too pointed? The prince was the sort of person who was certain to connect it with his gambling debt. What was there to do when he got home, anyway—read a book?

He saw Malini at the other end of the veranda, walking towards him, holding two tall glasses in her hands. She was dressed in white beach pyjamas, a halter, and sandals, and her face and arms and shoulders looked a lovely shade of copper, like an advertisement for suntan lotion. Gopal had met her several times at just such parties as this one, and had felt attracted by her; but he had shown no interest in her because everyone knew that she was the prince's mistress and that he was childishly jealous. But now he was in the process of making up to one of the Central European women and was showing unmistakable signs of dropping

Malini. Today it was Tanya whom the prince had wanted to sit by him, "to bring me luck," as he said. For a moment, as Malini came up, Gopal found himself wondering whether he would have preferred Tanya to Malini, if he were in the prince's place.

Malini came, walking delicately so as not to spill the drinks she carried, luscious, strikingly attractive; Tanya, on the other hand, was in the room at the other end of the house, snuggling up to the prince to bring him luck. It would be nice to take Malini on if the prince was really dropping her, Gopal reflected.

She stopped close to his chair. "All alone or waiting for someone?" she asked.

He liked her voice, husky and low-pitched. She must be trained to speak like that, he decided, for he knew that she often played small parts in films.

"All alone," he told her.

"Oh good," Malini said without smiling. "I came out with two drinks, one for myself and one for whoever would sit and hold my hand."

He laughed. "I wouldn't need to be offered a drink to hold your hand," he told her.

She gave him a hard, level look. "I hardly expected that you would turn out to be a friend: I always thought you were one of those who shy away from women." She handed him one of the glasses. "Cheers!" she said.

"Aren't you going to sit down?" he asked. "I can't very well hold your hand while you are standing up."

She lowered herself onto the arm of his chair very carefully, but even so some of the whisky from her glass spilled on the carpet. She must have had a lot to drink, he thought.

"Tell me," she said after a time, "are you allowed to visit your brother-in-law in jail?"

"He's not my brother-in-law," Gopal said.

"Oh, I am sorry; is there a hitch or something?"

"No, there is no hitch; just that I don't acquire a brother-in-law until the marriage takes place."

"Oh, I am so glad; really glad. Actually I should have thought it would be so exciting to have a convict for a brother-in-law."

Was she being bitchy? he asked himself; was that why she had come out, brought him a drink—just so that she could take it out on someone because her prince had discarded her?

"I thought you wanted to be friendly," he said.

"Oh dear! Have I said anything wrong? I was only trying to be companionable, but I seem to have offended you."

"Oh, no," he assured her. "I am getting quite used to people asking me about Debi-dayal."

"You're really not angry with little me, are you, sweet?"

"Of course not."

"Good, because you really are rather a pet. Let's take our drinks on the sand. What do you say to that? It's much cooler, out on the beach."

They both went out of the veranda and into the dark night towards the dim line of the sand, carrying their drinks with them. When they returned, about an hour later, and rejoined the others in the cardroom, they found them still bending over the card table with grim concentration. The men had fat black cigars stuck in their mouths and all of them had glasses of whisky at their elbows, while the two princes had the two women clinging to their chairs to bring them luck. No one turned to look at them.

"Banco!" someone called.

Malini gave an artificial yawn and wriggled her shoulders. "Darling, I am dead with sleep," she said to Amjid. "Mr. Chandidar is driving me back. Nighty-night."

No one turned. Casually they walked out of the cold room filled with cigar smoke and the fumes of whisky and the women's perfume. "Huit à la banque!" they heard someone shout in the cardroom.

Debi-dayal's trial caused a good deal of stir. Even the big national papers gave it prominence. They dug up their old files of the Meerut conspiracy cause and made elaborate comparisons of means and methods. On July 12, when Debi-dayal was sentenced to life imprisonment, almost all the evening papers carried his photograph.

Most of the Chandidars had implored Gopal to break off his engagement. They would find another bride for him, they assured him. He must be careful not to besmirch the family's prestige. Even his aunt, the Maharani of Begwad, sent him a long telegram telling him that he must not marry Sundari.

Gopal had taken no notice of their clamour. He had little in common with them. They would never have understood how difficult it was for someone like him to find the bride of his choice among the higher-caste Hindus. They matched couples through horoscopes, and as far as they were concerned looks took a second place to such considerations as caste and orthodox up-bringing. He had had to turn down dozens of proposals which they had regarded as suitable, and he certainly had no intention of starting all over again and ending up by marrying someone old-fashioned, someone like his aunt, who actually observed strict purdah.

Early in August, Sundari came to Bombay. He took her to lunch at Cornaglia's, and during lunch she explained to him that she had come to Bombay to visit her brother, who was in the jail at Thana.

That was the first time they had mentioned Debi-dayal's name. If Gopal wanted to say anything about breaking their engagement on account of him, this was the time to say it. He sat looking at her for a long time, without saying anything. Then he said, "I didn't know he was at Thana."

"They gather them there," she explained, "before being trans-ported. They will all be taken away in a week or so—for life."

There was nothing he could think of saying; this was some-thing they would have to learn to live with. He was glad that she had not burst into sobs or made a scene.

"Tomorrow is a visiting day," Sundari said. "And Debi has agreed to see me."

"Oh," Gopal said. "Oh, I see."

"The last visiting day. I don't know what I am going to say to him—what can one say? I have always loved Debi. You see, he and I have always been very close."

"Such a shame that he went astray," said Gopal.

Sundari stopped eating and looked evenly at him. "He did not go astray," she said. "He just happened to be one of the unlucky ones who were caught. According to his lights, he was only doing what he thought was his duty."

Unlucky, he thought, not wrong; someone deserving of pity, but not censure. The line of thought gave him a mental jar. "There is something in that, of course," he said weakly. "And yet—"

"Don't you see? He was trying to be sincere and brave. It is—it is our thinking that may be all wrong, those of us who are willing to live under foreign rule without qualms, people like my father. And yet, there are others; look at the patriots in Ireland, look at America, how she got her independence—by people protesting and fighting. If their young men had not striven to over-throw foreign rule, they would never have been free."

This was a new Sundari, earnest, impassioned. Where was it that he had read that a woman could look more tender than a petal and yet be harder than steel inside—in some Sanskrit romantic poem, surely; but that was what her face reminded him of. He went on staring at her, taken aback by her fervour.

"But Father will never see it in that way. He thinks that the Americans who fought to win independence were heroes, but that our own fighters are seditionists," Sundari was saying. "Can one blame Debi for being so bitter? He has refused to see Father."

Gopal, too, thought of people like Debi-dayal as seditionists. "I am sorry to hear that," he said. "Your father must be so upset."

"But I myself was not at all surprised. He and Debi belong to different worlds; he keeps wanting to apologize about what Debi has done, instead of being proud. I am the only one in the family who understands how Debi feels about—about these things. Do you think you could drive me over?"

The question came so suddenly that for a moment he was at a loss to say anything. He had resented being associated with the scandal. He had been educated in England and he worked in a British firm. He also held an honorary commission in the British-Indian army. As far as people like Debi-dayal, or even the followers of Mahatma Gandhi, were concerned, he was staunchly in the opposite camp. He could not afford to get mixed up with them, let alone visit them in jails.

"To the—to Thana?" he asked.

She must have noticed his hesitation. "Oh, never mind. On second thoughts, perhaps it would be better if I were to go by myself."

"But of course I will take you," he said.

"You know this has nothing to do with you. Actually, several people have hinted that you might even wish to break off our engagement. I just—"

"What absolute nonsense!" he protested.

"Do let me finish. I just wanted to say that if you do wish to break off the engagement, I would understand perfectly."

"Now stop being silly," he told her. "And try and eat some of that pomfret. I will certainly drive you to Thana, or anywhere else you want to go."

The next morning they drove to Thana. He stopped the car in the cobbled courtyard in front of the jail. Facing them was a long thirty-foot-high wall, and in the centre of the wall a great steel door. The big door had a small one-man door set in one of its panels, guarded by a yellow-turbanned policeman. A prison official met them just inside the door and led them through a long corridor smelling of sisal and coconut fibre, to a small room, where he left them.

From where they sat, awed and expectant, they could hear the sound of doors opening on creaky hinges and of footsteps in the corridors outside. The room had a small grilled window opening into another room, and behind the window there was a high stool for the prisoner to sit.

Gopal felt ill at ease, small, in the position of supplicant before a minor government official. He had never seen the inside of a jail before.

The superintendent came and introduced himself, and then he said, "I am sorry, Mr. Chandidar, but the prisoner will only see Miss Kerwad. That is his right, of course, to see or not see any of his visitors. If you would care to wait in my office . . ."

After all that waiting, the bracing up for an ordeal, the drawing upon reserves of good manners, it was like a slap in the face. He tried not to show his chagrin. "No, no; I shall wait in the car, outside," he offered, rising.

"I am sorry, but that is his privilege," the superintendent apologized. "I have to observe the rules."

"Yes, of course," Gopal said.

Fifteen minutes later, when Sundari came out, escorted by the superintendent himself, her eyes were wet with tears. All through the drive back to town she did not say a word to him. He drove angrily, concentrating on the mechanics of the drive, and did not attempt to speak to her or comfort her. They were held too far apart by their different bonds. They were separated even before they were joined together in matrimony, for their marriage was still more than two months away, when the auspicious season would begin.

[14]

"Beyond the Black Water"

IT was shocking to see him thus, thought Gian, the boy he had envied at college, now wearing a large red D on his shirt—a "D-ticket convict," as they called them. He had been brought in last, just a few minutes before the ship was about to move, escorted by two white sergeants; brought in with what the other convicts thought was something of a touch of fanfare, and he was handed over to the Andaman sentries who were to accompany them like a prize exhibit: a terrorist, a revolutionary working for the overthrow of British rule.

Even in a convict's nondescript garb—coarse grey undershirt and shorts—he looked different to Gian, not broken and ingratiating like the others, but proud, straight, and haughty. The white sergeants had exchanged pleasantries with him as they said good-bye and, incredibly, had even shaken him by the hand, while they had barely acknowledged the cracking salute given to them by the Gurkha sentry.

Yes, there he was, Debi-dayal, only son of Dewan-bahadur Tekchand Kerwad, in the hold of the prison ship on her way to the Andamans, lying without a whimper, only half alive.

On the very first day he had fallen foul of the head sentry, Balbahadur, a Gurkha with a mean, leathery, hairless face, for complaining to the escorting officer about their treatment.

One of the prisoners lying close to the barrel which served as their latrine had complained about the stench and asked to be moved. When the sentry took no notice of his complaint, Debi-dayal had said, "Will you please go and call the escorting officer here, so that he can see things for himself?"

Balbahadur came close to him and gave him a long, hard stare. "You want to see the sahib?" he asked.

"Yes, I want to complain to him. The stench is quite unbearable."

"You do, do you?" said the Gurkha, grinning, coming closer. And then he slapped him on the face, hard. "Complain, will you? Who do you think you are, the Aga Khan? Complain to my ————!" And he slapped his face again.

Debi-dayal said nothing at the time, but towards the evening, when the escorting officer had come on his rounds, he protested to him about the stench.

Rogers, the escorting officer, looked uncomfortable. He had no experience of India. This was his first assignment of its kind. It was, he felt, outside the scope of his duties to discuss complaints which evidently would cut across established procedure for transporting convicts to the penal settlement.

"A man of your sensitivities should have thought about all this before engaging in terrorist activities," he said with a touch of sarcasm. "The jail manual does not make provision for outside latrines."

"These are basic needs," Debi-dayal had said. "One does not have to look for them in jail manuals. Is this how they treat prisoners in England?"

Rogers felt weak. He had not bargained for such an exchange in the presence of all the convicts. "I'm afraid it's something I can't do anything about," he said. "You will just have to put up with it—only three more days."

"Can't you at least ensure that the sentries do not harass us?" Debi-dayal asked.

"What kind of harassment?"

"When I asked to be given an opportunity to speak to you, this man just came up and slapped me on the face."

Balbahadur was standing right behind Rogers. He obviously knew that they were speaking about him, even though he did not understand English. "Did you slap this man?" Rogers asked him, speaking in Hindi.

"No, sahib, this man is a liar, a badmash, trying to get the other prisoners to join in his protests."

"You can ask any of the other prisoners," Debi-dayal offered.

Rogers hesitated. His thoughts were confused. He looked from one to the other: the cocky young revolutionary and the sullen sentry, his face a wooden mask, his little eyes blinking. Rogers had never had much to do with prisoners in the past; he was a policeman. These convicts fully deserved what they were getting, and it was important not to interfere with ship's discipline. He remembered a pep talk he had been given before he joined the service . . . essential not to let the side down . . . important to back up your official subordinates—always.

"And he should be warned to mind his language," Debi-dayal went on. "The foul, obscene words he uses whenever he speaks to us—involving mothers and sisters."

"You should have thought about all this before you became a terrorist," Rogers snapped at him again.

After that it was just a matter of time before Balbahadur got his own back on Debi-dayal. Later that very night he and another sentry accused him of trying to commit suicide by tearing his blanket and twisting the strands into a rope with which to hang himself. It was true that Debi-dayal had torn the blanket issued to him because it bore large patches of dried blood, but the suicide tale had been made up by the head sentry as a sop to the escorting officer's conscience.

They took Debi-dayal out of the hold and it was nearly two hours before they brought him back, with fetters on both hands and feet. "Complain to the sahib again," Balbahadur taunted as a parting shot, "and we'll have another go at you."

He had not complained again; in fact, he had not said another word to anyone. "They must have beaten him with twists of rope," the man lying next to Gian whispered knowledgeably. "Covered him in blankets and then beaten him—so that the welts should not show."

In the gloom of the hold, Gian's eyes wandered. They came to rest on the inert bundle wrapped in a coarse blanket that was Debi-dayal. And then he looked at the sentry standing rigidly beyond the barred door. A feeling of revulsion came over him as he went on staring at the immobile face—the typical Indian sentry drunk with the authority vested in him. It was amazing how the Empire worked, held its sway, with a crop of honest, selfless officers at the top, and hordes of corrupt, subhuman minor officials at the bottom. Was that the India of the Indians? What would happen if the steel frame of British officialdom was ever removed, when India became free and her people held full sway? Then he suddenly remembered that he was leaving India forever; that her problems were no longer his problems.

The big Ramoshi with the gnarled teakwood face and the handlebar moustache clapped his hands for silence. He put his head back and began to sing:

> "Bolo jawanon kya-kya milat hai,
> Kale Panike bazaar?"

A dozen or so voices joined him in the chorus:

> "Arre Kale Panike bazaar, arre Kale Panike bazaar!
> Mofat-ki undi, aur mofat-ki brandy,
> Aur mofat-ki rundi hazaar!"

"Arre mofat-ki rundi hazaar!" the chorus took him on, now much louder as other voices joined in. "Arre mofat-ki rundi hazaar!"

They were already learning the prison song; the big Ramoshi, Ghasita, was teaching them. Ghasita was going back, a lifer for the second time. For the other forty-seven convicts, it was the first time they were going across the Kala Pani, the Black Water.

Only the literate among them, perhaps half a dozen all told, and, of course, Ghasita, had any precise idea of their destination: the Cellular Jail at Port Blair in the Andaman Islands. To the others, their destination was merely a place beyond the black water.

They came from all corners of India, a mixed lot speaking different languages, convicted by district courts and high courts to life imprisonment. Some of them did not even know that, according to a recent statute, a "life" term in a prisoner's sentence meant fourteen years, not all the remaining years of their lives; nor did they care. Many belonged to what the official manuals designated as "the criminal tribes." The big Ramoshi, Ghasita, was one of them.

They were a special breed of men, born to crime and to a life of violence; they were criminals first and human beings afterwards; unrepentant, unwilling to be reformed, incapable of reforming—the dregs of the social order. Crime was to them merely a way of life, ordained by God; it was even their religion, for they were the worshippers of Vetal, the god of criminals. Fatalists to the bone, they ascribed their captivity to the wrath of Vetal. Some lapse in the ritual of his worship had provoked his anger and Vetal had withdrawn his protection. It was unfortunate, but somehow it was only just, for it could not have been otherwise.

And now they were being taken to the mythical jail of the white man beyond the black water, a great prison-palace that was three stories high and in which, so they had heard, you lived in clean, airy cells, and from where, after a few months, you were paroled as a "feri," a freed-man or a pass-holder, and permitted to settle down in one of the convict villages in the colony. You could even get married if you could find yourself a wife from the women's prison.

It was the will of Vetal that they should go; they were ready to go, resigned, almost composed, disdainful of the other, lesser beings amongst them who looked dazed and who had set up a wail when the ship began to move.

Their familiarity with Indian jails had inured them to prison life; at least they were sure that nothing that the jail beyond the black water held in store for them could be worse than what they had already gone through. For months they had languished in little black cells infested with vermin, in the stench and filth of their own excrement, in the foulness of their warders' and fellow prisoners' linguistic depravity, getting accustomed to a vocabulary learned mainly from the walls of public lavatories; fettered, handcuffed, bullied, beaten, systematically de-sensitized, wholly powerless objects for the cultivated barbarism of those who were in authority over them. Then, from their city jails and district jails, they had all been gathered together in the Kalipada jail in Calcutta, a place of special horror where enormous red-eyed rats gnawed at their feet and hands during broad daylight, and fleas crawled along the floor in continuous, slow-moving lines.

Now they were on the open sea, even though they could not see it from where they were, in the great cage of their hold, body to human body, with the sentries who had come from the jail to take delivery of them strutting importantly, like marionettes blown up to life size, picking their victims at leisure. The heat, hanging like a vapour, and hunger, stark and rumbling, were their constant companions, for they had been already issued with what was their full quota of rations for the journey, parched rice and gram and blocks of jaggery. A half-barrel in a corner of the hold was their latrine.

Some of them had begun to weep when the ship weighed anchor, but Balbahadur and his men had come wielding their lathis and stopped them. That was when the big Ramoshi had laughed at his fellow prisoners derisively. Then he began to sing.

His voice was brave and strident, like a broken brass trumpet, Gian thought, and his face bigger than life size, like an unfinished statue roughly carved out of wood. He was coarse, defiant, a prince from the criminal tribes, the chosen people of Vetal. He had already done a full term in the Andamans, and now, within a year of his release, was going back for another term. The first thing he had done after reaching his village in India, was to seek out the man who had betrayed him to the police. He struck him down with an axe right in the middle of the bazaar and in broad daylight. According to his values, he had done only what was expected of him, for the demands of tribal justice had to be met. This was something that Vetal ordained, and he had made his offering in all solemnity. There was something in his face and bearing, an air of arrogance perhaps, that made him stand out, and there was, of course, his great size, for he was well over six feet tall and of large build. Even the sentries treated him not only with deference but with a little fear too.

And now he was singing again, and the other prisoners were joining in, one by one. What had they to sing about? Gian found himself wondering: the freedom from bugs and mosquitoes, the faint whiff of the sea breeze drowned by the odour of crowded humanity? The words of the song would have shocked Aji, he reflected, and then for a moment he was pricked by a sense of anxiety. Aji was the one person he had really let down—left alone in her old age when she had every right to expect to be looked after by the grandson she had brought up.

He wondered how she was getting on, now all alone in the Little House, waiting for her grandson, who was, if he got full remission for good behaviour, due to return in 1952. He knew that she had sold her gold bangles to pay for his defence, but the rice fields were still there, as far as he was aware. The fields should bring her enough to live on; there was, too, the Little House.

The song rose to a crescendo, drowning his thoughts. He had tried to hold himself aloof from their mirth, the bawdy songs, the vulgar badinage. How could they bring themselves to sing, when they knew perfectly well that what lay in store for them beyond the black water was not wine and women, but the dreaded Cellular Jail, transformed by the prisoners themselves into the "Silver"

Jail; the Silver Jail and its superintendent, Patrick Mulligan. Strict but just, that was what he was reputed to be; strict but just. In the last analysis, was not that what all British officials were—strict but just?

Gian was glad to know that the Silver Jail had a British superintendent, for he had nothing but admiration for British officials. An English magistrate had decided the Piploda case in Hari's favour, he remembered. The very fact that he was still alive was entirely due to the judge's sense of fairness. At the trial, the prosecution had made the strongest plea for the death penalty— a blatant, premeditated murder, the prosecutor kept repeating. But Gian's college principal, Mr. Hakewill, had personally testified to his character, and the judge had said that in view of his past record of exemplary behaviour, and taking into account his youth, a sentence of transportation for life would, in his opinion, meet the ends of justice.

But he remembered that his behaviour in college had been by no means exemplary. He had taken to wearing khaddar and had identified himself with the national movement. Mr. Hakewill had himself warned him that he might have to forgo his scholarship if he dabbled in anti-British activities; yet, when the time came, he had come forward to testify on his behalf.

Was it his youth that made him so shallow, he wondered, or was it a part of the Indian character itself? Did he in some way, represent the average Indian, mixed-up, shallow, and weak? Like someone out of A Passage to India, Aziz, or someone even more confused, quite despicable, in fact, like that boy whose name he had forgotten, Rafi, that was it. Was he like Rafi? His non-violence had crumbled the moment it met a major test, and now even his nationalism was wavering, just because the British officials he had come into contact with so far had been men of sterling character. Why could he not be like Debi-dayal, who held on to his beliefs with unswerving rigidity? He, on his part, had already begun to doubt whether India could ever do without the British. It was they who were so scrupulous about the ends of justice.

But what did it mean—the ends of justice? Should not the ends of justice have required Vishnu-dutt to die for Hari's murder?

From where he lay, wedged in by two coal-black South Indian

coolies who stank like rotting fish and who had been convicted for raping a teen-age girl, he looked at the faces of his companions one by one, all lying propped up against the sides of the hold or against each other, their feet stretched straight out before them because of the fetters they wore.

He was horrified. Most of them were singing and looked shockingly at ease, even as though they were enjoying themselves. He tried to catch Debi-dayal's eye but did not succeed. Debi was staring fixedly at the ceiling, as he always did; handsome and proud, he was now a motionless bundle in a blanket, like an Egyptian mummy that was still breathing.

Gian felt his limbs tremble—an unknown fear crawling through the rings of his fetters, like the lice and fleas in Kalipada jail.

The big Ramoshi clapped his hands once again. "Come on, brothers," he bawled. "Come on, friends; come on, kings; come on, lovers of your own mothers—sing!"

The rains had stopped, but clouds lay around them like a grey jelly, great wet sponges masking the horizon, and the gusty wind felt wet on their hands and faces. From down below, over the creaking of the woodwork and the lazy thump of the engine, came the sound of voices raised in singsong.

Sitting on the big chair beside the wheel, the captain in his grimy white cap sniffed the air with professional interest. He put away his binoculars and shook his frame like a dog coming out of water. "We could have seen them now," he pronounced, "if the clouds weren't so thick. An emerald necklace scattered over the sea—not much emerald about that!"

The young British police officer wearing a military-type Burberry shrugged his shoulders too, almost in imitation of the captain. "When do we get in?" he asked.

"We should anchor by nine tomorrow morning," the captain told him. "At night the entrance would be a little tricky—in this murk."

"I shall be damned glad when I have handed them all in, all counted and correct," Rogers said. "One of them tried to hang himself last night—tore up his blanket to make a rope."

"Now what on earth would a chap do a thing like that for?" the captain said without interest.

"He's an unfortunate case. His father is a big building contractor—a Dewan-bahadur. The boy is a revolutionary—was, rather. Now he is getting his deserts and can't take it."

"All these terrorists are pretty gutless when it comes to facing up. What did you do with him?"

"We had to put fetters on his hands too. The others have their hands free. Now he can do no mischief."

The captain pulled his cap low over his brow and cocked his head. "And yet they seem to be a cheery lot," he remarked. "Listen to them singing."

"I don't know. It is all rather—rather morbid, to hear them go on like that. I'd much rather they cursed and moaned. Somehow their singing makes one feel a little—a little less than human."

"What are they saying?"

"About wine and women, mostly. They—"

"Like sailors' songs," the captain interrupted. "I sort of like the tune, catchy, you know what I mean."

The big Ramoshi's raucous voice came from below:

"Bolo jawanon kya-kya milat hai,
Kale Pani-ke bazaar?"

"That means," Rogers explained, " 'Tell me, lads, what is in store for us in the bazaar at the Black Water?'—Black Water is their name for the jail."

"And what do they get?"

"Mofat-ki undi, aur mofat-ki brandy,
Aur mofat-ki rundi hazaar!"

came the words of the chorus.

"Listen to that," Rogers said, "Free eggs, free brandy, and a thousand mistresses—also free."

The captain chuckled. "I wouldn't mind losing my seniority for that sort of captivity," he said. "Who would have thought—what are they up for?"

"Murder, mostly, over women and land. Three or four are for rape, and the one revolutionary—sedition and sabotage; for burning down a plane and removing fishplates from railway tracks and that sort of thing."

"The bastard!" the captain said with feeling. "That type should have been hanged."

"I don't know. It's all so difficult. They're mostly from good homes, these terrorists, quite well educated, and they're all fervently patriotic. It's just that they are so misguided—and they spend their lives in jails. It seems particularly sad at a time like this, when we ourselves seem to be plunging into another war for a strip of land in Poland. Do you think we will?"

The captain shook his head. "Who can say?" His pale eyes scanned the sea around them. "How does one get involved in a war? The last time it was the murder of some prince or other that started it. No one had heard of the place, or the prince. Now it is the Polish Corridor. And yet they can hardly have forgotten the horrors of the last one. I had two whole years of it. Destroyers."

For a time, they were both silent. Then the captain asked, "Are there a lot of those in the country?"

"The terrorists? Oh, yes; they are all over the place. The people themselves seem sympathetic towards them, unfortunately. Almost hero-worship some of them—Bhagat-singh, for instance. That makes it difficult to dig them out. Once they know we're on to them, they go underground. Take this particular gang. We knew there were certainly more than thirty in it. But we—that is, the police—seem to have bungled it, rather. They operated from their club, a sort of gymnasium. When our men raided the place, only seven were there. The others had fled. It is rather funny, really; all seven were Hindus, not a single Mohammedan in the lot, which makes us think that there was some kind of a rift among them— What were you saying?"

"So only seven were caught?"

"Well, eight, really, because later that night they went and took this chap in his house: Debi-dayal. The others must have been tipped off—quite definitely. They usually have their sympathizers even in the force."

"You mean in the police!"

"Oh, yes, even in the police. Unfortunately their leader got away, chap called Shafi Usman, but of course that may not even be his real name—at least half a dozen aliases. Really unsavoury character—long record of terrorist activities and said to be homosexual too."

"Have you got all eight of them in this lot?" the captain asked, suddenly interested. "I should like to take a look at the bastards."

"I'm afraid not. We only have this one. Only one 'lifer'; the others got lighter sentences."

"Oh, in that case," the captain muttered, lifting his glasses to his eyes. "Nothing doing," he pronounced. "C'mon, let's get away where it's cosier." He waved a hand at the man attending to the wheel and slid off his high captain's chair. "The news should be on soon; let's find out whether we are already at war."

"I should like to stay on up here for a while, if you don't mind," Rogers told him. "Then I'll go and do my rounds."

After the captain had clambered down the steps in his waddling old-sea-dog gait, Rogers lit a cigarette. It felt limp in his fingers and the smoke was clammy on his tongue, like a sip of brackish water. For a time he stood smoking, looking at the immobile figure of the Indian second or third mate or whoever it was at the wheel. What was he thinking about? he wondered. About the coming war? The dangers of submarines and mines? Perhaps he was not thinking of the war at all, only of wine and women, like the prisoners in the hold. Gathering his raincoat tightly around him, he went down.

He paused in the doorway of the hold, peering into the gloom, bracing himself for the overpowering stench. Balbahadur, the Gurkha sentry, opened the barred door and stood hovering by his side, holding a rifle with fixed bayonet, a mixture of doglike reverence and servility and bravura; a strutting, cocky little terrier of a man who took his authority with terrifying seriousness and had been invaluable in maintaining discipline.

One by one, as they saw Rogers standing in the doorway, the convicts stopped singing, abruptly, in mid-note; like a wave, the silence rolled on to the far corner where the big Ramoshi sat. It stifled his voice.

They were all staring at him, making him conscious of their fear and hatred, like characters in some dance drama. He felt uncomfortable at the effect his entrance had caused, as though he had rubbed out the little spark of lightness in the gloom of the hold. He walked in, picking his way carefully between the lines of prisoners, the sentry striding importantly at his heels.

"Had your conna?" Rogers asked.

"Jee-sahib," they answered. By now the replies were conditioned, almost automatic. That was what he was expected to ask them, that was what they were required to answer—the Gurkha had seen to that.

"Any complaints?"

"Nahi, sahib."

"You'd better doss down and get some sleep. We shall be arriving tomorrow morning—and don't try any tricks tonight; maloom!"

"Nahi, sahib."

"But if you want to sing, bloody well sing!"

"Jee, sahib."

He dragged on his cigarette and realized that it had gone out. He flicked it into a corner where, as it fell, a hand closed over it. But the sentry was onto it like a flash. He stamped his foot on the erring hand, saying, "None of that, you!"

Rogers gave the Gurkha a withering look. "That was not necessary at all," he said sharply.

Meekly Balbahadur withdrew his ammunition boot and took his place behind Rogers.

"Thank you, sir," Gian said to Rogers, rubbing his wrist.

Rogers peered at him with sudden interest. "You speak English—of course, you were at college, weren't you?"

"Yes, sir."

"You all right?"

"Yes, sir."

"Like a cigarette?"

Gian glanced at the sentry standing like a statue behind the Englishman. "N-no, thank you, sir."

"Here," Rogers said, and thrust his packet of cigarettes into Gian's hands.

"Why, thank you, sir," Gian said gratefully. "But it is—it is of no use, sir."

"But you do smoke, don't you?"

"We are not allowed matches, sir."

"Oh, of course not, but here you are," Rogers chucked his box of matches at the convict. "But mind you don't try to set fire to anything."

"No, sir," Gian said. "Thank you, sir."

Rogers gave him a quick smile and turned on his heel. He hurried up the passage so as to be in time for the six-thirty news. The Gurkha followed him as far as the door and gave him a noisy salute. He bolted the door and waited outside, listening to the sound of the receding footsteps, his head cocked. Then he unlocked the door again and came striding in. He marched to

Gian's corner and snatched away both the cigarettes and the matches.

"You son of a thank-you!" he whispered. "Just because you speak English, I'll give you the Kaptaan-sahib's cigarettes to smoke, you ———! And remember I will put my foot on your hand whenever I want to, understand? A hundred times, if I want. On your hand or on your ———. I can even ——— you if I want, see? Or ——— your sister and ——— your mother."

He planted his heel carefully on Gian's thigh and turned it. His slit eyes narrowed in a grin of ecstasy. "Now let me hear you squeal. Squeal! Let us see who comes to save you!" He went on turning his heel, increasing the pressure, grinning tightly all the while.

Forty-seven men watched the performance with dead, unrevealing eyes. Almost any one of them would have risen to murder for less. Many had.

When, early next afternoon, they were marched up to the ship's deck, each prisoner carrying his roll of blankets and his enamel mug and plate, they had their first sight of the Silver Jail. It lay on a promontory from which the jungle had been shaved off, making an unsightly gash in the rain-washed green of the land, stark and bare against the swaying palms, the lush green jungle, and the low-hung clouds glutted with rain.

The jail dominated the landscape; beside it everything, even Saddle Mount, the highest peak on the land, looked stunted, unimportant, vaguely stagey. It towered above everything, a great seven-spoked, seven-sided wheel, three stories high, the spokes radiating from a central tower, the rows and rows of windows like countless eyes in the limbs of some animal, a gigantic iguana or a spider from a lost world, crouching on a bed of lava and rearing its head in anticipation of its unnatural food: the criminals of India.

They were all counted in the hold and again on deck and yet again in the tiny shed on the quay where they were formally handed over to the jail superintendent, who stood behind a table, wearing a quilted sola topee and smoking a black cheroot, tapping his boots with a thick black malacca cane.

That was their first sight of Mulligan-sahib. He was short and pug-nosed, round-faced, and beer-fat; an Irishman who had been soured and singed and wrinkled by the tropics and now never wanted to go home. Scorched by the sun, yellowed by malaria, reddened by whisky, coarsened by authority, he was a tough man in a job that called for toughness. He had begun in the army, and then, as a corporal at the end of the war, had changed over to the Indian police. Three years earlier he had been rewarded for specially meritorious service by being given the post of the superintendent of the Cellular Jail. Godfearing, conscientious, and, according to his lights, just, he was trusted implicitly by his official superiors. He openly boasted that the only book he had read since he left school was the Jail Manual, that he could lick any man his own age, and that he could drink any man of any age under the table; affable, hardheaded, touchy, swashbuckling, arrogant, he knew the Jail Manual by heart and rode roughshod over every single one of its provisions—a unique combination of virtues, vices, whims, and narrow-minded righteousness. It was impossible to think of the Silver Jail without Mulligan-sahib, to visualize any other man who could hold down his difficult job with as much efficiency and dispatch. Inspector-generals and chief commissioners notwithstanding, he was the real king of the penal colony.

Past Mr. Patrick Mulligan swinging his cane in slow arcs, they marched up the road that led up the hill. As they went past him no one sang, no one spoke. Even the big Ramoshi was silent. The only sound was the clanking of the enamel mugs against the shackles around their waists.

And thus they entered a new world, to the music of the chains that bound them, a world made up of prisoners and prison officials and paroled prisoners. The great main gate opened for them and they marched into the prison, this last batch of convicts that ever went to the Andamans.

The date was September 4; the year was 1939. Not one of them had any idea that the world they had just left behind had already plunged into another war.

The entrance was a high archway leading through the twin turrets, like the gate of a castle, with an inner gate at the end of the long archway. Inside the passage, the walls were decorated with the implements of captivity and punishment, proudly exhibited like trophies in a game room: chain and ball fetters, multiple handcuffs, and coffin cages designed to keep prisoners standing up. There were other kinds of fetters which prevented a man from sitting down even if his hands were free to move, and lighter chain-fetters to permit the free movement of the limbs so that a man could do his allotted work. There were, too, the flogging frame and the flogging canes kept polished and oiled.

These were the relics of an earlier era, like heirlooms preserved for reasons of sentiment. At one time their purpose was to shock and intimidate new arrivals and remind the inmates that this was a place of punishment, not of reform, for the wreaking of society's vengeance on those who had broken its rules, not for corrective treatment of those who had gone wrong; a place where hard labour, however unproductive, the suffering of the body, however unrewarding, was a legislative requirement.

But those of them who had thumbed through the copies of the Jail Manuals, which had to be made available on request, had discovered that the days of the coffin cage and bar fetters belonged to a less civilized past; now the most severe punishment that a convict could be given was flogging, and this was given only rarely, for the most serious breaches of discipline, such as attacking a warder or attempting to escape. Two successive commissions of inquiry had imposed reforms upon the administration of the Cellular Jail, and now the manual stressed that it was more of a clearing house for the rehabilitation of convicts in their new environment than a place of punishment: indeed, the prisoners now were more like colonizers than convicts, brought over to become citizens of the Andaman islands. But the new system of reform was about to receive its first jolt. The clock would be put back by the advent of war. The time for taking pains to make human beings out of criminals was already over. Now, with a war on, it was no longer necessary to be squeamish about the book of rules. This was the time for a commonsense approach of rough and ready justice delivered by the men on the spot, leaving the policy-makers in India free to devote their energies to higher problems.

The new chalan of convicts tramped through the portals of the jail; the gates shut behind them. For the moment, it was enough for them that they were freed from the control of Balbahadur and his men, enough that they were to be given their first cooked meal in five days, enough that they were liberated from the confines of their cage in the belly of the ship.

And above all, one luxury was suddenly theirs: the luxury of solitude, of an almost unhoped-for release from the press of other human bodies, from the reek of the sweat and breath and excreta of locked-in humanity, and, for some of them at least, the luxury of being able to lie back and let their minds wander.

Their cells, they found, were large and airy and, compared with the cells of Indian jails, scrupulously clean, almost like little hospital wards. They opened out of the long open passages running down the lengths of the seven spokes of the wheel. Through the bars of their doors, the prisoners could look into the passage outside. On the other side of the passage were more bars, and through these bars, beyond the obtruding segment of their jail building, were the open sky and the jungle. The cells measured twelve feet by eight, and on the back wall each had a minute grill about one foot square, flush with the floor, and a barred window fitted high up in the wall. The only furniture was a wooden plank to sleep on and an earthenware chamber pot.

For the first time in many weeks they slept, having by now learned to adjust their postures to the demands of the fetters they still wore. They slept as men will do, as much from sheer exhaustion as from relief at having come through a major ordeal.

Only the British could have thought up something like this, Gian reflected; only the British could deliver truly humane justice. In the days before they came, anyone who stole from another had had his hands cut off, and anyone who blasphemed or committed perjury had had his tongue cut off. Now even murderers were being rehabilitated, given another chance in another country; permitted—no, encouraged—to settle down, own land, raise families. Here, even as prisoners, they were far better off than millions of Indians who had committed no other crime than that of being born.

Their day began with daylight. They were taken to the bathing troughs, which had been filled with sea water by other prisoners, and permitted to take baths while the sentries stood on guard. After that they spent long hours in orderly, slow-moving queues being documented, fingerprinted, weighed, tonsured, fumigated for lice. In the afternoon they were taken to the prison workshop to be fitted with their Andaman chains.

The chains were about twenty inches long and an inch thick, and in the centre each bore an oval disc made of steel. On the disc was engraved the name and number of a convict, also the year of his anticipated release. The two prison blacksmiths fitted the chains around their necks, cutting the ends off and bending them inwards with pliers. Each man was warned to place his forefinger against his throat to ensure that the chain was not fitted too tightly, and after the chains were in place Joseph, the assistant jailer, and Mathews, the chief supervisor, went round and satisfied themselves that they could not be pulled off over the head.

The six "D-ticket holders" came last, under a special escort. They were led by the big Ramoshi, who greeted the blacksmiths with laughter, almost as though they were friends who were meeting again after one of them had been away on a holiday. Behind him came Gian and Debi-dayal. They did not say anything to each other because there was nothing to say—not that they were permitted to talk.

[15]

A View of the Beach

THE date had been fixed earlier, in consultation with the family astrologers, an auspicious date that could not be changed. And yet perhaps it was an almost inescapble coincidence. Sundari and Gopal were going on their honeymoon on the same day that Debi-dayal's ship sailed from Calcutta.

The wedding itself had been a quiet affair, even quieter than Sundari's father had intended, for not one of Gopal's numerous relatives had shown up for the ceremony or cared to send messages or presents.

Sundari felt miserable. She herself was going on her honeymoon; her brother was on his way to the Andamans. She had to remind herself that this was a time for joy and excitement, but it was difficult to drag her thoughts away from Debi.

The car was new, the luggage was new, the landscape was unfamiliar, and the man sitting beside her, concentrating on the driving, was almost a stranger. Everything was strange, unfamiliar, because everything belonged to someone else—even she herself now belonged to that someone else.

Only the dog, now curled up in its blanket on the back seat, was her own. It had come to her because its owner, Debi-dayal, had gone to prison. Debi was due for release in 1952. The dog, Spindle, was already five years old. It would certainly not be alive in 1952.

Spindle would not be alive now, she reflected, but for Debi. Its mother had belonged to Mr. Muller, who owned the ice factory and the pig farm. Both Sundari and Debi had hopped on their bicycles and gone to see the puppies on the very day they were born. Mr. Muller was on the veranda behind the pigsty where the puppies were kept in a tea chest lined with straw. He was weighing each puppy in his hands and feeling their bodies and

examining their heads and feet. One of the sweepers was cleaning the stone floor with a brush.

"Make the water really hot," Mr. Muller was telling the
sweeper as they went in. "Otherwise the little beasts keep swimming for a long time."

"Are you going to give them a bath, Mr. Muller?" Sundari
asked.

"Bath! No, dear. I am having one of them drowned. I am
trying to decide which one."

"You mean you want to kill one of the puppies?" Debi had
asked.

"It is no good keeping all of them; one has to think of their
mother. She can't feed more than three. It is a small breed, the
dachshund."

Sundari had avoided looking at her brother, knowing how
shocked he must be. It was important not to give Mr. Muller the
impression that they were squeamish about this sort of thing.
Mr. Muller was a German, known to be contemptuous of the
numerous weaknesses of the Indian character.

"Which one would you select—for destroying?" Mr. Muller
asked Sundari.

"They all look so small—so small and so pretty. Can't you
keep them all?" she asked.

"We can't keep more than three; she has given birth to four,"
Mr. Muller said blandly.

Sundari swallowed desperately. "The poor little things," she
managed to say.

"It is the kindest thing, really," Mr. Muller explained. "They
die quite quickly when the water is really hot; only one has to
hold them down for a minute or so. Otherwise they swim and
take a long time to die."

Sundari felt her body shiver. She glanced at Debi. His face had
gone pale, and he looked as though he wanted to be sick. Oh,
please, please, God, don't let him be sick here, Sundari prayed,
not in front of Mr. Muller. The sweeper came in with a large
bucket full of steaming water.

"I think this one," Mr. Muller pronounced, holding up one
of the puppies. "Though there is little to choose between them."

"Yes," Sundari heard herself saying. "I think so too." Mr.
Muller turned the puppy in his hands to determine its sex, and
its mother came up and began to lick its body.

"Come on, let's go," Sundari said to Debi. "Thank you, Mr. Muller," she remembered to say.

"Oh, are you going?" Mr. Muller asked, raising his big red face. "You needn't go. It doesn't take more than a couple of minutes." He handed the puppy to the sweeper. "Or are you afraid?" Mr. Muller asked very casually.

"Of course I am not afraid," Sundari had said, suddenly stung. "All right, we will stay on and watch, if you don't mind."

"No, I don't mind," Mr. Muller told her. "I don't mind. What about your brother?"

"Oh, come on Sundar, let's go," Debi had implored. "It is getting late."

"No, let your sister stay if she wants to," Mr. Muller said, looking at them in turn. "Perhaps she would like to hold the little thing down in the water." He felt the water with a finger. "No, not too hot," he pronounced. "Just right. I know that a German girl would not mind."

"Give me the puppy," Sundari said, putting out her hands. "I don't think I shall mind, either."

"Oh, stop being a show-off, Sundar!" Debi pleaded. "Please let's go away."

"You go if you want to," Sundari told Debi. "I shall follow you in a few minutes. Just as soon as this is over."

"I shall never speak to you again—never!" Debi had spluttered. Then he had turned to Mr. Muller. "You horrible German butcher! You killed and ate French children in the war —everyone knows that. You are mean and cruel and disgusting! —and when you lost the war the British should have killed all of you, every single one of you—monsters!" he screamed, shaking his fists. Then he had turned and fled.

For a long time Mr. Muller had sat speechless, his face redder than ever. And then Sundari had said, "I am sorry, Mr. Muller. I hope you will forgive my brother. He did not know what he was saying."

"He should have been you," Mr. Muller said. "And you should have been him."

"Shall we drown the puppy now, Mr. Muller?" Sundari had asked. "The water must be getting cold."

Mr. Muller shook his head. "No, we will not drown the puppy," he said. "We will rear it, and then when it is six weeks old we will give it to your brother."

"Oh, thank you, Mr. Muller! Thank you. I am sure he will be so pleased . . . and I shall make him apologize. . . ."

"Tell him it is a present from the horrible German butcher," Mr. Muller had said. "A monster!"

That was how Spindle had come to them, five years ago, and even though it was regarded as Debi's dog, it had fallen to Sundari to look after it.

It had always been so, Sundari remembered, ever since they were small; she was always doing things for him, taking the blame for him. But then, in all honesty, that was something she herself had loved to do, and at times she had wondered if there was not something a little unnatural in her fondness for her brother.

For instance, he had a habit, whenever he woke up during the night, of pretending that he saw ghosts in their nursery, and would not go to sleep until Sundari got into his bed. But then, if there had been anything sexual in their relationship, she would have found herself resenting his growing independence, she told herself. Instead, as soon as the initial shock of discovering that he had become a revolutionary had subsided, she had felt a surge of pride at his having surmounted his childhood weaknesses and become manly and brave. Now it was difficult to think of him as someone who saw ghosts in the shadows or shrank from handling grasshoppers and snails and little tadpoles as a child. Now he would not feel sick at the thought of a little puppy being drowned, or come begging to her to remove an anthill on their badminton court.

The badminton court was still there, even though it was rarely used now. The mali had gone on marking the lines on it, every week, just out of habit. But when they were at school they both used to play quite regularly. She remembered it was winter, because Debi wore a Fair Isle sweater, torn at the elbows, and was on tenterhooks because she had asked two of the girls from the convent to come and spend the day with them. Debi had come into her room, still looking sleepy but already dressed in white shorts, a shirt, and canvas shoes.

"Sundar, there is an anthill on the court," he had complained.

"An anthill?"

"Yes, and the Stanley sisters are coming. . . ."

"Oh, God!" She had never cared for the Stanley girls. "Break it down, then."

"But we can't. You see, it is their house. They built it; they are living in it."

"Yes, but they have no business to build their house right in the middle of our lawn. Go and ask one of the malis to break it down."

"There is no one about today; it's Sunday."

"Well, then, there is nothing to be done about it."

"Oh, please, Sundar, don't be mean," he had pleaded.

"You're always wanting me to do your dirty work," she had protested. But she had got out of bed all the same, and gone out with him. It was cool on the lawn, which had been watered the previous evening, and sure enough, between the white lines on the far side of the court was the anthill. It was almost nine inches high, with the mud still soft and wet-looking.

"Can't we—cannot we just let them be?" Debi had asked. "It is only in the lobby, and we need not play doubles. . . . Oh, what are you doing, Sundar! How can you!—the poor little mites!"

She had kicked at the anthill in sudden anger, anger at her brother's weakness of mind. He had no business to go on like that. He must learn to be tough, learn to be a man.

The little tower of soft earth had toppled over, like an over-turned toy castle, and the ants came scurrying out of hundreds of little holes and passageways. And she had gone on kicking, razing their township to the ground and then stamping on the ruins with both feet and crushing all the little white ants.

"Oh, how could you, Sundar! How could you!" Debi had yelled at her, his face tense and drawn. "Then why don't you do it yourself!" she had snapped at him. "Or get your Stanley girls to do it for you!" She had turned and fled into the house, unable to tell him that it was not the ants but he, her little brother, whom she had always wanted to grow strong and manly, that had made her stamp on the ants—or had it also something to do with the Stanley sisters?

Sundari was still thinking about Debi when they reached their destination, a small forest bungalow beyond Mahabaleswar. The keeper of the bungalow was waiting for them with garlands. Did they always have garlands ready or had he somehow discovered that they were a honeymoon couple? Sundari asked herself. Was it as obvious as that?

She tried to shake off her despondency, to step into the part of a newly married wife. But she did not feel excited or happy or eager, as a bride was supposed to, nor did she even look attractive, she told herself as she was undressing—her face had become puffy and looked smudged with tears.

Gopal had every right to feel disappointed with her, she thought as she bathed her face in cold water. How could he understand what Debi had meant to her; how could she prepare her mind for the delights of their honeymoon . . . beautify herself to receive this strange man who had now become her husband, when Debi's ship was heading for the Andamans?

Gopal was sitting on the veranda, nervously smoking cigarettes. Below him, the great Konya gorge was bathed in moonlight. He heard her shut the bathroom door and get into bed. He waited for a few seconds, then threw away his cigarette and went into the bedroom. She looked flushed and nervous, and gave him an eager smile. But as his fingers touched her body, she shrank away from him, and two large tears slid out of her eyes. Then she began to sob.

He tried to comfort her, to kiss away her tears, but he felt clumsy and unwanted. Her thoughts were obviously far away, and her body remained cold and unresponsive.

He left her bed and went for a walk round the bungalow. Afterwards he sat on the veranda again, drinking whisky. When, much later, he crawled back into her room, she was fast asleep, and Spindle came charging at him, barking furiously.

He slapped the dog in anger, slapped it hard enough to make it squeal, and she awakened from her sleep and screamed at him, "How dare you, you brute!" She took the dog into her arms and turned her back on him. Quietly he slunk out of the room and returned to the bottle of whisky.

That first night set the pattern of their honeymoon. It rankled in their minds, something grotesque and unseemly that would stay with them all their lives. And he rebelled against it more than she. His terrorist brother-in-law had already cut him off from the other branches of his own family and caused him considerable social embarrassment; now his shadow was coming between him and his bride, preventing them from getting to know each other as man and wife.

"How dare you touch him, you brute!" she had screamed at him on their first night together.

They both tried to make adjustments, and she offered to have

Spindle tied up on the veranda, but things did not improve. The purely physical process of defloration proved messy and was accompanied by a good deal of pain. The very next night Sundari managed to run a temperature, and he had to ring for a doctor. The fever lasted three days. During the last week, although the fever had gone, she looked wan and withdrawn, but she had not denied herself to him. Indeed, even in her fever she had shown a readiness to surrender to his passion. It was only when they were about to leave that he came to realize that on her part it was like a game of let's pretend, good manners taking the place of sexual appetite; that she was forcing herself to play the part of the happy, eager bride, trying to make out that she was enjoying what, in fact, she found painful and abhorrent. Even when he was in the grip of desire, her passionless surrender vaguely reminded him of rape.

They returned to Bombay at the end of August, when the rains were still at their heaviest. In the car, driving back, she was much more cheerful, and together they made plans for settling their house. He was unreasonably cheered when she said, "Darling, don't let's go out too much for the first few days."

"We will just pretend that we have not come back," he said, laughing.

"But I mean it," she insisted. "I know I really behaved disgracefully badly in Mahabaleswar. Now I want to make it up."

He patted her affectionately. "Oh, we don't have to go out unless we want to. Luckily, we are far enough away from the town not to be disturbed."

But they were disturbed, that very first afternoon. They were having tea and she was just about to go to her room to see to the unpacking, when the telephone rang.

"Acutally we've only just arrived—we haven't even unpacked," she heard Gopal say. He put his hand on the mouthpiece. "Malini," he told Sundari, and then he was talking into the telephone again.

"What! . . . Well, no; it is not raining at this very moment, but there are a lot of fat grey clouds about, and the breeze is quite cold. . . . What? Of course I am not trying to put you off. What an idea! Indeed he is most welcome. Do . . . Of course!"

He turned to her with a sheepish grin. "That was Malini—yes, she was at the wedding. She says that she and her prince want to come for a swim."

"Oh!" Sundari frowned. "Now?"

"I can't bear the prince—actually I thought he'd dropped her, but"—he shrugged his shoulders—"I couldn't very well tell her not to come. We—we know each other too well for that."

"Oh, no, you couldn't."

She was still in her room, unpacking, when Malini turned up, too quickly to have driven out all the way from town. "Darling! How wonderful to see you back in civilization," she heard her say. "You're looking wonderful—even though you shouldn't be."

Squatting on the floor in front of her open bags, Sundari had winced at the "darling" and then, as the meaning of her remark had become clear, had found herself flushing. She had heard that "darling" used by an actress did not necessarily imply an advanced degree of intimacy, but she found herself resenting Malini's air of familiarity, even possessiveness.

She quickly ran a comb through her hair and went into the sitting room. And there was Malini, wearing eye-shadow and crimson patches on her cheeks. In her pearl-pink sari and black choli, she looked smart and sleek and ready for a party. "Oh, please keep your dog away," she pleaded, shaking her shoulder in a gesture of revulsion. "I can't bear dogs—least of all these German sausages."

Sundari carried Spindle back to the bedroom and put him on her bed. When she came back, she asked Malini if she would like some tea.

"No, thank you, dear," Malini said. "I never drink the stuff, as Gopal knows. I have asked Baldev to bring me a whisky—he knows just how I like it."

Baldev was Gopal's bearer. Sundari still did not know the names of all the servants, and found herself resenting Malini's speaking of them with such familiarity. She felt dowdy and ill at ease, with the dust of the road still in her hair, her sari crumpled.

"Where is His Highness?" Gopal asked.

"Oh, poor Princy got involved in a game of poker, just at the last minute. So I thought I'd come by myself, so as not to disappoint you, even though, I must say, you didn't sound at all thrilled over the phone."

"Oh, no; we were delighted," Gopal protested.

"Don't tell me you are going to cut out all your old friends just because you're married," Malini said.

"Of course not, only I rather got the impression that it was the prince who wanted to drop in for a dip."

"Poor Princy," Malini said again. "Getting into his poker game just when I had persuaded him to come swimming. Come on, let's go in before the sun goes down—ah, thank you, Baldev." She beamed at the bearer who had brought her drink. "Looks wonderful. Aren't any of you joining me in this?"

"Yes, I think I will," Gopal said. "Give me one too, please, Baldev. Sundari hardly touches the stuff."

"Oh, my God! Don't tell me she is one of those—not a disciple of Morarji?"

"Oh, no!" Sundari protested. "I do take a sherry now and then, or a gimlet, and of course I don't mind others drinking."

"What about the swim?" Malini asked.

Gopal looked at his wife. "Would you like to?"

"I have so much to do," Sundari told him. "Besides, I don't feel all that well."

"Poor dear," Malini said pityingly. "How tired you look. The first honeymoon is always like that, they say. I wouldn't know, of course, being the bachelor girl."

Sundari laughed politely even though she found the joke a little coarse, and she still felt a little out of place in her own house.

"I was dying for Princy to see my new costume," Malini was saying. "Came all the way from Hollywood. A two-piece in what they call a stunning red—and my tan too. Don't tell anyone, but it is an all-over tan. Now I will only have unappreciative you to see it," she said to Gopal. "I mean the costume—not the all-over tan."

"Hardly unappreciative," Gopal assured her. "Please come and sit on the beach even if you are not feeling like a bathe," he said to Sundari.

"Why trouble the poor thing if she is not feeling well?" Malini pouted. "You are not looking at all well, my dear," she said to Sundari. "Just look at your eyes—and what have you done to your poor hair? And don't tell me you are one of those tiresome women who can't bear to let their husbands out of their sight, are you? No, of course not. Tell me, where can I slip into my costume?"

The costume consisted of two wisps of satiny cloth, and it

showed Malini off to perfection. She really had a stunning figure, Sundari conceded as she watched them walking towards the palms; and she carried herself well too, as so few Indian women do. And then for the first time, through the annoyance she had been feeling about Malini's intrusion on their day, she experienced a sudden prick of jealousy.

She saw him offer his hand to help her over the stile in the fence, and noticed that he did not let go her arm as they walked through the coconut grove beyond the fence, all the way to where the sand began, at least three hundred yards from the house. She saw them leave their chaplis and towels at the edge of the beach and walk over the strip of sand towards the dark blue waves, the red and blue of their costumes closer and closer with the distance. They waded into waist-deep water and then dived together, head-first, into an enormous roller.

Did their bodies mingle together in the waves? Sundari asked herself, remembering the look in Malini's eyes, her rippling, belly-dancer's body with its over-all tan shrieking for attention, the heavy, pointed breasts barely restrained by the outrageous strip of satin. Was it already enveloping that other body, clean and firm and youthful—contaminating something that was hers? She shook her head and tried to laugh at herself even though her eyes were brimming with tears. The sun was just poised to go down as she left the window.

She left the suitcases as they were and gave herself a hot bath. She felt much better as she dressed, even ready to laugh at her absurd jealousy. She daubed some cologne over her hands and made up her face and put on one of her pale Chanderi saris.

It was nearly dark by the time she finished dressing, but they had not returned. She thought she would utilize the time by putting Gopal's things away. His dressing room was on the other side of the bedroom from hers. It was full of built-in shelves and cupboards with his shoes and suits and shirts and hats all neatly arranged in their respective shelves. In a cupboard in one corner were his hunting clothes, and on a shelf next to them, his guns and boxes of ammunition and cleaning rods. He was a man's man, her husband, Sundari told herself, fond of the outdoors, he rode and shot and swam. . . . They were certainly away a long time swimming, she thought; and this time the feeling of jealousy came with a rush, making her face feel hot.

In the top shelf of the cupboard, where the boxes of ammunition were kept, she noticed a pair of binoculars and a short, chunky telescope mounted on a swivel stand. Now she felt angry and purposeful, suddenly rebellious at her own weakness; it was the sort of feeling that had come over her when she had offered to drown the puppy in Mr. Muller's backyard, offered to hold it down in the water, alive and struggling, until it stopped struggling.

She picked up the telescope and carried it to the glazed veranda opening out of the sitting room, its windows overlooking the sea. She put it down on the window-sill, noticing its heaviness and unwieldiness only after she had put it securely down. She bent down and began to scan the beach with its eyepiece.

For a long time she did not see them. The telescope was powerful, but it was highly selective, being designed to spot small targets during range practice and to ascertain where the bullets were hitting. It offered only a glimpse of a small round segment of the landscape at a time.

And then she saw them, her eye caught by the minute red splotch in the water. They were just coming out of the water. She saw Malini pull him towards her and, as he turned, bend his head down and kiss him on the mouth. They stood like that for a long time, in knee-deep water, until a wave came and engulfed them. Then she saw them again, and this time his arms were around her and their bodies were pressed tightly together.

Sundari stood glued to the telescope, following their movements, keeping them imprisoned in the circle of glass. She lost sight of them as they walked up to where their towels had been left, and it was some time before she was able to locate them again. And then she realized why she had failed to find them easily. They were not wearing their costumes now. In the last few seconds of the summer twilight, she saw them under the palms, far beyond the fence, the slim brown body obscuring the vulgar white, the male and the female mingling together.

Or was she imagining it all, was it some peculiar fantasy of a mind distorted by jealousy? For now there was no light left at all, except the soft white light of the moon which fell from directly above. The ground was covered with dark splotches and all she could see were the lacy tops of the trees under which she had seen them. She got up and went to her bedroom and lay back in bed, thinking, trying to piece together the relationship that appeared to exist between her husband and Malini.

Sundari was still in bed, with Spindle curled up beside her, when they came back. She heard their footsteps coming up the stairs, and then her husband was calling, "Aren't you ready yet, Sundari?"

"I'm just dying for a drink, aren't you?" Malini was saying. "A drink and then a shower." And she gave a girlish squeal.

Through the open door of the passage that led from their bedroom to the sitting room, she could hear them talking, and then she heard her husband's footsteps in the passage, and Spindle began to bark. "Oh, stop that damned row," Gopal said, half in anger, half playfully. "What are you doing, all in the dark here?" he asked Sundari.

"I was not feeling very well and must have dropped off to sleep," she forced herself to say. "Oh, no, please don't put on the light!"

"What a pity!" he said. "Shall I send you a drink or something?"

"No, I just want to lie down."

"It is not—not anything serious, is it? Have you got fever?"

"Oh, no; I just want to rest, that's all."

"Shall I ring for a doctor?"

"No. I'll be perfectly all right in the morning."

He paused in the doorway for a few seconds and then went out, his chaplis making little squeaky sounds in the uncarpeted passage. For a time there was silence in the sitting room, unless they were talking in undertones. Then she heard him exclaim, "What on earth is the telescope doing there! . . . Oh, my God!"

"The spying little bitch!" Malini said.

Sundari sat up in bed, her skin tingling. She had forgotten to put away the telescope, and there it lay, telling them the full story. Now that it had been discovered, she could not have wished it otherwise. She wanted them to look through the instrument; she hoped that the palm-trees under which they had been lying were still visible in the moonlight. She could have chortled with laughter at the little bit of luck that had come her way. If she had put away the telescope, they would never have known; somehow that would have been like admitting defeat from a woman like Malini. It was unthinkable.

Savouring her triumph, she soon fell asleep. She fell asleep even though it had struck her that their marriage was as good as broken. Oddly enough, it seemed unimportant. It was almost as though she wanted it so, that she wanted whatever had happened to have happened exactly as it did, so that when the break came, it could be clean and without pain.

For the first time since her wedding day, she fell asleep without thinking of Debi-dayal. She never knew what time Malini left their house that night, or if she had stayed there all night. Now, somehow, it did not matter.

"I am not going to let that slut come barging in here again," Gopal said to her next morning.

She gave him a long look and a smile, but said nothing.

"I mean it," he protested. "I am just gong to tell her point-blank."

"Oh, but we mustn't stop seeing your old friends just because you are married," she assured him.

He was disturbed by her lightheartedness. It did not tie up with her sullenness of the previous night, with the telescope placed neatly on the window-sill, aimed accurately at the clump of trees under which they had been lying. What had she seen?

"Malini is not exactly a friend of mine," he told her. "What were you doing with the spotting-scope?" he asked, trying to sound casual.

"Why, I was trying to locate you, of course," she explained. "I couldn't see a thing."

He was relieved by her casual tone; it was just his imagination, then. "Not if you try to see through it in the dark," he said.

"Yes, it was so dark when I thought of it; and then it is such an unwieldy thing. One doesn't know where to look."

"There is a knack to it," he told her. Then he added, "And all the time I have been thinking that you couldn't stand the sight of her."

"Who?"

"Malini. I thought you were really put out when she came. She is a little overpowering, I suppose, at first sight, a professional dancer—movie actress too, of sorts. . . ."

He stopped. For the first time that morning Sundari was looking directly into his eyes, and now there was no smile on her face. "Let us get this straight, since it is important to get such things straight," she said in a cold, very flat voice. "To be honest, I did think she was a little coarse, but beyond that I did not think anything about her. She is just someone one feels sorry for, but that is all; like—like someone out of *Yama the Pit* suddenly walking into our drawing room. One can only be polite and feel a little sorry for her. It is hardly fair to judge such people by conventional standards—like or dislike them for what they say or do."

He was conscious of her sudden sense of power over him. "I didn't know you were so snooty," he said.

"I was not being snooty," she said in the same even tone. "I was just trying to set things straight between us—put everything in its proper perspective."

[16]

The View from Debi's Cell

THE chink in the mortar between the two layers of brick must have been made by an earlier inmate of cell number twenty-three, barrack seven. By propping one end of the sleeping plank up against it and standing on the plank he could reach the bars of the window set high into the wall. Then, by pulling himself up, he could look down into the triangle between two spokes of the jail building. As long as his arms would support his weight, he could go on looking.

In the yard below, it was like market day. They were shelling and breaking coconuts and putting out the copra to dry. Looking down at them like that, from the third-story window of barrack seven, it was easy to think of those men as coolies in some well-run factory—a happy factory where the workers shared in the profits. They were a part of the noise and bustle, of the assembly-line efficiency: exhibit A in the prison reforms initiated by an enlightened government and enforced by Mulligan-sahib with unswerving zest.

In the centre were the two great mounds of coconuts—thousands upon thousands of misshapen green footballs which were now the playthings of the convicts, or, if you let your mind wander, like the pyramids of human heads built by Nadir Shah in the streets of Delhi. The peelers stood in a line, thin and wiry, their copper bodies glistening with sweat, expertly breaking the fibre by smashing each nut with a twisting motion against the line of spikes mounted on wooden stumps—breaking the fibre and yet not damaging the nuts within, for that would have led to their being fined for carelessness—and then, without turning their heads to look, hurling the naked, sand-coloured nuts at the tin wall of the shed behind them with resounding thuds. Squatting behind them were the rows of splitters who broke the nuts

145

with single deft strokes of their light axes and threw the halves, the brown cups containing the dazzling white meat, into the wooden trough, all in one continuous, machine-like motion, while the water from the broken nuts ran in a sluggish stream between them. Around the trough there was another horseshoe of human ants, the men who scooped out the kernels from the halves in triangular strips with the help of koytas, the heavy, curved coconut knives.

They worked in silence, for speech was forbidden. The thunder of the nuts banging against the tin wall of the shed and the sharp cracks of the axes splitting open the nuts formed the background to the twangy whine of the warders and petty officers.

"Get a move on, there! Next time I catch you with your mouth full, you'll be up for flogging. Come on, come on; don't dawdle, sons of whores, sister-rapers; stop eating or I'll send the whole lot of you to the kanji-house."

Balbahadur, the Gurkha sentry, was there too, strutting, shouting, raging, and all the while shovelling handfuls of coconut meat into his mouth.

Debi-dayal's eyes strayed lovingly over the weapons the convicts were wielding: the short-handled splitting axes and the heavy, curved knives—all useful weapons in an emergency.

How like cattle they were, he thought, cattle or some lower form of life, tamed into abject subservience; working mechanically, their brains feverishly working out plans for secreting some of the kernel on their persons, watching the sentries with hawk-like eyes, insensible to insults, the degrading prison epithets, docilely participating in the routine, helping instead of hindering.

There were at least a hundred and fifty convicts in the yard. The warders and the petty officers could not have numbered more than twenty. The convicts had the axes and the hatchets in their hands; the guards had only long, weighted sticks. What could not one do in a situation of that sort? If only he could find someone he could depend on, someone like one of the Freedom Fighters, the same herd of cattle could be so easily organized, taught to stampede at a given signal, make a concerted rush against the warders and others, and overpower them before the rifle squad at the main gate could intervene.

Was Gian the man, Debi wondered, the non-violent disciple of Gandhi who had been convicted for murder? He cursed and shook his head in disgust. Gian was certainly not the man. He was typical of the youth of India, vacillating, always seeking new anchors, new directions, devoid of any basic convictions. He had been dedicated, so he had told them, to truth and non-violence. He had already jettisoned non-violence; how far would he go with truth?

If only he could rely on Gian, between them they could easily turn the prisoners against the officials. He clung to the thought, organizing, in his mind, the details of a mass break-through.

It would be over in a moment. They would have to choose a time when Mulligan was going his rounds. It was important to finish off Mulligan in the first rush. After that, everything would be plain sailing—almost an anti-climax. Balbahadur, the Gurkha head sentry, would also have to be disposed of, but that was something he would like to reserve for himself; it was a purely private affair, selfish, even; it had little to do with the plan forming in his mind.

His arms trembled. There was a stab of pain in his right shoulder, and the backs of his hands were covered with large drops of sweat. But he ignored these warnings of physical tiredness, almost defied them; he concentrated his mind on the scene below.

The convicts were naked; naked except for the little strips of cloth running between their legs and secured by rope waistbands; naked except for the unremovable chains around their necks—chains which some of them now wore proudly as badges of rank.

Two men stood out in the crowd because they were not naked; they wore grey prison blouses and shorts, with conspicuous red Ds sewn on the backs and fronts of their blouses. One was Gian, the other was Ghasita, the big Ramoshi. Both were working in the line of splitters, both wielding the short, murderous axes in their hands—axes that could crack open a skull or a coconut with equal ease.

That must be the sort of weapon with which the big Ramoshi had killed the man who had betrayed him—killed him in the middle of the bazaar, as he proudly told everyone. In terms of his values, he had fulfilled himself, and he was stoically taking the consequences. That was the retribution Vetal had laid down for those who betrayed his devotees.

The man who had betrayed him, Debi-dayal, was his own father. It had come out during the trial that it was Tekchand's complaint about the missing explosives, and, even more so, his call to the Chief Commissioner when he said that the local police were not taking his complaint seriously, that had led to the raid on the Hanuman Club.

And the man who could have warned him, warned all the members of the club in time, was Shafi Usman.

Shafi had been tipped off about the raid: that was the talk of the prison during Debi's trial. All eight of them had sworn to avenge themselves. It would have been different if he had run away without warning any of them. In their sort of work casualties had to be accepted. But what he had done was a betrayal of everything that he stood for, had prepared the others for, with all that anti-religious talk.

He wondered what the Ramoshi would have done in his situation. Would he have confined his vengeance to Shafi? Or did Vetal rule that not even one's own father was to be spared the retribution for betrayal?

Shafi and his father; how unlike each other they were. His father, haughty, superior, well-bred; Shafi emerging from the gutters, embittered, coarse. And yet it was almost as though they had combined to betray him, him and the others. If they had been spared, they would have been able to play havoc with the British war effort. What could not he and Basu and the others have done to cripple the British.

He longed to get back. The urge to resume his work was even stronger than the desire for vengeance. He rebelled against his confinement. He had to get away; they would never succeed in breaking him down to the size of the other convicts—criminals reformed by an enlightened government and converted into useful citizens. They could never reduce him to the acceptable pattern of one of those men below—grovelling for the crumbs thrown at them by Mulligan, like that man Gian Talwar.

A swift wave of anger passed over him, drowning the pain in his shoulder. Gian too had been classified as a dangerous convict. How was he released from solitary confinement so soon, permitted to do work in the open, without fetters, with the other prisoners? And the big Ramoshi, who had committed two murders?

Exhibit B? he asked himself. Another instance of Mulligan's clemency, now heightened by the war? What provision of the jail manual could Mulligan have invoked to justify his letting out a "D-for-dangerous" convict within three months of his arrival?

"Sons of whores! Pigs from Hell! Sister-rapers!" The swear words came from below, hitting his eardrums with almost physical force. Almost perversely, he thought of his own sister, shocked at the connotation, inwardly guilty at associating someone like Sundari with the foulness of the warder's language. His thoughts flitted back to that day in the Thana jail, the last visiting day before he was to be sent off to Calcutta to be taken to the Andamans. He had turned down all requests from his father and mother to visit him in jail, but had agreed to see his sister. And he had cursed loudly when the superintendent told him that she had come accompanied with her own exhibit A, that glossy-haired rich boy they had found for her. He had taken a peek through the wire and felt his blood rising, for he looked almost like an off-duty British subaltern. He wore the regimental tie and blazer of some territorial battalion he had joined, and Debi-dayal could imagine his pride at being in the army with all the talk of war going on—typifying the despicable people who made the British empire a stark reality, captives who hugged the chains and imitated their masters, somehow far more contemptible than his own father who, in spite of his title, was still wholly Indian.

"But I want to see my sister alone," he had told the superintendent.

He had seen Gopal stride out, apologetic and well-mannered, accepting his dismissal with a smile, but he had not felt sorry for him.

Sundari had sat alone, her face like a mask, her lips trembling, her eyes filled with tears, and, knowing that he too was near to breaking down, he had been curt with her. She wore a simple white cotton sari, but looked so breathtakingly beautiful that he had found himself resenting her presence. It was not right for someone like Sundari, virginal, unblemished, refined, to expose herself to the sordidness and dehumanized atmosphere of the Indian jails, to the leers and lascivious thoughts of men who were no longer human beings, or smile at the superintendent, a lecherous-eyed Bengali hovering unctuously in the office, almost too eager to please.

When he had told Sundari that all he wanted was a copy of the jail manual, the superintendent had looked doubtful even though it was the right of every prisoner to be given a copy if he asked for it. But an anxious look from his sister had made him unbend. "I shall let him have my copy," he assured Sundari. "He can read it in his cell."

After the superintendent had gone, they had been alone hardly for five minutes, and just as they were about to part Sundari had whispered, "I will try and send you some money. I shall get it to you somehow. They say life is not too bad there if one has money."

She was so pathetically earnest about it that he had not the heart to decline her offer of help. But he could not accept any money from her, of that he was sure, knowing that it could only be his father's money or her husband's money that Sundari could send him.

"And Father wants to know if he can do anything—you don't know how lost he looks, quite shattered!"

He had shaken his head. He wanted nothing from his father. His father had done all the damage of which he was capable. In some odd, twisted way, he was even glad that his father had taken his conviction so much to heart. He was aware that, in his own way, his father had tried to help. His father's influence with the high officials had spared him the famed torture of the Indian police thanas; while the other members of the Hanuman Club were being beaten and starved to induce them to confess, one of the sentries smuggled a cake of soap and a slab of chocolate into his cell. Defiantly he had thrown both soap and chocolate out of the window.

But the Andaman manual was quite another thing. He wanted it because he had to find out exactly what they were in for. The superintendent brought him a copy.

It was comforting to realize that after the prison reforms of 1920 and 1929, the Cellular Jail was a place no longer of punishment, but where convicts were held for a time before being resettled.

All literate prisoners, the manual said, were usually given some kind of clerical work in the prison itself within six months of arrival, and after that they were not required to wear prison uniform. No convict, if he behaved himself, was kept in the jail for more than a year. He was made a pass-holder, or a feri according to local jargon, and permitted to reside in one of the other settlements on the island. Such prisoners were also helped to find work in the coconut or tea plantations or with the timber-extracting companies. They were even encouraged to cultivate their own land, to build houses, to marry the girls from the settlements, or even to bring out their wives from India.

The "D-ticket holders," however, formed a separate coterie. For them the treatment was considerably stricter. They were kept in solitary confinement for at least three months, after which, when they were permitted to work, they were not to mix with the other prisoners for at least another six months. They had to wear their blouses at all times, with the distinctive red Ds sewn on them. But even in their case, three years was the most they were required to spend in the jail itself. After that they too were made feris and permitted to settle down in the colonies on their own.

But one thing he did not find in the Andaman manual: there was no release from the island itself. No prisoner could leave the island until the full term of his sentence had run out. There were, to be sure, remissions of sentences: a month a year for good behaviour, and another month or so whenever there was an occasion for national celebration. That would take away about twenty months from his sentence—he would have to remain on the island for more than twelve years. Actually, the date etched out on the metal disc round his neck was 1953. Even accounting for an unblemished record, it could never be earlier than 1952. He would be thirty-two years old, he reflected.

He squirmed with rage at the thought. It was unthinkable to go on living here until he was thirty-two. And he had no wish to qualify for time off for good behaviour; had no intention of cooperating, marking time for twelve years, waiting patiently for 1952. He did not want to be given work in the prison office as a clerk or settle down in the convict colony as a plantation labourer, marry, raise a family. All he wanted was to go back and finish his interrupted work, until the sunrise of their freedom, as Shafi had described it that day; to join hands with the others in the ceaseless fight against the Raaj, all the more vulnerable now because of the war. If only the Gandhis and the Nehrus would discard their pacifism now and channel their energies towards driving out the British with violence, using the terrorists' methods, they could make short work of the Raaj.

But they would never do it. They were even more bent on

emasculating the nation than the British were. It was only men
like himself and Shafi—even if Shafi had gone wrong—who
would succeed in striking the final blow.

Through a blur, as though behind some opaque curtain, he
saw a sudden wave pass through the convicts and their guards
below. The tempo of work suddenly quickened as though by the
turning of some valve; the separate sounds of the coconuts banging against the tin wall, the sharp cracks of the splitters, now lost
themselves in a loud, ceaseless rumble; the peelers and the splitters suddenly sat straighter, straighter, and, at the same time,
more subservient. The warders began to yell louder and strut
about with upraised lathis, with Balbahadur imitating Mulligan's
swagger, more voluble, more alert, more aggressive than the
others.

Even without seeing him, Debi-dayal realized that Mulligan
was on his rounds. As he watched, the rounded, squat figure
under the thick topee came stamping through the archway, ignoring the warders' salaams, and stood in the shade, puffing a black
cigar, swinging a black stick. He watched them at their work,
without saying anything, and then he chucked the cigar-stub into
the rivulet of the coconut water where it floated away with jerky
movements. Then he stepped out of the shade and wandered
amongst the convicts, pausing now and then to pat one of them
on the back or to say a word.

Debi-dayal winced. He was talking to the big Ramoshi and
had his back turned to Gian, Gian who wielded the coconut axe.
Just one stroke, he prayed in his mind, just one slanting stroke
against the thick red neck, thick like the neck of a soldier seen
long ago in bright moonlight . . . and the rounded head with
its piglike eyes and pug nose would go bounding off into the pile
of broken coconuts, complete with its ridiculous topee. . . .

Far behind him, in another dimension of his mind, he was
aware of a break in the pattern of the silence, followed, seconds
later, by the faint crunch of footsteps at the end of the corridor.
He loosened his grip on the bars and dropped to the floor. The
blood rushed back into his hands and fingers with a surge of
pain. He had just managed to replace the sleeping board in its
usual position when the Pathan warder came stamping to his
door.

"Mulligan-sahib is coming," the warder said, gasping. He unlocked the padlock on the door and waited, the heavy hasp held in his hand, ready to throw open the door with a flourish. "For God's sake remember to stand up and salute the sahib," he entreated. "If you are rude, he takes it out on us."

He was a friendly enough man, unlike the other warders in the jail, but of course he might quite easily have been ordered to be friendly, to get into the prisoners' confidence.

He flung open the door and Mulligan strode in, followed by a petty officer. Debi-dayal did not rise to his feet. Nor did he raise his hand in salute.

The superintendent and the petty officer went round the cell. Mulligan stopped under the window. "Here," he said, tapping with his cane between the two layers of brick where the plaster had been chipped. "That's where he must have been propping the plank. I told you I saw his head from below. I know all their tricks."

He certainly did, Debi-dayal thought resentfully, and he must have eyes like a hawk, the swine. "Shall I have him put into another cell, sir?" the petty officer was saying. "Yes, do that," Mulligan ordered. "But check up first to see that the walls are smooth."

"Yes, sir."

"And five days' kanji for breaking prison rules," Mulligan pronounced as he stamped out onto the veranda, without a glance at the prisoner. Even the petty officer looked a little taken aback.

"Five days' kanji!" the Pathan warder said as he was locking the door. "That is just because you persist in not getting up or salaaming when the sahib comes. We know that all the cells have notches in the walls—that every convict looks out of the window by propping up the plank. Mulligan-sahib knows it too. He does not give five days' kanji just for that—he is a good man, Mulligan-sahib. But if you won't even salute him . . ." And he shook his head.

Debi-dayal was getting used to the kanji. It was almost a routine punishment for minor breaches of prison regulations. Kanji was rice gruel, thin and grey, and being given kanji house meant that you were given a teacup full of gruel twice a day and no other food. And, of course, the punishment was noted down meticulously in your prison record and counted against you in calculating remissions of sentence. It also meant that while you were undergoing the punishment you were denied other privileges such as sending or receiving letters, being taken out for exercise in the yard, or having a bath.

But he was determined not to bow and salaam, not to show subservience to this Irishman who represented the British Empire in the Andamans—a slave from another slave country working for his bread. He did not care about remissions of his sentence, for he was determined to escape from the prison. He was certainly not going to mark time for twelve years, bowing and scraping to the officials, qualifying for "good behaviour." And he did not care about not being permitted to write letters, because he had no intention of writing to anyone; nor did he care if he did not receive a single letter all the time he was there.

[17]

D-for-Dangerous!

THERE were two baskets of letters, one labelled "Vernacular" and the other "English." The letters in the vernacular tray overflowed the sides and spilled on the table and on the floor. No one particularly minded, for they were the convicts' letters; if the sweeper noticed them on the floor, they would perhaps be put back in the tray, but it did not matter either way. The English letters were in a neat stack, hardly four inches high.

The fat Bengali head clerk, Ghosh-babu, his chest and stomach outlined by sweat under his thin muslin kurta, looked over his half-moon glasses in disapproval, and pulled the "Vernacular" tray towards him with a jerk, spilling another half a dozen letters on the floor. "So much mail!" he complained. "That is because they are all allowed to write home every month, and receive a letter every month too. In Barrie-sahib's days, it was only one letter a year; one a year, and that too was stopped if they misbehaved during the year. Now government going too soft." He shook his body, a living brown jelly in a thin white shirt. "Here," he said to Gian. "You'd better look through the English ones before they go to the sahib."

"Yes, sir," Gian said.

"Remember not to let more than half go through," Ghosh-babu warned. "Mulligan-sahib not liking too many letters referred to him."

"Yes, sir."

"Hold back anything that says anything about war. Mulligan-sahib is most strict about that."

"Yes, sir," Gian promised.

He carried the tray of letters to the small room at the back, where he and the two other ex-convicts who worked in the rationing section had an office. His rise had been fast: indeed, for a

"D-ticket" convict it had been almost unprecedented. He had been released from solitary confinement within two months of arrival and permitted to work and eat along with the other convicts. Now he had been taken up as a lower division clerk. He still lived in the barracks, as the jail buildings were called, and was not allowed out of the jail between sundown and sunrise. He still had to wear the prison uniform with its "D-for-dangerous" sewn on it. But he was now on pay, seven rupees a month, and his work in the victualling office carried a lot of prestige amongst the warders and petty officers. The way things were going, he was certain that in a year or so he would be made a feri, and then he could go about in ordinary clothes. After that, if he could find a suitable woman from the women's prison, he could get married and settle down in one of the convict villages. . . .

Suitable woman! Gian shuddered as he thought of the few women he had seen in the settlement: ugly and stunted, almost deformed, a hotchpotch, almost grotesque product of the island of criminals, like cows bred through artificial insemination; and even they were outnumbered by at least four to one by the male convicts. In the jungles of the interior, retreating from the civilizing influences of the prisoners' settlements along the coastal plains, were the Jaora women, who were said never to wear any clothes. The thought of women—of hordes of women—going about in total nudity, gold and brown and shining, was tempting, almost erotic, evoking visions of unrestricted carnal delights, of a strong man seizing any woman he fancied and possessing her on the spot. And then someone had told him about the Jaoras, about their poisoned arrows, about their not having a language, and, above all, their size and shape. They were a short, stunted people, almost malformed by ordinary standards, anthropologically so undeveloped that they were said to be more akin to gorillas than to human beings, and most of them still had short protruberances on their tailbones—tails that they were still in the process of shedding.

No, finding a suitable woman with whom to settle down was not going to be easy. Here in the Andamans no one could afford to be choosy about women; they were a precious commodity and, because of their rarity, to be strictly rationed, like drinking water or kerosene, to be impartially apportioned amongst the applicants. Women belonged to that other world that they had left, and which was now at war. At the same time, he would have to keep his eyes open to see if there was someone from among the political prisoners in the female ward who would agree to share his life here.

The one thing he was certain about was that his future lay here, in the Andamans, that there was no question of his ever going back to India. Once one was resigned to that thought, it followed that one's sentence had only another year or so to run, not twelve or thirteen; for as soon as one was made a feri, there was nothing to stop one from settling down anywhere on the island.

What was there to go back to? The village of Konshet in the hill district of the Punjab was already fading away; a village where a withered old woman sat in a dark room praying to a brass god for her grandson's release. The god of the Little House had been powerless to save it from destruction. In a sense, it was he, Gian Talwar, who had brought about its ruin. But then, in destroying the Little House, he had brought about the destruction of all that surrounded it, even the Big House, for had he not with his own hands killed its last male heir while he was still sonless? He had dug up the roots of his own family.

Somewhere in the distance a gate clanged open and a sentry shouted an order. Mulligan-sahib must be doing his rounds. He would be in his office by eleven, when he would look through the letters that were put up to him. He had better get on with them, instead of allowing his thoughts to wander.

The letter that caught his eye was almost at the bottom of the pile of drab postcards and mean little government-issue envelopes. It was an opulent pale blue letter which looked as out of place on his bare dealwood table as a ripe mango on a stone slab. He picked it up and turned it in his hands almost tenderly. It was addressed in a neat, bold hand to Debi-dayal Kerwad, care of the Cellular Jail, Port Blair, Andaman Islands.

Carefully, inserting the tapering stem of a pen into the slit, he worked the flap open. Inside was blue letter paper, the same shade as the envelope, written on only side, and in the fold of the letter, a stiff packet wrapped in transparent tissue paper. Gian held open the letter and began to read:

Dear Chote-bhai,
    We have had no news of you since you went. Aba is most anxious even though he does not say so, and Mummy is pining

for news of you. Please write, if only a line to say you are all right. Aba spends most of his time in the museum when at home, but all day he spends in the office. I am sending you some photographs. Gopal's regiment is mobilized and he is likely to be called up soon. Please write, if you don't write to Father and Mother, at least to me. We all send love to you and pray for you.

Your loving sister
Sundar

Inured to the demands of prison censorship, Gian felt no qualms about reading someone else's letter. In any case, it was the sort of letter, studiedly innocuous, that people wrote when they knew it was going to be read by others. But as soon as he had opened it, his heart had begun to beat faster. It was from Sundari, that girl he had met when they went to the picnic. He had nearly kissed her then, in the museum she spoke about. It all seemed so long ago.

He wished the letter had not contained the reference to someone's joining a regiment and to the regiment's being mobilized; for that would have to be cut out. He read the letter over again and decided to show it to Mulligan. Then he opened the packet of photographs.

There were three photographs. One was of a smiling bride and groom, the bride dressed in the traditional draped-over-the-head sari of a bride, and the groom in military officer's uniform; the second was of Sundari's father and mother; and the third of Sundari playing with a dog.

Gian went on staring at the girl in the picture. She was like something out of a dream, something difficult to think of as having substance and reality, but it was a face he had seen, had so nearly kissed in that room with all those statues.

It was unfair, so soon after he had been thinking about the ugliness of women and resigning himself to spend the rest of his life with one of the women from the political prison, to be reminded that somewhere, girls like Sundari did exist. The sudden longing within him was akin to physical pain, and there was too a nick of jealousy for the smiling groom in uniform.

For a moment he toyed with the idea of keeping one of the photographs; the recipient would never know how many had been sent. But he pushed the thought away and replaced the photographs in their envelope.

While he was looking over the other letters in the tray, his mind kept straying back to the girl. All the same, he was careful to find fault with at least half the letters so that Mulligan-sahib should see how diligent he had been. Mulligan smiled as he took the letters in. He always gave the clerks a smile unless he happened to be in a temper.

"Mail?" Mulligan asked.

"Sir."

"Have you gone through them?"

"Yes, sir."

"Any that you find objectionable?"

"This lot, sir."

"Oh, damn! All those? What's wrong with them?"

"Bits about war, mostly."

"About Dunkirk, I bet."

"Not specifically; just references to major German victories."

"No, we can't overlook that sort of thing, the way rumours spread in this place. Everyone seems to want the damned Germans to win so they'll be set free. You don't know what the Germans do with their prisoners. How they heard about the bombing of England, I can't imagine. . . . Listening to them talk, you'd think the whole Royal Navy had been sunk. And now they know all about Dunkirk."

"Some of those who are permitted to work outside talk to the feris, sir, from the settlements. Then they spread the news in the barracks," Gian suggested.

Mulligan pointed to the letters. "That lot all right?"

"Yes, sir, except—I thought I would ask you about this one." He opened the blue envelope and placed the letter and the photographs on Mulligan's table.

"Photographs," Mulligan muttered to himself. He put on his glasses and studied them for a long time, his jaws making a steady grinding motion. He reached for a cigar from the box on his table and lit a match. Then he threw away the match and replaced the cigar in the box. He picked up the letter and began to read, muttering to himself. "Oh, our friend Debi-dayal. . . humm. How a character like him can have a sister so—so attractive . . ." He shook his head. "Says the man has joined the army," he said to Gian. "Nothing wrong with that. I wish more Indians would, instead of damning the government. Yes, it is all right about the photographs. I don't mind, so long as they show a pretty girl and a soldier—officer too—oh, no. Take them away."

"Shall I distribute them, sir?" Gian asked.

"Yes," Mulligan said, reaching for his cigar box.

In the courtyard the convicts sat on the ground in rows, holding out their plates and mugs. The servers were throwing chapatties into their plates, six to each man, and doling out the mess of pumpkin and chili powder that was to go with them. Gian went and sat next to Debi-dayal, who had been released from solitary confinement just that week and was permitted to work and eat with the other prisoners.

"There is a letter for you," he said and handed it to Debi-dayal.

Debi gave him a cold glare as he took the letter, holding it by a corner as though to express contempt towards this man who was so obviously a spy of Mulligan. They sat close to each other, without saying a word, concentrating on their chapatties and curry. As Debi-dayal held out his mug for the ladleful of curds that they received twice every week, Gian said in a whisper, "I think you can read it now; the head jemadar has gone to the other court."

Debi-dayal stared at him. Was this some trick to get him to say something about the head jemader? He was suspicious of Gian. He had heard him spouting truth and non-violence to Shafi when they had asked him to the picnic, hoping that they would be able to recruit him into the Freedom Fighters. But he was so clearly not the type, a man without principles, his non-violence a cover for cowardice, for a total absence of patriotic fervour. Now he had shown himself to be one of those who played along with the authorities to win petty favours. Why was this administrative spy singling him out?

Gian left him to his mood and went and sat among the warders. His new position carried its special privileges. He could eat his food in the warders' row, take as many chapatties as he wanted, and get an extra helping of the curds that had been saved up from the convicts' rations. From where he sat, he watched Debi-dayal eat. He saw him get up and go to the sea-water tap where they washed their plates, two uneaten chapatties still on his plate. That too was against prison regulations—you had to eat everything that was served. Debi threw the two chapatties into the dustbin and then, after a surreptitious glance behind, also threw away the blue envelope. Then he began to wash his plate.

After the prisoners had been marched off to their afternoon spell of work, Gian walked over the dustbin near the sea-water tap. He could see a corner of the envelope showing through the coconut husk and pumpkin peel and uneaten prison food that lay piled in it. He picked up the envelope, cleaned it with a bit of coir, and put it in his pocket.

Two days later, when he happened to be alone in the victualling shed, Gian took out the envelope hidden under the empty flour bags. He extracted the letter and tore it into little bits, throwing the scraps into the wastebasket. Then he unwrapped the packet of photographs.

The girl's face stared at him, the beginning of a smile on her lips, her eyes bright and full of life. It made him catch his breath. Again he felt a slight stab of jealousy for the man in the picture, the bridegroom in the lieutenant's uniform that had impressed even Mulligan, the smug vaguely anticipatory bridegroom-smile on his face proclaiming to the world his right to possess the girl beside him.

The government-issue pair of scissors on his desk was rusted and blunt with use. With these, he began to cut out the man's picture, taking care to keep the girl's intact. He had just cut through the white margin when he stopped, suddenly aware that there was something a little odd about the photograph. He looked at it carefully, bending it in his hand. Now he could see it. A piece of stiff white paper had been glued to the back of the photograph, forming an envelope. He picked up the scissors again. His fingers shook.

He cut through the margin on one side. By bending the picture, he could see the cavity. Inside was a hundred-rupee note, folded in four. Each of the other photographs also contained a hundred-rupee note.

His fingers shook more than ever, and the backs of his hands were wet with sweat. He inserted the notes in the blue envelope and tucked it into his waistband, under his blouse. It felt cold and stiff against his skin, as though made of metal. He sat for a long time, staring at the three photographs, collecting his thoughts. Now he too had violated prison rules. If anyone were to search him—and a convict could be subjected to a search at

any time—he would be caught with three hundred rupees secreted in his belt. It was enough to send him to the kanji house
for a week—it might even earn him a flogging; and, of course, all
his privileges would be instantly withdrawn.

He tore up the photograph of Sundari's parents and threw the
pieces into the wastebasket. Then he snipped off the picture of
the bridegroom from the other picture. The girl looked much
more beautiful now, all by herself, he thought, even happier,
freed from the presence of her man, like the girl in the picture
with the dog. He wrapped the two photographs in the tissue
paper and put them away in his wallet, beside his prison card and
other papers.

Later the same evening he found an excuse to go down to the
workshop. The wheel-pin from one of the ration carts had
broken and he had volunteered to go to a smithy and get a
replacement. On the way out he selected a massive jack-fruit tree
in which to hide his money. The tree was just a few paces away
from a culvert, and easy to mark down. On his return, after a
quick look all round, he climbed the tree. About twenty feet up
there was the sort of hollow that he needed—a hole which fur-
rowed upwards. He wedged the blue envelope into a crack inside
the hole and scrambled down the tree.

A great load was off his mind. Now he had no reason to fear
one of those surprise body-searches that were a normal feature of
prison life. It was, of course, perfectly all right to keep a girl's
picture in your pocketbook; indeed, most convicts carried a picture or two, usually cut out from magazines. Money was quite
another thing; possessing money was a serious offence.

On the darkening road tunnelling through the trees, with the
prison building outlined against the sky, Gian Talwar went striding. Soon he began to whistle for the first time in more than a
year. He, Gian Talwar, sentenced for life and classified D-for-
dangerous, was perhaps the richest prisoner in the Cellular Jail.
He also had in his wallet two excellent photographs of the loveliest girl in the world.

[18]

The Tail of the Serpent

IN the beginning, the war meant nothing to the convicts; it obtruded on their lives only in odd little ways: their lighting-up time was curtailed, their ration of molasses was cut, worms began appearing in their boiled rice and weevils in their chapatties—dark brown specks which looked like sesame seeds, tasted like sour mud and blistered their tongues.

The regular ships from India had stopped, and there were no fresh chalans. Ships had to be diverted to tasks more important than transporting criminals to the Cellular Jail. Hitherto, chalans—monthly drafts of new prisoners from India—had been the most eagerly awaited events in the colony's life. Even the warders and petty officers, once convicts themselves, sought out new arrivals from their own districts for news of their homes. Now news of home came only in letters brought by itinerant ships, letters that were mutilated by an ever-tightening censorship.

There were other changes. Spurned by the war itself, those outside its main current strove to prove their zeal. Mulligan and his underlings went about enforcing the law of the colony with unprecedented sternness, determined to bring home to everyone that, despite the reverses of the war, the British Empire was as enduring as the sun and the hills; making it clear to the convicts that, even though they comprised its rejects, they still were a part of the great Raaj, privileged to do their bit in the grand muster of the Empire. Their working hours were gradually stepped up, their privileges less gradually cut down, their punishments stiffened. The dreaded kolu, the human oil-mill, was reintroduced for all serious breaches of prison discipline, and flogging, which had been forbidden for years, was declared to be legal once more.

But by and large, the prisoners were ignorant of the progress of

163

the war. No newspapers were permitted, and their only source of information was the brief contact that some of them had with the settlers. And then, one day, the conflict of the outside world made a sharp intrusion into their isolation. On their way to carry a load of sisal from the store-shed near the quay to their own yard, a batch of prisoners came upon a slogan inscribed in charcoal on the wall of a culvert:

HITLER-KO JAI!
ANGREZ MURDABAD!

All of them saw it, and those of them who could read repeated it to the others. By afternoon, it had gone round the entire jail. "Victory to Hitler—death to the British!" someone had dared to write on the wall in this jail-town of British India. Mulligan had fumed, spluttered, roared like a bull, brandished his cane in their faces. Then and there he had dispatched a couple of warders to rub out the writing. He made a proclamation that anyone found repeating rumours to other prisoners would be put to work on the oil mill, that anyone found writing anti-British slogans would be publicly flogged.

But the very next morning, as the pumping gang was being marched to the sea-water trough, they saw on the white embankment wall behind the timber godown a charcoal drawing of a fat, solar-topeed figure, dangling by his neck from a gallows, and under it the slogan:

ANGREZ-RAAJ MURDABAD!

The figure was unmistakably that of Mulligan himself.

The prison grapevine shook with activity. Vague rumours began to circulate of a German spy landed by a submarine to write slogans; there were whispers of crushing defeats suffered by great armies, of mass sinkings of mighty ships, of teeming cities flattened down by bombs raining from hundreds of aeroplanes, of proud countries overrun and subjugated by a world conqueror: Hitler.

And with the defeats came hope, wild and unreasoning, fattening itself gluttonously on their yearnings. Any day now the British would collapse and their empire fall, crushing to death all who throve in its shadow, its Mulligans and Sadashivans, its Josephs and Balbahadurs, its warders with their seven-foot lathis.

The war had come closer; the picture of the saviour with his short moustache and staring eyes came into sharper focus, became transformed into that of some alien god who had come to liberate the oppressed, an avatar of Vishnu. Was this what the war would achieve—sudden and universal release from the beehive existence of the Silver Jail? The men who still believed in prayer began to pray to the new avatar.

"Long live Hitler! Down with the British Raaj!"

Mulligan and his assistants plunged into a fury of activity. They were determined to discover who had written the slogans. Stool pigeons were planted in all the barracks and in the settlements, like jungle animals trained to lure others into captivity. Trusted warders were directed to show sympathy with enemy victories in private conversation with the convicts. Jemadars went about offering forbidden cigarettes to those on the secret black list. All those with histories of anti-British activities, the political prisoners, were kept under special surveillance.

At the end of the week, during his evening rounds, Mulligan made a dramatic announcement: anyone who gave information identifying the slogan-writer would at once be made a feri; if he were one already, he would get a whole year's remission of sentence.

To those whose sole aspiration was now confined to becoming a feri, to live outside the prison, wear ordinary clothes, and lead their own lives, this was a very tempting offer. For those who were feris already, particularly those within a year or so of release, it was a promise of liberation, for it meant that they could, if they wished, ask to be immediately repatriated.

But the promise of Hitler seemed still more desirable. Mulligan could never match it, nor the chief commissioner nor even the viceroy. For a whole month nothing happened—a month during which the hope of a British collapse hung over the landscape like a permanent full moon; the month when the battle of Britain was at its fiercest. Then, with no more German victories to feed their flames, the fires began to die. The Andamans curled up for the annual fury of the southwest monsoon. And then one day the flame died out without a flicker, just as suddenly as it had come to life. The hopes in the prisoners' hearts spent themselves against prison routine.

The big Ramoshi, Ghasita, accepted a packet of Red Lamp cigarettes and whispered to his jemadar that he had some information he would like to give Mulligan-sahib. To Mulligan he reported that he had seen a man late one evening scrambling down the jack-fruit tree near the culvert that had the slogan written on it.

"When was this?" Mulligan asked. "The day before we saw the writing?"

"I think so—I cannot remember. It was so long ago."

"Why didn't you report it before?"

He was too old a hand to squirm under Mulligan's glare."I did not connect it with the writing on the culvert. . . ." He shrugged his shoulders, his benevolent, glazed eyes quite unrevealing.

They were the eyes of a habitual opium smoker. There were dozens of convicts in the jail who smoked opium, some of the warders too; Mulligan was aware of that. Some of the feris grew the stuff in the jungle, and warders sold it to the inmates at extortionate prices. The pay the convicts received was certainly not enough to buy opium with. Where did the money come from? There were some things going on in the prison that he would never know, he had decided long ago; perhaps it was just as well.

"Now I hope the sahib is going to make me a feri," the big Ramoshi reminded him.

Mulligan's face reddened. "So you can grow opium yourself and make money, instead of having to buy it," he retorted. "A D-ticket convict with a record of two murders—"

"Three," the big Ramoshi corrected him. "The first one was a double murder. Man and wife."

God, the nerve! "A murderer three times over, and you expect to be made a feri?"

"That is what the sahib had promised—made a public announcement, that anyone who gave information would be made a feri."

Mulligan had no answer to that one. He was sharp, the big bastard, sharp and unscrupulous. He too must have been waiting for a quick German victory to sort out all his troubles. Now that it had not materialized, he had decided to change sides.

"But you did not actually see who it was," Mulligan pointed out.

"It was dark, sahib. I could not see the man very well. All I saw was that he wore a D-ticket blouse."

"That's nothing to go on," Mulligan muttered almost to himself. "At least sixty of them here, about half of them permitted to work outside the barracks. That doesn't get us anywhere. You know you have been very wrong to keep this thing to yourself. It would have been much more useful to come out with it on the very day—it was your duty to report it."

"I did not connect it with the writing on the wall," Ghasita said blankly. "When will sahib make me a feri?"

"I don't know. We'll see if anything comes of this," Mulligan conceded. "Whether you get made a feri will depend on what we are able to discover."

Next morning, when Gian and the two other clerks were issuing empty rice bags for filling with dried copra, Mulligan strolled into the victualling shed. He was followed by his dog, a sour-faced bull-terrier bitch with pink eyelids. He sent away the two men with the rolls of bags that were already counted, and then perched himself on one of the bales of cotton cloth.

"Who do you think has been writing those things—the seditious slogans?" he asked Gian, sounding very offhand.

"I don't know, sir," Gian said, wondering for a moment if Mulligan was suspecting him.

"I didn't expect you to *know*; but who do you think it might be?"

Gian wanted to be helpful. "Might be one of the feris, sir," he hazarded.

Mulligan shook his head. "I have reason to believe it is someone from inside—a D-ticket walla."

Then Gian's heart began to thump. The prison was now riddled with spies and stool pigeons. Any jemadar who had a grudge against you could concoct something to report to Mulligan. And he was particularly vulnerable, having wormed himself into Mulligan's favour, a convict with a "Dangerous" classification working as a clerk. And then, as he remembered the money he had secreted, he had to gulp hard to overcome the sudden dryness of his mouth. He wished he had never touched the money. Before that, his conscience had been absolutely clear. "I would myself never do a thing like that, sir," he said. "Because—because I really want the British to win the war."

"No one is saying you did it, damn you," Mulligan assured him. "At least a dozen of you could have done it, from those who are employed on prison duties. And there are fifty others, not allowed out without escorts. But even for the others, it's easy to slip away from a working party for a minute or two while the sentry's busy and dash off. Dash off and write a few words on the wall—or, climb a tree, for instance."

The fear was right on the surface now, crawling on his skin, showing itself clearly. Mulligan could not fail to notice how nervous he felt, Gian thought. He tried to think of something to say, anything at all, but the words refused to come.

"I want you to keep your eyes open," Mulligan was saying. "They'll talk to you more easily than to the warders—only natural. You act as though you are in sympathy with them. You know, say things such as how you want Hitler to win the war and all that. Let me know if anyone behaves suspiciously, if you hear any rumours—anything at all. Report to me direct. I must get to the bottom of this."

The fear had passed, just as suddenly as it had risen; now there was only a flood of gratitude. "Yes, sir," Gian promised eagerly.

"Remember I shall make it worth your while."

"Thank you, sir."

"All you have to do is to keep your eyes and ears open. But your special responsibility will be to keep a watch on just one man. Keep him under surveillance without his knowing it—Debi-dayal."

Gian avoided his eyes, pressing down the feelings of nausea, trying to concentrate on Mulligan's dog, which was looking for rats, while Mulligan went on talking, his words coming out of the side of his mouth in sharp jabs because he was speaking in a confidential whisper, screwing up his face and rubbing his cheek with his right hand in a circular motion. "Tagged every minute he is out of the barracks, understand? He will be sent out a lot from now on, on outdoor jobs, just to give him enough rope, see?"

"Yes, sir."

"According to the record, you two were at the same college. But you must be careful not to show extra friendliness, or anything. He must not suspect. Is that clear?"

"Yes, sir."

"I want to catch him red-handed, if possible. Then I can make an example of him—stop all this seditious talk and rumours. Until then, I am going to do nothing—let everyone go about just as before, Debi-dayal and the others who are under suspicion.

But any time he is outside the jail compound, it will be your duty to keep a watch on him—never let him out of your sight."

They were fair, they were always fair, even under extreme provocation, Gian reminded himself. He could never visualize anyone but the British being so fussy. The Indian police would just have rounded up all the suspects, taken them to the thana, and beaten them to a pulp to extract confessions—the police, or even the sentries in the jail here, if given a free hand. The thought of what would happen to them all if the jail were left in charge of someone like Balbahadur was too horrible to entertain. And yet, he asked himself, was not that what the nationalist movement aimed to do: to remove all the British and put thousands upon thousands of people like Balbahadur in positions of authority?

"Here," Mulligan said. "You had better keep this. And don't let anyone know you have one: not even the jemadars here. None of them are to be trusted, really. Use it only in an emergency, only when you think it absolutely imperative, like—like catching someone red-handed."

It was a shining new police whistle. Gian accepted it with gratitude. It was a symbol of the confidence that Mulligan-sahib was placing in him. The whistles, like the prison siren, were intended for raising a general alarm and were a signal for the sentry-squad at the gate to rush to the scene of trouble. Only petty officers and jemadars were allowed to carry them.

"Thank you, sir," Gian said.

Even after Mulligan had gone, he was not particularly distressed by his new assignment. Once you got used to the idea of being a stool pigeon, there was nothing to it. For one thing, he had never thought that it was Debi-dayal who had been writing the slogans; and even if he were the man, could he not warn him that he was being watched?

Above all, Gian was thankful that Mulligan himself was carrying out the investigation, and not one of his subordinates. He admired Mulligan's thoroughness, and, even more, his restraint. He was convinced that Mulligan would never pronounce judgement on a man without incontrovertible evidence, and that in his hands, the ends of justice would never be in jeopardy.

[19]

Having Been Found Guilty

THE evening sun flooded the corridor of barrack seven, making a pattern of bars on the cobbled floor. Debi-dayal marched ahead of the Gurkha sentry, who carried his studded lathi. They went down the stairs and into the yard and out of the gate, heading for the administrative office halfway up the hill.

"Remember to salaam when you go in," Balbahadur warned. "Otherwise, you will have to reckon with me."

Debi-dayal wondered whether his old sentry had been changed as a matter of prison routine or because of some quirk of Mulligan's. It was just his luck to draw Balbahadur from the hundred or so prison sentries—this man with his sadistic urges and the atrophied, twisted mind.

In the office, Mulligan sat at his desk. The assistant jailer, Joseph, stood by his side, stooping slightly almost from habit, the picture of abject servility. Joseph held a sheaf of papers in his hands. On the table lay the blue envelope.

Debi-dayal was marched in. The sentry came to a halt with a crash of his ammunition boots. "Salaam karo!" he ordered.

Debi-dayal did not salaam. He stared at Mulligan's face in silence. For a moment Mulligan stared back at him, red-faced and champing his jaws. His face sweated. He nodded to the chief supervisor. The ritual of prison justice began.

"You, Debi-dayal Kerwad, son of Tekchand Kerwad, prisoner number four hundred and thirty-six of nineteen thirty-nine," Joseph began to read out, "are hereby charged with having committed multiple breaches of prison rules in that you, having come into possession of unauthorized sums of money, on or about the twentieth day of August, nineteen forty, broke bounds and deposited the said money in a hollow in a jack-fruit tree, approximately three hundred yards away from the confines of the

170

Cellular Jail and which, as an unparoled D-ticket prisoner, is out of bounds to you. And that, on or about the same day, you also wrote a seditious slogan on the culvert near the said jack-fruit tree."

"Do you understand the charges?" Mulligan asked.

"Yes," Debi-dayal told him.

"Do you admit them?"

"No."

"None of the three charges?"

"None of the three charges."

Mulligan held out the envelope. "As it happens, I myself saw this letter before it was delivered to you. I have ascertained that it was, in fact, delivered to you by convict Gian Talwar, who has testified that he did so."

"Yes, it is my letter, all right," Debi-dayal said. "At least it was addressed to me. It was delivered to me."

Mulligan took out the three currency notes. "Then the first charge is conclusively proved," he said. "Are these not yours?"

Debi-dayal shook his head. A wave of anger broke through his indifference. "Is this a frame-up or something?" he asked. "I received that letter, all right, but I never opened it. I never open any letters. I threw it into the dustbin." His voice quivered, rose a note. "If it did contain money, I know nothing about it. What is it that you want to pin on me? And if you do, why all this farce? Why not just pronounce the punishment and be done with it?"

"Khamosh!" Balbahadur yelled, and prodded Debi-dayal with his lathi. "Don't shout at the sahib!"

"But you were seen," Mulligan told him. "A man in a D-ticket uniform was seen climbing down the jack-fruit tree where your letter, with the money in it, was found quite close to the culvert on which the treasonable slogan was written."

So that was it; not just the money. They were trying to charge him with something much more serious, so that they could give him the sort of punishment they revelled in and still keep to the book of prison reform. Flogging! He shuddered, in spite of himself.

"Is that what you are trying to frame me for?" he asked, and his voice shook with indignation. "No, I did not write the slogan. Neither that one, nor the one next day. For one thing, I don't want the Germans; they are just as bad as the British. I had no opportunity; any number of people will tell you that I was with them, doing my work. It is all a crooked frame-up. Whoever says he saw me is a liar, perjuring himself for the sake of reward. No, I did not do it!"

"Your record says that in India one of your group's main activities was writing up anti-British slogans," Mulligan pointed out.

"I am merely saying that I did not write the slogan on the culvert, which is what you are charging me with—unless you are also combining the charge with what I did more than a year ago in India."

For a long time there was silence in the room. "Have you anything to add?" Mulligan asked.

"No," Debi-dayal told him.

"You still deny all the charges?"

"I do."

"That's all," Mulligan said. "Take him away."

"Salaam karo!" Balbahadur ordered.

Debi-dayal did not do his salaam. "About turn, quick march!" the sentry barked, and marched him out of the office.

"Arrogant swine," Mulligan murmured under his breath. "What do you think, Joseph?"

"The evidence is incontrovertible," Joseph assured him.

Mulligan opened the red padua-wood box on his desk and took out a cigar. He rolled it lovingly in his fingers and put it back and snapped the lid shut. "I don't know," he said, shaking his head. "He is an arrogant man, but I don't think he's a liar. He is not like the others—like that big Ramoshi, for instance, an inveterate liar!"

"He admits to having received the letter," Joseph persisted. "The other charges follow."

Mulligan shook his head slowly and looked longingly at the cigar box. "It may be that he did receive the money and hid it, though we have no conclusive evidence. Anyway, most of them have some such secret cache of money, as you know. Perhaps not as much as three hundred rupees, and ordinarily not in currency notes. They usually keep gold—sovereigns." He was quiet for a while, his jaws champing, and then he banged his fist down on the table with force. "But I don't like this business about the slogans!" he exclaimed with sudden vehemence. "Bloody treason! It deserves a flogging. That will teach them to spread their sedition here. Sedition must be put down absolutely ruthlessly, here, above all. But first I must be convinced. The evidence against this man is far from conclusive. The Ramoshi's word certainly isn't enough. For all we know, he may have been keeping the money up there himself. No, we shall have to wait. If Debi-dayal is our man, let's prove it; it shouldn't be difficult to catch him red-handed. I'm not going to put him back in solitary, or in handcuffs. Let him work with the others; he is bound to give himself away some day."

"Just as your honour says," Joseph said, inclining his head.

"I am having all these suspects trailed every minute of their time outside barracks; we shall find out soon enough."

"Yes, sir."

Mulligan took out a cigar and rolled it in his fingers, close to his ear, listening to the soft crackle. Then he bit off the end and lit it.

For a moment the sun lay poised on Saddle Mount, a slightly flattened ball on the nose of a seal, and then toppled down the other side. As they started marching back to the barracks, the quick darkness of the tropics was just a few minutes away.

"Jaldi-karo, you bud-tamiz," Balbahadur barked as soon as they were out of earshot of the office. "If I were the super-sahib, I would have put you on the oil mill for not salaaming," and he shoved his prisoner forward with his staff.

At first it began as a tingling sensation in the small of the back where the point of the lathi had dug, but it was not strong enough to break through the over-all feeling of injustice at the charge they were trying to bring against him. And then another prod of the lathi in the same place had brought it out in one quick explosion. The opportunity he had always dreamed of was here, his for the taking, screaming at him. All he had to do was to silence the sentry and make a dash for the jungle. It was like a mechanical puzzle which suddenly works out right when you are not trying, all the pieces fitting neatly into place.

And then, just as suddenly, came the thought of the jungles; the dark Andaman jungles which are like no other jungles in the world. They had beaten back three successive British attempts to colonize the islands. No prisoner had ever succeeded in making good his escape; not only were the jungles themselves impenetrably hostile, but the Jaoras with their poisoned arrows were forever on the prowl. These little naked men shot at sight; they had

made even the British fight for every inch of the ground they
had gained. They were there now, in the darkening forest, just
out of range of the guards' shotguns. To be sure, the judicious
use of bribes and bullets had enabled the British to pacify some
of the Jaoras near the coast. But these half-civilized men were
perhaps the most dangerous of all. They were required to bring
back any escaped convict they encountered, dead or alive, and
got a standard reward of a hundred silver rupees and a bag of
salt. Over the years they had brought back many prisoners who
had escaped, but not a single one had been alive. Farther inland
were other Jaora tribes, human beings without even a spoken
language of their own, who attacked all outsiders as a matter of
principle. No prisoner falling into their hands was returned
either dead or alive. They were said to be cannibals.

"Hurry up, you!" Balbahadur shouted. "Do you think your
mother's lover is going to do my chores?" and Balbahadur held
him by the shoulder and began to march him faster.

The touch of the hand was like a flame; his body shrank away
from it, rebelling. And yet it was important to keep calm, Debi-
dayal reminded himself; to think things out in advance. It was
not as dark as he would have wished, but the opportunity was
too good to miss. If he had planned it, this was just the time he
would have selected, the busy hour for both prisoners and officials as the working day was ending. The prisoners would be
doing their evening chores, washing up their plates, surreptitiously trying to wash some of their own clothes, lining up for
the latrines, which they were forbidden to use after dark, and
trying to bargain with the cigarette and tobacco peddlers among
the sentries. Meanwhile the sentries and the warders would be
hustling them about, getting all their charges safely locked up in
time for the "all-clear" report of the day.

He looked at the Gurkha with new interest: the hard animal
features; the skin tightly stretched over the cheeks; the flat gorilla
nostrils; the overdeveloped, bow-shaped legs. It was a special bit
of luck to have Balbahadur alone, at his mercy, he realized. He
would never get another chance like this—not the Gurkha and
escape both at the same time.

It had to be faced. Now was the moment. A hundred yards
more, and they would be in sight of the guard at the main gate.

"Oh, come on, pubic hair!" Balbahadur ordered and raised his
stick to goad him on.

He acted without conscious intent, almost through reflex action. He swung into him like a panther closing in on a clumsy buffalo calf. It was almost too simple, putting this elementary judo hold into practice. When an assailant raises his hand to attack you with a weapon, he is at his most vulnerable. The thing to do is to jump in closer, not away, almost under the upraised hand, and then hit at his windpipe with an upward clip of the edge of the right palm. A more severe, more deadly defence is the scrotum kick.

He chose the scrotum kick, and it was so easy to forget the oft-repeated warnings of Tomonaga: "No-evah use folce for da sclotum kick—no-evah!"

He used all the force he could muster. The Gurkha folded up like a jack-knife, without a groan, too stunned by the sudden explosion of pain in his groin; it was like a little bomb exploding within him, blinding him with searing pain. He fell where he stood, his legs doubling under him. For a moment he writhed on the ground, like a snake whose head has been crushed but is still alive, and then he lay still.

That was the scene that met Gian's eyes as he came trailing behind Debi-dayal and Balbahadur. For a moment he stood stock-still as though paralysed. It took another moment for him to realize what was happening, and yet another for his reflexes to take over. He took out his whistle and blew on it, harder and harder, until the great alarm bell on the central tower began to clang. From hardly twenty yards away, he and Debi-dayal stared at each other with the startled disbelief of animals caught up in a game drive. The clop-clop of the footsteps of the prison police squad was already in their ears, becoming more and more distinct.

And only then the full horror of what he had done came to him. "Oh, my God!" Gian gasped. "Oh, please forgive me, Debi, please. . . . I am sorry, sorry . . . oh, what have I done!" But the guards were already converging on their quarry, yelling their warnings.

All the prisoners were drawn up in three rows as on a parade, making a half-circle around the triangular scaffolding. The sentries marched the culprit into the yard and made him stand against the wooden frame. He was made to undress and then to stand facing away from the onlookers. His wrists were secured in steel rings fixed on the horizontal strut of the frame, and his ankles were caught up in similar rings at the foot of the step. A leather collar, suspended by a chain hanging from the central bar, was fastened round his neck.

Debi-dayal was now ready, straddled against the flogging frame.

The medical-room assistant was already there, carrying a bowl of disinfectant and bandages. The great alarm bell in the tower clanged for a full minute. Even before its sound died out, Mulligan, wearing his Sam Browne belt and a crisp, starched uniform, its brass buttons shining, marched into the courtyard, flanked on one side by the prison doctor and on the other by the cane-man, a short, squat gorilla of a man with a Negroid face, carrying his special flogging cane.

Joseph ordered the assembly to attention, marched up to the superintendent, and saluted. He was given the order to "carry on." Standing midway between the flogging frame and the ranks of the convicts, Joseph began to read out the charges.

"The convict, number four hundred and thirty-six of nineteen thirty-nine, Debi-dayal Kerwad, son of Tekchand Kerwad, having been found guilty of, A: assaulting a prison official who was entrusted with guarding him and of causing him serious injury, and, B: attempting to escape, is, by order of the superintendent, awarded twenty-five lashes of the cane to be administered by the official lathial of the Cellular Jail. The sentence will now be executed, with the permission of the superintendent."

"Carry on," Mulligan ordered.

The cane-wielder swung his cane high and brought it down with a whup, making a neat pink line across the naked buttocks of the man on the flogging frame.

"One!" Joseph began to count.

Swish-slap! Swish-slap! Swish-slap!—the strokes went on in a precise rhythm of their own. "Two! Three! Four!" Joseph went on counting.

At the fifth stroke, Debi-dayal let out a scream, and then for the next minute or so he bellowed and howled like an animal in pain, his whole frame twitching as the cane came switching down. The lines on his bare body were criss-crossed in a neat pattern, and then the blood began to trickle from the welts and blurred the precise lines, opening them wider and wider, exposing more and more flesh. Then the screams stopped, almost abruptly, choked off as though by a switch.

"Seventeen! Eighteen! Nineteen!" Joseph's voice went on.

Swish-slap! Swish-slap! the cane came curving down with a hiss, landing with a thick, wet report, and with each stroke the victim's body twitched, almost without volition now, more with the force of the stroke than with the victim's reaction.

"Twenty-four! Twenty-five!"

It was over. Even the lathial was bathed in sweat, his coal-black limbs glistening as though rubbed with oil.

The medical officer stepped forward. The warders unhooked the offender from the frame and laid him down on the ground, his back and buttocks an expanse of raw flesh, blue and white and pink, and curiously free of blood.

The doctor bent down, examined the man's pulse, and pronounced it to be satisfactory. He rejoined Mulligan, who, now that the ceremonial part of the morning was over, had lit a cigar. The medical jemadar daubed the wounds with disinfectant and covered their surface with a piece of gauze dipped in some sort of solution. Then the culprit was carried away on a stretcher.

Mulligan told Joseph to dismiss the parade and walked away, talking animatedly to the doctor. Joseph called the parade to attention and then dismissed it. The convicts marched off to their interrupted chores.

[20]

Led by the Pipers

THE shame was harder to bear than the ostracism; it was like an ulcer, permanently tender, seated deep within his body, causing him to whimper with pain, making sleep a time of recurring nightmares.

Overnight, Gian Talwar had become the most despised man in the colony; even the warders seemed uneasy in his company, this favoured stool pigeon of the sahib, who, unknown to anyone, carried the instrument of authority, the petty officer's whistle.

Gian was made a feri at least two years before he was due to become one, but even before that he had become the pariah of the colony. He no longer had to wear a uniform, and he could go and live in any of the feri settlements where he could find work. But there seemed nowhere for him to go. The settlements of the Andaman islands were run by convicts whose sentences had already expired but who preferred to stay on in the islands. They told him they had no room for him; the septuagenarian head man of the Phoenix Bay colony actually spat in his face. The saw mill at Chatham, the vegetable garden at Navy Bay, even the tea garden and the rubber plantation in the interior all turned him down.

For several days after he had become a feri, Gian found it necessary to live in one of the prison barracks, but in the end Mulligan found a room for him in a workers' chawl at Navy Bay, even though they would not take him on as a worker in the gardens. He went on working in the victualling office as a clerk, censoring whatever mail came in, and keeping an account of the stores, a leper in a world of criminals—this lowly spy for the British raaj.

Nineteen forty gave place to nineteen forty-one, making a discernible dent in the allotted sentences of the convicts. Mulligan gave them a talk on the progress of the war. The British army was immense, powerful, its resources inexhaustible; it had all the troops that were needed for the growing appetite of the war, to fight in Europe and Africa and the Arab countries, and to spare. And almost as visible proof of that might, in January 1941 a whole company from a Scottish battalion arrived at Port Blair, marching up to their camp to the music of bagpipes.

The camp had been pitched halfway between Navy Bay and the main jetty, in a grove of palms: a row of neat, individual huts for the officers, and another, longer row of clean white tents for the troops. With the arrival of the troops, the prisoners' hopes died; the sight of the soldiers, bronzed and swaggering, marching in step along the red road, or doing drill and physical training on the square of shaved grass, was like a physical blow to those who had entertained visions of a quick German victory. In the evenings the Jocks slouched about in the bazaar, looking for women and drink, whistling, laughing, singing snatches of song; later their mess-room radio blared loud music that could clearly be heard in the cells of the Silver Jail.

Suddenly, without even trying to, Debi-dayal had become the convicts' hero. He had dared to turn on Balbahadur, the most despised man in the jail, had sent him to hospital for three weeks, and, as they had all heard, inflicted on him a permanent infirmity. He was their benefactor; they gloated over his triumph, chuckled over what he had done to Balbahadur. When, after nine days in the prison hospital, Debi-dayal was brought back to join the others at work, they all rose to welcome him. They could see that he walked stiffly, his body obviously still a mass of aches, and that, when he sat down before the pile of coconut husks which had been put before him, his fingers could not grip the fibre. Without a word, one of the warders removed the pile and distributed it among the others.

Though none of them looked at Gian, he was aware of their contempt for him. He had slunk out of the yard, feeling like a whipped dog.

So it went on. The prisoners vied with each other to do little chores for Debi-dayal, washing his plate and his clothes, pressing on him little titbits saved from their own rations or bought from the sentries. It was touching to see how hurt they looked when he refused to take them.

The sharp eyes of Patrick Mulligan did not fail to detect the

new current within the jail. He went and talked things over with
Major Campbell, the commanding officer of the military detachment. When he returned to his office, he sent for Gian.

"The commanding officer wants a clerk, someone who can
understand both English and Hindi. I have recommended you.
Go and see him in the afternoon. If he takes you on, you can
start work from tomorrow."

"Thank you, sir," Gian said gratefully.

Major Campbell was young, perhaps in his late twenties, with
a frank, open face and an easy smile. Though unmistakably British, he was unlike any other white man Gian had ever seen.
When his new clerk came to report his arrival, the major held
out his hand.

It was with hesitation that Gian took it; he had never before
shaken a white man by the hand.

Major Campbell gave him a quick look. "I think you'd better
take that chain off when you start working here," he said, pointing to the chain around Gian's neck.

"We are not allowed to remove it, sir," Gian told him. "Not
until the date engraved on the disc has passed—and only a black-
smith could get it off. It's quite strong."

"Oh, I see. Well, perhaps you could button up your collar—far
less embarrassing. Will that be all right with you?"

That was the major's only stipulation; he did not want Gian to
feel embarrassed while working in their midst.

Next morning he reported for work, wearing his shirt buttoned
up at the collar. His pay, he was told, was to be sixty rupees per
month, on a par with that of the petty officers of the jail. It was
wonderful to get away from the hostility and contempt of the
convict world, even though he still carried the bile of shame deep
within him, hidden, like the Andaman chain, from view.

Gradually the routine of prison bells gave place to that of
bugle calls. There were perquisites he had not known or hoped
for: canteen cigarettes, and eleven-o'clock tea and biscuits, occasionally a real soldier's breakfast with tinned sausages and mash.

A few weeks after Gian began his new job, Major Campbell
asked Mulligan for the services of a messenger boy, and Mulligan
sent him Ghasita, the big Ramoshi, who had been made a feri at
the same time as Gian, and was now living in the colony at
Phoenix Bay. If there was one man in the entire colony whom

Gian himself would have chosen to have in the office, it was the big Ramoshi. At least he had no strong feelings about what Gian had done. He was coarse and jovial as ever, and it was good to have him sitting outside the tent, learning soldiers' swear words and asking Gian their meaning.

Every evening, when their work was over, Gian and the Ramoshi walked back from the camp, two men in Andaman civilians' knee-length shirts and dhotis, chatting about their work at the office. It was nearly a mile to the road junction where their ways parted, Gian's to his room in the Navy Bay chawl, the Ramoshi's to Phoenix Bay.

One day, on their way back from the office, Gian's companion was unusually silent. Normally he talked like a machine, almost without a break, whether he had any listeners or not.

"What's wrong with you today?" Gian asked him.

For a few seconds, Ghasita did not answer his question. Then he said, "If I get hold of a big sailboat, will you join me?"

"Join you!" He had no idea what the big Ramoshi was saying. The thought of escape was too remote from his mind just then. "Join you in what?"

"A boat with a big sail," the Ramoshi said earnestly.

"But where? How?"

"There are quite a few of them about. I think I have managed to find one. But first I have to make sure of—of other details. No use going ahead with the boat."

At last it had become clear. "Just you and I?" he asked.

The Ramoshi shook his head. "We will need at least one more man. But we can go about finding the third man later, when we are ready."

After that they walked in silence for a time, each wrapped in his own thoughts, through the palms and the jungle and the mild sea breeze. It was wonderful here, a paradise, people said, a paradise populated by convicts and wild men. He, Gian, had never once thought of leaving the Andamans. This was his land; he had wanted to settle down, grow old, and die here.

But no longer. Here he was despised even more than in India, where he had displaced himself; in this world he was lower than Mulligan's terrier.

He brooded on what the Ramoshi had suggested. Was this some trick of Mulligan's—a spy spying on a spy? He looked at the Ramoshi's face: a statue cut out of some dark wood and left unfinished. "You're just daydreaming," he said cautiously. "Why would anyone want to go away from here? You, a feri, earning what?—thirty-five rupees a month. Perhaps more than you will get in India."

The Ramoshi gave him a hard stare. His jaws suddenly hardened, his fists curled, his eyes narrowed; he looked more rigid, more like a statue than ever. "I have a purpose in mind," he said very slowly. "I must go. There is work to finish."

Gian's nerves tingled at the sudden glimpse of malevolence that was offered to him. Another murder? he asked himself. He gave the Ramoshi time to compose himself. Then he said, still taking care not to show any special interest, "I really don't know how you think you can make it. Calcutta's at least six hundred miles away."

His companion shook his head impatiently. "Not India. I was thinking of Burma."

"And how far do you think that is?"

"About two hundred miles; less, actually."

He seemed to have given it much thought. Gian tried to visualize the map of Southeast Asia, but found it difficult to calculate the distance to the coast of Burma.

"Five men escaped when I was here before," Ghasita was telling him. "In a stolen power-boat. They landed near Tavoy, in Burma."

"But you can never be sure of landing at any particular spot."

"Why not? One cannot go wrong during the southwest monsoon. In any case, there will be land wherever the wind blows us; a thousand miles of it—from Mergui to Akyab and then right down the Malay peninsula. And it is all inhabited land. After that we make our way back to India—easy."

"What happened to the five who got away?" Gian asked.

"They? Oh, they were caught, the fools!" the Ramoshi said with contempt. "But that was because they had no money with them when they landed—the fools!"

"But you too will be without money—not much of it, anyway, on prison pay."

"We do have the money," the Ramoshi assured him. "We certainly do." It was odd how he always used the plural in speaking about his plans, while Gian was careful to refer to it as "your scheme." "Oh, yes, the money's there, all right; for buying the boat and everything."

"How much will the boat cost?" Gian asked. "A big enough boat with a sail?"

"Six sovereigns. I have settled the price."

"Sovereigns!"

Ghasita looked at him in pained surprise. "But naturally. Who do you think is going to accept paper money? Neither here nor wherever we shall be landing. Prison money has special numbers. Didn't you know? Always traceable. We must deal only in gold."

"And where are you going to get the six gold mohurs?"

"Wait," the Ramoshi said. "Do you see that lone palm tree halfway up the road, the bent one, like an elbow; see it?"

"Yes," Gian said, turning his head. "You mean the one with . . ."

The big Ramoshi was laughing at having tricked him into looking the other way. He was holding out his hand. In his palm lay a gold sovereign, glinting in the sunlight. "Now do you believe me?" he asked.

Gian tried to hide his surprise. Surely there must be some simple explanation. He might have stolen it from the office, though how a sovereign could have found its way there was difficult to imagine. "Well, I don't know. You tricked me into looking the other way, and then took out a gold mohur you have been secreting in your clothes—a coin which you must have stolen here, since you could not possibly have brought it from India."

His companion frowned. "Babuji, you are even more suspicious than Mulligan-sahib," he complained. "But it is a good thing to be suspicious, for that is the only way we can survive. But between friends there should be no suspicion. There should be only open hearts. So I shall be frank with you, knowing that I am placing my neck in your hands. But I am anxious to show you that I am not trying to trick you, or anything. The truth is, I did not hide the coin in my clothes, nor have I stolen it—at least not stolen it here. I brought it with me from India in my khobri. In my tribe, almost everyone has one."

"What is a khobri?"

"Haven't you seen conjurers in India producing objects from their mouths? Where do you think they hide them? In the khobri. It's rather like the sack cattle have for storing food, just at the back of the throat, in the fleshy part. In our tribe, every male child has to have one; it's quite essential, even before we commit our first robbery to propitiate Vetal. You know that Vetal can be propitiated only with stolen gold."

"But how do you acquire a—" The word stuck in his throat.

"A khobri? Even as small children, we are made to go about with a lead ball in our gullets, suspended there by a thread coming out of the mouth—like a weight dangling from a fishing line. Every morning the ball is smeared with some kind of a corrosive juice which our priests have—an acid to burn the flesh, you know. The weight slowly makes a pocket for itself, just below the ear and slightly to the rear. As the pocket gets deeper, the flesh on top begins to close, and then only a slit is left on the surface. Within a few weeks the khobri is ready, a secret pocket within the body itself that can defeat the closest search. After that, it is just a matter of practice. Now look at this!"

And right in front of Gian's eyes the big Ramoshi put his head back and swallowed the sovereign.

"How many coins can it—can a khobri hold?"

The other man laughed. "Now you're asking, babuji! I can tell you we have enough to buy the boat and then enough for our needs after we land in Burma. After that, we shall have to depend on our own resources. Now, will you join me?"

Gian gazed at the setting sun behind the line of the palms. Two months earlier he would have said a firm no to any such invitation without a moment's thought. Now there was a sudden and overwhelming longing to escape; escape to Burma, anywhere at all, so long as he could get away from this land of shattered illusions, where no one wanted him; the land he had once decided to make his own, to settle down on it in some coconut grove such as the one they were passing through, build a cottage, take a wife—a wife like Sundari, whose photographs he still carried close to his heart.

But the land had rejected him. Here he was like a mouse painted with luminous paint and released so that the other mice shunned it. He was anxious to go, to leave this sunlit projection of the underworld far behind him.

The Ramoshi was still talking away, caught up in his dream. "Think about it," he entreated. "If you're willing to join me, I'll go ahead and make the arrangements. We shall have to get away in May, just when the monsoon wind starts, but before the rains begin. By that time, we must find another man—someone who wants to go back, not like those cattle who want to go on living here and breed. . . ."

Another man?

It came to him like a flash of lightning. A man who wanted to go back, a man who was daring: Debi-dayal. This was the one thing he could do for Debi; then the shame that clutched his heart like a limpet would release him. His duty was clear.

He would do it too. He would join this venture only if the big Ramoshi agreed to take Debi-dayal as the third man, not otherwise. He would help Debi to make the getaway if it was the last thing he ever did.

They came to the end of the grove of coconut palms. Here their ways parted. "I will think about it," Gian told the Ramoshi as he took the turning. "I will let you know in a day or two."

He was alone now, on the narrow track that led to the chawl in Navy Bay, and he was deep in thought. He must have gone about a hundred yards when he heard the Ramoshi shouting behind him. "Babuji, wait!" he was saying. "Babuji, wait!"

Gian halted and waited for the other man to catch up with him. "What is it?" he asked.

The Ramoshi came and stood very close and waited for a few seconds to get back his wind. He stood panting, towering over Gian, the sweat glistening on his face in tiny specks. Then he said, "Babuji, you are a wise man and have read many books, so there should be no need to warn you. But I just wanted to say this. I know I have put my life in your hands by telling you about my plans—that and the gold mohurs. I just wanted to give a warning, particularly after what you did to Debi-dayal babu. I do hope that—that you will not say anything about it to anyone."

"Of course not!" Gian assured him.

"I am only telling you in your own interest," the Ramoshi went on almost apologetically. "In our tribe, our god demands that anyone who betrays a confidence must be slain. There is no other alternative."

It was not a threat, merely a statement of fact, and on his face, there was no anger, arrogance, or even resolution; only perhaps a touch of regret that Vetal left his tribe no other choice. And then, before Gian could say anything, the big man had turned on his heel and walked away.

They were the plans of mice, plans which other mice before them had made, plans that had failed. But the mice who devised them were caught up in them now, as in a snare. For the next three days, whenever Gian and the big Ramoshi were alone together, they talked of little else. And as they talked, their plan had begun to emerge, taking shape by the hour. Its wrinkles were smoothed out, its gaps filled, its lines darkened. It began to stand out, a scaffolding; something like a gigantic flogging-frame straddling the Burma sea.

During the week all the convicts in the jail, excepting, of course, the D-ticket wallas, were put on land-clearing work behind Phoenix Bay. It was rumoured that another lot of soldiers was coming to the islands, a much bigger lot, a whole battalion, and that the site was being cleared for their camp.

One evening, before the outdoor gangs returned, Gian went into the jail to see Debi-dayal. He was sitting near the coconut shed, his plate and mug beside him, waiting for the evening meal which was going to be served as soon as the others were back. Gian went and sat close to him.

For two days now he had been thinking of what he was going to say. Now that he was going to say it, he was conscious only of the shame welling up inside him. Debi-dayal's face, staring at him in disbelief as he blew the whistle that time, kept haunting him—that and the memory of the flogging which followed. The words he had so carefully rehearsed escaped his mind.

"I came to say that I am sorry for what I did," he began, talking in a whisper. "I blew the whistle without thinking. It was all so sudden. I have been meaning to come and tell you how sorry I am even though I know how inadequate it must sound."

Debi-dayal was not even looking at him. He was staring straight ahead, at the central tower. Not a muscle in his face moved.

"But I have something important to say," Gian went on. "I have come to make a proposal. Listen carefully. I and another man are planning to get away; sometime in May. I cannot tell you the details now, but I feel the plan is bound to succeed. We have the money, we have a boat. I wanted to ask you if you would join us."

Debi-dayal did not say anything. For all the change in his expression, he might not have heard a word of what Gian was telling him.

"You must come with us, I beg of you. Give me a chance to do something for you—make me feel that I have been able to repair, in some measure, the injury I have done you." Gian looked hopefully at the other's face, the face that was like a metal mask except for the sharp look in its eyes, the eyes of a dog looking at something in the distance.

"This is a proper plan," Gian went on eagerly. "A plan with a chance of success. You don't have to do anything but get away and join us when we are ready. I shall make it possible for you to get away. In three weeks, a month at the most, you will be back in India. And remember, even if you had been able to make good your escape that evening, you would have been caught up in the settlement, or brought back by the Jaoras for the reward. Brought back dead—they never bring back anyone alive. They torture their victims before they finish them off "

Then Debi-dayal turned to look at him. It caused a quick flutter of hope in Gian's heart.

"Do you remember talking about truth and non-violence?" Debi-dayal asked. "You gave up non-violence when you killed a man. I don't know when you abandoned the truth." The contempt in his tone was like the lash of a whip. "I know that you are just trying to get me involved in some talk of escape because Mulligan has told you to do it. I know it's a trap."

"I swear it isn't," Gian protested. "I swear by everything—swear by Shiva."

"But even if you were in earnest, let me tell you that I would willingly rot in a cell here rather than associate with someone like you and become free. You are scum; you are far worse than Balbahadur because he at least is openly hostile—you spout truth and non-violence. You are the sort of man through whom men like Mulligan rule our country, keep us enslaved; you are a slave working for the masters, proud of the service he renders, hankering after the rewards."

"Please," Gian implored. "Please calm down. The gangs are

coming back now. I mean every word. How can I prove it, how can I convince you?"

"Why don't you blow your whistle?" Debi-dayal said.

The next morning, when Gian saw the big Ramoshi, he told him that he was not willing to join him in his bid to escape. The plan had gone the way of other plans of other mice; the frame that straddled the Burma sea had suddenly collapsed.

That very day Gian received a letter from the lawyer Ramunni Sarma, telling him that his grandmother had died.

It was almost symbolic, Gian thought; the last strand that had kept tugging at his heart had been severed. There was nothing to go back to now; the Andamans had become his land. It was here that he would have to live out the rest of his years, an outcast, a leper shunned by his fellow lepers.

[21]

Act of Liberation

SUMMER came, a hot wind from the west, a season of iridescent dragonflies and of flowers bursting through the green of the
forest like spilled neon signs. The site for the new camp was
cleared and levelled in its blaze. After that, the convicts were put
back on their normal labours.

Then came the monsoon, bringing a respite from the heat, but
claiming its own price; in no time at all it repossessed the cleared
camp site for the dripping jungle. It drove the population cower-
ing before its lash into their shelters, bringing with it malaria and
dysentery and unknown jungle fevers, making yet another assault
against the colonizers' puny efforts.

In October, the rains went. Men came out into the open once
again. Work on the new camp was resumed; an enormous camp
for a thousand men: officers' huts, sergeants' huts, barracks,
sheds, water-points, latrines, mule lines, kitchen halls, mess-huts
—even a guardroom complete with a flagpole.

The camp was barely ready before the battalion moved in, a
battalion of Gurkhas, carrying murderous-looking kukries slung
in their belts; slit-eyed, stumpy, swaggering, bow-legged, giving
meaning to the Empire's resolve to protect the islands from a
new enemy that none of the prisoners had heard of before, an
enemy who was not yet an enemy but was crouching thousands
of miles away and waiting: Japan.

In December things began to move with the speed of a land-
slide: a rumble and a roar and a sudden shifting of the earth
underfoot.

The enemy from a thousand miles away had sprung into action. Pearl Harbor was flattened. Indo-China, Malaya, the Dutch
East Indies crumbled like mud houses in a monsoon flood and
disappeared, leaving sad little heaps of unrecognizable debris and
thick, oily bubbles on the surface.

The new year came, and every day brought the enemy closer and closer. Early in March both the Scottish company and the Gurkha battalion were whisked away in a hurry, and with them went the women and children of the British citizens on the islands.

The ordered routine of the human beehive that was the Cellular Jail received a shattering blow. Anyone with the will to do so could have escaped; opportunities were there as never before. But no one made the attempt. The way things were shaping, to sit and wait for the Japanese to come offered the best chance of deliverance.

"Their women and children have already been sent off," the convicts told one another. "Now it's just a matter of days before the sahibs themselves follow them. They'll leave in the middle of the night—they're not going to wait and be slaughtered by the Japanese."

Women and children first, and then the men themselves; it was in the highest tradition of the men who ran the Empire; sinking ships or abandoning countries, the pattern was the same, almost sacred. The convicts waited with mounting eagerness for the process to be completed.

Once more the Andamans were entirely unprotected. At Port Blair the prison police were the only visible remnant of the Empire's might. Debi-dayal could easily have organized a mass breakout. Everyone turned to him for guidance now, ready to do his bidding, eager to follow him; even the warders and the petty officers were turning their faces to the masters of tomorrow. "We are only servants," they kept explaining to Debi-dayal. "We only did what we did because of the sahib's bidding. We shall serve other masters with equal zeal. We have no personal enmity against you."

But Debi-dayal was in no hurry. He chose to wait, knowing it would not be for long.

It was the Sunday after the troops had gone. Port Blair lay under a burning sun. The sweep of the sea that shone like silver brought to boiling point was without a ripple. The air came from landwards, laden with the scent of the new seasons's blossoms. Mulligan sent for Gian at his bungalow.

His wife and daughter had gone away, and now, in charge of a convict bearer, the house had lost its air of prim orderliness; it was unswept and bare, like a rest house into which the occupants had moved only a few hours earlier. The remains of Mulligan's lunch were still on the bare dining table, a feast for the fat, highly coloured tropical insects. A thin coating of dust lay on the polished coffee-table. The bull terrier bitch lay sprawled on the cool floor, fast asleep, her pink tongue showing out of her mouth.

Mulligan sent his bearer away. "I have something to tell you in the strictest confidence," he said to Gian.

"Yes, sir," Gian said.

"Sit down," Mulligan invited.

Was it an indication of the pass things were coming to? The super-sahib asking one of the convicts to take a seat? Gian hesitated and then sat down on the edge of the cane sofa, leaning forward.

"The Japanese have taken Rangoon," Mulligan said.

Rangoon? What did it matter? He had only a vague idea where Rangoon was. A city on a map, known for what? Rubies? Rice? But what did make a deep impression on him was the way Mulligan seemed to have taken it. His full face was haggard, his eyes rimmed with red; his pug nose trembled with the effort of breathing. His shoulders drooped.

"They have had to pull away the garrison from here—take them to more important tasks. Now we have no protection, none at all. When the Japanese come, there's nothing to stop them."

It was still not very clear to Gian. Why should the Japanese want to come to the Andamans? He slid back on the sofa and sat more comfortably, more sure of himself.

"No more ships will be coming to Port Blair," Mulligan went on. "Too open, too dangerous. The islands will be abandoned."

"What happens to the—the Cellular Jail?" Gian asked.

Mulligan spread out his hands, a gesture of despair. For a time he sat in silence, holding his hands in a spread-out position on both sides of his bulging stomach—hands gnarled and wrinkled and yellowed by fever. Like the talons of some bird, Gian thought, talons swollen by disease.

"I have put into operation certain plans, plans to get away, the moment they arrive."

The blunt admission had made Gian's mind reel. This was the man who had ruled the jail like a king, the man whose greatest boast was that during his tenure as the superintendent no one had succeeded in escaping from the jail. Now he himself was planning to escape, leaving all the convicts behind. "You mean plans to—to escape?" he asked.

Mulligan nodded. "Only after the enemy has been sighted. Not a moment before."

That was understandable. That too fell neatly into the pattern. Men like Mulligan never ran away a moment too soon. It would never do to run away and then discover that the island had not been occupied.

"They'll never come here, sir," Gian suggested. "Never." But even to himself his voice did not sound sincere.

"Oh, yes," Mulligan said matter-of-factly. "There is no question of their not coming. And then I just have to go."

Yes, he just had to go. It was dreadful to think what would happen to Mulligan if left to the fury of the prisoners, free to do what they liked with him; this man who had been strict and just and godfearing, who had awarded punishments and rewards with the same godlike detachment.

"There is no one I can trust in the colony," Mulligan went on. "Not even my officials. The moment it suits them to turn against me, they will do so. That is why I have sent for you, knowing that I can depend on you."

Gian's mind shrank from the compliment, aware that the only reason why Mulligan felt he could trust him was that he too had no friends among the convicts; it was just a question of one pariah trusting another. They were in the same boat. He too was one of those who would just have to go.

And, as though echoing his thoughts, Mulligan went on. "Last night Rangoon radio made a special broadcast for the colony. It promised deliverance to all the convicts and promised the prisoners that they would be presented with the British officials to do what they liked with. British officials, and also any traitors amongst them."

Gian winced. He looked hard at Mulligan. But Mulligan was staring out of the window at the silver sea in the bay. He was always a plain-spoken man, Mulligan. He called a spade a spade; a traitor, a traitor.

"I shall do anything I can," Gian offered.

"I too will make it worth your while," Mulligan said, looking directly at him. "You will be saved much unpleasantness here— even rewarded. What we have to do is this. The moment the

Japanese are sighted, all the remaining Europeans on the island are to make for the old Forest Department bungalow on the hill behind Port Campbell. That is the rendezvous. We are to wait there until the boat comes to take us away."

It was amazing how the British always thought of everything. Even as they had sent away the women and children, they had made plans for those who were left behind. A power-boat had been specially detailed to round up the remaining men on the island gathered in little groups near convenient beaches. They were to be taken to the jetty at Interview Island, where a destroyer would come to take them away.

"The boat travels only at night, of course, taking cover during the daytime. And we won't know when exactly it will come—not within two days. The whole plan comes into effect only after the enemy has been sighted. Two days' start is all we can hope for, really. I mean, if the boat doesn't come within two days, it will all be useless because by that time the Japanese will have found us."

The thought of what would happen if the Japanese did find them made Gian shudder; what the Japanese would do to Mulligan could not be worse than what the other convicts would do to Gian.

"One man will have to keep constant watch, day and night," Mulligan was saying. "That will be you. I shall also have to take another man with us, someone to carry our rations. There should be eighteen men in all at the bungalow—if they can all make their way there before the boat arrives. The boat will not wait—not for anyone."

"You mean, you were thinking of taking another man with you?" Gian asked, suddenly alert.

"I have to. I am responsible for the rations. I have got the man in mind, even though he doesn't know anything about it. I can't trust him that far."

"Not Debi-dayal?" Gian asked, in spite of himself.

Mulligan frowned and shook his head. "Oh, no, not him. He'll be the first to welcome the Japanese, I've no doubt; the first to lead them on our track. Oh, no, never Debi-dayal. I have another man in mind."

"Ghasita? The big Ramoshi?"

Mulligan nodded. "Yes, he's a good man to have in an emergency. Strong, too. But don't say anything to him; not just yet."

The beach where the boat was to come was all of two miles away from the forest bungalow. Gian was to keep a lookout for the boat and give a prearranged signal for it to send out a dinghy. The boat, Mulligan told him, would flash a signal: a green flash followed by a red flash every two seconds for half a minute. It would repeat it every half-hour for three hours. Then the boat would go away, unless, of course, there was an answering signal for it to come up: a green flare followed by a red flare.

It was Gian's job to fire the answering signal for the dinghy to be sent up. He would be given a Very pistol and shown how to use it.

"I'm afraid I'll have to leave Delilah behind," Mulligan said.

Delilah? Oh, yes, the dog, of course, lying stretched out on her belly. "She's far too old," Mulligan was saying, "and far too fat. . . ." He choked a sob, and began staring out of the window. He took out his handkerchief and blew his nose noisily. "I wish I could put her down," he said. "Put a bullet through her head as she's sleeping—but I know I won't."

They discussed the details of the plan for another half-hour, and after that Mulligan gave him tea—tea served by a convict orderly, complete with a wedge of tinned Dundee cake. And when he rose to go, Mulligan gave Gian a tin of English cigarettes.

The day was made for big things to happen, coronations or royal weddings or great military parades. The greens and the reds of the islands, the blue of the sea, had an almost artificial brightness, as in a colour photograph.

First came the planes, flying high, the tiny red circles on their wings barely discernible. There were two planes. Their quiet hum hung over the township for a long time. They circled the sky like lazy hawks looking for a kill. After a while they began to circle lower and lower over the township. Then they made tree-top sweeps over the Cellular Jail, releasing a shower of posters.

Men and women rushed into the open, cheering the planes, scooping the leaflets like village children running after circus handbills.

It was not until the afternoon that the ships came, a cruiser and two destroyers, flying the flag with the red dot, slowly, suspiciously, zigzagging and halting, looking for mines and other dangers in waters that were wholly innocuous. They came closer and halted again. Then came voices, magnified and distorted by the ships' loudspeakers, speaking in Hindi.

"Indian brothers, we want to set you free—free your land from the British tyrant."

A jubilant crowd of convicts and ex-convicts waited on the jetty, hysterically waving Japanese flags. Debi-dayal stood in the centre, megaphone to his mouth. He spoke in Japanese.

"Japanese brothers, we are waiting for you. There is no one on the islands but your friends. The British have gone away. The Andamans are yours. We welcome you!"

After that, things happened with breathtaking suddenness. Two fast boats were lowered from the cruiser and raced for the jetty, making white, curving lines on the surface of the water. The ship's loudspeaker blared again, this time with military curtness. "If there is any treachery, every single person in the town will be put to death!"

"There is no treachery," Debi-dayal hailed back. "We are your brothers, waiting only to welcome you. Japan-Hind, bhai-bhai!"

"Japan-Hind, bhai-bhai! Japan-Hind, bhai-bhai! Japan-Hind, bhai-bhai!" The prisoners took up the cry, jumping, waving their flags.

"Silence! Silence!" the voice snapped from the ship. "Hold your hands high. High! Yes, all of you. And face away from the ships. Away from the ships! Anyone who turns will be shot—will be shot. Anyone who lowers his hands will be shot!"

But there was no thought of treachery. The settlers and the convicts waited for the liberators, their backs to the sea, their hands held high, yelling hoarsely. It was their day of triumph. For them, the clocks had begun to run once more. They were free.

Puffing up the track skirting Saddle Mount, Mulligan paused to take a last look at the Cellular Jail. In the trembling heat of the afternoon, the flag on the mast of the central tower fluttered triumphantly: a white flag with a blood-red circle. Suddenly Mulligan turned his face away.

March. The month of reptiles, the breeding season of the tropical jungle; a time for the centipedes, the scorpions, the murderous little vipers, and the giant pythons to emerge, all in search of their mates. Only the rulers of the islands were going into hiding.

The three men, one white and two brown, marched all that day and half the night, having rested for a few hours just before dawn. Towards nine the next morning they came to the forest hut. Two other Englishmen were already there, supervisors from the rubber plantation at Pangore. Mulligan, his face red, his feet sore, his limbs aching, his legs swollen, lay down in an undignified heap, breathing heavily. The two men with him opened the boxes of rations and began to prepare a meal. Far below, the sheet of sea lay still as a pond, beyond the curve of Port Campbell where the boat was coming to take them away. When? If it did not come that very day, it might be too late. And would the other officials on the island, the men from the tea and the timber companies, be able to join them in time?

Yet another plan of mice was in operation, the mice grinding away at it in all earnestness. As they drank their tea in thirsty, gulping mouthfuls, the one thing that they did not want to think about was what would happen to them if the boat did not arrive in time. They knew that a Japanese patrol, assisted by enthusiastic volunteers, must be already on their trail.

[22]

A View from the Forest of Palms

GIAN lay in the forest of palms, scanning the sea below him. As it grew dark, his eyes began to play tricks. Hazy shapes loomed on the surface of the water, shapes that he had not seen there before. Rocks brought up by the receding tide? Or were they boats? He was expecting to see just one boat. It was to creep up in the dark, hugging the coastline, showing no light, except, of course, the signal. What were the shapes, then? A squadron of the Japanese Navy, suddenly come to foil their plans. The British were clever at planning, but the Japanese had proved themselves even cleverer. Could they be lying in wait for the boat? But did not ships always have some kind of light? They had to have lights inside. Could they be a pack of submarines, then, coming to the surface for air?

The sea was like a blanket of tar flecked with mica. The shapes he saw had again become one with the darkness. The minutes passed, slow as molasses spilling out of a hole in a barrel. His excitement subsided, giving place to a feeling of utter exhaustion. He wanted to lie back and sleep. But it was important not to fall asleep; he must keep awake, whatever happened. The rescue boat was going to flash its signal for only thirty seconds, he reminded himself—thirty seconds every half-hour. He could not afford to miss the signal. He got up and began to walk, trying to fight off sleep.

He wished he had a watch, to find out how much of the night had gone. He took out the zinc water bottle which Mulligan had given him and took a long drink. The water was warm and tasted of rust. He splashed some of it on his face.

The sleepy feeling kept coming in waves, even when he was walking. There were vague rustling noises in the jungle behind him, and once, somewhere far away, he heard a sudden rata-ta-ta-

ta cough of some animal, that made him nervously grip the handle of the coconut knife that hung from his belt.

He became aware of the sound of music, a music that was somehow a part of the sounds of the night, indistinguishable from the gentle roar of the waves and the breeze soughing through the palm fronds and the chirp of the tree-frogs. He stopped and listened, trying to locate the direction of the sound. It was like a caress, soothing, almost hypnotizing. He suddenly realized what it was, even though he had never heard it before: a Jaora feast.

His skin tingled. He closed his eyes, surrendering himself to the spell of the night: somewhere the Jaoras were having a dance or a sacrifice or something of the kind, and this was their music, primitive, haunting, man's first crude efforts at reproducing the music of the elements. He shook his head and rubbed his eyes and took a deep breath. This would not do. He was dropping off to sleep. He began to walk.

The breeze changed. The music grew more insistent without growing louder. Its beat quickened, the notes of some reed instrument now mingled with the other sounds—a damsel with a dulcimer, he thought to himself. Then other instruments joined in so that the sound seemed to become richer and mellower, and oddly enough, hauntingly familiar. It was somewhere to his left, perhaps beyond the rise of the next hill, hardly a mile away. If he climbed a little higher, he could keep an eye on the beach and also get closer to the music. It was even possible that he might just be able to see the feast or whatever orgy the Jaoras were having. The thought occurred to him that he would be one of the very few men ever to have done so, for when the Jaoras celebrated they posted sentries with poison-tipped arrows all round. Few men had seen one of their feasts even from a distance; fewer still had lived to tell the tale.

He realized that he had been walking in the direction of the music, attracted towards it as a cobra is drawn to the notes of the pungi. Now fully awake, he increased his pace. Very soon he began to run, crashing through the undergrowth, stumbling, cursing. The music sounded clearer now, divorced from the jungle noises. It was unlike any other music he had heard, without being weird or discordant. He was at the crest of the hill now, and still running. Then the trees opened with startling suddenness. He stopped.

They were not more than three hundred yards away, in soft white sand that now looked grey-green: men, women, and children, dancing stark naked.

The beat of the music came from drums, skins stretched tightly over hollowed wood and rubbed with thongs which, from the distance, looked like animals' tails; the notes he had thought to be those of reed instruments were human voices, men and women sitting to one side and making a continuous nasal wail comparable only to the sound of bagpipes.

In the centre was a circle of fire, and close to it at least a dozen drums of varying sizes and a number of men who clapped at intervals and made jungle cries and other sounds: the sharp crack of bull-whips, the calling of monkeys, the roar of tigers, the piercing cry of jackals, the mournful honk of the python in search of a mate.

Around them was a circle of women, dancing hand in hand, and, outside the women, another, much bigger circle made by the dancing men. They jumped and they postured and they cooed at intervals, each as wildly as any animal of the forest, totally unrestrained, and yet contributing to the over-all pattern of music.

And every so often, as the drums rose to a crescendo, the big whips cracked, and the music and the dancing stopped with dramatic suddenness, each dancer holding the pose that he or she had acquired, like figures in a photograph, not moving, until the whips cracked again and the drums rolled.

It was weird, almost spellbinding, and, in its own way, perfect. A dull half-moon had risen in the sky and the faint yellow circle of fire cast a one-sided light on the dancers, lighting up only half of their bodies at a time. The women who were said to be ugly and diminutive looked from that distance almost perfectly formed, their bronze bodies glistening as though smeared with oil: maidens offered to the lust of a hundred dancing devils, men who were only half human. This secret theatre made by the narrow inlet of the sea, the beach surrounded by a forest of palms and with hills rising on all sides, made a striking setting. Endless civilizations receded and fell away to the beginning of time, when primitive man first surrendered to the ecstasy of bodily submission to rhythm and made of it a pagan ritual.

The big drums thundered, the bull-whips crashed, the dancers held their poses as though turned to stone. The night was stabbed by a moment of silence. Gian's skin tingled. This was something he had seen before: a tableau of bronze gods and goddesses suddenly coming to life. And then he remembered where he had seen it: in the private museum at Duriabad, with Sundari standing by his side.

This must be a ferility dance, virgins being initiated to strange sexual practices, an orgy of selective mating; the best in the breed chosen to fertilize the crop. He wondered how and when it would end. No wonder many a white man had risked his life to see a Jaora dance.

The thought of a white man jolted his mind. A sudden cold panic came over him. How long had he been watching the dance? Had the boat come and gone?

The whips cracked, the drums crashed, and once again the dancers were switched into motion. Gian turned on his heel and began to run, aiming for the crest of the hill showing faintly against the sky, crashing noisily through the undergrowth, not caring if he got a poisoned arrow in his back.

Even as he topped the crest of the hill, he saw it: a green flash, a red flash, and a green flash. He stopped. Carefully he unslung the Very pistol and inserted the green cartridge into its chamber. He fired the two flares as quickly as he could load the shells. Then he ran down the slope of the hill.

When he reached the sand, he flung himself down beside a dry log and waited. He was panting, but the fatigue of his limbs had vanished. Now, with the misty light of the half-moon, the surface of the sea looked quite blank; not even the rock shapes he had seen earlier could be seen. Very soon he heard the faint slap of oars dipping in water, intermittent at first, and then in a steady rhythm. He peered hard in the direction of the sound and could make out the blue-black shape of the dinghy. Then, almost immediately, he heard the sound of the canoe crunching against the sand. Two men got out and pulled the boat onto the sand. He could see another figure in the stern. He rose to his feet and coughed. "Mr. Mulligan sent me," he said.

For a second or two there was silence. Then a gruff voice said, "Come closer, in the open, and stop when I tell you to stop. Oh, there you are. What's your name?"

"Gian, sir."

"Who are you?"

"Mr. Mulligan sent me."

"Have you brought a letter or anything from him?"

"Yes, sir, if I may come closer."

"All right, Dicky, let him come up," another voice said. It was a much younger voice.

Gian delivered the letter Mulligan had given him, and the third man flashed his torch and glanced at it in its beam. "Where are they? Mr. Mulligan and the others. How soon can you get hold of them?"

"They are about two miles away, sir," Gian said. "Half an hour to go, another half an hour to come back. One hour—perhaps a little more, on the way back."

The men looked at the luminous dials of their watches. "Plenty of time for that," the younger voice said. "Go ahead, then. Get back as soon as possible—don't want to hang around here too long. How many are there in all?"

"I don't know, sir. Mr. Mulligan said seventeen were to come, but there were only eight when I came away in the afternoon."

"We should be able to manage that. Tell them to hurry, and to leave all their stuff behind. What was the matter with you? We made the first signal nearly an hour ago."

"I must have missed the first signal," Gian said.

"Snoozed off, I bet," the younger voice said.

Gian began to climb the hill at the back on the way to the forest bungalow. When he had left them, earlier in the afternoon, only six others had joined them. He wondered how many more had come by now. He ran and walked all the way, walking only long enough to regain his wind.

The forest bungalow looked unnaturally white in the moonlight, and it was also unnaturally still. Even as he walked into the clearing in front, Gian experienced an odd sense of fear. He halted, not knowing what had prompted him to halt. He gave a low whistle.

No one answered his whistle, and yet, from where he stood, he could see someone crouching beside one of the pillars of the veranda, stiff as a sentry aiming a rifle. He gulped his fear down, telling himself that he must hurry.

"They have come! The boat has come!" Gian shouted, throwing caution to the winds. "They want us to hurry."

He heard his own voice tremble, but no one stirred. Gian took out his coconut knife. Cautiously he edged towards the hut, crouching, ready to pounce, trying to overcome the fear that was now in all his limbs, making him shiver. He climbed the steps onto the veranda. The man-figure against the pillar loomed over him, now quite distinct. It was the big Ramoshi. Even before touching him, Gian knew that he was dead. He crouched beside the post only because he had been tied to it, with his hands secured behind the post. They had bayoneted him; how many times, it was difficult to say. His guts trailed from his stomach, sparkling like a living diamond necklace in the moonlight. He must have taken a long time to die, Gian thought, as he looked at the dead man. And then he realized with a twinge of horror that his intestines sparkled as they did because of the luminous lines of ants crawling upon them; lines of squat, iridescent ants, busily curving in and out like housewives at a sale, while behind them, long orderly queues of other ants waited patiently for their turn.

He turned and fled indoors, looking into all the rooms, shouting out Mulligan's name. But there was no trace of Mulligan and the others. They must have been taken away, prisoners of war, live dummies for bayonet practice, Gian reflected.

He leaped out of the veranda and ran, not looking behind. At the edge of the clearing he came to an abrupt halt. There was something he had just remembered.

For a moment he hesitated. Then he turned and went back towards the bungalow, clutching the coconut knife in his hand. He walked up to the body of the Ramoshi, now stiff against the post, with the neck conveniently bending forward. He began to cut through the neck, working round the bone, and then inserted his fingers past the bone to locate the khobri. He found the coins without difficulty and prised them out, one by one. They were sticky with the fluids of the body, but they shone dully in the light of the moon.

He did not count the sovereigns. He tore off a piece of cloth from the Ramoshi's shirt, bundled the coins into it, and tied the bundle to his belt. He wiped his hands on the dead man's shirt, but the stickiness of the blood was still upon them. He felt something crawling up his foot. The luminous chain of ants had already formed around his feet, and some of their scouts had climbed up to his right ankle, where they were probing method-ically with their feelers. He brought down the flat of his hand hard against them, crushing the ants. Then he hurried away from the bungalow.

At the edge of the clearing he stopped again and turned to take a last look. The half-severed head of the big Ramoshi now lolled drunkenly on one side, mocking him in the moonlight. He unbuckled his flare pistol and hurled it in the direction of the bungalow in a gesture of anger and defiance.

"Well, that's a bloody mess," the man with the gruff voice said.

"Waste of bloody time coming all this way," said the other.

"Well, what're you waiting for?" the young man at the back said with a touch of peevishness. "Hop in, damn it; we haven't got the whole night!"

Gian's knees wobbled as he climbed into the dinghy, and he had to keep his fists clenched to prevent his hands from shaking. The two men pushed the boat until it was free of the sand and then waited for the third man to jump in before getting in themselves. The slap of the oars broke the silence of the night. The moon was just going down.

Late in the evening, six days later, the destroyer turned into the channel for Madras harbour. The sea around them was full of catamarans and tiny fishing boats. In the destroyer there were at least two hundred evacuees, men, women, and children gathered from Singapore and Rangoon and Penang. No one asked Gian a single question. As soon as they berthed, Gian was one of the first ashore. No one noticed him or missed him.

He had been thinking of this moment, planning for it. Back in India at least ten years before his sentence was due to expire, he had no wish to expose himself to any awkward questions. He had had his fill of prisons. But now he might be thrown into some Indian jail to serve out the remaining term of his sentence. The British were strict but just; they would have no option but to send him to jail. There was no one now to come to his rescue and explain that Mulligan-sahib had promised him a special remission of sentence as a reward.

He wondered what they had done to Mulligan.

[23]

Brothers from Japan

THE new masters of the Andamans did not do things by halves, nor did they waste much time. On the very day of their arrival, even as the citizens of Port Blair were celebrating their liberation, they got down to work. The commanding officer, Colonel Yamaki, passed an order imposing a state of permanent martial law. Every sector was to be segregated; anyone found outside his own sector was to be put to death.

The population was divided into two lots. Those with known pro-British leanings were herded into the prison; the others were impressed into a labour corps. Work on constructing an aerodrome began within three days.

Anything that bore the taint of British occupation was ruthlessly eradicated. Old newspapers, books, magazines, anything written in English, were brought out for burning. Huge bonfires were made in the main square of the bazaar. All radio sets were confiscated. The people were warned that anyone caught spreading rumours or expressing pro-British sympathies would be bayoneted in the main square.

It was like the refrain of a song, the threat of the bayonet.

Yamaki looked so much like a Japanese version of Mulligan that many people thought he had been specially selected for taking over command of the islands, and spoke of it as just another example of Japanese thoroughness. He went about in a little command car, flying his flag on the bonnet, dispensing the justice of victors; he soon became the most dreaded man in the islands.

Teams of English-speaking Japanese came and pored over the prison records. With them they brought their own records too, containing black lists, white lists, and grey lists. The work of grading men and women of the colony went on for many days. Everyone was fingerprinted, and there were constant parades for checking identification. One name kept cropping up: Gian Talwar, a known collaborator of the British, a protégé of Patrick Mulligan. Then the teams of experts went back to Rangoon, taking away some of the prison records with them, and ordering that the remainder should be burned under strict supervision. Yamaki had the records destroyed in the prison incinerator. He also announced that anyone giving information leading to the capture of Gian Talwar would be paid a reward of five thousand victory yens, while anyone found giving him shelter, or suppressing information of his whereabouts, would be bayoneted. Copies of Gian's photography taken from the prison files were posted on notice-boards and on all important street corners.

On the same evening, Yamaki sent for Debi-dayal.

Debi-dayal sat on the same sofa that Gian had sat on barely two weeks earlier. But this time the house was spick and span and free of dust. On the coffee table stood a spray of flowers, arranged with Japanese artistry and fussiness. On the wall was a portrait of Hirohito.

Colonel Yamaki himself remained standing, his short, stubby arms resting on the back of a chair. He peered at Debi-dayal through thick rimless glasses.

"We have seen your record," Yamaki told him. "Excellent! We too have a dossier on you—our own Kempitai at Tokyo. Excellent! I understand you speak Japanese—yes?"

"A little," Debi-dayal said.

Yamaki waved his hand, as though whisking a fly. "No matter. It will not come in your way—not knowing our language. I take it that you are willing to cooperate." He smiled. It was more a hiss than a smile, a mere baring of stumps of teeth followed by the sound of suction. It remainded Debi-dayal of Tomonaga, his judo instructor. Is that how all Japanese smile? he wondered.

"In what way?" Debi-dayal asked.

"In a way you have yourself chosen—have chosen in the past."

"Yes, of course," Debi-dayal said eagerly.

"Japan wants to free your country from the British oppressors. Is that not what you want?"

"Of course."

"We have already liberated the people of Malaya and Burma

from the British. And Indochina from the French, and the Dutch Empire from the Dutch." Again there was the baring of the brown teeth, a quick hiss.

"And the Andamans," Debi-dayal reminded him.

"Ah, yes, the Andaman Islands. So many countries set free, one almost forgets. Asia for the Asians, living in a sphere of prosperity, all on their own."

"And now India?" Debi-dayal asked.

"India, Ceylon, Australia," Yamaki told him. "But India first, because Japan loves India, wants her to be free. India first. Japanese soldiers are ready to die for India's freedom. We love the people of India."

It would have sounded far more convincing, Debi-dayal thought, if they had not been making a practice of bayoneting any Indian who did not fall in line. But this was not the time to remind Yamaki of the ruthlessness with which the Japanese had enforced their particular brand of liberation.

"Now we have Indians in our army," Yamaki said. "Maybe you too will join our army, serve your country—in the Indian National Army. The Indian National Army," he repeated.

"Are there many Indians in the Indian National Army?"

Yamaki straightened his back and took a deep breath. The government chair creaked as the weight of his arms shifted. "Last month, in Singapore, sixty thousand, seventy thousand— they all joined. We will get more, all the prisoners taken in Burma—soldiers trained by the British. They will all join; another fifty, sixty thousand, maybe." He clenched his fist and thumped the back of the chair. "They have become our brothers. Soldiers in our army—our Indian army. You have heard of Bose —Subhas Bose?"

"Yes, of course. He is one of our greatest leaders. We call him Netaji—the leader."

The fist came down again. The chair creaked. "There you are. Subhas Bose will lead the army, the Indian National Army—lead it all the way to Delhi. That is what we will do, we and you together—capture Delhi. Now I invite you to join this army." Yamaki straightened himself and then bowed stiffly from the waist.

"I should love to—I mean, it is an honour. But I have no military training. Perhaps I could be given training."

Yamaki closed his eyes and leaned over the chair again. "That we shall see. People like you can do much more than soldiers—much more. They can work from behind—just as you used to." The eyes opened, stared at him, blinking, distorted by the thick lenses, like the eyes of an owl in daylight, Debi-dayal thought. Hope suddenly sprang within him. "You mean in India?" he asked.

Yamaki nodded several times. "Working from behind the enemy lines. Blowing bridges, sinking ships, burning down aeroplanes—I understand you did that once. Good! Good!"

Debi-dayal's mind reeled. This was something that his system had yearned for—the havoc of sabotage behind the British lines, crippling their war muscles.

"Now is the time," Yamaki went on. "The British are ready to quit, just as they left the Andamans. The Gandhis and Nehrus will never make them quit. The British do not understand passive resistance. They have not given in an inch to your Gandhi for the last twenty years. Look how much Japan has taken from them—in no more than two months."

"But how can I get behind the lines—to India?" Debi-dayal asked, his thoughts snapping back to the main theme. "How is it possible?"

Again Yamaki bared his teeth and hissed. He released the back of the chair, and it went toppling down to the floor. He kicked the chair away with his boot. "Easy," he pronounced. "The Kempitai have their own methods. They will do all that. I think they will take you to Assam, to the borders. Thousands of refugees are still on their way, fleeing to India. You will be one of them. Then you go to Bombay, Calcutta, get into touch with your friends, Shafi Usman and the others." He stopped abruptly and shot a quick glance at the door behind him. "I don't know the details, of course," he said, as though he had already said more than he wished to reveal. "I am not supposed to know them."

Debi-dayal's hands shook. What wouldn't he give to come face to face with Shafi! This was something that he had not dared to dream of.

Yamaki bent down and straightened the chair carefully and sat down on it. "From here you will be taken to Rangoon, to see the general there. After that, I cannot say. The general will tell you the plans—what he wants you to do, how you are to do it, everything."

He clapped his hands. A short Japanese soldier in a green

blouse came out with two bottles of Ashahi beer, still cold from the ship's refrigerator. He must have been waiting outside for the signal, Debi thought. Solemnly they drank to the health of the Japanese Emperor and then of Netaji Bose, and over their beer they talked, sitting on the veranda of the house overlooking the harbour, the victor and the collaborator. Before they parted, they shook hands and bowed to each other.

The very next morning Debi-dayal was on board a destroyer on the way to Rangoon. The first leg of his journey to India had begun.

[24]

The Grace of Shiva

ONCE again the train chuffed through the familiar hills. Gian sat smoking, his thoughts straying over the happenings of the past few weeks.

He was dressed in a pair of khaki slacks and a white shirt, the shirt buttoned up at the neck to hide his Andaman chain. He had had many opportunities to have the chain cut off but had decided against it. In the first few days of his return, a bit of human flotsam in a flood of humanity, it seemed the only thing that gave him an identity. Now the chain round his neck had become an important factor in his plans, something of an asset, really.

He was aware of a sense of finality. He was a man coming to the end of his tether. Unless he could get a job within the next few days, he would have to starve—starve, or give himself up. As he had planned it, his getting a job would depend on the Andaman chain. And if that did not succeed, the chain and the disc would make it easy for him to give himself up, establish proof of his identity without too much fuss.

It was now the middle of April. Five weeks had passed since he had landed at Madras, a man without a name, grateful for the immensity of the city, its poverty, its heat, and, above all, for its overcrowding. No one took much notice of a half-naked man sleeping on the pavements, sheltered by the arches of the great shops. There were hundreds, thousands of other half-naked men sleeping on pavements; women too, hugging little brown children to their bodies, grubbing for food.

The weeks in Madras had been harrowing; the return to the world of the free, a constant strain. He could not have endured those weeks if it had not been for the big Ramoshi's gold.

Even to think of that time brought on a gush of bitter anger:

209

a picture of a man driven to desperation by hunger, haunted by fear, his bare feet blistering in the hot streets—himself. And then the picture of that same man, tramping through the goldsmiths' bazaar, turning surreptitiously to look into the shops, at the fat, sweating men sitting on clean white mattresses, the gleaming, delicate-looking balances in glass cases, the mirrored shelves of gold and silver ornaments, and the blackboards near the entrances marked with the day's rates: GOLD—83-12-3, SOVEREIGN —58-2-0.

Sovereign fifty-eight, he kept telling himself as he walked, sovereign fifty-eight. His stomach rumbled with hunger. He had ten of them. Five hundred and eighty rupees, he kept counting, five hundred and eighty-one and four annas.

And how many times had he passed that particular shop, trying to pluck up courage to go in. The big Ramoshi would not have hesitated, he kept reminding himself. He had carefully tried to think out what the Ramoshi would have done in his place.

The shop was a little apart from the other jewellers' shops, separated from them by a teahouse and a betel-nut stall. It looked mean and dingy, its wares shoddy. He noticed the crowds were getting thinner and that the shops had already begun to put up their shutters, one by one. He must act quickly, unless he wanted to spend another night without food. And again his nerve had failed. He had decided to make another round, to walk up to the end of the road by the silk mart and then come back. If the shop was still open, he would risk it.

It was open.

The fat man with the gold-work cap had risen to his feet, but when he saw Gian he squatted down again. "What is it?" he asked frowning. "This is not the first of the month! I saw you passing the last time."

For a moment Gian did not know what he was talking about. He stood nervously, clutching a sovereign in his hand, ready to make a dash if there was any danger of being challenged. Something in his attitude must have warned the shopkeeper that he was not whoever he had mistaken him for. His frown turned into a smile. "Oh, you have come on business," he said. "For a moment, I thought you were from the police—come for his hapta. Do come in." He squatted down on his white mattress.

That had been a lucky break. In his faded Andaman blouse and shorts, he must have looked like a plain-clothes policeman.

Boldly he walked up the remaining steps and held out the coin. "I want to sell a sovereign," he explained.

The man gave him a hard stare and took the coin from his hand. He turned it expertly in his fingers, almost without looking. "I'll give you thirty rupees," he offered.

Gian shook his head. He had lived with criminals long enough to know that a goldsmith who had to pay his montly bribe to the police was always open to a shady transaction. "No, thank you," he said and sat down on the bench. "It says fifty-eight rupees on the board."

"Take it or leave it. The other shops will not be so—so accommodating. They will send for the police."

With studied deliberateness, Gian pulled out his coconut knife and placed it beside him on the bench. "Send for the police, then. I will tell them you offered thirty rupees for a sovereign."

The man made as if to return the coin and then turned it over in his fingers again. "All right, fifty, then. A man must live."

"Fifty if you will buy ten sovereigns."

The fat man looked at Gian's face and then at the knife. He nodded. Gian took out the other nine sovereigns and gave them to him. He thumbed them expertly and kept them on one side, in a neat pile. From under his mattress he took out a bundle of hundred-rupee notes and began to count them.

"I want the money in tens," Gian told him.

"They always do," the man muttered. Without even looking at him, he put away the hundred-rupee notes and pulled out another bundle from under the mattress, this time of ten-rupee notes. He counted out fifty notes and gave them to Gian. "Any time you have any business, you know where to come," he said with an ingratiating smile.

"Of course," Gian had said. "I will remember." He pocketed the notes, tucked the knife away into his belt, and walked out.

After that he began to eat regular meals. He bought himself clothes, a razor, and a small tin trunk. The trunk gave him a sense of respectability; he was now a man with possessions. But even after that he hesitated a long time before moving from the pavement to the cheapest hotel in Madras. This necessitated his taking on a false name: Maruti Rao.

He chose the name after a great deal of thought, a name that would not sound outlandish in South India. There must be hundreds of Raos in Madras itself, he had told himself, thousands. For a few days all went well, and then, just as he was beginning to feel secure, he nearly gave himself away.

They were all waiting for the second sitting in the dining room, and Gian was looking over the dog-eared and grease-stained sheet from the morning's *Hindu* that lay on the table. The room-boy had come for his keys.

"The room-boy wants your keys, Mr. Maruti Rao," the manager had called from his desk.

He had gone on reading, and then he heard the voice again. "Can the room-boy have your keys, Mr. Maruti Rao, so that he can tidy up?"

Gian had looked around him to see who the manager was speaking to. The others in the room were all looking at him, the dark South Indian faces with bemused smiles on them. "*Mr. Maruti Rao*, your keys," the manager said again.

"Yes, of course," Gian said. He took the keys from his pocket and walked over to the manager's desk.

"Thank you," said the manager with exaggerated politeness. "Thank you, Mr. Maruti Rao."

Sleep had been difficult that night. The incident had pinpointed his problem. He was a man without a name. Madras, an unfamiliar city for anyone from the north, was not the proper place to begin a new life. His accent and appearance were conspicuous. His money was running out. For several days past, he had been looking for a job. There were numerous openings in Madras just then, with new ordnance factories going up. But they never took on anyone, even as a coolie, unless he could produce a verification of his character from the police.

Towards the morning he had been able to formulate a plan. It was by no means perfect, and much depended on a number of imponderables. But there was a very good chance of succeeding. He was going to try and get a job, preferably in a big city. And if he could not get a job before his money ran out, he was going to give himself up.

Suddenly it was all as simple as that. He felt free and light. He could easily have gone to sleep now, but it was too late to think of sleeping. The trams had already begun to clang in the streets below.

He packed his tin trunk and went to the office to pay the bill. The manager had asked him with a casualness he thought was studiedly elaborate, "I hope you are leaving a forwarding address, Mr. Rao, in case there are any letters."

"There will be no letters," Gian told him. He went to the Central Station and bought himself a third-class ticket to Duria-bad. After paying for the ticket he had exactly one hundred and seventy-one rupees left.

He would never have gone to Konshet if it had not happened to be on his way to Duriabad. Even as it was, when the train stopped at Pachwad junction he was seized with a sudden fear which made him hang back in his carriage until the guard blew the whistle for the train to start. Then, just as the train had begun to move, he jumped out.

He watched the train crawl away, wishing he had remained in it. It was at Duriabad that his plan was to be put into operation; stopping at Konshet was merely a détour which had no place in his plans. Why had he jumped out, when he had no desire to visit his own village? Was it because he was secretly afraid of what Duriabad held in store and wanted to put off arriving there?

He remembered the last time he had got out at this station, almost exactly three years before. What had then been occupying his mind were such topics as how he would have to give up cigarettes for the holidays, Debi-dayal's sister and those other men at the Birchi-bagh picnic, his next year at college—all the little inconsequential subjects which college boys think about. Now, so much had changed. The three years had been like a lifetime.

The station was crowded with the traffic of a country at war. It was easy enough to slip away, a man carrying a little tin box shoving through the crowd at the ticket gate. Who could think that he was a fugitive, a convicted murderer hiding from the law?

Until evening he loitered in the jungle on the hill behind the station yard. He concealed the tin box behind a tree and marked down the place in his mind. Then he began his ten-mile trek.

The road was the same, the forest was the same; the last time, he and Hari had walked side by side along the same road, jubilant at their success, discussing plans for the pooja that Hari had planned. They had walked because Hari had wanted to spare the feet of his bullocks, Raja and Sarja. Raja and Sarja, whose bodies had been scarred for the production of smallpox serum and who were later sold to the butcher at Sonarwadi.

The Big House loomed out of the shadows, a light shining through an upper-story window. He wondered who was living in the Big House now. In the dark, with the solitary lamp, it looked forlorn and deserted. The thought crossed his mind that, with Vishnu-dutt gone, he was the only remaining male heir in both families. Did that mean that the Big House belonged to him? He felt a little sad to see the house deserted and he hurried on.

He walked down the village street, his feet scuffing in the familiar dust. Now and then a dog barked idly at him from some farmer's hut, but there were no lights in any of the houses. He felt like a ghost, haunting the scene of its past. At the turning of the road was the peepul tree, its leaves shimmering in the pale moonlight. Once Vishnu-dutt had stood under the tree and taunted him as he passed by. Now there was no one about, only the rustle of leaves in the wind and the faraway yelping of a dog.

In the moonlight the Little House looked just as neat and well kept as in Hari's day, the shadows obscuring its blemishes. He could almost picture Aji waiting behind the door, clutching the tray with the oil lamps and the parched rice to propitiate the evil spirits.

Gian paused by the gate, gathering his thoughts. It was important not to let one's mind wander. He had work to do, work he must finish quickly and get away; get away because he had been foolish to come; get away because almost anyone who saw him was bound to recognize him. He crept to the side of the house, to the room Hari had always occupied. He knew that by lifting the panel of the window he could release it from the hollow groove in which it was anchored. He put his hands under the edge and forced the whole window up. The frame slid out of its groove as he knew it would. He removed a panel and placed it against the wall. Then he entered the house, flashing his torch.

There was nothing in the house except a layer of dust. All the rooms and both the verandas were absolutely empty. There was no furniture of any kind; not a single bed or a chair or a table. The cooking pots from the kitchen, the big copper handa for heating the bath water, the farming implements in the storeroom at the back, everything had gone.

His legs felt weak as the explanation came to his mind: a

demonstration of the government's revenue collectors' tremendous zeal. They alone had the power to distrain all movable property from a farmer's house if the tax on the land was not paid. That was what must have happened after Aji's death. The taxes on the rice fields must have fallen due, and the men from the tehsildar's office had come and taken away everything. He could picture the men coming, scavengers of a system, proud of their calling; they must have meticulously listed everything under the eyes of the "panchas" or respected witnesses, and then taken the things out and put them up for auction. They were like vultures. Once they had come and gone, only the bare bones remained, picked clean, shining white in the moonlight.

He sat down, almost sinking to the floor, looking at the wreck of what Dada and Hari had tried to preserve. A sudden wave of anger came over him. That was what the Japanese had done to him. He had been happy in the Andamans, a feri earning sixty rupees a month, holding down a job in a British regimental office. From the blackness all round him, the sunlit land of convicts beckoned to him. That was where he had made something of himself, working with zeal and honesty, that was where he belonged. Now he would have to resort to deceit, even to get himself a job. Could he not have stayed on in the Andamans?

But that was where he had disgraced himself too, he suddenly remembered. The petrified face of Debi-dayal, crouching over the fallen Gurkha, and then glaring at him in utter disbelief; Debi-dayal dangling naked from the flogging frame, his back and buttocks covered in blood. The shame of what he had done came back with such force that he had to grit his teeth to fight it down.

He stood up, aware that the Andamans too were a chapter from his past: the land itself had discarded him, discarded him after giving him a legacy of shame to carry through life. He wondered what the Japanese had done to Debi-dayal, to all the other convicts. He thought of the body of the big Ramoshi with his lolling head laughing at him, the fluorescent ants crawling up to feast on his entrails. Was that what the Japanese did to all their prisoners?

Almost forcibly he brought his mind to the present. The Little House had nothing to offer him. There was no use lingering, feeling sick over the past. It was time to go.

It was almost an afterthought, a surrender to a quirk of sentiment, that made him go into the prayer room behind the
kitchen; here, in the beam of his torchlight, stood Shiva.

They had not dared to take Shiva away. The certainty of the
wrath of the god of destruction had deterred them. Relief
flooded his mind. They had spared the family god—perhaps the
most valuable single object in the Little House.

Gian lifted the statue. It was lighter than he had thought. He
carried it out of the house. He went back and replaced the
window pane he had removed. Then, with Shiva cradled in his
arms, he crept away from the house.

The office was big, opulent, air-conditioned. The floor was covered with a dark red Persian carpet. Near the window were a
large stuffed sofa and two chairs and a blackwood coffee table
with flowers in a vase. Above the opposite window was an oil
painting of the new Kalinadi bridge. On the wall behind the
polished desk was a portrait of a woman with flowers in her hair.
That must be Sundari's mother when she was young, Gian
thought. On the desk itself, in a double silver frame, were the
photographs of Sundari and Debi-dayal. On the high-backed
chair behind the desk sat Dewan-bahadur Tekchand.

Tekchand looked at the young man who sat opposite him, and
then at the statue of Shiva on the floor. He got up and walked
up to the statue for a closer look. He ran his finger over its back
and then tapped it with his fingernail. "Could you put it on the
shelf there, by the window?" he said.

Gian jumped to his feet. "It might scratch the surface, sir," he
pointed out.

"Yes, it might." Tekchand walked back to his desk and picked
up an issue of *Fortune* magazine that lay in a tray. "Here, put
this underneath," he said.

After Gian had placed the statue on the shelf, Tekchand sat
down and motioned Gian to a chair. "What made you bring it to
me?" he asked.

The deception came easy. It was a part of his plan not to tell
him that he had been to his house and seen the museum. "I have
heard people talk of your collection. Better than the Lahore
museum, they say."

Tekchand peered at him and then at the statue. "Excuse my

saying so, but you must be really hard pressed to be wanting to sell it, Mr.—"

"Talwar," Gian told him. "Gian Talwar." The details had been worked out in his mind. He must give his correct name and tell as few lies as possible. The plan depended on his being able to establish his identity.

"Oh, yes, Mr. Talwar."

"As it happens, I am quite hard up. But I did not realize that it was so—so obvious."

"Hindus don't go about selling their gods, Mr. Talwar. I can see that the idol has been worshipped, worshipped till quite recently—all the marks of paste and ochre are still there."

"I am not very religious. Few things are sacred to me."

"At your age! How old are you?"

"Twenty-three, sir."

Tekchand gave him a long, hard stare, an inspecting, searching sort of look, almost like the one he had given the statue. His eyes took in the work-hardened body, the callused hands, the deep tan given by long hours in the sun, the width of the shoulders. A frown came over his face and cleared away again.

"It is quite brave to say 'few things are sacred to me.' Particularly when one is twenty-three. And there is still the point that you must be pretty hard pressed to wish to sell a household god, something that other members of your family—your father or mother, perhaps—have worshipped."

It was difficult not to flinch under that cold, probing stare. "It is true that I am out of a job," Gian confessed.

"That too does not fit in—not these days. A bright young man, obviously with education, used to hard work—no. Hundreds of jobs, with all this spate of work—excuse me!" He picked up the white telephone on his desk, which had given a discreet burr. "Yes?" he said into the mouthpiece. "Send him in in a minute, will you—well, three minutes. I should be finished by then." He replaced the receiver and turned to Gian.

Gian had just been on the verge of blurting out everything, telling him who he was and what he wanted, when the telephone intervened. He could see that Tekchand was suspicious; he remembered that he had always had a reputation for his shrewdness. It was just as well to get it over. He hesitated, knowing that this was something that had to go right. He had to sell his story to this man; and this time there was no question of drawing out the coconut knife.

"Do you mind leaving the statue here for a while? I'd like to show it to some people—experts—before making an offer."

Gian was stung by the insinuation. "It is not a stolen idol, Dewan-bahadur-sahib."

"I have no doubt about that. At the same time, it is just as well to be sure what one is buying. It looks rather a special piece to me, and I would like to get a second opinion before making an offer."

"Would anyone else's opinion on old bronzes really influence your own judgment, sir?" Gian asked.

Tekchand gave him a sharp look, a look almost of approval. "If only to put a fair valuation on the piece," he said.

"I would much rather you judged it for yourself—paid me whatever you think is fair. . . ."

"Have you any objection to leaving it behind?"

He felt cornered. "No, none whatever."

Dewan-bahadur Tekchand rose to his feet. He walked over to the shelf and looked closely at the statue. From the side, and bending down like that, he looks so much like his son, Gian reflected. The same figure, the same cast of head, the air of breeding.

"There is a mark, quite sharp, on the shoulder—the left one." He lifted the image in his hands and turned it upside down. Then he put it back on the shelf. "It must have been hit with great force by some kind of steel instrument. Otherwise the mark wouldn't be there. They are almost indestructible, because of the five-metal alloy. Bullet-proof, absolutely, and so light too. They should make helmets of the stuff, for soldiers, and vests for the governors. Shall we leave it at that, then? Come over to my house—yes, I think you had better do that, let me see, tomorrow about five; yes, five in the evening. I have a meeting at four, but I shall have finished by then. Would that suit you?"

"Yes, sir," Gian said, rising.

"My house is in Kerwad Avenue, you know, near—"

"I know where it is."

"Good! Five o'clock tomorrow, then. And if I am not there, perhaps you wouldn't mind waiting."

"Not at all."

"Oh, and in the meantime, Mr. Talwar, if you would like

something in advance, say a hundred rupees or so, just to tide you over . . ."

"No, thank you, sir; my need is not quite so—so urgent."

As soon as Gian had gone out of the room Lala Tekchand lifted his telephone. He told his secretary to get him the curator of the Lahore museum. He was still speaking to the secretary when the next visitor was ushered in.

25

Some Things Are More Important
than Money

DEEP down was a tiny ember of guilt, perversely alive, which made him hesitate before the gate. A hardened criminal had no business harbouring a conscience, he reminded himself. His future hung in the balance; the choice was between security and long years in jail. He walked in, wondering if he was too early. Without a watch, it was difficult to time things exactly.

The drive was just as he remembered; even the gul-mohors and the jacarandas were in bloom, creating a cool tunnel of shade after the heat of the bare, wide road. In the pillared porch a servant asked his name and showed him into a long high-ceilinged room behind the curving staircase. As he sat down, he heard the pendulum clock on the wall chiming the hour.

The room was dim, with curtains draped over the two windows and dark panelling on the walls. There was a faint smell of camphor and furniture polish. Everything was faint, subdued, muted; in character, he thought, spelling out how many generations of affluence? Even the velvet covering on the chairs looked faded, and his cheap yellow shoes were an affront to the Persian carpet. From where he sat, on a straight-backed chair of carved wood, directly under the slowly revolving fan, he could see out of the door and into the garden. The flowers reminded him of the Andamans, lush as cabbages and brightly coloured; violent pinks, yellows, and reds: cannas, dahlias, Easter lilies, and others unknown to him.

So this was what Debi-dayal had turned his back on. He had become a revolutionary, knowing that at the end of the road lay the Cellular Jail and a life sentence which, now that the islands had fallen to the Japanese, would perhaps never end. The important thing to remember was that Debi-dayal would never come back. It was doubtful if he was still alive. If he had managed to make himself hated by Mulligan and his sentries, he would not get very far with the Japanese. The stiff, leaning figure of the big Ramoshi, his guts spilling on the floor and the ants crawling in and out of belly, his lolling head with the face that had seemed to laugh at him in the night, came back to Gian. That was the Japanese answer to their rules' being broken, their routine punishment, the equivalent of Mulligan's kanji house.

He was confident of success, elated at the way he had played his cards so far. Shiva had strengthened his hand, had become a pawn in his designs—Shiva, discovered almost by accident, originally intended to be sold for whatever he would fetch, had been worked into the plan and had already helped him to get over the first, all-important hurdle.

The minutes passed. The feeling of guilt had now almost wholly evaporated. His elation grew. He waited, resolute, ruthless, braced for any eventuality. His fingers touched the Andaman disc, now under a tie and shirt, almost as a devout man touches a talisman.

There was a scamper of feet on the carpet behind him, and a small chocolate-coloured dog came and began to sniff at his toes, wagging its tail. Gian was not used to dogs; he was suspicious of them, was secretly afraid of them—perhaps the relationship of the criminal to the watchman, he said to himself. He jerked his foot back, almost involuntarily. They were in opposite camps, dogs and men like himself, hereditary enemies. No wonder the criminal tribes were said to sacrifice dogs to their deity. . . .

The dog backed out and began to growl; the hair on its spine stood up; the tail stood rigidly out. Suddenly it occurred to him that he had seen the dog before, on the day of the picnic, knew its name too: Spindle, Sundari's dog. For a moment he wondered if she too was there, in her father's house. Her presence would certainly complicate things, if she remembered him from the Birchi-bagh picnic. He had gone over his plan with care, and he had been prepared for Tekchand and his business shrewdness. But not for this. He hoped everything would not be ruined by her being there. He did not want to be recognized before he was prepared to disclose his identity. But she was bound to be in Bombay, he reassured himself, with her husband.

There was a sound of footsteps coming down from the stairs,

and then a woman's voice calling out, "Spindle! Where are you, Spindle?"

Gian sat up, rigid with apprehension, confronted with the sudden fear of failure. His heart thumped wildly, and sweat broke out all over his body. Was he going to be recognized now, before he could tackle Tekchand and say to him what he had rehearsed a hundred times? The dog, sensing his nervousness, began to bark. He gingerly put a hand to stroke its head. It was useless.

"Oh, stop yapping, Spindle!" the girl was saying in mock irritation. Now her footsteps were behind him, on the carpet, coming nearer. It was inevitable, he felt, fate taking a hand, consigning him to a future of misery, sending him back to the jails of India. . . .

She came in, almost running, tall and slender and more beautiful than he remembered her. He stood up and folded his hands, not daring to say anything, going through the motions of greeting a lady as practised in civilized Hindu society.

"I am sorry," Sundari said in Hindi, stopping abruptly in her stride. "I didn't know there was anyone here."

No, there was no one in the room, only a runaway convict, he told himself with bitterness; she could not have known about his coming because she had not heard a car drive up. No one came to the house on foot, as he had done. "I am waiting for the Dewan-bahadur," Gian said.

"Oh, yes, you must be the gentleman he is buying the statue from. He was saying something about it at lunch. I do hope Spindle hasn't been worrying you."

"No, but he wasn't very friendly, either."

The girl laughed. In spite of himself, Gian stared at her face, went on staring. How many years was it since he had seen a pretty girl laughing? She bent down and picked up the dog and cuddled it in her arms. "Abaji should be here any minute. Sorry Spindle has been worrying you; he is quite friendly, really." She walked away towards the staircase and then stopped and turned. "Haven't I seen you before?" she asked.

His heart fluttered, sensing defeat. And yet, somewhere within him there was also a glow of gratitude to her for remembering him. Was this the end, he asked himself, or just a beginning—a beginning of something he had never dared to aspire to?

"Oh, yes, now I remember. You came and had tea here, with Debi, and then we all went to Birchi-bagh and—and you swam all the way beyond Aswini rock, to the other bank. Don't you remember?"

Did he not remember? There was very little else he remembered so vividly, very little else he so much wanted never to forget. Was that all he had meant to her—someone who had gone swimming beyond Aswini rock? Gone swimming to hide the shame of being found wearing a janwa?

The silence hung around them; both went on looking at each other, the man with the convict's work-hardened body, the blunted sensitivity and dead soul, and the girl from the world of fragrance and laughter. Outside on the gravel, wheels crunched and came to a smooth halt, doors opened. There was a sound of footsteps approaching. Gian stood still, waiting for the spell to break, aching for it not to be broken.

"Ah, there you are!" Tekchand said, looking at his watch. "I hope you haven't had to wait too long. This is Mr. Talwar," he went on. "My daughter, Mrs. Chandidar."

Gian folded his hands and bowed. Sundari acknowledged his greeting and then excused herself and went out, carrying her dog.

"Let's go upstairs," Tekchand said, leading the way, and Gian followed him. Here, too, it was all as he remembered: the wide, curving, carpeted staircase, the long passage with the bronze and brass figures on both sides; the private museum, at the back of the house, with its high scalloped ceiling and banks of shelves.

And the statues. They were all round them, a parade of gods, standing, stooping, dancing, blessing, killing, eating, embracing, copulating; Shivas and Vishnus and Brahmas and Gokals and Ganpaties and Narasimhas and Lakshmis and Saraswatis and a hundred others. And on a waist-high pedestal painted white, placed in a corner where the light came in a shaft from the skylight, stood Shiva from the Little House. Beside Shiva, looking prim and shining with jewellery, stood Sundari's mother, Radha.

"Mr. Talwar," Tekchand said. "My wife."

"I have just ordered tea," Mrs. Tekchand said, "when I heard the car downstairs."

It was so much like that other time: servants in white coats bringing in the trays, plates of cakes, sandwiches, and pakoras, the shining silver tea service, the fragile cups and saucers. Mrs. Tekchand sat on the fan-backed sofa, its gilt legs placed on the edge of a blue and green carpet. Both the sofa and the carpet must have been specially made for the room, Gian told himself, for the design of the dragons on the carpet was also repeated in the tapestry that covered the sofa. He sat on the frail gilded chair, worrying whether he was doing anything wrong, afraid that he would drop his cup. He watched the servants moving about, handing round plates with small pink napkins folded like flowers, and little silver forks.

For the past three years he had avidly held out his enamel mug for the tepid grey liquid that the Andaman jail served as tea. Now he was sitting in a private museum, on an antique chair, in the aura of the perfume that Sundari's mother wore. And again there was that slight twinge of conscience which he had experienced when standing at the gate. What business had he to break into these people's lives, contaminating them by his presence, like the man with the beard who had been here that other time, Shafi Usman, carrying with him the shadow of evil?

For a moment he felt sorry for them, these people who were being so good to him, permitting him such an intimate glimpse of their lives, he who was planning to feed upon their distress. But he shook the thought away. This was no time to be squeamish. He had not shrunk from cutting a dead man's throat for his gold. Now it was the relatively simple matter of playing on the anxiety of a man and his wife. He looked at the wife, who was offering him a slice of cake. She was soft, beautiful, elegantly dressed, and jewelled; she would be much easier to deal with than her husband, he reflected; he could not imagine her being cautious and businesslike, allowing her righteousness to come in the way of sentiment.

She gave him a pleasant smile. "Oh, do have another slice—you must."

"Thank you." Gian held out his plate. The fork rattled slightly with the shaking of his hand.

It was not as though he was going to do them any harm, he consoled himself. At the hand of their son, they had already suffered all the harm that was destined for them. If anything, he was going to make it easier for them by giving them hope. A few lies more or less did not matter.

"Where is Sundar?" Mrs. Tekchand asked. "Isn't she coming up to tea?"

"She must have taken the dog out," her husband said. "I saw her downstairs."

"Mohan, go and tell Sundar-baba that we are having tea in here," she ordered one of the servants.

Now he was calm. The room with the high scalloped ceiling and the two enormous chandeliers was not there. Suddenly, it had taken on the shape of a beach at midnight, with a moon poised above the coconut palms. The statues blurred and receded and focused themselves again, dancing round a campfire. The drums had stopped with the crack of the whips, and now they were all turned to stone, holding their postures, until the music would begin again.

The spoon slipped off his saucer and fell softly on the carpet. The dream ended, having reminded him that he had stolen a glimpse of the Jaora dance, a primitive fertility rite. Now he found himself on the brink of another world, surrounded by luxury. He was hungry, excited, braced for whatever challenge the moment held. This was something he was not going to allow to go sour. He would fight, fight with all his seasoned criminal's cunning. Even the girl coming in did not worry him now.

A servant brought him another spoon, placed on a tray. Tekchand rose, picked up a magnifying glass from one of the tables, and walked over to Shiva's pedestal. He began to examine the figure, moving the glass slowly.

Sundari came in, followed by Spindle. Gian got up, balancing the paper-thin cup and saucer with ease. "Oh, there you are," her mother said. "This is Mr. Talwar."

"We have met already," Sundari said, taking one of the gilt chairs.

"Met?" her mother looked up from pouring tea.

"While I was waiting downstairs," Gian said.

The ritual of afternoon tea went on, polite, unhurried. They talked of the war, of the heat, of the freedom movement. Then the women left and servants began to clear away the tea things. One offered him cigarettes, fat, exotic-looking cigarettes from a heavy silver box. He took one and lit it, remembering the time when Balbahadur stamped on his hand when he reached for a butt.

The noises ceased. He was still sitting in the chair facing the fan-backed sofa, smoking, aware that a moment of crisis was at hand. And yet, he was almost startled when Tekchand addressed him.

"Well, Mr. Talwar, I have decided to make you an offer. And

I think you will find that the price I am offering is fair." He was still standing close to the statue, still holding the magnifying glass in one hand.

Calmly Gian drew on the cigarette. He felt supremely confident of success, a man in a position to bargain. Shiva was just a preliminary, as you will soon find out, Dewan-bahadur, he told himself. You are someone I am going to make use of, and nothing is going to stop me from doing that. Shiva is merely a happy coincidence, a handy pawn pressed into service. Whatever I have planned is going to happen; it was inevitable even if Shiva had not been there, for to me it means survival. Shiva has merely paved the way.

"I had the curator from the museum here for lunch and we were both able to have a good look at the piece. It's early sixteenth century. Made by Kumarappa's son, at Tanjore. Not by Kumarappa himself, as I had originally thought. That would have made it rather awkward."

"Awkward, sir?"

"Because in that case I might not have been in a position to make an offer. The price would have been beyond me."

"Oh, I am very glad it is not as precious as you originally thought, then."

Tekchand deposited the magnifying glass in its velvet bag and came and sat in the chair that Sundari had occupied.

"That is a somewhat unusual wish, if I may say so, but perhaps you have your reasons. At it turns out, it is by no means a unique piece. Mind you, the sons, both of them, were good craftsmen in their way. But never as good as the father. And they were far more prolific, if that is the word. They sold at least a hundred of these Shivas, which, purely from a collector's point of view, reduces their value. You see what I mean."

"Yes."

"I myself rate their work high, much higher than Maheswari, even Nityanand. There is a certain vitality, virility, almost, nothing of the romanticism of the Ajanta school, the sexual obsession of Khajuraho. It is starkly primitive. . . ."

"Like when man first began to dance," Gian suggested.

"Exactly. They have two of these figures by Kumarappa's sons at the Lahore museum—at least, only two that can be authenticated."

"Is this one—er, authentic?"

"Oh, very much so."

"How much would it be worth?" Gian asked. He was not really interested in the price. He would have been very glad if Tekchand would have accepted it as a gift. But he knew that any such suggestion would be repugnant to him. It was Tekchand, not Shiva, who might be of use to him.

"It's rather difficult," Tekchand was saying. "There is no price, as such. But if I were buying a Shiva made by the younger Kumarappas, say, from the Bhadrapore or Lankadaman galleries, I myself would place a limit of two thousand rupees. I think that was what the museum paid for the second of their figures. Supposing I give you two-five?"

The figure staggered him. He had never thought that Shiva would be worth much more than a couple of hundred rupees. He was also surprised by the other's frankness—his gullibility, almost.

"I have a similar figure, made by Maheswari, almost a contemporary of the Kumarappas. I would like to buy this one so that I can put both of them at the entrance near the foot of the stairs, side by side in the hall as you enter—that is, if you are willing to sell."

"That is most generous of you. Of course, I shall sell. I would be quite willing to sell for two thousand."

"No, no; that wouldn't do at all."

"Frankly, I had never thought that the figure would be worth anything like two thousand—that it was anything special."

"Oh, very special," Tekchand said. "Indeed, if it had turned out to be the elder Kumarappa's work, it would have been worth—well, fifteen thousand, at least, maybe more. Some American paid twenty-five for one of them, two years ago."

"Even if it had been, I would much rather have sold it to you," Gian said, "for whatever you were willing to pay."

Tekchand looked at him, a question in his eyes. Then he said, "Is there anything special you want from me, Mr. Talwar?"

It was coming, and he was prepared for it. "Yes, sir, I want a job," he said, almost with relief.

"What sort of a job?"

"I don't mind what it is. As a clerk, or as a supervisor of labourers on one of your construction works—anything. I don't mind even working as a coolie. I am used to manual labour."

For the first time Tekchand looked uncomfortable, suspicious.

Was he one of those desperate young men who were engaged in terrorist activities? What was his reason for wanting to get work on a construction job—even as a coolie?

"Anything else?" he asked.

"Yes, the job has to be somewhere away from this place, and—"

"Oh, I see." There was a moment's silence. Gian waited for the next question, feeling relaxed and confident.

"Is there, by any chance—are you trying to hide from something?"

"I am trying to rehabilitate myself."

"Is it anything to do with how the statue came into your possession?"

"No, sir."

"Can you tell me how it came into your hands?"

"You don't think I have stolen it, do you?" Gian asked with a touch of resentment.

"Well, no. Actually, I have ascertained that it is not stolen—at least not from a museum or a temple, or a private collection. The curator had no knowledge of any such theft. They are always kept informed, whenever an identifiable piece is stolen. But still, there is an air of mystery surrounding all this. . . ."

"Why is it necessary to clear the mystery?"

"For one thing, it is important for a collector to learn details of the pieces he owns. You will find that every one of the figures you see here has a card pasted underneath, giving a brief description—who made it, how it was discovered, who were the owners, and so on. It is essential to give each piece an identity, a name, and address and a background, just like a human being. A man has to have a name, a record, a background. Otherwise—he's just a nobody."

"I will tell you all I know about it," Gian said. "It is not much. It was discovered by my grandfather while he was digging in his field. The nick on the shoulder was made by Grandfather's pick."

"Yes, it intrigued me, that nick. You know, of course, that Kumarappa's main business was to make armour, something thin and light that would yet break a spear on impact. Where is this field?"

"At a place called Piploda, in the Sonarwadi district."

"That is up north somewhere, isn't it?"

"Yes, in Himachal."

"That's at least two thousand miles away from where Kuma-rappa lived. Just shows how Hinduism had already unified India, even before the British did so. In what year?"

"Pardon?"

"When your grandfather came upon the Shiva."

"Around nineteen-hundred."

"What else?"

"That is about all. Since then it has been in the family, in the shrine."

"An object of worship?"

"Yes."

"And you are, you said, a non-believer."

"Yes."

"And that is all you can tell—or are prepared to tell?"

"That is all I know about the figure."

For a few moments Tekchand stared at the figure of Shiva, and then at Gian. "And it seems that you have brought it to me not so much because you want to sell it for a good price but because you hope to get a job."

"That is quite right."

"A job somewhere away from here."

"Yes, sir."

"Why do you need a job so badly, Mr. Talwar? There are hundreds of jobs going these days. For a young man like you, there should be no difficulty—no need to offer one's services as a coolie."

Gian said, "You said just now that a figure like that Shiva has to have an identity, just like a man: a name, a family background, a history. That is what I am seeking—an identity."

Tekchand gave him a sharp, searching look. "What is wrong with your present identity," he asked, "as Gian Talwar, who comes from a village in the Sonarwadi district, in the Himachal state? You have been to school there, so there should be a record there; then, presumably, you have been to college too. Some-where you have held a job, working with your hands. Why can-not you go before the employment people and offer your services, as Gian Talwar? What is wrong with your present identity, Mr. Talwar?"

"This is what is wrong with it," Gian said very evenly. He loosened his tie and opened out his collar, baring his neck. "This is what is wrong." He held up his Andaman disc.

They were on the private balcony behind their bedroom, over-looking the garden and the grove of casuarina trees, with the curve of the river in the distance. Tekchand was pacing up and down, dressed in his kurta and pyjamas, his yellow velvet chaplis making a soft phut-phut sound on the bare tiles of the floor. His wife sat hunched in a rattan chair, her feet drawn up on the seat.

"I don't like it," Tekchand pronounced. "Don't like it at all." He had said the same thing several times before.

"But you must do something," his wife said, "since Debi told him to come to you. You cannot let your son down." She too had said the same thing several times before.

"But don't you see? It all seems so—so underhand, for some-one in my position."

No one knew more than she how vulnerable his position was. He was a Dewan-bahadur, and had Debi not been involved with the terrorists, he would almost certainly have been knighted be-fore this. Now all that had blown over; his work for the war effort, his civic zeal, his donations to public causes, had overcome that setback. Now he was on the rise again. They could scarcely help giving him a knighthood as soon as the war was over; that was what everyone said, even the officials. Sir Tekchand Kerwad, that was what he was going to be, and she would be Lady Ker-wad.

He looked resentfully at her, sitting with a flushed face and an injured look, suggesting by her manner that he had done some-thing to upset her.

"Most dangerous," he muttered almost to himself. "With the war going so badly, to be employing a known murderer who's escaped from jail . . . most dangerous."

"What is the danger?" his wife asked.

He stopped in his stride and scowled at her. "Anything might happen. How do we know he is not one of the terrorists? He may well be if he was friendly with Debi. Almost certainly was one of their—er—set; you know, the boys Debi went out with, who led him astray. But even if he is now reformed, as he says, as soon as they discover him, they are bound to create trouble. Might even

make difficulties about my contracts. Think of the money involved—lakhs of rupees!"

"You can make him promise not to do anything
foolhardy. . . ."

"The word of a convict!" he snapped.

"He seemed such a nice young man. Even Sundari says you
must do something."

He began his pacing again. The frown on his face was deeper.
"Did he tell you how he managed to escape?" his wife asked.

"Oh, yes, something about being made what they call a feri—
you know, paroled, allowed to move about freely in the colony.
It seems he and another feri got together and bought this sailboat—some cock and bull story about this other man keeping
sovereigns in his throat. He says he offered to take Debi with
them, but that he refused. Quite sensible too, with all the risks
involved."

"My son would never have held back from anything because
of danger," his wife interrupted with a touch of asperity.

He lowered himself into a chair. "I was only trying to save
your feelings," he told her very quietly. "According to this man,
it seems that Debi was not worried about the danger. It was just
that—just that he did not want to come back or to have anything more to do with us. He does not even open any of the
letters he receives. All right; then how could he have told this
man to come to me for a job?"

"He has a right to," his wife pronounced with feminine perver-
sity. "A son can surely ask his father to do a little thing like that.
How did they get away?"

"Those two? In the boat. Landed on the Burma coast, at a
place called Tavoy. It was just a week before the Japanese over-
ran Burma, and everything seems to have been in a bit of a mess;
otherwise they were bound to have been caught. As it was, the
disruption of the administration in Burma seems to have helped
them. They just got mixed up with the refugees streaming out,
thousands of them. No check on who was who. That's how they
got back—you don't have to look like that!"

Her eyes were wet with tears. "If only Debi had decided to
come with them, he would be here now."

"But don't you see? That would not have done at all. We
would have been bound to report him; we could not have—"

"Never!" his wife snapped with anger. "I would never have let you do that." She dabbed her eyes with the end of her sari. They were silent for a while, both aware that they were on the verge of a quarrel. Then she asked, "What do you think is happening to Debi now, under the Japanese?"

He breathed freely again. The danger had passed. They had been quarrelling too often lately. "It's difficult to say," he told her. "No one seems to know, even in Simla. I expect the Japanese will treat them just as considerately as the British did—no reason why they shouldn't. I have never believed all those atrocity stories myself. Anyway, Mr. Talwar doesn't know. He got away just a few weeks before they took over. Before that, on the whole, the convicts don't seem to have had too bad a time, not like the jails here."

"We must do something for him, just for Debi's sake. How can we face him when he comes back—if he ever does come back?" She dabbed at her eyes again and blew her nose. "Remember how hurt you felt, when he was in Thana, when he refused to let us visit him. How can anything be more important to us than the happiness of our children?"

There was reproach in her tone, mixed with the anguish. He knew what she was thinking about. Not Debi alone, but Sundari too. Sundari had returned from Bombay two months earlier, ostensibly on one of her visits home, and later told them that she was not going back.

At least that part of it had nothing to do with him; no one could put the blame on him. That was something about which he and his wife never quarrelled. They were both partners in this, conspirators almost, because they were aware that neither could be held responsible for whatever had happened, and they were always thinking out ways and means to make her want to go back, to give her marriage another chance. They had both tried so hard to do the right thing by their children. Where had they gone wrong?

He got up from his chair and walked to the balcony, knowing that the question had no answer. The trickle of the river beyond the casuarina grove was thinner than ever; it would remain thin for another month, when the largesse of the flood would make it strong and turbulent again. A cyclist went past the white wall at the back. The heat lay like a blanket, covering everything, and he shut his eyes against it.

Sundari had to go back. Her marriage must be saved. How had he managed to spawn two such self-willed children, determined to get their own way even if it led to ruin? he wondered. His wife was saying something. He opened his eyes and turned back. "What were you saying?"

"Sundari has agreed to go back," she told him.

It was like a breath of cool air through the oppressive heat, and for a few seconds he remained where he was, savouring its caress. And then he was overcome by a sudden sense of gratitude to his wife, knowing that he himself would never have been able to speak to Sundari about her estrangement. He sat by his wife and took her hand.

"Does it mean that they are reconciled, that Sundari will try to make a success of her marriage?" he asked.

"I don't know. But she now realizes how much it means to all of us—they will always say that her husband left her because her brother turned out to be a wrong one. Who would go on living with a girl from a family such as ours—who would put up with a daughter from this house? That is what they will say, even if it is Sundari who leaves him."

"What does she mean to do?"

"She is prepared to wait. She will live in his house, not that it means anything."

"Why doesn't it mean anything?" he asked in irritation. "If they live together—as husband and wife."

"Because Gopal is not going to be there. He is with his regiment, and he may be ordered to the front any day. Anyway, he won't be in Bombay."

"What has gone wrong? Won't she say?"

"She is definite on one point; she refuses to live with him any longer."

"Then what is she going back for?"

"Because I told her it was the right thing to do, for the sake of what everyone will say. Who knows, they may yet become reconciled. The important thing was to get her to give her marriage another chance."

"Why haven't we been able to make either of our children happy?" He asked her the question he had left unanswered himself. "God knows we have both of us tried."

"Who can say? One can only keep doing one's best for them."

They were both silent for a time, aware that they were close to each other once again, sharing the glow of a minor victory. Then she said, "About this man whom Debi sent to you. You must do something. We cannot let Debi down."

How matter-of-fact could women be? Were their minds divided into watertight compartments, which they could open and shut at will? It was almost as though, now that some temporary solution had been found, she had put Sundari's problem aside and was telling him they must now concentrate on the other problem.

But this time he detected no suggestion of reproach, and for that reason his sense of guilt increased. She had always been nearer to the children. If only he had always consulted her . . . and yet, how could things have been different? Once he had reported the theft of the explosives the thing was out of their hands.

The feeling of guilt tormented him. The failure was his, for he should have read the danger signs in time. The boy had always been a stranger to him, and he had made no special effort to bring him up to share his own values.

He himself had been a staunch supporter of British rule in India, not by force of circumstances and least of all for personal gain, but from the conviction that there was no alternative. He shuddered to think what the nationalists would make of the country—people who had not a single constructive thought in their heads and were nothing but agitators mouthing slogans. In the chaos that would follow the withdrawal of British authority, Hindus and Moslems would be at each other's throats just as they had always been before the British came and established peace. Men like Churchill were not fools; the alternative to the British rule in India was civil war.

And there were the terrorists who had attracted his son, pitting their puny rage against the might of an empire, wasting themselves like flies round a roaring fire. Painful as it was to admit it, the British were quite right in putting down the terrorist movement ruthlessly. It was for the good of the country, but how many Indians could be found to say so openly? The papers only registered shock at the firmness with which the revolutionaries were dealt with.

How had his son become a revolutionary? Where had he failed him? Why could he not be like millions of other young men in the country? Tekchand had never understood him.

But he was conscious that his son had not understood him either; the only person who had been close to him was Sundari; even as children they had always stuck together, he remembered. He and his wife were both outsiders, however hard they tried. Suddenly he felt sorry for his wife, for she too had failed, in spite of all her diligent efforts to keep the children happy. They were partners even in this particular failure, but somehow her failure was greater. Impulsively he raised her hand to his lips and kissed the open palm.

"Debi will never forgive us if you do nothing for Mr. Talwar," she said.

Her mind was like a machine, he thought again, the compartment was now open only to the problem of finding Gian Talwar a job.

Was it any use worrying about whether Debi would forgive—Debi who might never return, Debi who had so casually plunged them in shame and sorrow? Debi had nothing to forgive them for; it was they who would have to forgive him. He fretted at the twisted logic of her remark, and yet he knew that she was being entirely herself, ready to forgive, prepared to make sacrifices.

"What happened to the other man?" she asked.

"Which other man?" he asked, suddenly roused from his thoughts.

"The other man who came in the boat."

"Oh, I never thought to ask."

"Darling, it is no use even thinking about it. Our duty is clear. He is a friend of Debi's, and we cannot turn him away. And it seems he is a friend, not just someone who happened to be in the same place at the same time, and who is trying to take advantage of the fact. He even offered to help him to escape."

"So he says."

"And in a way it is our fault for trying so hard to do the correct thing—that is what kept Debi from coming back. Not because of the risks, but because he does not want to have anything to do with us, and also . . ."

"And what?"

"And I don't think Debi trusts us enough to be sure we would not have given him away again if he had managed to escape."

He was grateful for her use of the plural, implying that they were both equally to blame.

"What a horrible thought," she went on, "that our own son

should distrust us. And remember he knew our son before all this happened. They were in the same class at college. This is the least we can do for Debi."

He knew he was losing, and yet he was not angry with himself or with his wife. It was almost as though he had already made up his mind and was glad of her support.

"And what is the danger? What can anyone do, even if they do find out that he is working for you?" his wife asked.

"If they find out who he is, they will almost certainly send him back to jail. As for me, even if they can't prove that I took him on knowing who he was, they will certainly suspect it. That means an official black mark, no recognition, no rewards—possibly even the cancellation of all government contracts."

"Money!" his wife said contemptuously. "What is money? Some things are far more important than money—or titles."

In a way, that was exactly what he too had been trying to say. But the things that were important to him did not seem so to his wife and children. There was prestige, there was business integrity, a reputation for honesty. These things were certainly far more important than money.

He glanced at his wife in hurt surprise; she had been so artlessly captivated by money and all it could buy that he had always thought of her as Lakshmi, the goddess of wealth. In his mind's eye she even resembled Lakshmi, as conjured up by Ravi Varma in his famous painting. Now she was telling him that money was nothing. It was as if the goddess of wealth had suddenly turned her back on gold.

26

Identity Card

THE job was specially created for him; he was appointed ship-ments supervisor for the Kerwad Construction Company in Bombay, with responsibility for speeding up the unloading and onward dispatch of steel and machinery sent out from England for use on the company's projects. Shipping schedules had been disrupted by the war, and movements of ships were kept secret. Until a ship was actually sighted, its arrival was uncertain. There was also an acute shortage of railway cars, and even though the company had high priority, someone had to be on the spot to ensure there were no hold-ups.

The pay was four hundred rupees a month. It suited Gian to be in Bombay, where he was unknown, and the work kept him busy. He liked the bustle of the harbour and the anonymity of being a man in a crowd. Above all, he now possessed an identity card, entitling him to enter the docks.

His name, according to the new card, was Gian Joshi. It was like leaving half your past behind, Gian thought, for he was Gian still; but not Gian Talwar from Konshet village, but Gian Joshi, with a job and a bank account and a small two-roomed flat just outside the Yellow Gate.

At the moment he wanted nothing more from life. He was secure, sheltered, free, leading the humdrum, perfectly normal life that he had longed for; just one of fifty thousand men working on the docks, one of a thousand other Joshis. He had discarded the Andaman chain, the caste-mark of the convict, as he had discarded his Brahmin's janwa; now he carried an identity card.

He loved crowds, as though compensating himself for the loneliness of convict life. In the evenings he went for long walks along Marine Drive, ending up at Chowpatty, savouring the smells and sights, the heady welter of humanity. Only at night, in the loneliness of his room did he sometimes feel oppressed and debased. Some day he would have to leave all this and become wholly free, disengage himself completely not only from his past but from his humiliating obligations to Debi-dayal's family. But the practical difficulties were forbidding. This was a time for a faceless anonymity, a time for waiting—like a tortoise going into a hole for the summer, to lie for months, hibernating.

Oddly enough, unlike himself when he was in the Andamans, he was not disturbed by thoughts of women. The only woman who now existed for him was Sundari, someone wholly out of reach, already married. He had carried her photographs with him for over a year, almost as if they were a talisman. At times he wondered if he was in love with her. He would drop off to sleep, exhausted by his work and his walk, his last waking thoughts of her. And yet, how could he be in love with someone he had seen only twice—love her from afar, like someone in a Victorian novel? Did the loneliness of a condemned man, abetted by a couple of photographs, add up to love?

The fifty-ton crane was coming down, smoothly even if noisily, with ponderous gravity. Its looped chains held a long, swaying girder. Gian watched it, fascinated, marvelling at its precision, knowing that the cradle would descend exactly where the other girders lay, that the girder would be deposited within inches of the others, in the correct position for being loaded into cars.

Someone touched his sleeve. A year ago he would have started with fright. Now he merely glanced at the man who was trying to tell him something, his voice drowned by the clamour of the dockside. He was already a new man, filling out his new personality with ease and assurance.

"What is it?" he yelled.

"A lady is waiting to see you, Mr. Joshi. At the end of the yard, near the oil tanks."

"A lady! To see me? Are you sure?"

He nodded. "She gave your name."

Even as he walked towards the oil tanks, he was sure there was some mistake. Then he saw her, standing in the shade of one of the Alexandra warehouses, fresh as paint against the dirt-smeared oil tanks, wearing a pale blue sari which was so pale that the blue showed only in the folds of the material.

It was Sundari.

He experienced a surge of resentment. It was wrong of her to be there, introducing an unwanted complication in his new life and opening up old scars. He could feel his new self shrinking, becoming conscious of an older self that had been contaminated.

"You look as though you are seeing someone you detest," Sundari said.

"No, of course not," he said guiltily. "It is just that I was seeing to the unloading of the beams—I wasn't expecting anyone."

"That is exactly what I came to see you about. Abaji rang up. He is worried about something called Craddock girders and wants me to ring back and tell him when they might be expected."

He felt instantly relieved. "Tell him not to worry. I have already written to the office. The ship only came in last night. They will get there in six days—seven at the most. The last lot is being unloaded now. That is just what I was supervising."

"Do you have to be there when they are unloaded?"

"Well, unless they are all stacked in one lot, there's no end of trouble when it comes to loading them on to the railway. They also have to be in the correct position so that they don't have to be turned round when they get there."

"He will be so pleased. Can't we go and stand where you can still see to your work and talk there? I have never seen a ship unloading."

She had given her message, and he had given her the assurance that the beams would be dispatched on time. What else was there to talk about? "Of course." He shrugged his shoulders. "If you don't mind the racket."

They went back to where he had been standing, on the greasy dock between the curving black side of a liberty ship and a high wall of cement sacks and tar barrels. The smells of a great port, the bustle of humanity, the noises of scores of derricks, winches, cranes, and donkey engines surrounded them. They stood side by side, the man in his soot-stained overalls who was a part of the background, the slim girl in blue and white, freshly perfumed, the outsider.

"Are those the Craddock girders?" she asked.

"Can't hear you," he yelled, shaking his head. "You have to shout!"

She repeated the question, shouting out the words, and inevitably they began to laugh. Sundari wanted to know all sorts of things about how ships were unloaded.

It was nearly eleven before the last girder was down. He hesitated before he said, "Do you think we could go and have a cool drink somewhere, or a cup of tea?"

He had to repeat the question because she did not hear him the first time, and somehow that made the question sound even more awkward to him.

"I would love to. I am quite hoarse, yelling at you."

"I'll get a taxi," he offered.

"I have a car outside."

They threaded their way out of the clutter of dockside goods, to the high wall of the customs warehouse, beyond which her two-seater Ford stood in the parking lot.

"That's where I live." He pointed as, in the car, they waited for the gate of Yellow Docks to open.

"You mean there? In the old brick building?" she asked.

He was instantly ashamed of himself. The house was a mean, three-storied building, coloured an unrelieved mustard, next to the railway track, and it had an outdoor staircase. The outdoor communal latrines, one to each floor, had their doors open.

"Pretty squalid, isn't it?" he said.

"Oh, I didn't mean that, but—but surely, is it really necessary for you to live in a house like that? The noise, for instance!"

"I like the noise," he told her. "I know what you are thinking. That I could easily find a couple of rooms somewhere nicer. I don't know. I have to save as much money as possible so that . . ."

"So that what?"

"So that I can leave the job whenever I wish to—to be free again. Not to be under an obligation to anyone."

"But you are not obliged to anyone. You have to put in hard work. And look at what you offered to do for Debi."

The little train with its flat cars puffed by, its engine belching smoke against the yellow house. The hamals ran and pulled the gates open. The dammed-up stream of traffic began to move again. "Where do you want to go?" she asked, throwing the car into gear.

"I've no idea," he said. "I mean, I don't know where a man

can take a girl like you for a cup of tea simply because I have never taken a girl like you out—or any other girl for that matter. And also . . ."

"And also what?" she arched her eyebrows.

"And also we'll have to find a place where they won't chuck me out. Look at my clothes!"

"Why, you look very nice in them; handsome! And just for that, we shall go to the Taj. I've promised to meet someone there—and no one cares how anyone is dressed."

It was quite true. The ground-floor tearoom was quite full, but no one took the slightest notice of his clothes. The waiters hovered over them just as solicitously as though he had been wearing the linen-shirt-slacks-and-sandals that had become the uniform of Bombay's elite. They sat over cold lemonades and talked.

"I have been meaning to ask you," she said. "Why were you so anxious not to be recognized when you came to the house to see Abaji?"

He had been thinking what to say if she asked him to explain, and had decided to tell her the truth. "You see, it was important for me to find a job; find someone who would take me on without having the police check my record. Under the wartime ordinances, no one can be employed unless the police have verified his records. I wanted to establish my bona fides with your father before revealing who I was. If he'd found out about my past before I was able to tell him that I had offered to help Debidayal to escape, he would quite likely have sent me away."

"It doesn't sound very plausible to me," she said, but he was glad to see the smile on her face.

"No?"

She shook her head. "Not when you wanted to tell him who you were anyway."

He laughed. "It was just a question of timing. I had planned it most carefully, exactly how I was going to tell him. Seeing you there was something I had not bargained for. It was—it was quite upsetting."

"Tell me, was all that you said about your asking Debi to escape with you quite true?"

He found it easy to be frank with her. "Partly," he said. "The essentials were all true. I did ask him to make the attempt with us. He refused to do so."

"Yes, he is very bitter," she said. "I can understand that he had no wish to come back."

"And I must thank you for not letting me down," he said. "If you had said you had met me before, it might have made things most awkward."

She said nothing for a few seconds. Then she asked, "What do you do with your evenings? I doubt if you have any friends here."

"I have no friends—not a single one. I go for walks, most evenings, to Chowpatty. Then I eat somewhere."

"And then?"

"Then I go back to my room. I know what you must be thinking, but that is how I like it. It is so much better than what I have been used to."

"Would you like to come and see me some time? It might be a bit of a change. We could talk about Debi; there are so many things I want to ask you. You see, I was the only person he was really close to; I would do anything for him, really anything. It was so comforting to know that someone like you was there with him, a friend."

His fingers around the glass were white at the edges, and he relaxed his grip. What would she think of him if she knew, found out that he had prevented her brother from escaping, had been the cause of his being flogged? Out at sea, through the arch of the Gateway of India, he could see a battle cruiser with patches of camouflage paint, surrounded by half a dozen smaller ships; their masts looked strangely like the flogging frames of the Cellular Jail.

"When would you like to come?" she was saying.

"I don't know," he said. "I don't know what your father would think."

"I don't see how that matters. Abaji's just an old woman, always so fussy about wanting to do the right thing."

"Also, I am sure Mr. Chandidar would not approve—if he were to know who I am."

"He doesn't."

"Most people are fussy when it comes to an escaped convict visiting their houses."

It was almost pathological how he could not get away from his convict's past, and he wondered if that was what she was smiling about.

"As it happens," she said, "my husband is away with his regiment, in Egypt. But even if he were here, it would have made no difference. You see, my husband and I never try to keep each other away from our friends—we both agree we mustn't drop our old friends just because we are married."

Friend? he asked himself. The flogging frame with its leather fittings for the neck and arms and ankles was still before his mind, a barrier to friendship; that and the crack of the blue-black whipping cane as it came down to hit the body, making it twitch like a wounded snake.

It was important to say something, something innocuous, to drag his mind to the present and prevent himself from making a false move.

"It is nice to hear that," he said. "Yours must be the sort of happy marriage one reads about in books."

She remained silent for a while. Then she said, "Yes, it is rather like something one reads about in books."

She looked sad, he thought, sad and lovely, so that he wanted to go on looking at her. "To me, you and your family are people one reads about in books," he said. "I never thought that you would remember me."

"But of course I do!" she protested. "So elegant in your bathing trunks; and then you were so painfully shy about the janwa and went off in a huff, showing off your crawl. And when you came back you'd thrown the thing away and wouldn't speak to anyone. You were ever such a serious-minded young man."

It was nice to be remembered; he savoured the delicious feeling of a bygone triumph, however slight.

"Ah, there's the prince," she said, waving her hand.

He watched the fat man who had appeared in the doorway turn his dark glasses in her direction and wave back. He wore a cream bush shirt and beige linen slacks and white sandals.

"The Maharaja of Pusheli," she explained, as the prince came waddling up to their table, bringing with him a wave of some strong perfume.

"My dear girl!" the prince exclaimed in a piping, almost girlish voice. "And to think I have been whiling away my time, knowing that you'd keep me waiting." He held her proffered hand and kissed it and then beckoned to a waiter to bring an extra chair.

"Mr. Joshi." Sundari introduced Gian. "The Maharaja of Pusheli."

"How do you do," the prince said, barely turning to look and putting out a soft hand. "My dear, it's not twelve already, is it?"

"No," Sundari said. "Mr. Joshi wanted me to have a drink. . . ."

"I sent away the car, remembering that you had offered to drive me over. Shall we go, they must be waiting." He rose to his feet.

"Do come sometime," Sundari said to Gian. "Just telephone and say you are coming. The name is in the book." The prince solicitously pulled her chair from behind her as she rose. "Would you like me to take you back to the docks?" Sundari asked Gian.

"No, thank you, I'll find a taxi."

He watched them go, the slim, delicate girl and the fat, uncouth prince. The perfume he wore still seemed to hang in the air. Gian noticed that her white chaplis bore a smear from the sludge of the dockside. In a way the prince had seemed even more out of place in her company than himself. She had come on a mission and had been polite to one of her father's employees. Now she was going off to a party, accompanied by a maharaja, unaware that her chaplis had been soiled by contact with his kind of life.

The prince had taken her arm as though guiding her through a crowded street, and in the doorway he must have told her something funny because they both stopped and laughed.

She wanted him to visit her so that she could talk to him about her brother. He had no wish to talk about Debi-dayal; he did not want to go to her house. Old friend, she had called him. What was the prince? Was he too an old friend?

He paid the bill and rose to his feet. He walked out of the tearoom, carefully keeping his eyes turned away from the cruiser out at sea. The little red Ford two-seater in which he had come was speeding past the Gateway of India.

Sundari's visit had left a mark on his colourless existence. Her talk, artless and gay, her easy laughter, her familiarity with the maharaja, her casual invitation to visit her house, had sparked a new desire within him. He was tormented by a longing for her company and was guiltily aware that the longing bore strong overtones of sensuality.

For a whole week he had tried to fight it off, knowing that it was unworthy of his love for her. But the new hunger within him had made him restless, prodded him on: why should he hold back from what might turn out to be a delightful experience just because of a suburban conscience? People like the prince certainly did not suffer from such qualms; they usually got all the fun they wanted out of life.

And he had given in; he had dialled her number and asked to speak to her. Even as he waited for her to come to the telephone, he was aware that he was facing a turning point in his life.

On the following Sunday he went to Juhu by train and taxi. He had bought himself a bush shirt and linen slacks almost exactly like the Maharaja of Pusheli's, and he wore dark glasses and white sandals. He felt gay and debonair, a young man in search of romance, in tune with the glorious early winter afternoon.

Sundari looked genuinely pleased to see him. Over tea, served on the back veranda overlooking the beach, they chatted pleasantly about Duriabad and about his days in the Andamans, almost as though they really were old friends. For him the promise of the afternoon had already come true. It was an exhilarating experience to be sitting alone with a girl like Sundari, good-looking, sophisticated, making small talk with the waves and tall palms murmuring in the background.

"Wonderful day for a swim," Gian commented idly.

"Oh, what a pity you didn't suggest it when you rang up," Sundari said, glancing at her watch. "I would have loved to spend the evening on the beach. It is just that the maharaja will be here any minute—too late to put him off. He can't bear the sun, or any form of outdoor exercise. Unfortunately, Sunday happens to be the day of his weekly party, and he gets really upset when anyone drops out."

"It was just a thought," he assured her, "brought on by all those palm trees and the sand."

"We'll go swimming next time, I promise. When can you come?"

"I'm afraid only on a Sunday."

"Come next Sunday, then. Bring your swimming things. We'll spend the evening on the beach, and then you stay on to dinner. Shall I ask some people? . . . No, perhaps not."

"What about—what about the maharaja's Sunday party?"

"I'll tell His Highness I can't come. His parties bore me to death, and all his women friends seem to detest me."

He went to Juhu again on the following Sunday, and they spent the evening on the beach. They lay under the palms, sipping beer-and-ginger-beer shandies and smoking, abandoning themselves to the warmth of the sand and the caress of the breeze. It was long after sunset when they came back to the house for a shower and change. And after that they sprawled in cool cane chairs in the veranda, listening to gramophone records, hardly saying a word to each other.

Gian experienced a sense of contentment he had not imagined possible—like a dog slumbering before a fire, he told himself, a stray dog discovering the blessings of a home. And yet he was careful not to linger too long. As he walked the dark, deserted road to the station, he was pleased with himself that the evening had ended as it had; he had not done or said anything to make him feel ashamed of himself. In retrospect, the way in which they had spent their day was much more rewarding than if he had tried to make love to her.

He went to Juhu again a few weeks later, and after that almost every other Sunday. The pattern had remained the same, even if they were aware that they were drifting closer and closer to each other with the inevitability of the tide coming over the sand. It was almost as though they were waiting for the tide to catch them up, rather than walking into the waves on their own, deliberately holding back so as to savour the full flavour of an experience that was new to both of them.

[27]

Chalo-Delhi!

HE was going to be sent to India. At one time it had looked doubtful, as though they had begun to have second thoughts about him. Now he had been told he was going. He wondered what had made them change their minds.

The room in Rangoon's West End Hotel was straight out of Maugham's East: high-ceilinged, cool, spacious, the open doors and windows draped with bamboo blinds to keep out the glare, the furniture heavy and solid; "made in the East to British specifications," everything seemed to shriek.

But the British themselves had left, almost casually, like tenants vacating a house. They had never had any stake in the house itself. On the other hand, even in their hurry, they had actually made efforts to destroy whatever they had laboured to build—all the vaunted gifts of their occupation—not caring how the people of the land itself would live after they had gone. But, like everything else, even their efforts at a scorched-earth policy had been clumsy and amateurish. True, the oil refinery had been totally gutted, but the Rangoon docks were already in use, and the electric power station was functioning normally. The fan in the hotel room revolved at maximum speed.

The contact with the Japanese had been something of a disillusionment; at times he had even thought of making his own bid for escape. But in the countries they occupied there was nowhere an Indian could hope to go into hiding. Nor had there been any opportunity. He was never left unguarded; at all times a Japanese sentry was somewhere close by; a soldier was standing at the head of the stairs now.

And yet, could he not have got away if he had really wanted to, he reproached himself, as Patrick Mulligan had got away?

Mulligan's escape had caused quite a stir in the Andamans. At

247

first the Japanese had stoutly denied that he had run away, and then, almost naïvely, Yamaki had come out and announced a reward for anyone giving information that might lead to his recapture.

Mulligan had been their prize catch. Instead of putting him to death as everyone had expected, they had done their best to make him lose face by putting him to work as a manual labourer, a coolie. Whenever the gangs of freed convicts were marched off to the site of the airfield that was being constructed, they had to pass through the main bazaar so that the people could see for themselves how the once-proud, swaggering super-sahib had been humbled; hobbling along without shoes in the long line of cool-ies, his head hung low, his face haggard, his skin falling in folds like that of an aged elephant.

And then they had heard that, while working on the runway that was being cut through the hills, Mulligan had strayed away and made a dash for the jungle and escaped, risking the fire of the sentries, who had opened up with their tommy-guns as soon as they realized what he was up to.

It was difficult not to feel a grudging admiration for Patrick Mulligan, who had managed to come out the victor in the Orien-tal game of "face," preferring torture and death at the hands of the Jaoras to Japanese captivity, but somehow it was even more difficult to think of someone as tough and plucky as Mulligan letting himself be killed by the Jaoras either.

Debi-dayal wondered what had happened to Mulligan; Mulli-gan, who had escaped while he, Debi-dayal, had stayed back as the esteemed guest of the victors.

Even from his position of privilege, he found them uneasy companions. They were ruthless, overbearing, and cruel—far more cruel than the British could ever be; he had no doubt about that. He had been befriended by them, given special food and comfortable rooms, treated with a kind of stiff Oriental cere-moniousness. But it was difficult to reconcile their flagrant disre-gard for the other prisoners in the Andamans, or for the unfortu-nate Burmese citizens here in Rangoon, with their scraping and bowing, their toothy smiles, their excessive courtesy. He had seen coolies mercilessly flogged for minor misdemeanours, by strutting, jackbooted soldiers, respectable men and women press-ganged into a sweeper corps to clean the city's streets; he had been hor-rified by the callousness—glee, almost—with which they bayoneted their prisoners, and had squirmed at the tortures they inflicted on anyone they suspected of working against their interests. Mulligan's dog, which had dared to bite one of the soldiers, had had its front paws chopped off; at this time it was quite usual to see cattle with great chunks of meat hacked out of their sides because some soldiers could use a few pounds of fresh beef, but still wanted the animals kept alive for future use. He had almost fainted with shock when he had first come across one of those bullocks.

The British were kind to animals, kinder than they were to human beings; one had to concede the fact even if one hated them, but that did not necessarily make them preferable to the Japanese. For one thing, their military performance had so far been anything but creditable. Wherever they had come up against the Japanese, they had been routed. More often they had preferred to withdraw, without even offering a fight, so that even their staunch supporters had turned against them.

The short, balding Indian who had come to see him moppped the sweat from his brow. He wore a crumpled uniform too tight for him, with the badges of rank of a Japanese brigadier.

"We must consider it a privilege—a great honour," he said, "to be fighting side by side with them. They are our saviours. They will liberate our motherland." He uncrossed his bulging legs and loosened the belt of his trousers. "Don't you agree?"

Debi-dayal did not know if it was a trap to get him to speak out his mind about the Japanese. But his visitor appeared not to expect an answer. "Look at me," he went on. "I was an officer under the British, in the Indian army, a captain. We were sent all the way to Malaya—"

"What were you, infantry?" Debi-dayal asked.

"No, the Supply Corps."

"Ah, I see."

"As I was saying, we were sent to Malaya, just to save a part of the British Empire—just think of that! All the way to Malaya, away from our country, our wives and children—for what? To save Malaya for the British. And what happened?" He rolled up his handkerchief and wiped the beads of perspiration from the backs of his hands.

"What happened?" Debi-dayal asked.

"We were routed. Killed like flies, surrounded, caught up. Those lucky enough to escape were made prisoners by the Japa-

nese. But we are prisoners no more. Now they have organized us
into an army of liberation—eighty thousand strong. All trained
soldiers, formed into battalions and brigades and other units,
with our own equipment. And look at me." He tapped his chest.
"Look at me: a brigadier, at thirty—a brigadier. The British have
never made an Indian a brigadier yet. Not one has gone beyond
the rank of major. Just look at the difference!"

Now, whom did he remind him of? The talk was something
like Shafi's—the same earnestness, the same zeal. But Shafi was
hard, openly contemptuous of men like the brigadier. No, he
reminded him of someone else.

"What happens when you run into your own brethren?" Debi-
dayal asked. "Those who are still in the Indian army. Will you
oppose them?"

"But of course! It is the duty of all patriots, of all those who
love the motherland, to put down every obstacle that stands in
the way of liberation. For the sake of our beloved country, we
must be prepared not only to fight the men from India, but if
need be our own fathers and mothers. 'Chalo-Delhi!' That is our
war cry: 'Destination Delhi!' Anyone who stands between us and
Delhi must be destroyed." A drop of sweat gathered on his forehead and ran down his nose. He mopped it up expertly before it
could fall.

The line of talk was straight out of Radio Tokyo. Yamaki had
said the very same things. This man even talked like Yamaki; at
any moment now he would bare his teeth and hiss.

No, he wasn't like Yamaki either, Debi-dayal decided. He was
soft and fat and dripping with perspiration. Yamaki was hard as
wood, alert, a soldier to his fingertips. And this man was too
much wrapped up in being promoted to brigadier at thirty to
make a good soldier. He could not help thinking that only a few
weeks earlier the brigadier had been on the side of the British,
currying favour and mouthing the same sort of platitudes. His
proximity brought on a creeping sense of revulsion. He was the
embodiment of all that was servile in India: the Moghuls, the
British, the Japanese were all the same to them. How many such
creatures did India possess? Thousands upon thousands. Was
that why he had looked so familiar—the picture of India's in-
grained, traditional servility?

"Even the British had no choice," he was saying. "Even
Churchill was compelled to do it."

He must have missed some important bits. "What was Churchill compelled to do?" Debi-dayal asked.

"Why, when Russia was attacked by the Germans, he instantly declared himself on Russia's side: any enemy of Nazism is a friend of Britain. We too have to take a lesson from the enemy. Anyone who is out to destroy the British nation—the Germans, the Japanese—should be welcomed as our friends. We must assist them, fight on their side. It is the duty of all patriots."

"Yes, of course," Debi-dayal managed to say with a measure of eagerness. The sentry outside was joined by another soldier, and they were talking to each other in Japanese.

"We're lucky, both you and I, to be trusted, placed in positions of responsibility. I am sure Netaji himself would have liked to see you. But he is so busy. There is so little time, so much to do. I am glad I was sent to have this discussion with you, before you went back. One thing I wish to repeat: unquestioning loyalty to the cause. We have to prove it, show our zeal in every action. That is Netaji's exhortation to all of us. You don't know how much I envy you—how I wish I were in your place."

So that you could have changed sides once again, Debi-dayal thought to himself, put yourself in the hands of the British, adopted another line of talk.

The brigadier droned on. Even his voice was flabby, Debi-dayal reflected, like that of a eunuch in a harem. Was he one of those? He might quite easily be, with those bulging thighs and puffy, rounded face. How could anyone, either British or Japanese, trust such a man?

The brigadier rose to his feet and hitched up his trousers, pressing down the bulge of his stomach to do up the buttons. He put on his British officer's cap with the Japanese officer's badges of rank on it. He bowed from his waist and put out his hand.

"I am honoured to have met someone like you, sir, a patriot whose zeal has been tested, someone who has made sacrifices for the cause of his country—our country."

Debi-dayal took the proffered hand, pudgy and light like a piece of stale cake, the moisture still clinging to it, and felt a little unclean by its contact. That was what was wrong with India, the shame and sorrow brought on by this special breed. They represented all that was rotten and degrading in the country: its softness, its corruption, its dishonesty. Surreptitiously he wiped his hand.

"Just one thing," the brigadier said. "Remember that where you are going you will be under constant watch—we have agents everywhere. And we judge by results. If the results do not come up to our expectations, then—perhaps there is no need to tell you what happens."

"None whatever," Debi-dayal said.

"The highest priority must be given to the destruction of the river craft in East Bengal. The life of East Bengal is totally dependent on its local shipping."

He had been told all that before, by the Kempitai colonel himself, speaking American English. They wanted to soften up the country, to prevent a British build-up. The traffic in the estuary of two of Asia's greatest rivers was entirely based on the paddle boats and canoes of the villagers. The riverside villagers were almost amphibian. Destruction of the boats could paralyse their life.

Blowing up a bridge or destroying an aeroplane were somehow different; his mind shrank from the idea of causing havoc among the poor Bengal villagers, reducing them to starvation to let the Japanese march into India.

"And you happen to be particularly vulnerable with your—er background," the brigadier was saying. "There is no need to tell anyone as intelligent as yourself that if your performance is not up to expectation, a letter will go to the Indian police, telling them where you are, what you are doing. You know how easy it is to arrange for such a letter to fall into the right hands."

"Oh, yes."

"Good-bye," the brigadier said. "Sayonara!" He gave another Japanese bow, made awkward by the swell of his stomach.

The neck was ideally positioned for a guillotine chop, a quick jab with the side of the palm; just one quick, downward swing, and the brigadier would no longer spout his brand of patriotism.

Debi-dayal rose to his feet and bowed. "Sayonara!"

"Chalo-Delhi!"

"Chalo-Delhi!"

It had been like a turning in the road. He could never become a part of that particular form of degradation. He could understand Mulligan, and he could understand Yamaki. In a way, he could even understand Shafi. What could one make of the brigadier?

A few days later he received another jolt. It was as though the coin had been turned to show him the other side, demonstrating that there was little to choose between two brands of conqueror. Which was more repellent, the ugly blotches showing through the white, or the flagrant yellow of the Japanese?

He had never had much stomach for human misery: filth, squalor, hunger, disease made him squirm. Now, in his trek back to India, just one among thousands upon thousands of refugees fleeing from Burma, they were his constant, inescapable companions. No power that had occupied another country had ever disgraced itself so thoroughly as did the British in their withdrawal from Burma, Debi-dayal kept telling himself; it was far more callous and shocking than the massacre of Jallianwala. An arrogant, unbalanced, bitter man on the spot, ordering his machine gunners to mow down a mob, was somehow less evil than were the authorities in Burma, where a government, its mask of respectability and self-righteousness torn away by a shattering military defeat, had been exposed as an ugly spectre, making the starkest distinction between brown and white.

"Whether you were to be saved or not depended on the colour of your skin," the refugees told him with bitterness in their hearts. "It was not merely a matter of 'white first,' but 'white only.' If the others were slaughtered by the Japanese, it did not matter."

What had happened to the book of rules, to the haughty awareness of the white man's burden? Debi-dayal asked himself. The veneer of centuries of civilization seemed to have been flung to one side. Women or children, old or infirm, it had made no difference. The essential qualification for being evacuated was white skin.

His anger and bitterness mounted with the tales of discrimination the refugees had to tell. In the past, even though he had hated the British, he had still felt a grudging admiration for their tradition of fairness. Now, curiously enough, he found himself a little ashamed at the way they had handled the Burma evacuation.

Even before the fall of Rangoon, the big trading corporations had set the pattern by beginning to evacuate the women and children of European officials. Soon afterwards the Burma government woke up to its responsibilities to its own kind, and it too carried out an organized evacuation of the families of officials.

The Indians were left to fend for themselves. As it happened, they too were outsiders, just as much as the British were, having gone to Burma in the shadow of the flag, following their British masters. The Burmese hated them, if anything, worse than the British. Once the British had gone, the Indians and everything they possessed were at the mercy of Burmese hooligans. While the battered Burma army was in headlong retreat and the government radio was exhorting everyone to keep calm, not to panic or run away, refugees were pouring out of the country in thick swarms, choking the roads.

On the way they died like flies; they were butchered by Burmese strong-arm men for their little trinkets, decimated by cholera, smallpox, dysentery, and malaria; their womenfolk were taken by anyone who fancied them. But most of all they were destroyed by hunger, falling in their tracks and never rising again. Those who fell were left to die. Of the torrents that left Burma, only a pitifully thin trickle reached their destination, a thousand miles away, having walked all the way through jungle and marsh and mountain. There they were herded into camps and forgotten, like luggage piled up in an abandoned railway yard. They had crossed the great rivers of Burma, clinging to rafts, their children tied to their backs, while the planters, the oil men, the timber wallahs, and the administrators rode back in boats and motor lorries requisitioned by the government, and long processions of elephants trudged all the way from Burma to India, bringing up the whites who were left behind.

The ugly worm of hatred which he had carried within him all his life reared its head once again, now more grotesque than ever. If ultimate proof of the wrongs of foreign domination were needed, here it was. Beside it, the barbarity of the Japanese paled into insignificance. People of one colour had been ruling those of another, vehemently justifying their rule, proudly asserting that they were there only for the benefit of the ruled. But when disaster struck, a disaster brought on by their own decadence and incompetence, they had no time to worry about the obligations of a government to the governed. They had decided to abandon everything and clear out.

Their plans for evacuation, such as they were, envisaged only the evacuation of their own kind, though this did not deter them from seizing all transport, private or public, regardless of whether it belonged to those being left behind. Even his father, staunch supporter of British rule, would have been shocked, Debi-dayal felt.

He had much time to think as he made his way back to India over the mountain paths. What puzzled him most was why the callousness of the British evacuation of Burma had shocked him even more than the Japanese atrocities he had seen. Was it because the British were always to be judged by their own code of conduct?

They had decided to leave the country to its fate and pulled out. That sort of thing could never happen in a free country. Its officials would hold on to their posts if only because they had nowhere to go; they would have no other choice than to stay there and fight, to keep doing their jobs.

And yet, would they? He thought of the Japanized Indian officer who, a few months before, had been an Anglicized Indian officer. Under the British he was a captain; under the Japanese he called himself a brigadier. Would that sort of man ever stand and fight? Or would he always be ready to change sides and rush forward to welcome the victor? What difference did it make to such a man if his country was ruled by the British, the Japanese, the Germans, or even some other people like the Chinese?

The Japanese escorted him right up to Kohima. Only a few miles farther on, he ran into the swarms of refugees. He had a background story of having worked as a clerk in an Indian store in Rangoon. He had no papers to prove his identity, but neither had the other refugees. Unlike them, he had plenty of money with him, separate bundles of hundred-rupee and ten-rupee notes, secreted in his belt. He had been warned not to touch the money until he reached India. He went with the crowd, buffeted, questioned, documented, marked down in a register for employment, and finally forgotten in one of the dumps along the Manipur road, piled up with human flotsam from Burma.

After six weeks in the camp, he was once again on his way, carrying a cyclostyled letter from the Commissioner of Refugee Employment, in which his new name had been inserted in the blank space intended for it. It said that the bearer, Kalu-ram, an evacuee from Burma, should be provided with a job.

In the northwestern corner of Assam one of the assistants in the Brindian Tea Company interviewed him and sent him off to a tea garden called the Silent Hill, as an assistant stockman. His superior was a meek little Indian called Patiram.

By now Debi-dayal had made up his mind. He was not going to choose between two brands of world conquerors, between playing the role of the Indian brigadier to Yamaki or of Gian to Mulligan.

He was grateful for his new-found anonymity and remoteness, and yet he was gnawed by an inner uncertainty. What had happened to him, he who loved to be in the midst of strife, to make him want to shun it now? He wanted nothing of either the British or the Japanese. For the moment he was prepared to sit back and wait, while the two titans fought out their battle for India.

He was determined to keep out of the struggle, not to side with either the British or the Japanese; that much was clear. But, in doing so, was he like someone waiting on the sidelines for his own turn—a wrestler waiting impatiently for the main bout to finish before his own match was called up—or was he a mere onlooker who had no intention of entering the arena? He wondered whether all the exposure to what Gandhi had described as man's inhumanity to man had converted him to his doctrine of non-violence. Or was it just his feeling of revulsion against his fellow Indians, men like Shafi, the brigadier, and Gian Talwar, that had made his spirit curdle?

He did not know the answer, the rights and wrongs were so inextricably mixed up, but he was conscious of some great change that had come over himself. He felt weak, like someone waiting for outside guidance, as he tried to convince himself that the matter was out of his hands and that the war between the Japanese and the British would not be affected either way by his own puny efforts. He would lie low till it was all finished. That would give him time to think things over. Once the struggle had been resolved, one way or the other, the issues would be less complicated. That would be the time for him to jump into the fray and resume the struggle for the liberation of his country. Until then, everything would have to wait; even the settlement of his score with Shafi would have to wait until the war was over. For the present, it was enough that he was back in India.

And even in that remote corner of the country, so far away from its heart, he could see signs of the national ferment. The walls of the small bazaar of the Silent Hill estate were covered with thick black slogans scrawled in Hindi, Bengali, Assamese, and English.

QUIT INDIA!

"Quit India!" It had almost made him laugh. The British had left Malaya and Burma, but certainly not in response to such slogans. Those who had called on them to quit were now languishing in prison. The British would never quit a country just because a lot of men dressed in dhotis and white caps implored them to do so. The appeal could be regarded as either pathetic or ludicrous, according to whether you were Indian or British. The British would give in only to force. If only the terrorist movement had gone on and had flared up as widely throughout the country as Gandhi's non-violent agitation seemed to have done, this would have been the time for the final assault on the British. They would have needed just one last push. In Assam, he observed, many of them had already begun to evacuate their women and children. It was almost as though they anticipated the last, unthinkable contingency—mass withdrawal from India.

And so Debi-dayal waited, marking time for the war to finish, filling out his new personality as Kalu-ram, a refugee from Burma who had been made assistant stockman at the Silent Hill Tea Garden in northwestern Assam.

[28]

"The Docks Have Gone!"

SUNDARI was bending over the table, cutting out a choli according to the paper pattern, when she heard the explosion. The walls of the house shivered as though a giant had shaken it, and the glass panes rattled. Somewhere below, a door banged with the report of a rifle shot.

She ran to the window. The sea was a bright blue-green under the baking April sun, and still as glass. But even as she watched, the tops of the palm trees shuddered as a great wind swept from over the sea, and then she saw the faint white ridge on the surface of the water, crawling towards the shore. She stood entranced, holding the side of the window, conscious of the sound of footsteps and of agitated talk below stairs. The white line rolled on, with incredible speed, gathering size; it soon became an immense wall of water, rushing towards the shore. It caught up a tiny sailboat and swallowed it, leaving no sign, and then rushed up the beach with a hiss and a roar, sweeping over the fishermen's puny canoes drawn up on the sand and the nets spread out to dry, rushing muddily through the palm trees lining the shoreline, to spend itself in the garden below.

Baldev, the bearer, the maid, and the mali all came running into the room, open-mouthed and dazed, chattering incoherently, but at the sight of the water rushing right below them, at least two hundred yards beyond the normal waterline, their babbling stopped. They stood behind her, watching.

The wave receded, almost reluctantly; now, on its return journey, a mass of yellow scum like an overflowing drain, back to the sea which was no longer blue-green but dirty, the colour of boiling sulphur.

"What is it? What's happened?" she asked.

258

"It must be bombs," Baldev said. "I heard the explosion. I felt the shock."

"It must have been an earthquake," wailed the maid. "Hai-hai! May God spare my dear ones!"

They ran downstairs and into the garden. People from adjoining houses were already out, their heads turned towards the city. A tiny black cloud towered high over Malabar Hill.

"That's smoke," the mali said.

"The bombers have destroyed the city. The Japanese have reduced the city to dust," Baldev said.

Even as they watched, the cloud billowed up until it was an enormous grey-black cabbage, blotting out the outline of the city.

"It's a fire, it can only be a fire," the mali said.

"Hare-ram! It's the greatest fire anyone ever saw. The whole city's ablaze—every house is burning; look at it!" Baldev said. "Look at the smoke."

"Everyone must be dead." The maid moaned. "Ayaya, what could have happened to my sister? With a newborn child, too!"

Realizing something terrible had happened, but still unaware what it was, they stood watching. On all sides, people were coming out of their houses, excitedly asking what it could be. The smoke was like a giant playing in the bright blue sky, assuming frightening shapes to scare them.

"They say the docks are on fire," a cyclist yelled from the road. "Some ships in the docks have blown up!"

At first the words were just a part of the background, a new voice added to the nervous chatter of the onlookers. "What is it? What did he say?" asked Sundari.

"The docks have gone!" someone answered. "Finished!"

Then it registered. "The docks!" Sundari gasped. "Oh, God!"

It was almost useless to think about it. The young man in the soiled overalls standing on the wharf, the dingy crumbling house with its outdoor latrine near the railway track. She ran to her car, parked in the porch. She had to go, to see for herself what had happened.

She drove fast. The smoke was now tinged with red. Even on the Worli stretch, she could feel the taste of dust and ashes in her mouth. Now and then a tongue of fire would leap up in the smoke, losing itself instantly. How many fires were there? she wondered.

The roads leading to the docks were jammed with cars. Men
and women were milling about in panic. At the corner of Craw-
ford Market she found it impossible to turn left, where the traffic
had come to a standstill. She turned right, sped along the almost
empty road past the art school, only to encounter another traffic
jam in front of the post office. She wheeled back again, was
sworn at by a lorry driver who had to screech to a halt to avoid
hitting her. She drove into the car park at Victoria Station and
parked the Ford there. Then she ran back into the milling
stream of traffic, threading her way to the docks. At the end of
the road the traffic again came to a halt. No one was allowed to
proceed farther. She pushed her way to the front, broke through
the police cordon, and ran up to the Victoria Docks Bridge,
which stood empty before her. A helmeted British soldier barred
her way. The bridge had been damaged, he told her; parts of it
had already fallen down; the remainder would crumble at any
minute. No one was allowed across it.

She stood for a moment, glaring incredulously at the red-faced
soldier, when behind him she suddenly saw the centre of the
bridge cave in just as he had said, and a cloud of dust appear.
Then she saw the devastation all round. The dust and the pun-
gent fumes from the fire made her nostrils smart. Not a single
building seemed to be intact. Many had fallen down, and dust
was still rising from their debris. Others had had their roofs and
walls blown off in segments. A crumpled railway car was lying
beyond the railing of the bridge, upside down, like a beetle on its
back, with its wheels and springs exposed to view. The nearest
railway track must be at least a hundred yards away, she
reflected. She turned to the left, peering in the direction of the
Yellow Gate, where the railway track was. She could see nothing
because of the thick blanket of smoke and dust.

She turned back and almost stumbled on a man lying close to
the wall, sprawled out like one of the hundreds of homeless men
who sleep on the sidewalks of Bombay. But he was a white man,
and stark naked. It was only after she had passed that she realized he must be dead.

She ran back through the crowd, jostling, cursing, pushing her
way, not caring what they thought or said. When she came to
the edge of the crowd, at first she did not know where she was,
because there was nothing familiar about the locality. Then she
realized that she was right in front of the main Alexandra Docks

Gate. Again she ducked, broke through the crowd, and dashed to the entrance.

The enormous steel gates were lying awkwardly twisted on their hinges, and the high walls enclosing the dock area were full of gaping holes. Again there was the ubiquitous British sentry, standing squarely in her path. "You can't go in, miss," he said cheerfully. "They're expecting the whole place to go up in flames."

She felt trapped, on the verge of tears. "I just have to go," she pleaded. "I have to find someone. . . ."

"Them's orders, miss. No one can go in, except for wives and mothers."

"My husband works there," she told him. "My child is there— please, please!"

He waved her on. "Don't stay long, ma'am," he said. "And good luck!"

She thanked him and rushed past. The paved yard felt hot under her feet, and she realized she had lost her chaplis in the scramble. Now there were more bodies, some grotesquely mutilated. They were all completely hairless and all were white. Only a few of them seemed to have any clothes on. Then she realized that they were not the bodies of Europeans. They were Indians burned white by fire.

"Oh, God!" she said. "Oh God!" She ran towards the Yellow Gate.

The great cobblestoned yard was completely deserted. The railway track had been torn up and the rails twisted into grotesque shapes. The wooden sleepers on the track were still burning. The damage was more severe as she went closer to the Yellow Gate. Not a single house seemed to be standing. Somewhere a bell was ringing; a loudspeaker had come into action, and someone was shouting instructions in a distorted, foghorn voice. Nothing was familiar. She stood uncertainly near the railway gate for a few seconds before she realized this was where she had stopped her car, waiting for the gate to open. In the place where the three-storied building had stood was a heap of rubble. The doors and windows of the building were still on fire, making jagged, geometric patterns of red.

She stood rooted to the ground, staring at the fallen house and coughing in the heat and smoke.

The bell was ringing again, much more loudly. All around her was the sound of running footsteps. The loudspeaker had gone on blaring without let-up, telling them, in Hindi and English, something about the outer perimeter wall. Almost involuntarily she tried to concentrate on the words: ". . . close to the customs shed wall inside the main gate of Alexandra Docks . . . safe from blast."

Someone was speaking to her urgently, almost angrily—one of the men running. He had stopped and was trying to say something. She turned upon him in irritation. He was black with soot and oil, and his clothes were charred and in shreds. "What are you doing here?" he was saying. His voice was thick and gruff.

"Oh, leave me alone!" she said viciously, angry at being accosted. And then she realized that there was something familiar about the face and figure. It was Gian. She flung her arms around him and pulled him tight to her chest.

He held her shoulders and pushed her away from him roughly. "Come on, they're expecting another explosion," he told her. His voice was a hoarse, throaty whisper. His clothes were drenched with oil and his boots were squelching. There was a spot of fresh blood on his shoulder, and as they began to run she noticed that he was limping.

Arm in arm, they joined the throng of dockworkers all running in the same direction, yelling to each other, "Run! Run!"

The firemen were dragging back their hoses, hoping to save them for other fires, long black snakes following the running men, glistening in spite of the gloom and the smoke. The loudspeaker was more insistent now, announcing only in English, "Make for the wall! Lie flat down! On the other side—on the side of the street! Down flat, down flat!"

At last it loomed before them, the high wall surrounding the main customs shed, a part of the original wall erected in the days when the British fort of Bombay was built for defence. About a hundred men were lying prone against the wall. They flung themselves down, in the press of other bodies, clinging to each other, while more and more people kept coming and throwing themselves down on both sides of them.

They waited, panting, not daring to speak, their bodies wringing wet with sweat, in the midst of strangers, like lovers locked in each other's arms in a crowded railway carriage. The minutes passed. The clamour of the loudspeaker was like a record stuck in

a groove. ". . . make for the customs shed wall near Alexandra
Gate . . . lie down flat . . . down flat . . . on the street side
. . . on the street side . . . down flat . . . make for the . . "

And then everything was drowned in the convulsion for which
they were waiting—a hundred express trains converging, roaring,
hissing. They were lifted up and flung away by the earth rising
under them; and suddenly the air was full of smoke and dust and
pieces of burning cotton.

The men lying all around them were on their feet—running
away. Sundari raised her head. Things were still falling, whistling
through the air. Drums of burning oil soared up and fell down in
slow arcs; a heavy bar of some metal came and smashed against
the wall, only to drop harmlessly, bent into an L. The loudspeaker had stopped.

Suddenly they were alone; everyone had gone. "Come!" she
called out. "They've all gone!" And then she realized that he lay
limp in her arms, his eyes closed. God, was he dead? She grabbed
his shoulders and shook them. "Come on! Wake up! Everyone's
gone!"

He opened his eyes and blinked, almost coming out of a sleep.
In her relief, she bent down and kissed him on the mouth.
"Come on. Get up!"

He pushed himself into a sitting position, panting with the
effort. Then he said, "Look! They've all gone. You had better go
now. It is quite safe . . . so they say . . . until another ship
blows up." His voice cracked.

"What about you? Where will you go? Your house . . ."

"I'll find somewhere to go. They are bound to make some
arrangements. I don't know, not just now. Just now I want to sit
here and rest, do nothing." He leaned back against the wall.
"But please go away from here. Please; it is dangerous to hang
about here."

"Isn't it dangerous for you?" she asked.

"I belong here." He slid back into a more comfortable
position, and his eyes began to close.

"Steady! You're not going to black out again, are you?" she
asked.

He blinked and shook his head but said nothing.

"You are coming with me. I won't leave until you get up.
Make the effort, now! Come on—that's better." She almost

pulled him to his feet and began to lead him away from the wall.
"Try not to put any weight on the leg," she told him. "Lean on
my shoulder." They began to pick their way through the debris.

The car was hardly a quarter of a mile away, but it took them
an hour to get to it, stopping every few steps because of the pain
in his leg. His face was bathed with perspiration, and his hands
felt cold. She wiped his face with the end of her sari before she
started the car.

Gian lay on the sand, wearing linen slacks and a bush shirt,
making furrows with the toe of his white chapli, preparing his
mind for what he was about to do. He glanced at Sundari, lying
next to him, relaxed, unsuspecting.

He could never be like the prince, he had decided. His upbringing, his background of Hindu orthodoxy, the narrowness and
rigidity of a schoolboy conditioned by Aji and Hari, had
triumphed over his new-found disregard for convention. This was
something he had to do, if only to salvage his ego.

The heady plunge into unrestrained sexual intimacy was something he had accepted avidly, not knowing where it would lead
him and not caring, consoling himself with the thought that he
was incapable of resisting it. It was as though their venture into
romance had broken away all barriers. Now, he told himself, she
was like a she-leopard who had found a foster-cub, showering her
love with a fierce possessiveness, sheltering and protecting him.

She had no business to come barging into his life that day of
the fire, he kept telling himself; after that it was almost inevitable that they should abandon all restraint. He had allowed himself to be taken back to the house. She had put him to bed and
sent for a doctor to examine his leg. There had been nothing
seriously wrong; a small splinter of metal had cut right through
his calf. The doctor probed and dressed the wound and gave him
a sedative. He had dropped off to sleep instantly. But he could
easily have left the next morning; he should have insisted on
doing so, Gian told himself.

Instead, overcome with languor, he accepted her hospitality
and stayed on in the secluded house on the beach, knowing that
her husband was away somewhere in the Middle East, and savouring the anticipation of a romantic idyll.

But now the thought that his romance was built upon a
foundation of deceit tormented him; he reminded himself that

he had not hesitated to take advantage of her vulnerability. This was the moment to cry a halt, the time to thrash things out. He had made up his mind. He was going to open his heart to her and tell her he loved her. After that it was up to her. He could no longer continue with a substitute for love.

After the intimacy of the past four days, it was going to be like tearing out a part of himself, but he was elated at having brought himself to face the situation and to find that his suburban rectitude had surmounted the corrosive damage suffered in the Andamans.

"I just have to do this," he told her, "for my sake as well as yours. Because I love you."

She had been lying beside him, not saying anything, letting him talk away. Now she leaned over on her elbow and looked at him. But he went on staring at the sea, not daring to trust himself to the impact of the blood-red swimming costume that was so daringly brief, the bare brown body with long, slender legs and small-boned arms and that almost Spanish face with its pointed chin and high cheekbones—so much like that of her brother.

"Love," she said flatly, "is not an emotion for grown-ups. It is something only for schoolboys and girls, and for poets who died before they grew up."

"I don't know about the love of poets. I know my own love, and it's like a fire—something that keeps a lonely man going."

She reached out and patted his hand. He turned and looked at her. On her face was a smile, a smile almost of amusement. "In any case, you don't have to feel guilty. I love you too."

What did she mean by that? Was she thinking of the momentary, wholly sensual intimacy of the past few days, or of the desperation with which she had pulled him to her chest in the docks?

"But you don't realize," he protested. "I've loved you ever since I first saw you. I swear I've never thought of another girl—not even in all those days in the Andamans. It was you, you, all the time, even in my dreams. You don't believe me? No, no; I tell you I am about to make a sacrifice—giving up what I most want—knowing what is best for both of us." He produced his wallet and pulled out the photographs. "Look! Do you remember sending these to your brother?"

Sundari held the photographs in her hands. The colour had

gone from her face, and there were two tiny furrows above her nose. "But I sent these to Debi—with money hidden inside!"

He did not hesitate. The lie came easily to his lips, since he knew that he alone would suffer from it. "I begged Debi for the photographs, and he gave them to me, knowing how I felt about you. Yes, he knew. There were few secrets between us."

The lie had come and gone. It left no aftertaste.

Sundari leaned back and lay on the sand, her eyes closed. She looks so pure and helpless, he thought, and yet, it was because she was so vulnerable, so trusting, that it was important to make her realize that his love too was pure.

She had removed her rubber bathing cap and the wet strands of stray hair clung to her forehead. Her limbs glistened with flecks of fine sand. A thought, wholly sensuous, crossed his mind. That was the sort of impulse that had made him forget himself so irrecoverably three days earlier. He shook his head. A moment earlier, he reminded himself, he had been speaking of love that had to be pure, telling new lies to prove how pure his love had been.

He went on, stung by his own sense of guilt. "And when I speak of love, I mean an open, world-defying love, not a clandestine, hole-and-corner affair. I want you always, yes, always, forever and forever." Suddenly he leaned over and gripped her shoulders, his fingers clamping tightly like brown claws on the bare flesh. He saw the bright flecks against her closed eyelashes, but did not know whether they were tears or moisture from the sea.

He let her go, and she lay back as she was, rigidly, with her eyes still tightly shut. "Doesn't it mean anything to you at all? I want you to be my own, share my life. Doesn't love mean anything to you at all?"

She could not tell him, because she did not know herself. What was love? Love was a little girl's crush on Ronald Colman, something kindled by a glance and a smile from a man from another world, a flame kept alive through the frustrations of a honeymoon by tenderness and self-flagellation, and then smothered in one evening by a hard-faced woman in a satin swim-suit; it was something that could be shattered by a society whore, a perishable, tender thing for tender ages.

After that, love was a game, a game strictly for grown-ups, so that if you were not sufficiently skilful you could be broken by it;

heady, exciting, polychromatic, a thing of retaliation, of playing a card in the same suit, and if your card was higher, you won the trick. For a queen card in a stunning red costume, a king card in dark glasses; an overripe society bitch mated with a brown and handsome man in soiled overalls.

You had to learn about love, as you had to learn about drinking; and that was not something you could learn in an affluent family house in Duriabad or in the Silver Jail. It thrived best in the circle of the rich and the gay, took its proper place as an exciting accompaniment to life, but never as life itself. What was love but a sparkling, synthetic companion of an evening, a sneaking away from a dance to go for car rides and not returning until the small hours of the morning . . . ?

Or was it the hollow feeling deep within one that made one want to cry out, the desperate rush to a scene of convulsion to see an old building, the impulsive flinging of your arms around a man in a dirty, oil-soaked work suit, and the sudden wave of gratitude that followed.

"But there's another side too," he was saying very quietly. "And that too has to be faced. I have little to offer, but if you ever become mine, we shall be comfortable. I have money saved. Not anything that can run to this, but a small flat and middle-class living. I can buy a business of my own, make money—and who knows, even this, a big house, servants, may be possible. With you, nothing would be impossible; without you, life will mean nothing. As soon as the war ends, I shall go back to the Andamans."

"Andamans!" She looked up with sudden interest. "I would like to go there. Debi will be there."

"That is what it means to me," he said. "With you, an assumed name, happiness, who knows, even prosperity. Without you, the Andamans."

"But you don't have to go there, even without me," she pointed out. "Why can't you go on living here?"

"Because I shall have nothing to live for here. Why should I remain here, a man who never was? I shall go back to the Andamans proudly, buy a cottage, a beach of my own. And I shall have served the ends of justice."

She gave a nervous little laugh. "The ends of justice!" she repeated. "Such a terrible phrase—so sinister; the ends of justice."

"That is what I had to say—all I have been meaning to say. But I have my pride too—some semblance of it, I suppose, for pride is a queer luxury in one who has worn the Andaman collar. To me, there is something shameful in what I have done, taking advantage of you, forgetting myself. I want to be able to hold my head high, if such a thing is still permissible to someone like me; to be able to go and tell everyone—the world—that we are in love."

He was so desperately earnest, still the college boy who had been offended because they had joked about his sacred thread, she caught herself thinking. Why did he keep on mixing it up with love, thinking it was something to be ashamed of? He had committed murder and had spent time in jail, yet he was afraid to flout convention. She, on her part, would have had no objection to her husband's knowing about it. Was it not he who had written the rules of behaviour in their marriage?

But she could see that Gian would never understand. Instead of taking what was there to take, he was determined to let it go on hurting him, like those short-lived poets of love. For his kind of love there was no easy, uncomplicated solution.

"I plucked up courage to say what I did because I saw that you cared; otherwise I would never have insulted you by offering my humdrum life against this sheltered living, the car, the servants. Why should you give up all this? Why? There can be only one reason: because you don't love him. Otherwise . . . otherwise what has happened would never have been possible. That was my only excuse, the reason for bringing all this out; that was what gave me the courage. When you brought me out from the docks, looked after me, when we kissed, lay together—did not all that mean anything to you?"

"Of course it did," she told him. "It meant a lot to me."

"That is what I wanted you to say, longed for you to say. Now the choice is yours. And this is how I want it to be between us. It is best to leave it like this, before I forget myself again and degenerate merely into a creature of lust. Don't you agree?"

She nodded, ever so lightly. How little he had grown; how much he still resembled the boy who had petulantly dived into the river. The drops of moisture on her eyelashes were now fuller, and the flecks of sand on her limbs shone like stars in the dying sun. The two photographs, now yellowed and curled, were still clutched in her fingers. She was so desirable, so forlorn. He longed to put his arms around her and kiss away her tears. Instead, he stood up, dragging the leg which now had a large plaster across the gash, and tightened the straps of his chaplis.

"I want to leave it like that," he said, "and I promise you will never be disturbed by me again, never. But one thing I do ask; I think I have right to ask after—after what has happened. If you ever decide to share my love, marry me. You only have to say so. I shall come."

He turned and walked away, without a backward glance.

The Process of Quitting

NO one was supposed to know anything about the Bombay explosion. The newspapers were forbidden to publish reports or pictures; even the casualty figures were a secret. In the midst of a war, any mishap in a great port was an official secret, to be kept from reaching the enemy.

But within a few days, everyone in the country seemed to have heard about it. Its causes were not known, its details outrageously garbled; but everyone was aware that it was one of the greatest disasters of the war: the port had been almost wholly wrecked and its shipping brought to a standstill; dozens of ships had gone up in flames, complete with their cargoes, and buildings all around the docks had been flattened.

Hundreds of Indians had lost their lives, but very few of their countrymen bothered about that; the sacrifice was insignificant compared with the results. Inwardly most of them chortled with glee; the destruction was a blow to the ruling power. In the spring of 1944 the British had very few friends left in India. The Empire was ready to fall like a ripe mango into the hands of the waiting Japanese.

The face of India was covered with the slogan, crudely painted in clay, chalk, vegetable dye, charcoal, or red ochre, across roads, on the trunks of trees, on walls, on motor buses, and around telegraph poles.

QUIT INDIA!

Debi-dayal realized that the slogan which, when he first came across it, he had dismissed with contempt as the humble submission of a milksop organization had by now taken the whole country by storm and acquired new significance.

Somehow things were moving inexorably to a climax of violence; it was almost as though Shafi Usman's prediction were coming true. "In the midst of non-violence, violence persists," Shafi had told them. Was this what he had meant?

Debi-dayal had been astounded and secretly frightened by the change. He had tried to analyse it, poring over the papers in the reading room of the Silent Hill library, discussing the situation with anyone who was prepared to talk to him.

In their anguish and frustration, fired by their anger at the mass arrests of their leaders, goaded by the thought of the Japanese armies poised for an offensive, the people had chosen to discard their vows of non-violence. At least a part of the heat was generated by the authorities' repressive measures: the callous prison sentences pronounced on Gandhi and Nehru, the methods used to break up demonstrations. It was almost as though the British had forsaken their proverbial restraint and had suddenly decided to entrust the administration of the country to hundreds of General Dyers pressed into service to smash the national agitation. They had imposed a reign of terror upon the populace. Passive women blocking the streets of Bombay were dragged away by grinning British tommies; all meetings were invariably lathi-charged by the police. At Ballila, in the United Provinces, someone had even brought Dyer's technique up to date and had a crowd machine-gunned from the air; the Benares Hindu University was delared closed for alleged subversive activities and its premises taken over by the army; hundreds of Congress camps and offices were burned down under official supervision; crippling collective fines had been imposed on entire villages for sympathy with the movement.

The repression had clearly backfired. It had provoked the mobs into acts of violence. There were hundreds of instances of railway stations, post offices, and police stations burnt down, telephone and telegraph wires cut, and, in one place, a policeman burnt alive.

Meanwhile those who had the power to restrain the people, to persuade them to refrain from violence, were kept securely locked up in prison.

The authorities had swung into action with unprecedented virulence. The prisons of the country overflowed with its patriots. Sixty thousand people were arrested in the last four months of 1942. After that the arrests went on with warlike resolution, but the figures were not made available to the press. The Calcutta *Statesman*, mouthpiece of the ruling power, published a daily list of nationalists who had courted arrrest. The paper headed the column "The Crank's Corner."

It was almost as though the British were striving to convert the non-violence of the leaders of India into the violence of the terrorists; to discredit the movement in the eyes of the world by forcing it to become violent.

For Debi-dayal, it was like a dream come true.The nationalist movement was hardening, being transformed into a revolutionary movement. The British themselves had brought it about. You could not keep the spirited men of a nation tied down for long to bullock-cart speed and to the vegetarian logic of the Indian National Congress.

The time was ripe. The British were fighting with their backs to the wall, suffering humiliating reverses everywhere, losing thousands of tons of shipping every day. Never had their rule been more abhorrent to the people of India; freedom was closer at hand than at any time since the revolt of 1857. The Japanese army, mightier than ever in victory, was at the very gates, gathering for a final blow. India was ready to receive them, to welcome them as the Burmese had welcomed them.

And now they had blown up the docks in Bombay. He was convinced that it was the terrorists' work. He admired their planning, preparation, and patience. Hundreds of men working secretly, waiting for the moment, knowing that some of them would have to sacrifice their lives. They had gone to their deaths cheerfully. It was heartening to think of such men; so long as they were there, India still had a future.

The thought of his own lack of action tormented him. It was nearly two years since he had been sent back to India, charged with specific tasks and provided with ample funds. He had allowed himself to be swayed by the arrogance and the ruthlessness of the Japanese into a position of neutrality. How could he hold his head high in a Free India, knowing that he had spent the crucial years of the struggle in the placidity of an Assamese tea garden?

It was almost as though he had turned to non-violence himself, he thought with a shudder, while the Indians whom he had pitied for being non-violent were shouldering the weight of the struggle and softening up the ground for the Japanese march to Delhi.

"Chalo-Delhi!"

And almost inevitably, like a spectre, the image of a fat Indian in a crumpled uniform, sweating at every pore, marching at the head of the column, came to him, like a bad smell curdling his enthusiasm. What would the Japanese bring? What would they do in Delhi once they had marched up to the Red Fort? The same sort of freedom they had brought to Burma? To the Andamans? Would he ever be able to hold his head high if the Japanese became the rulers of India?

He had wavered, racked by confusion. He had gone on working methodically and diligently in the tea-garden, comforting himself with the thought that he could never prefer Japanese rule to that of the British. At the end of 1944, when Patiram, the stockman under whom he worked, was made assistant manager, Debi-dayal was offered the post of stockman. He had been so used to the perquisites of unimportance and anonymity that promotion came as a jolt. But he took on the new job, knowing that he would not hold it for long.

For once again the wheel had turned. The Japanese, who barely a year earlier had seemed invincible, had been dealt a series of shattering blows by the British and the Americans. The opening of the second front in Europe, which no one had thought probable, then had come to pass, and the Anglo-American and Russian armies were already deep inside Europe, bearing down upon Germany from all sides. It was only a question of time before the Germans would be vanquished. Then the Japanese would experience the full fury of Anglo-American might.

It made his mind reel, but it was true. And although it was not his, Debi-dayal's war, the prospect of an Anglo-American victory was somehow less abhorrent than that of a Japanese victory. He had seen the Japanese from too close to wish that their rule should replace that of the British in India.

Admittedly, even as things were going, the war would still last a long time, for the Japanese were determined and resourceful fighters. He felt thankful that there was still much time before he would have to face the issues squarely; it was only after the war had ended that he himself would have to plunge once again into the struggle for freedom.

The complications were being resolved, and yet, the thought of involvement in revolutionary activities had made his mind shrink. Two years of softness, of introspection, of worrying about rights and wrongs, had only increased his uncertainty; for the rights and wrongs seemed to be still as hopelessly mixed up as ever. He would have to talk it over with some of the others, seek their guidance to help him to make up his own mind. How long did he have? How much longer would the war go on?

And then came Hiroshima and Nagasaki, reminding him that the time for decision was at hand.

He left Silent Hill on the very day the war against Japan ended, threading his way carefully through the bazaar, where the coolies were waiting in long lines for the ration of rum they had been promised to celebrate the victory.

[30]

Founder Members

THE two-room tenement in Talkatora overlooked one of the
bustees of Calcutta, a welter of rusting tin and fabric and card-
board, where men and women and their cattle, dogs, and cats
lived, procreated, and died. One of the rooms was the kitchen
and had a tap for their baths and for washing their kitchen
utensils; the other was the bedroom and sitting room.

Basu's wife brought out cups of tea and a plate of sondesh,
keeping her face covered with the palla of her sari as though she
observed purdah. The two children went in and out of the two
rooms, excited, babbling in a mixture of Hindi and Bengali.

"I could take ten days' leave," Basu said at last. "Since you are
so keen."

"But aren't you keen yourself?" Debi-dayal asked. "Don't you
want to see him?"

"I can't afford to get mixed up in anything like that just now,"
he said. "Look at that!"

"That" was the dark, frail woman who was his wife, sitting by
the smoking kitchen fire, her face still covered by her sari, rolling
the flour for the loochis; "that" was the quivering poverty of the
house, the smells of the bustee, the two unkempt children, the
pile of washing that lay under the kitchen tap.

"Would you consider it presumptuous if I offered you some
money?" Debi-dayal asked.

His host laughed. "Oh, you don't have to be so sensitive about
it. Of course I wouldn't. I'm too far gone to worry about things
like that."

"It is not my own money, anyway," Debi-dayal told him. "Ill-
gotten wealth. Would a thousand rupees be any use? Of course, I
could give you more."

"It's as much as I earn in a whole year! Yes, a thousand would
be most welcome."

"And I don't want you to think that it has anything to do with what you have agreed to do. I mean, I'll pay you the money even if you don't want to come with me."

"But of course I want to go with you, see the ———'s face when you confront him. It is just that I am so tied down and helpless because of all that." And again he waved his hand towards the kitchen.

Debi-dayal could understand his hesitation. Basu was one of those who had got off with a lighter sentence. He had not been sent to the Andamans but was allowed to serve his term in the Baripada jail. He was still on parole, though; he must not get implicated in any activities which might bring him into conflict with the law.

"I don't think we shall have to do anything particularly violent," Debi-dayal tried to reassure him. "I'm not going to pick a fight with him—if it can be helped. But still, on second thoughts, I think it would be just as well for you to keep out of this."

Basu held out his hands. "Do you think I have started wearing bangles?" he asked dramatically. "Become like one of those people who have taken a vow of non-violence? Of course I want to be in on this. I promised myself when I went to jail—that's why I checked on his whereabouts carefully. It's just that I'm so tied down with family life."

"I don't think you should get involved with people like myself again."

"Oh, no, I want to be in on this."

"As you like."

"Besides, they won't let you in. I am known there. The durwan—the watchman at the door—knows me. I used to tip him well."

"Are they very strict about letting strangers in?" Debi-dayal asked.

"Oh, very. No one more particular than one of these old-fashioned brothels. They check every visitor. You have to be—sort of introduced."

It was difficult to reconcile Basu with his older self—as a debonair young man who prided himself on his prowess with women and boasted about his credit rating in houses of ill fame in Delhi and Lahore.

"Does he live there permanently, do you think?"

"I was told he doesn't. He comes and goes. Whenever he is in Lahore, he stays there."

"What a pass we have come to, fighting amongst ourselves, just when we should be concentrating on the British," Debi-dayal lamented. "It is almost as though just when they are on the point of leaving the country, the British have succeeded in what they set out to do. Set the Hindus and Moslems at each other's throats. What a lovely sight!"

"Do you want to see a lovely sight?" Basu asked, suddenly roused. "I'll show you one. Dipali!" he called. "Dipali! Come here. Come out and be introduced to my friend!" He jumped up from the bed on which he had been sitting and darted into the kitchen. He came out, holding his protesting wife by the hand, the two frightened-looking children trailing their parents. "Look! Look at this lovely sight!" Basu said. He pulled the sari away from her head, exposing her face. "Look!"

Debi-dayal winced. One side of her face was like a large wound that had healed, the skin all puckered up and shiny, with the eye a small pink slit like a wound still open. It was as though some wild animal had clawed the side of her face. "She was a lovely sight!" Basu was saying, "Lovely as a Bankimchandra heroine. And now look what they have done to her!" He let her go with an expression of disgust, and she hurriedly covered her face again and scrambled out of the room, the two children now clinging to her legs.

"I am very sorry," Debi-dayal said. "How did it happen?"

"Someone threw acid at her face—an electric bulb filled with sulphuric acid. That is the standard weapon of the Hindu-Moslem riots, don't you know? That is what has happened to the face of India—the mutilation of a race conflict."

"Did the Moslems do it?"

"Who else? Who else would attack a Hindu house? When a race riot starts, it is the time for settling private scores."

"But how did it happen? Where had your wife gone?"

"She had gone nowhere. She was here, leaning out of the window, looking at the lovely sight you see below, one of our greatest bustees, with the hooligans of both sides going for each other. That was when someone threw the bulb at her face. Possibly some Moslem buck with an urge to seduce her, working it off. That is what made me join the Mahasabha, parole or no parole. I could not keep out. We have to become aligned, in sheer self-defence. Hindus against Moslems."

"And to think that we used to sit together and partake of beef and pig—to symbolize our unity."

"But this is how things have developed in this country," Basu said heatedly. "What had been aimed against the British has turned against itself. And the ugliest thing it has bred is distrust. No Hindu can trust a Moslem any more, and no Moslem trusts a Hindu. The country is to be divided. That is what Jinnah wants; that is what the Moslems want. But before that division comes, every town, every village, is being torn apart. The Moslems don't want freedom for India unless it means the carving out of a separate state for themselves. They fear the Hindus will domi-nate them. They insist that when the Congress ruled, just at the beginning of the war, they treated the Moslems as a subordinate race."

"What is going to happen, do you think?" Debi-dayal asked.

"Isn't it clear as daylight? The moment the British quit, there will be civil war in the country, a great slaughter. Every city, every village, every bustee, where the two communities live side by side, will be the scene of war. Both sides are preparing for it, the Hindus and the Moslems. The Moslem League and the Hindu Mahasabha are both militant."

"It almost makes one think that non-violence is perhaps the only answer," Debi-dayal commented.

"Non-violence!" Basu said with scorn. "How can anyone be so blind? How can you go on striving for perfection and at the same time believing it's already there? You can't change the human race overnight. Non-violence is merely a pious thought, a dream of the philosophers. I shudder to think what disillusion confronts them; what Gandhi will feel when he sees the holocaust that will engulf this country. He will die a thousand deaths, I tell you, he will suffer for each single man that suffers, Hindu or Moslem but will he ever recognize that mankind is not prepared for true non-violence—will never be prepared? No! No! He will go on living and preaching his dream. Would you remain non-violent if someone threw acid at the girl you loved? Would Gandhi?"

"We may not hold with his philosophy," Debi-dayal said. "But no one can doubt his sincerity. Personally, I don't think he would retaliate with violence—"

"Sincerity! Are we not confusing sincerity with a delusion, something brought on by wishful thinking, endowing the human race with virtues it does not possess? And then again, has Gandhi himself not expressed doubts about it? 'What if,' he says, 'when the fury bursts, not a man, woman, or child is safe and every man's hand is raised against his neighbour?' That is exactly what is going to happen, what is already happening today. And the only thing we Hindus can do about it is to get ready for it, as the Moslems are doing. Unless we are prepared to meet violence with violence, we will perish. If our answer to Moslem fury is to be non-violence, then we shall be a slave race again, within weeks of the British leaving us. Non-violence is all very well, if the other party too plays by the rules. It may prove an effective weapon against the British because of their inherent decency. How far would it have gone against Hitler? Yes, tell me, what would non-violence do against brute force?"

"I don't know," Debi-dayal said weakly. "The Jews are said to have tried it."

"Yes, and what happened to them? Did you see the pictures of Buchenwald? Of Belsen? Read the accounts? They were exterminated like some kind of pest. . . ." He stopped.

His wife brought out the brass thalis with the mounds of loochis and katoris of bagoon-bhaja and macher-jhol and placed them on the little bedside table. He stared at her for a long time, as though at a stranger who had interrupted their talk. Then he gave her a smile. "Come on," he invited Debi-dayal. "I don't think you will have tasted spiced fish quite like this. It is a speciality from Dohazari, that is where she comes from."

But Debi-dayal still had a question to ask. "Tell me," he said, "do you think the Congress movement has been just as much of a failure as ours?"

Basu took a deep breath before he spoke. "It is an even greater failure. But will they ever admit it? They will take all the credit for achieving independence when the British finally leave, as though all that the others have done, the Mahasabha, the League even, means nothing. But there is a greater failure still: the emasculation of the people—making them into a nation of sheep, as Shafi used to tell us. That is what our organization, the Hindu Mahasabha, is attempting to remedy. But it may be already too late. The results of what non-violence has done will be seen—seen as soon as the British leave us to our own devices. For every Hindu that had to die, five will die because of the way the doctrine of non-violence has caught on. More women will be raped, abducted, children slaughtered, because their men will have been made incapable of standing up for themselves."

"The loochis are getting cold," his wife reminded him.

"And what will Gandhi do? He will go on a fast," Basu went on, ignoring his wife. "A fast to purify himself, perhaps a fast unto death. But will he ever admit failure? That non-violence itself has failed? No. And one thing more. What is the future for a country nurtured on non-violence in a world of mounting violence? Tell me that. How are we to survive, defend our borders? Can a non-violent nation have a violent army, a navy? We will be sitting ducks for anyone who chooses to pick a quarrel with us; Burma, Ceylon, this new country, Pakistan. If non-violence is the bedrock of our national policy, how is the fighting spirit to manifest itself only in our services?"

"The loochis are getting cold," his wife said again.

Basu glared at her. "That is the spirit of non-violence for you!" he said to Debi-dayal, pointing a finger at his wife. "Her face has been ravaged by a hooligan, and I, her husband, have done nothing to avenge it. But will she ever be angry with me, tell me I am a no-good bastard who cannot look after a family? No! She is Mother India, dammit—non-violent! All she is worried about is that I should eat my food while it is still hot!"

[31]

To Fold a Leaf

SHAFI USMAN lay stretched on a charpoy put out in the courtyard of a house in the second lane in Anarkali. He was wearing
knitted cotton underpants and nothing else. Mumtaz, one of the
girls from the house, was rubbing sandalwood oil on his arms and
legs and back. Shafi lay sprawled with his eyes closed, surrendering himself to the heat, the soft fingers kneading into his back.

The courtyard itself was in shade now, but the walls were
throwing out the accumulated heat of the day. From outside
came the noises of a city beginning to stir after the torpor of the
summer afternoon. Doors shut against the heat were being
thrown open to let out the used-up air; the streets were being
sprinkled to keep the dust down; the famous halwai shops of
Anarkali were removing the moistened cloth covers from the
man-high mounds of sweets, yellow, white, pink, green, and
brown, overlaid with gold and silver foil and dripping with
grease; the Sikh food shops were getting ready for the evening
rush; the fruit venders were assembling the baskets of mangoes
and custard apples and Lucknow melons under little awnings.
The smell of the summer day was everywhere, unmistakable,
heady—a mixture of khas, mango-blossom, spices, frying food,
sweating humanity, horse manure, rotting vegetables, and open
drains.

Outside the house, a three-storied burnt-brick structure with
pigeonhole windows, there was a red and yellow board saying
that it was out of bounds to all troops. That was the way all the
city brothels were marked, as some said, to make it easier for the
soldiers to find them. From street level half a dozen stone steps
led up to a heavy wooden door. When the bell rang a peephole
in the door was opened to establish the visitor's identity before
the door was opened.

He was now fully relaxed, almost asleep under the pressure of the kneading fingers, enveloped by the scent of sandalwood oil. He was at peace with himself, aware of a sense of purpose and direction. He had changed, almost inevitably, as the whole of India had changed. The fervour of youth had been tempered, its follies rectified. The Hanuman Club, the partaking of a beef-and-pork dish, belonged to an uneasy past. As far as Shafi was concerned, it was almost a lucky coincidence that the police had caught up with them, for he had now become convinced there was no possibility that the Hindus and Moslems could live to-gether. The days of religious unity, trying to organize the Hindus and Moslems and the Sikhs and the others to snatch power from the rulers, were gone. The Hindus had shown their hand.

The talk with Hafiz had opened his eyes. Hafiz was his friend, and now they were working in the closest collaboration. He had begun to see things for himself, subordinating emotion to logic, countering anger with cold facts. The facts were there, unassailable. The Hindus and the Moslems were traditional ene-mies. They would never be able to live together. That was what the trial spell of provincial government had demonstrated. Now the Moslems must fend for themselves. They were unquestiona-bly the superior race. They had conquered the whole of India, ruled it for centuries before the British came. It was unthinkable that they should now allow themselves to be relegated to a posi-tion of inferiority, crushed by sheer weight of numbers.

He had been saved just in time, Shafi told himself; even if he had arranged the whole thing himself, he could not have done it better. Neatly, at one stroke, all the Hindus in the Hanuman Club had been arrested and put into jail. That had been the recompense for the police atrocities in Bombay that Hafiz had told him about. But after that it had been necessary for him to lie low. Those whom he had betrayed knew too much about him. He had shaved off his beard and discarded his turban, and with it had gone the kada, the kirpan, and the kangi of the Sikh religion. How absurd it had been, he kept telling himself, going about as a Sikh, when one detested them even more than one did the Hindus.

But now the danger had passed. Once again he was as active as ever, building up his groups, patiently biding his time. Until it came, it was necessary to lie low. The warrant for his arrest was still pending. Besides, it was all the more important now not to expose himself to danger when everything was working out so neatly. It was clear that the British were ready to pull out of the country. Only the terms of the transfer of power were to be agreed upon. The Cripps mission had made it clear to the Hindus that they would not have it all their own way. The Congress had been desperate to grab power and create an India ruled only by the Hindus so that they could ride roughshod over the Moslems who once ruled them. It was the vengeance of sheep. The Moslems would never agree. To them independence was worth nothing unless it also ensured freedom from the domination of the Hindus. They would never live in an India where they were only a tolerated minority.

For Shafi and millions of other Moslems, the resolution of the Moslem League in which Jinnah had demanded the creation of a separate state carved out of India had crystallized the issues. When Hafiz had talked about it, six years earlier, it had seemed an absurd conception; now it was the bedrock of their political faith. The British were going away. Now the fight was no longer against the British, but against the Hindus who were aspiring to rule over them. It was Jehad, a war sanctioned by religion, a sacred duty of every true believer.

Jinnah had given direction to their struggle. But Shafi, Hafiz, and the others were not the men to abide by Jinnah's discipline. To strive to achieve their goal by constitutional means was one thing; it was the politician's way, slow and tortuous, like a legal battle in the courts. Unless it was backed by terrorism, the Hindus would never concede their demands with grace. It was essential to draw blood, to shed blood, confront their adversaries with fire and steel, the prick of the spear.

They were already operating in Rawalpindi and Multan and Bhawalpur. The Hindus had already begun to leave the districts. The task had just begun. They had to ensure that not a single Hindu remained in the part of India that was going to be theirs. But with the British still firmly in the saddle, it was necessary to work in secrecy. The moment the British left, they could come out into the open and make an all-out effort to purify the land. The organization was ready for its tasks.

When would that time come? Shafi asked himself. It was already the beginning of 1946. How long would it take for the British to clear out?

A year? Two years? Then they would plunge into their war, as he had no doubt the Hindus too were planning to do. But the Hindus were pacifists at heart, their leaders fond of extolling secularism. They were soft and shrank from bloodshed. They would never be a match for the Moslems in civil war—not even the Mahasabhaites, Shafi told himself, with all their talk of a pure India, which was nothing but a retort to their own demand for a pure Pakistan. Even their militancy was a pale imitation of the creed of the League.

In the meantime, there was work to do. Money was the most urgent need, but the Hindus seemed to have it all. People like Dewan-bahadur Tekchand—he was worth millions, and growing richer every day, with all his contracts.

But this was no time to think of money, he reminded himself, or of work. This was an interlude of relaxation in this pleasant establishment with its garish "Out of Bounds" board at the door. Some said it had been in existence in the days of the Moghuls, and even in those days out of bounds to troops because it was a training ground for the concubines of grandees. Those were the days, Shafi ruminated, when the Moslems ruled the entire country, and were not struggling for just a portion of it. But he was sure that even in those days the girls in this place could not have been more desirable.

And there could hardly have been anyone as beautiful as Mumtaz.

Shafi smiled as he thought of Mumtaz. He rolled over on his back and screwed up his eyes against the harsh glare of the afternoon sky and closed them again. For a moment he thought of himself as a Moghul nobleman, lying on a divan, with the harem favourite rubbing sandalwood oil into his body. He opened his eyes again. Mumtaz was bending over him, her breasts straining against the white cups of her choli. Her upper lip was beaded with sweat; wisps of copper hair stuck against her forehead; her hands were smeared to the wrists in oil.

She was something like one of those paintings in the Anarkali shops, he thought, fair and small-boned and slim. Who could have sold her into prostitution, he wondered, to be trained in the art of making herself agreeable to men? His glance travelled round the courtyard. The door leading to the back of the house was closed. There was no one on the outdoor staircase leading to the first-floor entrance, which was a sort of emergency exit. He reached out and made a quick grab for Mumtaz, but she must have guessed what he was up to and nimbly jumped out of his reach. She stood back, leaning against the wall, laughing and frowning at the same time.

"Come here," Shafi ordered.

Mumtaz shook her head. "I have finished," she said.

He found himself resenting her aloofness. Was it just a part of the training, to show reluctance to such advances in order to make herself even more desirable to her customers, or was it a genuine aversion to himself? He had noticed it before. "What's wrong with you? Come on," he said irritably. "Or do you want me to get up and drag you here?"

"Have some shame," Mumtaz admonished. "In broad daylight, here, in the open—like fowls!"

"In the evenings you get involved with—with the routine of the house," he complained. "I hardly ever get to see you."

"There is a living to earn," she said. "I have to entertain anyone Akkaji tells me to."

"You tell them to go to hell. You just keep yourself free, see?"

"I can't help it if I am the most sought-after girl in this place. You have to settle it with Akkaji. Your money is as good as anyone else's."

"You are not really the most sought-after," he taunted. "What about Azurie? Yes, and Nisha?"

She made a face, as if to register disgust. "Everyone to his own taste. Anyway, Azurie's gone. Already sold. That marwari from Jaipur. Eight thousand rupees. Fancy anyone paying eight thousand for Azurie. She has already had two babies."

"You're just jealous because the marwari bought Azurie when he could easily have bought you."

"There is no accounting for tastes," she said, "if a fair-complexion is all you want in a woman." She shrugged her shoulders. "They're all like that, the marwaris. He was such a nice man too, almost sixty. And rich! Oh, he was rich! Lucky for Azurie."

"You should have been paraded without clothes, as they do in Paris.Then he might have chosen you."

"Disgusting!" she commented. "This is a respectable house. Who will take off one's palla, just to be looked over—thu!"

It had always amused him, this pretence of respectability in a whorehouse. "You might as well not be wearing anything, the way the old woman makes you dress in the evenings—all that gauze."

"That is the traditional costume, designed by the Emperor Shah-Alam, so they say. The older women, like Azurie and Nisha, are thankful for the gauze," she taunted. "A girl's best friend, they say—hai, the sun has already gone down. I'll have to go and bathe and get dressed."

As she was passing him he made a grab for her and pulled her on the bed against him. She struggled, panting, beating her hands against his chest, pushing herself away. "You keep yourself free this evening, see!" he warned. Then he let her go.

"Why don't you settle that with Akkaji?" she protested. She was breathing heavily and her clothes had become dishevelled. "What is the point of pestering me, when—"

"Akkaji's after money, the bloodsucking old hag!" he snapped.

"Shush!" she warned. "She has the ears of a donkey. What do you think she runs a business for? She has to charge for what she gives."

"Money! Money! Money!" he said in sudden anger. "It's only these Hindus who have money. The banias and the marwaris, fat lecherous swines, sit respectably in their shops all day and then come here, slobbering at the mouth, making offers to buy up girls as if they were sheep or cattle!"

"What do you think we are here for?" Mumtaz retorted. "Not to spend the rest of our lives in this house! Who will look at us when we are old? We have to find a man who will keep us to look after him and make him happy."

"One of these days I'll come here myself, loaded with money, and make an offer for you," he told her.

"You!" She laughed. "You are not the type who buys. You come and go, paying for an occasional malish. What will you do with a woman of your own? I don't even know how Akkaji lets you live here whenever you come, free."

"Money!" Shafi spat in disgust. "Damn all money and damn all women who run after it!"

Money was one thing he lacked. But not for long, he consoled himself, not for long.

Just as they turned into Anarkali, Basu clutched his sleeve. "Remember what you promised," he entreated. "Please."

"Yes, yes," Debi-dayal said. He looked strangely relaxed. Basu did not like it.

"You know how dangerous he can be."

"Of course I shall be careful."

"And if there is any trouble, a scuffle or anything, clear out. We will meet in Dabbi-bazaar, in front of Lachhi Ram's shop. Oh, I know you can lick three men like Shafi, if it comes to a scrap. But we have to keep out of trouble."

"There won't be any trouble," Debi-dayal assured him. "Not at this meeting anyway. Remember Shafi's a wanted man too. He'll think twice before starting a row. We'll just tell him we know everything and see what he has to say. It's something I have promised myself. Then I shall plan how to play it."

"It goes against the grain not to pick a row with him right away," Basu said ruefully. "But we must wait; the time to come into the open is when the British leave."

Debi-dayal nodded, almost absent-mindedly, but did not say anything.

"There it is." Basu pointed to the "Out of Bounds" sign. "I will knock. I am known—at least they used to know me."

Shafi heard Akkaji's tortured breathing as she came up the stairs. She entered his room without knocking. "Two men out there say they want to see you," she announced.

"What sort of men?" he asked, suddenly alert.

"No, no, they're not from the police." She gave a toothless grin. "There's no one at the back entrance. When it's the police, they always have a man at the back entrance first, before they come in."

"Did they give any names?"

"Don't be ridiculous! It's a rule of this house that no one is ever asked his name. Who would give his real name here? They gave made-up names. One said he was Ram, the other said he was Rahim."

"Oh!" Shafi gasped. "Oh my God!" He shot a quick glance at the door beyond the courtyard, at the outside staircase that ran down to the street, wondering if he could slip away without anyone's knowing. "Didn't you try to put them off and say you knew nothing about me? They don't even know my name; I mean, my real name."

"I don't know your real name either," she commented. "But why are you so nervous? They may not know your name, but they described you. They say they're old friends. If I'd had them thrown out, they might quite easily have gone to the authorities. And then where would I be—a respectable house like this?"

"That type does not go to the authorities," Shafi pronounced bitterly.

"Yes, but they can always make a telephone call, or send a letter without signing it."

"What do they look like?"

"Very respectable, and one of them has a lot of money. He took out a bundle from his pocket—all hundred-rupee notes. They said they'd come to help you."

Shafi glanced nervously at the staircase once again. "Is the courtyard door locked?" he asked.

Akkaji gave another grin. "They're not from the police, and they look quite harmless. Why don't you take a look, from behind the screen—where the clients sit to look at the girls. Who knows, they may really have come to help you, to give you money."

"All right," Shafi agreed. "I'll take a look, from behind the screen." He rose to his feet.

The terrace where they sat was straight out of a Sher-Gill painting. The seamy side of a city lay exposed beneath them: cows, dustbins, nursing mothers, clotheslines, outdoor privies, and the walls of houses plastered with cow-dung cakes, all rendered romantic by the perspective and the pink and blue effects of the summer evening. A hundred yards beyond the huddle of houses at the end of the Khan Market, they could see the narrow one-man staircase leading up to the third-floor room of Sehgal Lodge, the red brick structure with pigeonhole rooms opening off the passages on each floor. That was where they had been staying till an hour earlier.

"I really don't think Shafii would go as far as that," Debi-dayal pointed out. "After the first few minutes, he seemed quite eager to be friendly, wanting us to have a meal—"

"How could anyone be so brazen as to think we'd sit down to a meal with him, after what he did?" Basu shook his head in disgust.

"Even if they do come after us I doubt if it will be tonight," Debi-dayal said.

Basu shrugged his shoulders. "We'll just have to wait and see.

Luckily, we can see everything that's happening—the way the street light falls on the staircase."

"Personally, I no longer feel any real hatred for the man," Debi-dayal remarked. "He's just like everyone else in India now, in one camp or the other. I thought he seemed genuinely repentant."

"And cagey as hell, too, wanting to know what we were doing and exactly where we're staying. Too eager, I thought."

"Somehow even that does not strike me as odd," Debi-dayal said. "We'd traced him, so in a way he had a right to know where we were living. Fancy holing up in a place like that! In a house of ill repute!"

Basu laughed. How squeamish Debi-dayal was, in spite of becoming a terrorist and going to jail. "I thought it was very sensible. Obviously he knows the old woman well; maybe she's some sort of relative. Evidently he's never here for more than a few days at a time, and what you call a house of ill repute is often the safest place for anyone wanting to lie low. It's always under police protection; if their hapta is paid regularly, they guarantee not to interfere. What better hiding place could you wish for?"

"No wonder he resented being discovered. But otherwise I didn't object to his behaviour."

"But surely when he insisted on coming all the way back with us to where we were staying, didn't you feel he wanted to check for himself? Then he could make an anonymous call to the police and tell them that a runaway convict and a paroled terrorist are living in Sehgal Lodge."

"I really can't imagine he could bring himself to do that. He said he was sorry, explained why he had to give away only the Hindus, because the police already had our names on their list—"

"You don't know how things have changed in this country in the last six years," Basu said, shaking his head. "It's as though, as far as you were concerned, the clocks had stopped; as though the Hindus and Moslems were still united instead of nursing hatred for each other, only waiting for the signal. . . ."

"The clocks had stopped for me," Debi-dayal said, "but the Japanese started them again. It gives me an extraordinary feeling that we should be nursing so much hate against someone we used to venerate; he was like a dedicated prophet, and the fervour with which he talked was spellbinding."

"He is still everything we thought him to be, make no mistake," Basu cautioned. "Only, he has changed his targets. He is still the dedicated visionary who lets nothing come between him and his mission. But his mission is different. That's all."

"He certainly seems to have fallen for that girl."

"Mumtaz? I may say I can't altogether blame him. He's dying to take her out of that place."

"I don't know how he is going to manage that," said Debi-dayal. "He doesn't look as though he has money, yet he was saying it will cost about eight thousand. Who on earth do you think would want to buy a girl from a place like that?"

"Banias, mostly," Basu explained. "They are what you might call the principal props of the system. It used to be Moghul noblemen; now they are all impoverished, and the Hindus have taken over. They have all the money; and, poor things, they themselves are married off terribly early, to girls even younger than themselves, children, almost. They prize these girls highly and take them as concubines. Even their wives are said to approve."

Debi-dayal made a face. "Fancy falling for a prostitute. How could one ever fall in love with someone who'd been brought up in a house like that? And the girls too? How can they go off and live with anyone who pays the price?"

"That sort of girl does not understand love as you and I do. The men are happy enough to take them because they are trained to sing and dance, trained in what they call the art of making love. The girls are content to go with whoever pays the price. The house, for them, is only a sort of finishing school. It works out well in the end. Many of them find places in the harems of one or the other of the princes; some, no doubt, get tied up with dirty old men; some, when they lose their charms, are driven into the streets; but the large majority become the mistresses of rich merchants and live in comfort, almost as members of the household. It's all in the game."

"So all Shafi need do is to find the money?"

"Oh, yes, that's his only worry. It doesn't matter whether she wants to go with him or not."

An hour had passed. The clamour of Anarkali had died down. The city was preparing to sleep. Debi-dayal was dozing, but Basu remained watchful, like a sniper waiting for his target to appear.

At times even he experienced a flatness, as though he were playing some children's game and waiting for make-believe robbers to
show up.

The Sher-Gill street scene had been submerged by a blanket of
hot darkness and dust. The street lights had come on, making
long, uneven lines in the darkness, hiding the ugliness and the
dirt and the squalor of the bazaar. In the distance, one of the
lights shone clearly on the open staircase of Sehgal Lodge, showing it up as a pattern of black and white rectangles.

Basu stifled a yawn and cupped his hands to his eyes. "Oh my
God!" he cursed. He nudged Debi-dayal. "Look! The swine! The
bloody, double-crossing crook!"

As Debi-dayal sat up and looked where Basu was pointing, his
face, even in the half-darkness, was deathly pale.

A man in white Punjabi clothes was climbing up the stairs
slowly, pausing at each step to listen before taking the next.
Even at that distance he was recognizably a Punjab policeman in
plain clothes; they could see he was still wearing normal uniform
chaplis. His shadow broke the even black-and-white pattern of
the staircase.

When the man was halfway up, another figure, this time a
uniformed policeman, appeared and stationed himself at the foot
of the stairs. They saw the first man go up to the room they had
occupied and knock on the door.

After that, things happened quickly. Whistles blew; black police cars came screeching and blocked both entrances to the lane;
squads of policemen jumped out and stood in groups on each
side of Sehgal Lodge.

Basu turned to Debi-dayal. He was startled by the pallor on his
face. "I told you this would happen."

"Yes, you certainly did. And my God, you were right!"

"I'm sorry; I mean, I'm sorry I turned out to be right."

"I'm sorry too. Yes, this explains a lot."

It did indeed. This was not something that had just happened
to them; it had happened to the whole of India, multiplied
hundreds of thousands of times, wherever Hindus and Moslems
lived. For a long time they lay there in the darkness without a
word. It reminded Debi-dayal of the time when he and Shafi had
crouched behind the tree, looking at the burning aeroplane. At
last he stood up. "Come on, let's go," he said to Basu.

"You mean leave Lahore? Now?"

"No, there's something that must be done. I am going back—to the house of ill repute."

Basu put a hand on his shoulder and shook it. "Are you crazy?" His voice trembled. "We'll pay him back, but there's an easier way. A letter to the police, telling them where he's hiding. Then wait for a chance to leave the city."

Debi-dayal shook his head. "That's not my way of paying people back. Besides, just now he is bound to be there. Later, when he knows this has misfired, he won't—you can bet on that. He's too clever to stay put when he realizes someone's gunning for him and that his whereabouts are known—just as we were, in clearing out of Sehgal Lodge."

"But he's bound to go back there—for that girl. You know how crazy he is about her." Basu thought he saw a smile cross Debi-dayal's face. "But what do you mean to do?" he asked. "Kill him?"

Debi-dayal shook his head. The smile still lingered on his face. "No, I don't even mean to see him," he said. "Not unless he comes butting in."

"Then why go back? What do you mean to do? It's dangerous!"

"Just now it's as safe as it will ever be for us. Tomorrow might be dangerous. He'll certainly clear out, but the next thing whoever tipped off the police, his accomplice, will do is to make the police keep watch at the brothel for when we come back. Just now you can be sure they've been careful not to mention the place at all. You know how the police work. So does Shafi; if they'd realized that the tip had come from the brothel, the first thing they'd have done was to keep it under surveillance. That, neither Shafi nor the old woman would want."

"I still think it is a great risk," said Basu. "Why go looking for trouble?"

"Of course, you needn't come with me," Debi-dayal told him.

Basu turned on him angrily. "You don't think I am like Shafi, do you?"

"Don't be silly. But this is my business—almost private business. Why should you risk your neck? You're a free man. You don't want to risk jail for something like this. It's different for me."

"Don't insult me, Debi. I want to come, whatever the risk, if you're going. And for me there is no risk. They wouldn't send me back to jail just for going into a brothel." He paused. Then he added, "Unless you mean to kill him."

Debi-dayal gave an audible sigh and patted his shoulder. "No, no; of course I don't mean to kill him. I'm just indulging a whim, really."

"You're not planning to break his neck or anything, are you?" Basu asked anxiously. "One of your Japanese tricks."

"Not unless it becomes absolutely necessary. No, there'll be no rough stuff, I can promise you. But I really wouldn't like you to get involved. I can manage this on my own."

"Don't be absurd! Damn it, I want to come! I wouldn't miss this for anything. Not after coming all the way here from Calcutta."

Debi-dayal gave him a quick smile. "All right, then," he said. "You guard the outside. If there's any danger, anyone suspicious approaching, just give me the warning. You remember our old drill, don't you? Just say 'Jai Ramji-ki!' as though you were greeting the man, loud enough for me to hear. Then I can make my own way out and we meet here. All right?"

"If you insist. But I'd have liked to be with you and see Shafi's face. How long do you expect to remain inside?"

"Not more than ten minutes or so, I hope. But we'll have to hurry, particularly if what I propose to do is not to take more than a few minutes. And remember: after I have left the place, keep waiting for a few minutes to see that Shafi doesn't follow. Then make your way here and wait."

They circled the house twice before Debi-dayal went up the steps. The watchman at the door let him in with a smile and salaamed when he was given a rupee. In the sitting room, done up in Moghul style, with velvet curtains draped on the doors and large brocade-covered bolsters placed neatly against the walls, were the girls, now dressed in voluminous gauze pyjamas and silk scarves covering their breasts. The light was dim. A sitar player was tuning the strings, repeating a note over and over. It was still a little early for customers.

Akkaji rose to greet him, bowing and touching her forehead, giving him a smile reserved for a client who was known to carry money. So it wasn't she, Debi-dayal reflected, who had passed on the message to the police. Shafi must have found someone else to do his dirty work.

He gave a quick glance around the room. The girls sat demurely, eyes cast down, self-consciously prim. Then he nodded to Akkaji. She led the way to her own room at the back, and they squatted down on the carpet. The preliminaries were over. The business of the evening could now begin. The queen of the house was in her counting house.

"Well, whom do you wish to fold your paans for you this evening?" she asked politely. "You have seen the girls."

The initial move in this sordid business had been made. The girl you took up for the evening was only supposed to fold the betel leaf for you to eat; the price you discussed was not the price of an evening's debauch, but of the paan, the folded betel leaf a girl made for you with her hands, in the reception room, in the presence of the others. You paid the price then and there, in advance, before proceeding to one of the cubicles at the back of the house.

"I am not eating paan here," Debi-dayal said. "I am taking someone home to fold my paans for me for the rest of her life."

"Oh!" The woman was silent for a while. She gave him a long look, her head trembling slightly. "You realize, don't you, that a girl from a house like this is a lifelong responsibility, it is almost like taking a wife. Once they step out of here, there is no coming back."

Debi-dayal nodded. Like crows, he said to himself. Once a crow went out of the circle, it could not go back; the other crows pecked it to death.

"Older men can perhaps arrange it better," she was saying, her voice still serious. "They have wives and children. They provide handsomely for the girls they take out. Are you a shikari—a hunter?"

Was this some kind of euphemism, he wondered, like the folding of a paan? He shook his head. "No, I am not a hunter."

The woman grimaced and wiped the saliva from her chin with the end of her head scarf. "The hunters have a saying: 'Save a life and make yourself responsible for its welfare.' When they kill a tigress, if there are cubs, they have to kill the cubs too. If they take pity and save them, they have to provide for the cubs—keep them as pets, bring them up."

He drummed his fingers impatiently on the faded red velvet bolster. What had all this to do with him?

The woman smiled again and wiped her lips. "This is what I

have to explain to everyone who comes to take one of the girls away. It is the rule. Sometimes a young man with money takes a fancy to a girl and takes her out. In no time at all he's fed up; his people threaten to stop his money. Then she is on the streets, destitute. It is always kinder to kill a tiger cub than to leave it in the jungle to fend for itself."

He frowned with impatience and looked pointedly at his watch. "You are certainly a man in a hurry," she chided. "In this kind of transaction, no one should hurry. Even the men from Calcutta and Bombay, they take several days—"

"I *am* in a hurry—I have a train to catch."

"And who is the lucky girl?"

"Mumtaz."

He thought he saw her flinch. "Mumtaz, yes; a very well-behaved girl; sings well, dances well. But I have another—you saw her outside—whose paans, experts say, are more delectable."

He was getting irritated by her palaver. "Look, I have come for Mumtaz. I want to take her away now, this minute."

"I must congratulate you on your taste," the old woman remarked, her face composed again. "It's just that—would not tomorrow do?"

He shook his head in annoyance. "Tomorrow certainly won't do—even another ten minutes won't do!" He glanced at his watch again.

"It is just that she is now with your friend, engaged. Only for the evening, of course."

"Then you'd better go and bring her out; tell her she's wanted for a few minutes, anything. It's up to you." He took out a roll of notes.

The woman eyed the money avidly, but after a moment turned her eyes away. "How can I?" she said uncertainly. "It would look so uncivil."

"What a pity!" He put away his money. "I understand you would have agreed to give her her freedom for eight thousand rupees. I was going to offer you ten." He rose to his feet.

"Please wait. I never said it could not be managed. Ten thousand, you said."

"That is what I said, but I can't wait much longer."

"Please sit down, only a few minutes." She rose, pushing herself up from the carpet, and shuffled out of the room. Outside, in the reception room with the silk screen equipped with eyeholes, the beat of the tabla had joined the sitar notes, and the rhythm was taken up by the tinkle of the tiny bells around the dancers' ankles. He looked at his watch again. His ten minutes were already up.

Akkaji came back, holding Mumtaz by the hand. "Do your kurnisat to this gentleman; he is your master now," she ordered. Mumtaz did a Moghul bow, bending low and touching her forehead with her right hand. Then she raised her head to look at her master. It was odd how the etiquette of this place had been influenced by the Moghuls, Debi-dayal reflected as he watched her face. Her eyes were flooded with tears.

Akkaji was still counting the notes when the door of the room was flung open. Shafi came up, his face contorted with anger.

"What's the meaning of this!" he demanded of Akkaji. Then, as his eyes fell on Debi-dayal, he drew back. "You!" he said. The blood drained away from his face; his fists clenched.

"Jai-Ram," Debi-dayal greeted him. "Surprised?"

"Very much so."

Debi-dayal grinned. "Put something on over those ridiculous clothes," he told Mumtaz. "We are going out."

"What do you mean?" Shafi expostulated. "She's with me tonight. No one can take her away."

"I'm taking her away."

"I'll see you damned first." Shafi came closer to him, panting, his eyes red with anger.

"None of that!" the old woman said in a screeching voice. "Not in my house, you don't. I'll have to call the watchman, the police."

Shafi grabbed Mumtaz by the arm and pushed her towards the door.

"Don't touch the girl," Debi-dayal said very evenly. "Let her go, at once!" Then he brought the edge of his right hand sharply against the other's elbow.

Shafi's hand fell limply by his side. The skin on his face looked yellow-white, like the belly of a snake.

"Ah, that's much better," Debi told him. "No need to call your watchman," he said to Akkaji, "or the police. Just bring a shawl or something for the girl."

The old woman gave him a look almost of awe. Her toothless mouth trembled, and there was a dribble of saliva on her chin. She went out of the room, stooping, resting her hands against her knees. Shafi gave a queer little cry and made as if to hold the girl again.

"I shouldn't," Debi warned. "That one was almost a gentle tap, something one does in practice. When administered correctly it's supposed to break the bone."

"I'll kill you for this! I shall pay you back for everything!"

Debi-dayal gave a contemptuous snort. "Not you," he said. "You can only work through others."

The old woman came back, carrying a woollen Kashmir-work shawl, and wrapped it round Mumtaz's shoulders. The girl bent down and touched her feet. The ritual of leaving home was over. "He seems a nice man, my child," Akkaji said, putting a hand on the girl's shoulder. "He has promised to look after you. Bless you!"

They went past Shafi and out of the door. Debi-dayal turned back. "Basu and two others are watching the house," he said to Shafi. "People from the old crowd. Don't try anything. They have instructions to shoot you at sight; indeed they're eager to do it. Don't forget that if they find you dead in the street, even the police will be happy. Remember there's a reward—even for your dead body."

They walked in silence. At the corner of Dabbi-bazaar they stopped.

"Have you anywhere to go?" Debi-dayal asked.

She stared blankly at his face and shook her head.

"Where are your people?"

"Karimganj, in Bhawalpur; that is where I come from."

"Is there someone who will look after you if you go back there?"

She shook her head, looking as if she was ready to burst into tears.

"Well, you'll just have to learn to look after yourself from now on. Don't get involved with anything like this. Find yourself a husband, some villager, an honest man. Live a normal life."

"But don't you—don't you want me for yourself?"

"No." He shook his head.

"Then why, why did you take me out if you did not mean to look after me?" There was disbelief in her voice, pain too, he thought. Oh, God, was she going to come out with all that nonsense about the tiger cub spared by the hunter? "I just wanted to buy you your freedom," he explained. "Here's some money. Take this for yourself."

"You mean, you took me out just for a whim? To leave me destitute on the streets!"

He shrugged his shoulders. "Well, you can go back if you wish."

"How can I go back? With what face? What will all those others say? You don't know how bad it can be." She began to sob.

He remembered about the crows, a crow that had left the circle could never be taken back. "Don't cry," he said. "Nothing can be as bad as that place. You can always—" He turned with a start.

There was a sound of footsteps behind them. And then there was Shafi's voice, yelling, "So you want her for yourself, do you? Take her! Take her!"

Even as he braced himself, the thing came hurtling out of the darkness, a glassy object, swirling, aimed with force and accuracy from hardly ten yards away, straight at Mumtaz's face.

Instinctively he put out a hand to ward it off. His hand was shot through with pain as the glass bulb burst against it and the acid spurted out, wet and hot on his palm and forearm.

"Take that, you slut!" Shafi cried again. "That will make you more beautiful than ever!" And again there was the broken electric bulb filled with sulphuric acid that had become the favourite missile in the race war, aimed at the head and body of the girl who stood white-faced in the night, and again Debi-dayal put out his hand, this time catching it in mid-air. He hurled it back into the shadows where Shafi had stood.

The bulb dropped harmlessly a few feet away, exploding with a crash. Only then the pain came over him with a full rush; at first it was like thousands of ants crawling on his hand, still clinging to it, stinging, and then it was as though he had thrust his hand into a roaring fire. "I'll make up for this, Shafi!" Debi-dayal shouted into the night. "You have brought it on yourself!"

It may have been his imagination or some trick sensation conjured up by the pain in his body, but he thought he heard the other man's defiant, mocking laughter in the distance—though it may have been merely one of the ordinary nighttime sounds of a city stirring in its sleep.

"Look what you've done!" the girl was saying. "Just to save me. Oh, that I had died in trying to save you, my lord."

"Oh, shut up!" he snapped at her in anger. "Come on, let's get away from here."

"Look at your beautiful, beautiful hand!" She moaned.

He felt irritated by her concern. He had not done it to save her. It had been almost instinctive. He looked at his hand. The scars were already showing red, and the hand had begun to swell. His body was covered with perspiration.

They hurried through Dabbi-bazaar. "Buy some coconut oil," she told him when they came to a shop that still showed a light. "Say it is for my hair."

He bought the oil and she poured it over his hand, dabbing it with a piece of cloth torn from her scarf. Then they began to walk again, without saying a word. A quarter of an hour later, they were in the room overlooking Anarkali. Basu was already there.

"Oh, my God! The bastard!" he said, when Debi-dayal told him what had happened. "He must have sneaked out of the back door."

The hand had swollen grotesquely now. "He is going to pay for this," Debi-dayal said. "But meanwhile you'd better do something about this girl."

"First we'll do something about your hand," Basu said, avoiding looking at the girl.

"He did that to save me; it would have exploded in my face," Mumtaz said.

They poured more coconut oil on the hand, and she tied the scarf loosely around it. "We will need some ointment, something for a burn," she said to Basu. "Shall I go and get some?"

"No, I will go," Basu said eagerly. "There must be an all-night chemist in Anarkali."

Debi-dayal heard him go. The pain seemed a little less, unless he was just becoming used to it. He leaned back, closed his eyes, and for a minute or two he must have dozed off. When he opened them again, she was fanning him with a folded newspaper. He saw that her eyes were moist.

"Have you nowhere to go?" he asked.

She shook her head. "Nowhere."

"Your village?"

"Only an uncle there. He sold me—I was an orphan—when I was eleven years old. Now I am nineteen. Where can I go? Where can someone like me go—except with those who have the money to buy us?"

"But there is nowhere I can take you either," he pointed out. "I have no home."

"I shall live where you live," she pleaded. "On the streets, if necessary. I shall not be a burden."

A tiger cub he had saved, he reminded himself. Now it was up to him to protect and provide for it; unless, of course, he was willing to leave it in the jungle to fend for itself.

"You paid the price," she said. "You must have liked me. Now why do you want to cast me away?"

"I never wanted you for myself," he told her. "I did it just to hurt Shafi."

She hung her head and did not say anything for a long time. Then she said, "I know I am nothing to you, and that I have to go where you tell me to go—"

"I am feeling sleepy," Debi-dayal said. "I must sleep. All this can wait till the morning."

"And what is wrong with me?" Mumtaz continued very humbly. "I am not asking to be your wife. You don't have to love me —nor even sleep with me unless you want to. I can sing to you, cook food for you, dance for you. I can press your limbs when you are tired, amuse you with stories. I can be a servant in your house—"

"I have no house, no servants."

"Whatever you want me to do, I shall do. I will even go away, if you want me to—but where to, dear God?"

He had already dozed off. He was still asleep when Basu came back with tubes of burn ointment and lint and bandages an hour or so later.

[32]

The Coils of Sansar

THEY left Lahore by the first bus next morning. In the afternoon they were in Kernal. The first night they spent in a hotel in the city. Basu spent the next morning looking for a house. He found a small two-roomed cottage near the dairy farm, and by evening they had already moved in. That night Debi-dayal had high fever.

Ill as he was, Debi-dayal resented her being there, ministering to his needs with pathetic eagerness as his own helplessness increased his irritation. He should have left her in Lahore, he kept admonishing himself. To have put off leaving her, even for a few hours, was a mistake. It was like being kind to some animal in the jungle which could not fend for itself. Once it became attached to you, you could never bring yourself to send it away.

And yet, even through the distortions of fever, he could see that he had no choice. Indeed they could scarcely have carried on without Mumtaz, for it was she who took care of them and looked after the house, cooking, washing, and sweeping. She learned to dress the wounds on his hand and put on Basu's medicine and tie the bandage expertly. Was it already too late to send her away, he wondered? How long would he have to remain tied to her, like one of those leg fetters they put on in the Andamans to prevent you from running away?

Even Basu grew more and more dependent on her, almost in spite of himself, getting over his initial violent aversion to the fact of her being born a Moslem. But then, he reminded himself, many of the girls brought up in brothels were Moslems, and most of them were taken on as concubines by Hindu merchants, marwaris and banias from highly orthodox backgrounds. That was what he tried to explain to Debi-dayal just before he was due to go back to Calcutta.

301

"She is highly capable and intelligent," he said. "I don't know what we could have done without her. I could never have left you here, like this, and yet I have to go. Now I can leave without any qualms, even though you still have fever."

"She will have to go," Debi-dayal said, "as soon as I am able to move about."

"You must not worry about her being a Moslem," Basu went on. "In a courtesan-school they are taught to be secular; no religion is practised. Even the most orthodox marwaris, men who would not sit at a meal with you or me, take them on as concubines."

"I don't want her as a concubine, damn it," Debi-dayal had retorted. "Whether she's a Moslem or a Hindu makes no difference to me, so long as she goes on doing her work."

That was all she was to him—a servant. Debi-dayal grew used to her. Resentment gave way to listless resignation. It was nearly a week before the fever subsided, leaving him limp and weak, hardly able to walk. It took nearly another month for the swelling to go. And for weeks after that his hand looked tender and pink and white and grotesquely pitted, while the fingers were pink suppurating stumps, like a leper's.

But it was healing. The weeks passed into months. The hand acquired a semblance of its former shape and colour, and all but the forefinger became straight and supple again. Gradually he began to train himself to use it, learning to curl his fingers at will, to grip a rolled-up handkerchief in his fist, groping tenderly with his fingers, trying to recapture the sensation of touch, like a blind man learning to use a stick.

He was helpless and vulnerable, wholly dependent on Mumtaz, knowing that Shafi would leave no stone unturned to discover his whereabouts. He began to realize that there was no anonymity like a householder's; a man and wife were the hallmark of respectability. That was what they were, to all appearances, a man and his wife living unobtrusively in the little cottage by the dairy farm.

"I brought bad luck to you," Mumtaz would tell him. "If it had not been for me, you would never have damaged your hand."

Looking at the hand, he could imagine what the acid could have done to her face—just what it had done to Basu's wife's. And yet, what she was telling him was true. If it had not been for her, the hand which he had so assiduously hardened by banging it against wood since he was thirteen years old would never have been maimed and made powerless.

Two months after his arrival in Kernal it was almost fully healed. Now only the diagonal pink scar burned by the acid remained, running from the wrist to the middle finger. One day he told her to go and buy a cricket ball, and then began spending hours playing with it, throwing it up and catching it again and again. At first his attempts were clumsy. The ball would drop out of his hands and he would wince with pain. But as the days passed, he began to catch it more easily.

One day he called Mumtaz out to the open ground behind their cottage and told her to throw the ball high in the air. Her throw was misdirected and not very high, but he ran and caught it expertly. "Not like that, you fool!" he snapped. "Can't you throw it higher! Like this?" And he threw it as high as he could and, as it came down, caught it without flinching.

"My hand is completely healed," he told her and held it out for her to see. "I can do anything with it now. Look!" And he threw up the ball and caught it again.

That evening, when she had washed up after their evening meal, Mumtaz came into the outer room. Usually in the evenings she had kept to herself, sleeping in the room where she cooked.

"Now that your hand is all right, am I to go away?" she asked him.

He glanced at her in sudden annoyance. "Go?" he asked. "Where do you want to go?"

"I don't want to go. It is you who told me to go."

"Where will you go?"

"I told you I have nowhere to go, except possibly back to Akkaji. That is the only home I know."

Back to a brothel, a roost of crows, to be pecked to death by the rightful inmates, he thought to himself. Why did she have to confront him with this just when he had begun to feel so light, almost jubilant at the way his hand had healed?

He was silent for a long time, gnawed by confusion. Was this how people got involved? he asked himself. Three months earlier he could never have imagined having anything to do with a girl like Mumtaz, but now the thought of sending her away suddenly seemed callous. Was that how Basu had got his Dipali? Had he tied himself irrevocably down because he could not make a harsh decision?

"Do you wish to go?" he asked.

She shook her head. "I wish to stay. I want to serve you, be your slave. I shall do anything for you. But if you want me to go, what alternative have I?"

It was just as he had feared. The decision was his responsibility alone, and he must harden his mind to whatever self-reproach might follow.

"I don't want you to go," he told her. "I want you to stay."

It was touching to see the relief in her face. "I shall stay as long as you want me to. When you tell me to go, I shall go."

He felt a quick flutter of relief at her staunchness. He had become so used to having her there that suddenly it was difficult to think of life without her, despite her background.

And yet he had seen nothing mean or greedy in her. She had worked faithfully and unobtrusively for him, making no demands and asking no questions about his hole-and-corner mode of living; indeed, all she was asking now was to be allowed to continue being with him. Debi-dayal, on the other hand, had not given her a single word of affection but gone on taking everything she did for granted, as though some kind of recognized slave-and-master relationship existed between them.

He looked at his hand, pitted and scarred and tender, and then at her face, smooth, unblemished, pale, unpainted, the eyes bright and eager as though freed of tension, and suddenly the thought of her leaving him was difficult to bear.

"I am sorry I could not throw the ball high," she apologized. "But I can sing. Would you like me to sing?"

"No, thank you," he had told her. "Not tonight." But he went on staring at her, as though taking strength from her serenity to dispel his own confusion, and something in his stare caused her to blush and turn her head away.

She went back to her room after that, and he lay awake in bed for a long time, haunted by her blush, wild with a sudden desire to take her into his arms. But he was aware that on that night it would have seemed sordid, even vaguely mercenary, as though he were expecting to be compensated for his kindness.

Gradually he realized he was no longer a free man, and deep inside himself he was glad, not sorry. Like the beggar in the fable who had acquired a cat to get rid of the mice in his hut, he had now become involved in the coils of what they called *sansar*—the web of responsibility. You could not keep a cat without providing it with milk: that was the lesson of the fable. You had to keep a cow too, and then a servant to look after the cow, and so on.

He had now become a man with ties. From now on he would have to live as other men lived, doing humdrum jobs, wrapped up in domesticity, not allowing themselves to be distracted by political iniquities—not even nursing the compulsion of unsettled scores.

And then it hit him like a revelation: he had acquired a woman of his own, a wife—yes, a *wife*, he told himself defiantly. Once the thought had struck his mind, he held and savoured it, like a mango that had tasted sour when he first bit into it, but was delicious once he got used to the flavour. For the first time since he had hurt his hand, he felt wholly relaxed.

"Look!" he called out to her. "As soon as my hand is completely all right, we will go and see my sister. I would like you to meet her."

"Your sister!" He could feel the note of anxiety in her voice, the shadow of fear.

"Yes, she lives in Bombay."

She was silent for a while. Then she asked, "Is that where you are going to leave me?"

"I am not going to leave you anywhere," he told her. "I am going to keep you to myself. It is just that I would like you to meet her."

"Is she as nice as you are?"

"You will have to find that out for yourself." He chuckled. "I think you'll like her."

"I am sure I shall."

"After that, we ought to go and see my parents."

"Your parents?"

"Yes, in Duriabad. It is not going to be very easy—in fact, quite awkward."

"Oh!"

"It has nothing to do with you. It's because of many things that happened before I met you. That's why I think it would be better to see Sundari—my sister—first. She will prepare the ground for my mother and father to meet you."

"Will they want to see me?"

"It is customary for parents to wish to see the girl their son has brought home—their daughter-in-law."

She did not say anything after that, but he could tell she was not asleep. After a while he thought he heard her sobbing, but he knew this was not the time to intrude, that her emotion was too private to be assuaged by words of comfort.

It was odd to have a wife sleeping on a charpoy in the kitchen, away from her husband, he reflected, particularly a wife as lovely as Mumtaz. And then he began to think of his father and mother and sister.

He had not seen them for more than seven years now. He had gone on hardening his mind towards them, drawing some inner satisfaction from his determination to keep himself aloof, clinically segregated from their world. They represented the opposite camp, the contaminated, the faithful allies of the British; like the thousands of Indians who joined government service and diligently, even proudly, helped to enforce alien rule; like other thousands who had joined the services and fought in the war for the preservation of that rule—like Gopal Chandidar, his sister's husband. He, on the other hand, had openly revolted against the British. To have wanted to see his parents or his sister would in itself have been an admission of weakness, of defeat.

And yet, there were gaps in the wall of his privacy. Seven years was a long time, he admitted to himself; almost half a "life" sentence. And not all the members of his family were in the opposite camp. There was Sundari, who had always understood him, and, he was sure, sympathized with him, and there was his mother.

His mother was the one to whom he had caused pain wantonly, for she was like the vast multitudes of the women of India, totally unconcerned about politics; she had no side to take between pro-British and anti-British. He had read in the papers that his father had been knighted. He was now Sir Tekchand Kerwad and his mother was Lady Kerwad. She must think a lot of being addressed as "Lady" Kerwad, he could not help thinking, for that was the sort of thing that was important to women. A title was almost like an ornament, a blue diamond ring or a pink pearl necklace, a mark of one's wealth and prestige. That it was a foreign title, the recognition shown by an alien king which almost stamped its recipient as being anti-national, could not even have occurred to someone like his mother, who had never given a thought to who ruled the country.

Or his father for that matter. He too was in for a rude shock, Debi-dayal reflected. He had been staunchly and openly pro-British all his life. The coming of independence would find him sadly out of his element. The new rulers could not be expected to show much tolerance towards men such as his father who had prospered under British patronage and had been singled out by the British for special recognition.

But was the rest of the country geared for the coming of independence? Debi-dayal asked himself, and braced for the division of the country? He experienced a sudden sense of foreboding as he thought of the ordinary citizens of India, millions of men and women and children who had hardly ever given a thought to politics, being rudely exposed to the forces of disruption let loose in the country, with the Hindus and the Moslems ready to fly at each other's throats the moment the British began to pull out.

The trend of his thoughts disturbed him. For a moment, he found himself wishing that the British would not withdraw in too much of a hurry but phase their departure in such a way that there would be an orderly transfer of power. It was their responsibility to ensure that there was no sudden collapse in the administration, in the rule of law and order; it had always been their responsibility to maintain law and order in the country.

But he instantly found himself being ashamed of his thoughts. Was it not a sign of a moral weakness, merely a habit of a mind nurtured in slavery, that made one look up to the British for the safety of life and property? This was certainly no time to be wishing that the ruling power should stay on, rule just a little bit longer.

For at last the British were going. Independence was only a few weeks away. The date was already announced: August 15. After two hundred years in India, they were responding to the call of India. They were quitting; and they were leaving everything in the care of those who had called upon them to quit. Only, they were dividing the country before leaving it, tearing apart what they themselves had helped to unify.

Another View of the Beach

AT the end of the war the regiment to which Sundari's husband, Gopal, belonged was ordered to Java, where the Dutch were trying to re-establish their rule. Evidently he had volunteered for service in Java. Sundari, for her part, did not mind how long he stayed away. She spent the winter of 1945 with her parents in Duriabad, and returned to Bombay late in March 1946, just a week before Gopal was due back from war service.

For a man with his kind of background, Gopal had done all the right things. He had won the Military Cross in the fighting for the relief of Tobruk, and was now retiring only after all the fighting was over, with the rank of major. His British business firm acknowledged his war service with the offer of a directorship. His friends welcomed him back with a party at the Willingdon Club. Even members of his family who had tended to ignore him since his marriage wrote letters telling him how proud they were of him.

Gopal had come through the war unwounded, and yet he was not the same man; it was as though the war had given him some inner scar, and at the same time helped to fuse the two sides of his personality, the orthodox Hindu upbringing and the Western education, to make him a mature, well-rounded person.

Sundari could not help being conscious of the artificiality that had crept between them. Even when they made love, it seemed to be more from politeness to each other's susceptibilities than for love or self-indulgence.

Almost from the very day of his return, he plunged into the life of his set with a new restlessness and what seeemed to Sundari an altogether new zest, sharpened by association with soldiers. It was almost as though he wanted to be surrounded by

other people, using race meetings and card parties as a kind of
shield to avoid being alone with her more than he could help.

Did this happen to all marriages which were about to break?
Sundari kept thinking. Could he not read the signs just as well as
she? His apparently docile attitude towards the whole situation
preyed on her mind.

She knew now that he did not love her, had never been in love
with her. Was he also making an effort to give their marriage an
appearance of success, much as her parents had enjoined her to
do herself? She had come to accept that a Hindu wife must
subordinate herself for the sake of convention; but did the husband too have to become a party to the fraud? What about the
Hindu male's special prerogative—the religious and social authority to break up a marriage at will? It would be much easier for
him to take the initiative.

Or was he one of those who believed that once two people
were married, they must live together until death parted them
—an unhappy grafting of Western rules of behaviour on Hindu
orthodoxy? If a mistake had been made, did he hold that it must
be lived with, not rectified, the deceit perpetuated, not exposed
to the light of day?

Perhaps he just felt less strongly about it than she did. The
thought made Sundari acutely conscious of the difference in their
ages: he was now in his thirty-fifth year, a mature, greying,
slightly bald man who had obviously acquired a degree of emotional stability that she lacked, and who could bring himself to
be kind and generous to her without being in love with her.

And that, she kept telling herself, was where the danger lay.
The longer you went on living together, the easier it was to make
adjustments. Would their marriage grind its way into a groove,
adjusting itself to the outward requirements of convention, drift
beyond the point of no return?

And that was the point at which she would shrinkingly admit
her infatuation for Gian; Gian, who was simple and sincere, a
living refutation of all that was artificial, of everything in Gopal's
dark-glasses-and-white-sandals set which had become so repugnant to her.

For days she had been nervous and irritable, conscious of her
own burden of guilt, and yet resenting what she could see was a
growing intimacy between her husband and Malini. Did they

think that she did not know they had been lovers, or did they simply not care?

One evening she had been shockingly rude to Malini.

Sundari had always regarded her with undisguised conde-scension: the typical girl from the slums who had found her way unerringly into the false glitter of their circle by making the most blatant use of her fierce, sensual earthiness. She had won her way back into the prince's favour after a fierce and unrelenting battle with Tanya, and was now the acknowledged high priestess of their set, a she-leopard once more on the prowl, businesslike, self-assured, knowing that she could pick and choose. She had chosen Gopal almost as though by right—a woman turning back to her first love, Sundari thought.

"You can't afford to throw stones at others," Malini retorted very evenly, loudly enough for all the others to hear. "All of us haven't got our own houses to receive our friends in while our men are away."

Too late Sundari realized it was pointless to match crudities with someone like Malini. She tried to salvage what was left of her dignity. "Will you please take me away?" she had called out to Gopal. "I can't stay here and be insulted by this type of woman."

Malini merely sniggered and shrugged her shoulders to signify her triumph, and then turned to give Gopal a private smile, almost as though to explain that she was not to blame for what-ever had happened.

Sundari swept out of the room, and Gopal, who had been involved in a game of chemin-de-fer, found someone to take his place and followed her. They got into the car and drove home. They said not a word to each other throughout the drive until, just as they were turning into the porch, he asked, "I wasn't listening. How did it all start? What did Malini say that annoyed you so much?"

"She asked me if it was true that Debi had been helping the Japanese in the war."

"You mustn't be so sensitive about it," he said. "Everyone's saying it."

"I can't help being sensitive," she snapped. "He is *my* brother and she is not *my* girl-friend."

He brought the car to a halt but did not switch off the engine

"But what did you say that made her call you—made her say what she did?"

"I'm afraid I called her a whore and a tart—that's what she is! —for daring to suggest that I am just one of them!"

"They're saying that too, many of them," he told her quietly. "You can't stop people from saying things. They live on gossip and rumour—like the sort of thing that you suggested, that there is something between Malini and myself."

She had glared at him in the darkness, angry enough to want to lash out at him, but she controlled herself. "I never want to go there again," she told him. "If you want to, you must go by yourself."

"I am going back now," he replied, reaching across and opening the car door for her. "I asked Bob to take my hand only until I came back."

"Then why didn't you stay on?" she taunted. "I could have found my own way back."

"No doubt you could," he said, "but not all of us can afford to despise convention as you do."

He had gone back. She had fallen asleep, exhausted with rage, still ruminating over his last remark. Convention! That was all their marriage meant to him. She did not know what time he returned. The next morning she stayed in bed until she heard his car drive off to the office.

It was long past eleven when she heard the telephone ring. Baldev came and told her that someone was asking to speak to her. She took the call on the sitting-room veranda. Her heart gave a sudden leap.

"Debi!" She gasped. "Debi!"

Debi-dayal and Mumtaz left Bombay on a Friday morning. On Saturday, Sundari rang Gian. "I want you to come and see me," she told him, "this evening."

They had not spoken to each other for more than a year now, not since Gian's outburst on the beach. She had often longed for him to telephone, but had been too proud to make the approach herself. And at that it was a narrow escape, she had to admit. Now that particular complication had been neatly sorted out, as though by a surgical operation, leaving behind, too, the pain and the shock of surgery. Debi's visit had opened her eyes. Pure love, she kept telling herself—was there anything more impure than love? There was always deceit in it, a question of how much you could get for how little.

She noticed his hesitation. "I don't know," he said. "I am not sure that I should."

She was conscious of the sudden rush of blood as she heard his voice, an emotion inconsistent with her seething anger. "But you just have to come," she entreated. "You promised—said you would come when I had something special to tell you."

He was silent for a while. "Have you something special to tell?"

"Very special. I simply must see you."

"I have a feeling it will only complicate things," he said, "just when I am beginning to learn to live without making myself miserable over you."

He sounded so sincere as he said it that again she felt a spasm of regret at whatever had happened, a sudden feeling of emptiness within her. She clutched the receiver hard. "No, no; it will only help to uncomplicate things." She laughed to reassure him. "Come for a swim first, so that we can have a talk. My husband will join us about six. Then—then we can talk it over."

She knew that that was something that would draw him; the suggestion that they were both to go to her husband and tell him they were in love. He had told her they should not see each other unless she was ready to become his wife. That was exactly what she was now promising him. "Don't be late," she warned. "I particularly want you not to be late. Gopal is always so punctual, and I want a little time to ourselves—to talk to you."

"No, I won't be late," Gian assured her, and now his voice sounded suddenly eager. "And thank you for calling. I love you, darling," he added.

She felt limp with conflicting emotions. As she replaced the receiver, she noticed that her hand was trembling.

Gopal was going to the club for a game of golf. Just as he was leaving his room, he called out to her.

"Sundari, who is this man you have asked?"

"A friend of Debi's. Why?"

"Nothing. I thought it was rather odd that he shouldn't have been here before."

"He has been here," she told him. She felt composed now,

sure of herself. "In fact, I went and brought him once. That was during the fire. He stayed in the spare room. That's what Malini and the others have been talking about."

If he wondered why she was telling him, he made no comment. "Has he been in Bombay all this time?"

"Most of it. Are you going to be late?"

"No. I should be back at six or soon after."

"Don't be late."

"You know I'm never late."

Yes, that was quite true; he could be depended upon to be always on time, Sundari admitted to herself with a sudden pang of compassion. He was a creature of habit; that was why she could be sure that her plan would go through without a hitch.

"Why did you ask?" he was saying.

"I might have a little surprise for you."

"Surprise, darling? Pleasant, I hope."

"I hope so too."

He paused at the head of the stairs, then came back. "What's the matter?" he asked looking intently at her. "You're looking so tense—excited."

She advanced towards him and placed her hands on his shoulders. He could feel the warmth of her body close to him. She was looking directly into his eyes, and there was a cruel, almost malicious twist to her lips. He felt uncomfortable under her steady gaze.

"Why are you smiling?" he asked.

"I was just thinking . . . of something that happened years ago. One of our neighbours was drowning a puppy because there was one too many. And when Debi burst into tears, he called us weak and sentimental. I offered to drown it for him, just to show that I wasn't weak."

"Did you drown it?"

"No. In the end he changed his mind. He gave the puppy to Debi. That's how we got Spindle."

"What put that into your mind?"

"I was thinking that when the time comes to do something harsh, one should go ahead with it and not delay, which only makes it more difficult."

He laughed nervously. "That sounds like something they used to teach us at the military staff college," he said. "Why hasn't this man been here all this time?"

"Mr. Talwar? Because he's old-fashioned and rather earnest. He thought you wouldn't approve."

"What nonsense!"

"So I told him."

"Told him what?"

"What you just said: 'What nonsense!'—that ours was a modern marriage, that we both maintained contacts with our old friends almost as if—as if we weren't married. Don't we, darling?"

"Look," he said. "I am only going to play golf with Malini—in a foursome. Surely you are not objecting?"

"But of course not! What an idea!"

"Then why all this talk about who we see and all that?"

She dropped her hands from his shoulders. "I don't know why you thought I objected. I was just trying to tell you what I told Mr. Talwar."

"Why should he suppose I'd object to his seeing you?"

"Perhaps he has a guilty conscience. He says he's in love with me. At least he used to be."

He laughed. "It will be interesting to meet him."

It was a few minutes after six when Gopal came back, pleasantly tired after his round of golf. It had been a hot afternoon, and his clothes were wringing wet.

"Where is the memsahib?" he asked Baldev.

"Memsahib has gone for a swim, sir."

"All by herself?"

"No, sahib. With another sahib. Mr. Joshi."

"Yes, of course." Gopal nodded, remembering their talk after lunch. Baldev had mixed up the names, surely? She had said his name was Talwar. "Has memsahib told you whether he's staying to dinner?"

"No, sir, I mean he is not staying. I asked memsahib."

"Oh, somehow I had thought . . . Bring me a drink, will you, a whisky, and then turn on my bath."

After a bath, he changed into linen slacks, sandals, and a cellular shirt. He was glad that they were going to be by themselves for dinner. Afterwards he could just nip across to the prince's shack for a game. It might have been awkward if Sundari's visitor had stayed on to dinner. It would have meant dawdling over the food, coffee afterwards, perhaps a brandy. Now it seemed that he could just have a drink with them after their swim and then leave.

When he came into the sitting room the sun was just going down. Baldev had already put out a tray of drinks and switched on the lights. He was a little annoyed that Sundari should still be on the beach herself when she had told him to be back at six. He picked up a magazine and walked onto the veranda overlooking the sea. He switched on the lights.

Even as he turned, he felt that something was wrong, and then his eye fell on the short black telescope on the window-sill, like a miniature piece of artillery. For a moment he stood in the doorway, hardening his mind against the thoughts that came flooding over him. Then, steeling himself, he advanced to the instrument.

It was locked in position, aimed at the patch of palmyra and coconut at the edge of the high ground shelving down to the beach. He was aware, even as he applied his eye to the telescope, that he was looking at exactly what he was meant to see; that the scene that had been put on would not have been complete without his own participation. Sundari and a man lay in the thicket of reeds and palms, leaning against the trunk of a tree. They lay on towels spread out on the short grass, and neither of them wore a stitch of clothing. They looked relaxed and contented, as though wishing to give the impression that their passions had been assuaged, and, almost as a corroboration, he noticed that her hair was disarrayed. They were not even talking to each other. The man was gazing blankly towards the sea, and she was looking in the direction of the house, her right hand shading her eyes. And then he realized that she was looking directly at him, seeing him bending down to the telescope. He drew back from the window and switched off the veranda lights.

So this was her way of getting her own back, delivering the death-blow to their marriage as she had once offered to destroy a puppy, ready to hold it down, squirming, to watch it wriggling in a bucket of hot water, as she was watching him now. She had always pretended that she had not seen Malini and himself that day; now, after all these years, she was telling him that she had.

He remembered how cool and deliberate she had sounded, putting her hands on his shoulders, when she asked him not to be late. He felt defeated, curiously humbled; it was somehow far worse than if she had created a scene that day. Instead she had waited for this kind of revenge, calculated and openly retaliatory, staging a scene for his benefit which shrieked of artifice, and yet made it clear to him that she would have no hesitation in giving herself wantonly to a stranger just in order to get her own back on him.

The cigarette burned his fingers and he came to with a start. She had waited six years, he kept telling himself, for the entire duration of the war, to tell him what she had meant to say all along: that their marriage was irreparably broken and that it was he who had broken it.

Sundari had been watching the window of the glazed veranda where she had placed the telescope, and when she saw the light go off she turned to Gian.

They had said nothing to each other for a long time. He too had been conscious that he was at one of the crucial moments of his life; it was almost the exact feeling he had experienced when he had set out to kill Vishnu-dutt after finding the axe, and later, again, when he had got off the ship at Madras. In a few minutes now they would get up and dress, and then walk back to the house to wait for Gopal, the husband he had never met but whom he had already wronged. After that would come the straight, man-to-man talk, with Sundari by his side. He was ready, elated.

"Darling," he said. "I have waited for this moment all my life."

She sat up, putting her arms round her knees. He wanted to reach out and take her into his arms, but something about her expression made him hold back.

"I too have been waiting for this moment," she said. "Perhaps not all my life, but for several years."

He saw from her tone that they were not speaking of the same thing, and he was about to say something about it when she went on.

"I saw my brother, Debi-dayal. He came to the house. He told me all about—about what happened in the Andamans."

The change that had come over her face made his flesh creep even before he was aware of the full meaning of her words; and her voice had become suddenly cold and high-pitched. He could only stare at her, unable to say anything.

"I saw the marks on his body," she was saying. "The marks of flogging. They will be there all his life."

"Oh, my God!" He gasped as the surge of emotion caught up with his thoughts. He felt defeated and humbled. His head throbbed, his limbs felt weak and clammy, as though bathed in perspiration.

"What had we ever done to you?" she was saying. "Debi or my father or myself? You even said you were in love with me."

He went on staring at her face. The colour had drained from it and it was like a mask, even though her eyes had an unnatural brightness.

"I can explain everything," he said weakly. "Everything."

"And those photographs. Debi never gave them to you. You opened the letter, took the money. I had sent money to Debi in it. And then you gave him away." The trembling in her voice showed that she was close to tears.

"Please!" he implored. "Please!" Even to himself his voice sounded like a whimper.

"And then you came to Duriabad, saying that you had escaped —oh, so many lies! And the talk of love. Love! Love for what?" she asked with sudden bitterness. "My father's money? You thought his son would never come back—was that what it was?" Her voice had risen to a thin screech, making him flinch, as though someone had scratched a pin over glass. She closed her eyes tight, making a visible effort to prevent herself from breaking down.

He had got his wind back now; the creepy, defeated feeling had passed. He even caught himself feeling sorry for her. "Have you finished?" he asked.

She opened her eyes and sat up, rigid with anger. "There is just one thing more. Last time, you asked me if it meant nothing to me that I had slept with you. I want to tell you about that. I want to even out the score—to make you feel as small as you have made me feel. On the day we returned from our honeymoon, my husband lay here, exactly here, with a low woman. That was six years ago. Ever since I have been waiting to avenge myself. Today I have succeeded. I arranged that he should take a good look at us, you and me, while we were here, making love, or giving the impression of it, naked. If you hadn't been here, anyone else would have done. But you happened to be handy and you happened to have few scruples. So that is what you were to me—a male whore; that is what your great love has meant to me." Suddenly she hid her eyes with her hands and began to sob.

"What had we ever done to you?" she asked in an anguished voice.

He felt strangely composed now. For a second or two he watched her, her face hidden, her shoulders heaving. "No, you did nothing to me," he told her very quietly, and then his voice rose to a tremor. "You did nothing, but you have now. I had just begun to believe in myself, taking courage in the fact that somewhere, in spite of all his weaknesses, there is in every man something that he can value. You have now destroyed that faith."

She lifted her face and stared at him through her tears. She went on looking for a few moments before she spoke.

"And what about what you have destroyed in me?" she demanded in a very flat voice.

Her gaze made him turn his eyes away, realizing that she was accusing him of destroying something that was equally precious to her; and again he caught himself feeling sorry for her, knowing that whatever she had said had in some manner hurt her just as much as it had hurt him; that in trying to even out the score, she had only succeeded in making a sacrifice of something that was deeper and more intimate than a woman's vanity.

She got up and grabbed the towel and wrapped it around her, and then she walked away without a backward glance, erect and defiant. He watched her, feeling numb with emotion, wondering if she thought she had won or lost. He waited until she was out of sight, until the sound of her footsteps had ceased. Then he rose to his feet and began to dress.

[34]

The Anatomy of Partition

IN the grey light of dawn, Tekchand stood at the window of his bedroom balcony, looking at the smoke of the fires in the distance, darker plumes mingling into the wispy blue lines of the clouds. The stillness of a town under curfew surrounded him. It was like a wall around the house, a persistent reminder of their isolation.

The disturbances had now been going on for more than a week. At first he had not been worried. His house was too far from the centre of the town to be affected by the riots. Sporadic disturbances between the Hindus and the Moslems were something that they had all learned to live with. Over the years, whenever either community had some kind of festival, there was inevitably a flare-up: processions, demonstrations, slogan-shouting, even a few killings. Then the authorities stepped in. The police made a lathi-charge or two and dispersed the crowds with tear gas; the magistrate imposed a curfew on the affected localities, and it was all over until the next Hindu or Moslem festival.

But these riots, as he could now see, were different. These riots were occasioned by the cutting up of the country. A vast landscape packed with people was now being partitioned according to religious majorities: the Moslems in Pakistan, the Hindus in India.

Every citizen was caught up in the holocaust. No one could remain aloof; no one could be trusted to be impartial. When men and women of your own religion were being subjected to atrocities, you could not be expected to remain friendly with adherents to the religion of the oppressors. The administration, the police, even the armed forces were caught up in the blaze of hatred. Willy-nilly, everyone had come to be a participant in what was, in effect, a civil war.

Tens of millions of people had to flee, leaving everything behind, Moslems from India, Hindus and Sikhs from the land that was soon to become Pakistan: two great rivers of humanity, flowing in opposite directions along the pitifully inadequate roads and railways, jamming, clashing, colliding head-on, leaving their dead and dying littering the landscape.

As a background to this great two-way migration, religious civil war was being waged all over the country—a war fought in every village and town and city where the two communities came upon each other. The most barbaric cruelties of primitive man prevailed over all other human attributes. The administration had collapsed; the railways had stopped functioning because the officials and technicians had themselves joined the mass migrations. Mobs ruled the streets, burning, looting, killing, dishonouring women, and mutilating children; even animals sacred to the other community became the legitimate targets of reprisals.

It had been building up under the surface, building up for years, and now the fury had burst, as Gandhi himself had long ago feared it might. Any sensible man could see it now, as Tekchand was seeing it that morning of August 1947. The freedom they had longed for was only a day away, a freedom that would bring only misery to millions of them. The entire land was being spattered by the blood of its citizens, blistered and disfigured with the fires of religious hatred; its roads were glutted with enough dead bodies to satisfy the ghouls of a major war.

They could have gone away. His wife had actually suggested it. But he had laughed at her fears. Now that he himself wanted to go, it was not easy. Your car would almost certainly be waylaid at the very first village; a log across the road or an abandoned bullock cart would suffice. Men and women blind with hatred would come rushing from all sides to hack its occupants to pieces and rob whatever they possessed. They would disappear just as quickly as they had come, to prepare themselves for the next car that arrived.

Tekchand had never imagined that such happenings could be possible now, in the middle of the twentieth century, after more than a hundred years of the sanity and orderliness of British rule, after thirty years or so of the Mahatma's non-violence. . . .

Now he could see that, as far as the people of India were concerned, Gandhi's message was merely a political expedient, that for the bulk of them it had no deeper significance. At best, they had accepted it as an effective weapon against British power. It seemed that the moment the grip of British power was loosened, the population of the subcontinent had discarded non-violence overnight and were now spending themselves on orgies of violence which seemed to fulfil some basic urge.

Over these disquieting generalizations came regret at his own failure to heed the signs. It was he who had told his wife he would stay behind and see it through. "Why don't you and Sundari go?" he had said casually, knowing that she would never leave him to face danger alone—not that, even two weeks ago, they had really thought there was any danger.

"Dhansingh can drive you all the way to Delhi in a day," he had said.

Was it only a fortnight ago that he had said that? Why had she not gone then? Why hadn't they all gone? It was as simple as that, just two weeks ago. Get into a car and drive away.

His wife had not even answered his question. She had merely given him a look, half-amused, half-reproachful, which told him that there could be only one answer to such a suggestion. She would not leave him, and the thought had made him inwardly happy.

Now Dhansingh was not there to drive them. He had still not told his wife what had happened to him. Indeed, he had even complained to her, forcing himself to sound suitably indignant, that Dhansingh had taken the Buick and gone away.

"He must have arranged with some of his friends to go away," he had said. "That story about bringing his family to live here must have been all made up. He wanted the car; that was all."

As he thought of what had happened to his chauffeur, his legs felt weak. Dhansingh had sought his permission to bring his family to stay in one of his servants' quarters because the other Sikhs in his locality were leaving. He lived in Chandpura, separated from the rest of the city by a sprawling Moslem bustee. He had never come back.

On the return journey the Buick was stopped beyond the bridge, and Dhansingh's wife and two children were dragged out. They stoned the children to death in front of their parents, and then poured petrol over Dhansingh's hair and beard and burned him alive. After that they had taken his wife away.

The car had been found where it stood, beyond the bridge, a burned-out shell; those who had killed Dhansingh could have had no use for it. The police had told Tekchand that he could take away the wreck; the other details he had ascertained from one of the Sikhs who had been watching from a distance. There was no room for doubt. The servants knew all about it, of course; they always knew everything. He had warned them to say nothing to his wife.

And now they were facing it all together, his wife and daughter and himself, for no better reason than that he had refused to leave earlier.

Why had Sundari come back, just at this juncture, bringing her dog with her? Even if she had left her husband for good, as she had told them, this was no time for a Hindu woman to be coming into West Punjab, when everyone else was leaving. And yet, he was secretly pleased that Sundari was with them. It was surprising how unperturbed she looked, as though nothing out of the way was happening. Suddenly he felt a little ashamed of his own anxiety.

He flung himself into one of the cane chairs; his fingers had left wet marks on the polished wood of the balcony.

He thought of the night that had just gone. They had not slept much. Even from their bedroom window, they could see the red glow in the sky, like a winter sunset, the glow caused by the houses burning in the city, and now and then they could hear the roar of the mob, like the din of a migrating swarm of bees, punctured by shrieks, catcalls, and the occasional report of firearms. What had happened during the night? What was happening now? There was no way of knowing.

There was the soft pad of sandals behind him, and his wife came and stood near his chair. "Darling!" she said. "The servants have gone."

He stared at her face. It was like wax. "There is no one in the house now," she was saying, "except the three of us."

He sprang from the chair and ran through the long passage and down the stairs, shouting, "Kamruddin! Kishen! Nathani!— where are you? Nathani! Kishen! Hamid! HAMID!"

He stopped. He was behaving like a fool. They had all gone, his cook, the malis, his own bearer, everyone. How could they, after all these years? He had never known a time in his life when they had been without servants.

Where had they gone? What would they do? Who would look after them?

And with the doubt came relief. Perhaps it was as well that they had gone, leaving him free. Hitherto it had been his responsibility to look after them, give them food and water and protection. Most of them were Moslems. How long could they remain loyal to him against the rising pressure of their own people?

As he climbed the stairs he felt more composed, and his heart had stopped pounding. At least they had been spared the fate of his chauffeur, he consoled himself. They had gone out of his life and freed him of a burden. He walked into Sundari's room. She was already up and dressed. Spindle jumped up, wagging his absurd ratlike tail.

"Sundar," he said, trying to control his voice so as not to alarm her. "Beta, you had better come and sit in our room. The servants have fled. They are bound to return when the scare is over—they have nothing to fear. I thought you were a little far away here, in this room. You had better come and sit with us."

"Of course," Sundari said. "But I'll get you some breakfast first. Tea or coffee?" she asked. "Whichever you can stand without milk—coffee, I think."

"Yes, coffee would be better. That was a horrible thing to have done," he complained, suddenly remembering. "Killing all those Saiwal cows just because they belonged to the Hindu gowalas. And now there is no milk, for either Hindus or Moslems."

"There is a tin of condensed milk, but we had better keep it for the journey," his daughter said.

It was heartening to hear someone talking about condensed milk and breakfast. He looked at her fondly, thinking how grown up she suddenly looked, grown up and so sure of herself. What had happened to her, to change her from a girl to a woman, someone who had known pain and suffering? It seemed only a few years since she was a little squirming thing who used to be brought to the sitting room by the ayah to kiss him good night. How many years had gone by in a flash to make him what he was today, fifty-one years old and tired and demoralized, the man of the house, responsible for looking after his wife and daughter.

"Sundar," he said. "Do you mind changing into something a little old and drab? And try to put some stuff on your face—I mean some kajal or something. Make a smudge or two."

She gave him an amused smile. "What's wrong with you? Don't worry, no one's going to abduct me—not when Mummy's around. You had better talk to her instead—tell her not to look so devastating."

He nodded. "Yes, she too will have to get into something inconspicuous," he said very seriously. "And Sundar, please take off those bangles and things. It's dangerous to wear gold."

"Are you going to send the jewellery to the bank?" she asked.

"Bank!" He shook his head. "None of the banks is functioning. We'll just put everything in a box and take it with us. We will give a party the day we arrive in Jullunder. And then you will both need your jewellery."

"That's much better," his daughter said, patting his shoulder. "That's the way to look at it: to think of when we reach there, not go on mooning over what is happening here. What can go wrong when we're all in convoy, escorted by the army right up to the border?"

"Nothing should go wrong," he agreed. "There is a boundary force that is still under the British. The army is still relatively unaffected by all this."

"There you are! There's nothing to worry about!"

He shook his head, unable to share her optimism. "One cannot help worrying," he said, "because no one can be trusted any more. And besides, there's the feeling that I myself have brought all this on you. Your mother wanted us to leave a whole month ago. Even two weeks ago, we could have done it—just driven off. I could have brought over all the trucks from the works here, and we could have loaded them with everything we wanted to take from here. I told your mother to go, but you know how pig-headed she can be. And then you came—"

"I would have hated myself if I'd left you and Mummy to face this by yourselves," Sundari assured him.

"And now we have to wait for a convoy organized by the police, and that seems to get put off from day to day. According to their original plans, we should have left two days ago—we'd have been through by now. There is still no sign of it."

"Oh, but the poor things must have so much on their hands just now," his daughter said consolingly. "You really have been spoilt all your life, haven't you, getting your own way every time. Come. You go and hold Mother's hand while I get you something to eat. You will feel much better."

And again he thought how comforting it was to have Sundari with them just then. It was she who seemed to think of all the practical things. "Sundari," he asked, "do you think we should all shift to the downstairs rooms?"

She gave him a level look. "What on earth for? If they come and set fire to the house, whether we are upstairs or downstairs won't make much difference."

"Don't talk of such ghastly things!" he snapped.

"But isn't that what you were thinking?"

"That it should have come to this!"he said angrily, aware that his voice was dry and husky. "After a lifetime spent in this part of India, in this town, and giving oneself to it and taking from it, letting one's roots sink deeper and deeper. There is a street named after my father, a library after me, a maternity home and a girls' school after your mother. This is my city, as much as that of its most respected Moslem families—the Abbases, the Hussains, the Chinais. I, my family, have done as much as any of them to make it prosperous and beautiful. And what are they doing? Burning it down! And look at us! Waiting for police protection because its citizens want to finish us off."

Sundari was taken aback by his outburst. "Abaji, please, please don't talk like that!" she said.

"Damn it! I have to talk about it to somebody—talk or my head will burst. I trusted them and scorned your mother's fears. They are my brothers, I told her. Why did I not listen to her? Because I wanted to keep all this, all that my family and I myself have built. One of the best houses in town, a name honoured in the whole province, the best private collection of Indian bronzes in the whole country. And suddenly someone has decided that this land which is mine should be foreign territory—just like that! And merely because some hooligans take it into their heads to drive all the Hindus away from their land, I have to leave everything and go, pulled out by the roots, abandoning everything that has become a part of me."

"Don't forget, Abaji, that you are luckier than most others," his daughter reminded him. "After all, you have a good deal of money. You have a house in Delhi, somewhere to go. You are not like the thousands—millions—who have to find shelter and work."

"Money!" He flung up his hands in disdain. "Do you suppose all the money in the world will make up for this? My house, my bronzes—I could spend hours just looking at them, over and over again, feeling an inner peace, a religious exaltation, almost, to be in the midst of all that beauty. True art that lived a thousand years ago and still lives and breathes."

He stopped, checking himself with an effort of will and gave a dry, forced laugh. "Yes, you are right, my child. I *am* lucky. I don't have to start all over again. We shall never be in want. We can go on living as we do here, in Delhi, Bombay, anywhere. Yes, I am lucky."

"That's the way to look at it," Sundari said with obvious relief. "Come on, I'll get you something to eat, and you ring up the police and find out the latest news about the convoy."

She took his arm and accompanied him along the passage, the dog leading the way. "I shall ring up as soon as it is light," he told her. "It's too early now." Sundari let his arm go and turned into the sitting room, which now served as their kitchen. For a time he stood staring absent-mindedly at the door through which she had gone, and then, as though he had suddenly remembered something, turned and walked into his museum. Once in, he mechanically went straight to the windows, threw open the curtains one after the other, and the morning light fell in streaks upon his collection. Then he turned.

There they stood, the Bramhas and the Vishnus and the Shivas; the creators, the preservers, and the destroyers; the Ganeshas and the Vithobas and the Hanumans; the Radhas and the Apsaras and the Asuras; men and women and in-betweens; elephant-headed, monkey-headed, eagle-headed; two-headed and four-headed; four-armed and eight-armed and ten-armed; gods and goddesses and demons and half-gods and half-devils; dancing, sleeping, blessing, preaching, bowing, fornicating; naked, bosomy, grotesque, beautiful.

To him they were like living creatures, more alive than many people he knew. He felt at home in their midst, for they meant something to him—they held a message for him, a message that was the secret of this life and the next and the many lives that lay beyond.

Their serenity made him conscious of his own weakness. He stood with bowed head, exposing his mind to its innermost promptings.

The only thing he could think of was the futility of resistance. He toyed with the thought of letting his wife and daughter go with the convoy. He would stay behind, with his men and women and half-beasts and half-gods of metal. He would like that; somehow he would be able to manage. It was his land, his town; its people were his people. They would come to their senses as soon as this wave of hatred had passed; they would realize he was one of themselves and not to be spurned.

But Radha would never leave me, he thought with a start. Never!

He felt sick with emotion. His duty lay with his wife and daughter; they had to have a man to look after them, and that man was now himself. If Debi-dayal had been with them now, he would have thought seriously of staying behind, confident that Debi would be able to deal much more adequately with the present situation. Debi would have accepted the challenge, revelled in it.

He shut his eyes, deliberately denying himself a last look. He would leave them like that, just as they were, never allow himself to be swayed by their spell from what was clearly his duty. He turned, his eyes still closed, and groped his way towards the door. He shut the door behind him and then, opening his eyes, went to the telephone.

"But we have already told you that we shall let you know when everything is ready," the police inspector said.

"But everyone who is to go in the convoy has been ready for the past three days," Tekchand pointed out.

"We have to wait and see how the other side is behaving. There is still no information that the convoy of Moslems from Delhi is on its way."

"Does it mean," Tekchand asked, "that we are being treated as hostages to see that the authorities on the other side send out your people safely?"

There was a long silence at the other end. Then the inspector's voice came on again. "You can call it what you like; but if they won't play, we won't either."

"Oh, my God! If you wait for them, and they wait for you, we shall be here forever!"

"I can't help that—and listen; I like neither your tone of voice nor your words."

"I am sorry," Tekchand said quickly. "I meant no offence. But can we expect to leave today?"

"I don't know about that," the officer said gruffly, making it clear that he had not forgiven him. "Everything depends upon how they treat our people on the other side. I hear a train was attacked in Patiala by the Sikhs, a convoy butchered in Amritsar. If that sort of thing is allowed to happen, how can we protect the Sikhs here from the fury of the mobs? Tell me that."

"I quite see your difficulty."

"Can you blame our people for trying to get their own back? Are we to be traitors to our own kind?"

"No, of course, not," Tekchand said politely. Then he added, "I am sorry about what I said just now; I meant no offence."

That was another indignity you had to learn to put up with; the insolence of petty officials. Though he had at least three senior retired police officers serving as security men in his company, he now had to be ingratiating to an inspector.

He made his way towards the sitting room, trying to overcome his despondency. Sundari was bending over the sigri, and the way she was concentrating on turning the toast made it clear she had heard him speaking to the inspector. He sat down and waited for his breakfast.

In a corner of the room stood a barrel of water and a bag of wheat flour. On the sofa and on the chairs were stacked boxes of candles, tins of sausages and beans and soup, and a bag of sugar, and on the floor a stack of chopped wood and a crate of charcoal.

That was one emergency they seemed to have made provision for. His wife had had the sitting room turned into a store and kitchen so that the cook should be near by, instead of in the kitchen, which was down in the basement. Now the cook had gone, and Sundari was cooking breakfast over the primitive sigri fire as though she had been doing it every day of her life.

That was what was important now, water and food and lighting; as though they were in a jungle camp, Tekchand reflected. Everything was there to keep them going for at least two weeks. The Kashan and the Kermanshah carpets which had covered the floor and were now rolled up, carpets that he had been collecting with a connoisseur's fussiness and avidity for the past twenty years and more, carpets that had come to him from his father and grandfather, were now worthless, as were the other possessions they had prided themselves upon: the Spanish silver candlesticks, the baccarat chandeliers and the Georgian tea service, the Minton dinner set and the rosewood dining table that seated twenty-four.

In the garage downstairs was the car, the brand new Ford V8 which, because of his influence, he had managed to buy out of the very first lot of postwar cars to come to India. That car too was something to be grateful for. It stood behind locked doors, packed and ready, its tank full and with cans of spare petrol, oil, and water for a long journey. The car too was far more important now than the furniture or the statues in the house, or the house itself.

Most important of all was the fact that his wife and daughter were with him, giving him strength and a sense of purpose, enabling him to overcome his emotional involvement in the land of his birth, his material possessions. A wave of gratitude passed over him as he looked at his daughter bending over the coal fire. Her mere presence was reassuring.

"The coffee's ready now," Sundari said, "and there are toast and pickles. I have even made you a fried egg on toast, just as you like it. No use keeping the egg any longer. Mummy is having a bath; you'd better have your breakfast."

The smell of coffee suddenly made him hungry, but just as he went over to the card table on which Sundari had put his breakfast, the telephone rang. His heart gave a sudden leap; it could only be the police, with news about the convoy. He gave a quick smile at his daughter and ran to the telephone in the passage. There was such a humming in his head that for a time he could not make out who it was or what the speaker was trying to say. It certainly was not the inspector's voice.

Then it began to be clear. Sardar Awtar Singh, one of his friends, was ringing up to ask him if they would like to come and stay in his house.

"We are at least fifty here—about a dozen men," he was saying. "We have three shotguns and a pistol—just in case—and the men take it in turns to keep guard, night and day."

"Why, thank you!" Tekchand said gratefully. "Of course we would like to. It is most kind of you. . . . What did you say?"

"How many will you be?" Awtar repeated.

"Only three of us—besides myself, my wife and daughter; oh, there is her dog, too."

"A dog?" There was a short pause at the other end. "What a pity! What we need is men here, as many as we can assemble."

Tekchand felt suddenly light. "You say you have twelve of your own men," he pointed out. "Surely a dozen Sikhs are as good as a score of other men!"

Awtar did not laugh. "As good as a hundred," he said very

evenly. "But we may be attacked by five hundred—five thousand! Come as soon as you can. Have you any firearms—a rifle or pistol or something?"

"Firearms! Oh, no!"

"Never mind. Bring whatever food you may have stocked; everything helps. We have to cook meals for fifty here—over a dozen children. And listen, couldn't you leave the dog behind?"

"Oh, no! No, we couldn't do that. But he's a very little one," he said apologetically.

"We have been telling the others to put down their pets, before coming here—oh, well . . . do bring all the food though."

"Of course! We have a lot of provisions stored," Tekchand told him, and then he remembered what the inspector had been telling him. "Listen!" he said. "I was just talking to the police. I don't want to alarm you, but the inspector said something about the people in the city being particularly roused against the Sikhs. There was some trouble in Patiala and Amritsar, so he says, and they want to retaliate."

"Oh, my God!" Awtar gave an audible gasp. "They already hate us so much! Look, I will understand if you don't want to join us. Perhaps it would be wiser to keep away from us just now."

"Nonsense!" Tekchand said. "Of course we will come. I just thought I would warn you to be extra careful—not do anything that might provoke trouble."

"Thanks," Awtar said. "I shall be expecting you, then. The food will be very useful, but it would have been so much better if you could have contributed a weapon."

Tekchand sat down to his breakfast and ate hungrily. He gave his wife a bright smile as she came in, bathed and dressed, and now wearing no jewellery. "We are going to Awtar's house," he told her. "We'll wait for the convoy there—with the others."

It was a great relief, and he wondered why he had not thought of it before. Where they were situated, right out of the town, with no other house within half a mile, they were almost wholly isolated—a little island of Hindu affluence in the midst of the wastes, a ready-made target for the random whim of any village gang. Now they would be in the company of others; strong, virile men, men with guns, ready for all emergencies; everyone waiting with his own car for the convoy to form up.

"Another cup?" Sundari asked.

"Yes, thank you."

Then the telephone rang again. He pushed back his chair and sprang to his feet, spilling his coffee. He ran to the instrument and began to shout into the mouthpiece, "Hullo! Hullo!"

It was Awtar again, his voice hoarse and cracking. "They are already here . . . hundreds . . . thousands!" And over the hammering of his own heart, Tekchand could hear the buzz of the crowd surrounding Awtar's house, punctuated by the cracks of shots and the hoarse yelling of a mob thirsting for blood.

"My God!" Awtar was saying. "They are setting the house on . . ."

"Hullo—hullo—hullo—Awtar!—Hullo!" he kept shouting into the telephone. "Hullo—hullo—hullo—what's the matter?" It was a few seconds before he realized that the line had gone dead.

"It was good of him to try to warn us," he told his wife. "At a time like this—when they are already there."

"They will drag out the men and pour petrol over them and burn them alive," his wife said. "Just as they did to Dhansingh. That's what they usually do to Sikhs."

He avoided her eyes. So she knew about Dhansingh. The servants could not have heeded his warnings, because no one else could have told her. Suddenly he felt weak and helpless.

For the first time since the riots started, he looks a really beaten man, Sundari thought as she looked at her father—someone who had given up all pretence of courage. It was awful to see him looking like that: the eyes with the permanent frightened stare, the slight trembling of the head, the fingers twitching nervously. She ached to comfort him, to say something that would shake him out of his gloom and make him smile again. Was this, she wondered, the time to tell him about Debi-dayal?

She knew how overjoyed her parents would be to learn that Debi was alive and back in India, a free man, because, now that the British were going, there was no danger of anyone's denouncing him for anti-British activities. If anything, he would be hailed as a patriot who had taken part in the struggle for independence. But how was she going to tell them about Debi's return and keep the details of his marriage secret?

She and Debi had planned it together, first in Bombay and

then in Kernal, where she had spent two days with him. She had undertaken to go to Duriabad to prepare their parents' minds to accept Mumtaz as their daughter-in-law. Debi and Mumtaz were to follow her four days later.

Even at the time, it had seemed a formidable task. And when she had seen the communal discord that raged in the Punjab, her mind had shrunk further from it. She realized that, in the climate of suspicion and hatred, her parents would never accept Mumtaz as one of themselves. The fact that she happened to be a Moslem was far worse than her being someone their son had picked up in a brothel; even Debi's conviction as a terrorist could not have shocked them more.

She had hesitated, and after a few days there had seemed no point in her mentioning anything about it. The riots had flared up. Two days after her arrival the incoming train had been attacked by a mob, and after that all railway services had come to a stop. Now there seemed no possibility of Debi's being able to make the journey to Duriabad—in the opposite direction from the flow of the migration.

And yet, knowing her brother, she was not so sure. In the face of all that was happening along the border, would he still try to come? The thought kept haunting her.

For a long time Tekchand sat rigidly in his chair, while Sundari and her mother went about their chores. Then he went onto the balcony and stood gazing outside, holding the wooden railing tightly. Was that a good sign? Sundari wondered. Did it mean that he had at least begun to take an interest in things again?

"You had better go down to the garage and see that everything is in order," she said, trying not to betray her anxiety about how he would respond, "so that we can get going the moment we have news of the convoy."

He turned with a start. "Yes, of course," he said with alacrity, and went running down the stairs, obviously grateful to be told what to do.

The Ford was in the garage, gleaming, the paintwork and upholstery still smelling new. He thanked the day he had installed the strong roll-down shutters on both the garages, and also the Chubb locks. The second garage was now empty, the Buick having gone. But this was no time to think about the Buick or his chauffeur. He got into the car, pressed the starter, and the engine responded instantly. He let it run for a few minutes and then shut it off. He brought the shutters down and locked the garage door.

They spent the rest of the morning looking out of the windows towards the town and running to the telephone every now and then to see if it was working again. "How are we going to know when they want the convoy to assemble," Sundari asked her father, "now that the phone is dead?"

He had been thinking of that. In fact, he had been thinking about little else. "Oh, the police will come to escort us," he said. "They know it will mean baksheesh. Anyway, the telephone is bound to be put right soon."

"Can't we try to telephone from the Khans' place down the road; or the Mullicks'?" she asked.

"I don't know. How can one tell if their telephones are working—and in any case, who will go?"

All the Moslem houses were tightly shut. Any one of them found sheltering a Hindu would have been regarded as a fifth columnist and subjected to special indignities. It was not fair to seek help from one's Moslem neighbours; it would put them in a false position.

"Why, I shall go," Sundari offered.

He shook his head. The nearest bungalow was at least half a mile away. "I shall go this afternoon," he told her, "if the phone is still not working."

"Isn't it terrible," his wife said, "to think that none of us have said anything about what happened at Awtar's house—whether anyone was saved. We are all so—so immersed in our own problems."

It was quite true, even though it was a shameful thing to have to admit it. They had already put Awtar and the other Sikhs out of their minds. Did nothing matter, when it came to a show-down, apart from saving one's own skin?

As though in answer to his doubts, his anxiety for the Sikhs gave place to a purely personal fear. He had committed himself to leaving the house. Someone had to go, and it was clearly up to him, since it was unthinkable that Sundari should do so.

Now, alone in the bathroom, he was more than ever conscious of his limitations. It was a pity that he was so soft, so useless. It was all very well to have built up the biggest construction business in the Punjab, but it was clear that he was not fitted for the demands of this kind of emergency; even his daughter seemed far less affected by it than he was. But then, did the women really have any idea of what the dangers were? Now, if it had been Debi . . .

And once again he found himself thinking of his son—Debi, tough as they came; he would not have been daunted by any odds.

He took a cold shower and put on the khaki slacks and shirt which he always wore whenever he went to inspect one of his projects. In the passage behind the sitting room, his wife was cooking chapatties on a smoking wood fire. She was still trying to save the sitting-room floor, making her fire outside. Seeing her like that, her eyes squinting against the smoke, her hands encrusted with dough, brought on another wave of self-reproach. He found Sundari in the open passage that ran all along the front of the house.

"You know," he said, pointing toward the museum, "when I was in that room this morning, I wondered to myself for a moment about the futility of going on struggling. Why not regard this as a signal from the gods—the signal of defeat—and recognize that this is the end, instead of struggling to keep things going? I have had a good life and a full life, and it would be improper for me to go on hanging on to it—indecent, almost, according to our philosophy. At my stage in life a man should be prepared to turn his back on sansar—the involvements of the world. Of course, that is all nonsense; I realize that I cannot give up. One has to go on living, struggling, if only for the sake of those who are near and dear to one. There is your mother, yourself . . ."

"And your son," Sundari blurted. It was out of her hands now, for whatever pleasure or pain it would give him. "Yes, your son too," she said, looking hard into his eyes.

The eyes remained expressionless. "My son," Tekchand said very flatly. He shook his head. "We don't even know if he is alive. Eight years now, and do you know, sometimes I get the horrible feeling that I have killed him with my own hands. Anyway, what I was telling you is that it is not easy to give up, however down and out one may feel, when one is caught up in the coils of sansar. There are ties of love that bind one . . ."

Sundari felt a twinge of alarm at the way he was rambling on. "I have not said anything about it to you before," she said. "I think you should know that Debi is back."

He looked into her eyes with a smile that made him appear even sadder than before. "You are a sweet girl and you are only saying it to cheer me up," he told her.

"I am doing nothing of the kind. It is true. He came to see me in Bombay. It is a long story, but the Japanese sent him to India to work for them. But he has done nothing to help them. He lived in Assam all the latter part of the war, in hiding, because the Japanese would have given him away."

"You actually saw him, you say?"

"Of course I saw him! He rang me up at my house. We had meals together; we went for walks. I went and saw them at their room at the Ocean Hotel."

"Them?" he asked. "Them?"

"He and his wife. He is—he is married."

Now that it had come out, she wanted to get it over. "Debi went to Lahore, to see someone, and there he met this girl. A very nice girl—I am sure you will like her. It is just that—that she is not from our kind of family."

But her father was paying no attention to what she was saying. "Tell me, how was he looking? Is he—is he all right, after all that horrible life?"

Sundari's face clouded. "Yes, he is as handsome as ever, very brown and slim. Only . . . his hand, his right hand. It is pitted and there is a scar, and a finger slightly crooked."

"We mustn't say anything to your mother about that, just now," he was saying. "What did they do to him?"

"They didn't do anything—I mean it didn't happen in the Andamans. It was in Lahore. Someone threw one of those bulbs filled with acid at—at his wife. He caught the bulb."

"Debi would. Of course he would," Tekchand commented with a touch of pride. "Is it—the hand—very deformed?"

"It is not deformed or anything. It has healed very well. His wife nursed him through it."

"But why didn't he come here? Why didn't you bring him with you?"

By now she was prepared with the answer. It would never have done to tell him that his son should have been with them a whole week earlier, that it was almost certain that something had happened to prevent him from coming.

"I was supposed to break the news to you; I mean, about his having married the girl, and then write to him. After that he was coming here—both of them. Kernal is hardly a day's journey from here—at least it was."

It was as easy as that. She felt grateful for her father's lack of curiosity. Almost as though she had manipulated it, what had come out in their talk was just what would please him. The unpalatable details still remained unrevealed. She had not told him that the girl was from a brothel, nor that she happened to be a Moslem.

"And now, of course, no one can send a message or a letter," he said. "But how stupid of him—both of you. You should have told him to come, Sundar, brought him with you. We would never have said anything."

It had come and gone, and she felt the better for it. There was no doubt that when her mother came to know about it, she was bound to ask for more details, but at the moment it was wonderful to see the effect it had on her father. The colour had come back to his face, and the slight trembling of his head had passed.

"Does your mother know?" he asked.

Sundari shook her head. "But, Abaji, it is for you to tell her. I wanted you to know first. Go and tell her, now."

Suddenly the pattern of gloom was broken. The load of unresolved guilt which he had carried for the past eight years was to be lightened by his son's return. He no longer thought of death, or that he had had his time, a full innings. The future had acquired a meaning; it was worth struggling for.

"Yes, I should like to do that. I will go and tell your mother. This will make her very happy." He rose to his feet with a quick movement.

"One moment, Abaji," his daughter was saying. "Wait!"

"What is it?"

"There's someone on the road, on a bicycle. Look!"

He turned. It was quite strange to see someone on the road. They had not seen a single human being on the road all day.

"It must be someone going to the Mullicks' place," he said.

"No; he's passed the turning. I think he is coming here."

"I wonder who it could be."

"Wait! I think I know who it is. Gian— Mr. Talwar."

For a moment the name meant nothing to him. Then, as the cyclist came nearer, he saw who it was. The young man who had sold him the statue of Shiva and who had persuaded him to give him a job. He was glad that he had done so, now that Debi was said to be back. His son would be pleased about it.

"I wonder what he wants," Tekchand said.

"I'll go down and find out. You go and tell Mother about Debi. Tell her that he is fit and bronzed and more handsome than ever—and Abaji?"

"Yes?"

"I shouldn't mention anything about his hand—all right?"

"No, I won't."

"Nor about the marriage," Sundari said, making up her mind on the spur of the moment. "Just tell Mummy that Debi is back —that he is waiting for her when we get to the other side. Let us not complicate things just now."

He stood blinking at her for a few seconds. "Just as you like," he said. "Perhaps you are right."

"And explain that now that the British are going, he can live here openly; there's no danger of his being sent back to jail."

"Yes, that should please her."

Tekchand turned towards the sitting room and then stopped. "Sundari, do you think he is quite . . . safe?"

"Who? Mr. Talwar? Oh, yes. I'll tackle him, send him packing. Don't you worry."

The dog was already barking and making darts towards the stairs. Sundari went running down. Gian was just getting off his bicycle when she opened the door. As he saw her, he let his bicycle go and it keeled over slowly and fell down. He stood looking at her, panting. His face and limbs were covered with sweat.

"What is it?" Sundari asked. "My father is hardly in the mood for visitors."

Gian wiped his face with a handkerchief before he spoke. "I am not a visitor," he said. "I have come to stay."

"Stay! What are you talking about?"

He stood in the porch, still panting and wiping his face, but looking strong and determined. "That's right," he announced. "I am going to stick here like glue, right up to the time when you join the convoy. If necessary, sit on the doorstep."

Sundari's hands shook with anger. "I see. That means you want to attach yourself to the convoy."

"Look," he said very evenly, for by now he had regained his

breath. "I am not attaching myself to your house or to the convoy or anything. As soon as you are out on your way, I shall drop
out. And may I point out that it is not at all safe for you to be
standing like this, in the doorway? Anyone hiding in the trees
can take a shot at you. I think you should let me come in, or
shut the door and we will shout through it at each other. I mean
to remain here. You can't get rid of me by being rude now—not
for a while yet."

For a moment she hesitated; then she opened the door wider
and stepped aside.

Without a word, he picked up his bicycle and wheeled it up
the steps. Sundari closed the door behind him and bolted it. He
left the bicycle leaning against the wall and went into the room
behind the stairs where he had waited for his interview with her
father. At the foot of the stairs, as though standing guard on
both sides, were the two Shivas, one from the Little House, and
the other by Maheshwari, both dancing the dance of destruction.
His gaze lingered briefly over the family god, who looked as
though he belonged where he stood, dancing while the world was
being destroyed. The clock on the mantelpiece had stopped at
nine minutes past eight.

"I shall sit here," he told her. "You can lock me in, if that
will make you feel safer."

She had followed him into the room. "Why this sudden eagerness to help?" she asked.

He stood facing her squarely. "Look," he said. "This is something you won't believe, but it happens to be the truth. I don't
know what possessed you, that day of the explosion, to come and
look for me. That is exactly the sort of thing I am doing now. I
have just arrived from Delhi; it took me a whole week. And the
things that are happening everywhere, there as well as here, are
not such that your father and mother should be exposed to. It
came to me all of a sudden, in the middle of the night, when I
discovered that you people were still here. So I came, to give
whatever help I can."

"The thought just came to you," Sundari said with sarcasm;
"here is this family in distress; let me go and give them help."

"It sounds pretty awful, the way you put it; but that's about
what it is."

"How I wish I could believe in you, Mr. Talwar. You have
never done anything without a selfish motive. You even pro-

fessed to fall in love, with a mercenary motive; you sold my brother to secure favours and then—"

"You have said all this before," he pointed out.

"You are making it necessary for me to repeat it."

"Since we are talking about my degradation, may I tell you that that is partly the reason why I have come?" Gian said. "To try and prove, if only to myself, that there can be some good in the weakest of human beings. Don't you see that I am trying to make up?"

"You say that is part of your reason; what makes up the rest?"

He gave her a hard, almost challenging stare. "I hardly know myself. It's the same feeling that prompted you to come looking for me in the docks; I am certain of that. It might even be love."

Sundari said, "I do not need your help, not any more. I think you had better go."

He walked over to the sofa and sat down. He smiled at her, a slow, gentle smile, and shook his head. "I am not going."

"I am going to tell my father all about you," she threatened. "This is just a trick to get taken on our convoy, knowing you've no chance of getting a lift otherwise. This would be the safest bet for anyone caught up on this side, Mr. Talwar."

"You can tell your father all about me, but that is not going to make me go away. And remember that I was not caught up on this side, as you say. I came."

He was still smiling. The smile, the assurance, the arrogant awareness of being in command made Sundari tremble with anger. "Yes, there are a lot of things in the house that are valuable! But remember, there are bound to be other claimants." She stopped, conscious of having drawn blood, knowing that she had made him lose his aplomb.

He had jumped up from the sofa but then sat down again. "You nearly succeeded." He laughed. "That was the one thing that would have made me forget myself—made me go away."

"Then why don't you go away?" she taunted.

"Because you are a silly, spoilt girl saying these things just in order to score off me. No, I am not going."

Sundari turned on her heel, walked out of the room and up the stairs. "What does he want?" her father asked. "I didn't see him go away."

"Nothing," she told him dryly. "He says he just wants to keep us company. He's come all the way from Delhi to do it."

"He must be mad to come into something like this!"

"He certainly sounds unbalanced," Sundari said. "He has parked himself in the waiting room."

"Well, I think it's most kind of him." Sundari's mother joined in. "Another man here, at a time like this. A friend of Debi's. Can he drive a car, do you think?"

"I think so," said Sundari. "He had a small car in Bombay."

"Why don't you ask him up?" her mother said. "He can share our meal. I think I have made enough chapatties."

"You can ask him, Mummy," Sundari told her mother. "I don't feel very friendly towards him—not just now."

"I'll go," Tekchand offered. "I'll go."

"That's a fine thing to say," Sundari's mother said in a tone of irritation. "Why shouldn't you feel friendly towards someone who has come all the way to help?"

"The Sunrise of Our Freedom"

THE train was unlike any train they had ever been in. It was made up by coupling together whatever carriages a skeleton railway staff had been able to assemble from half a dozen station yards; a hotchpotch of derelict passenger carriages, cattle wagons, and timber flats. It was protected by a dozen or so Madrassi soldiers travelling on it in order to keep away the mobs that prowled around the railway stations.

And it was packed with humanity as no other train could ever have been packed before the holocaust that had descended upon them. Men, women, and children were squeezed into windows and doors, stood precariously on the running boards, clung to the fittings between carriages; even the rooftops were packed.

It had been halted at the platform for hours now, looking like an enormous dead snake with myriads of ants clinging to its body. Although no one knew when it would move on again, none of them dared leave their places for fear of losing them.

A week ago they had all been citizens of India, men and women jubilant at the advent of the long-awaited, long-fought-for freedom. Today they were just a small section of a seething movement of humanity. Here, they were the Moslems, the counterparts of the "displaced persons" on the other side, who were Hindus and Sikhs, both sides making for a border that was yet to be officially demarcated. They were, at the moment, stateless citizens, hounded out from the land of their birth as much by collective fear of racial massacres as by the actual outrages perpetrated upon them by their erstwhile fellow citizens. Political expediency had suddenly transformed them into refugees fleeing from their own land as though it had been invaded by an enemy. They left behind everything they possessed: their lands, houses, cattle, their household goods. They also left behind scores of thousands of dead and dying, sacrificial offerings to freedom. They fled without caring for the weak or the lame who had fallen by the wayside.

The dark-faced guards stood with fixed bayonets, listlessly eying the passengers. The passengers huddled together, almost by instinct, like rats on a floating log. They were hungry, thirsty, tired, and sleepy, and many of them were sick and wounded. But they clung on desperately, wallowing in the reek and filth of crowded humanity, degraded, dehumanized, dumb, resigned to the present with a total lack of resistance, as though stunned by the horror which, like a fellow traveller, had arrived with their freedom.

They were already cut off from their environments as effectively as by a surgical operation. They could dream only of a future in a promised land which most of them had never seen; a pure and free land that was going to be their very own: Pakistan.

"A million shall die!" Debi-dayal kept remembering. That was what Shafi had predicted. "A million shall die!" he had told them; perish as a result of the violence that lay hidden in the midst of non-violence.

The date was August 12, 1947; their freedom was only three days away. On August 15, the sun that had not shone for them for more than a hundred and fifty years would rise again. How many more men and women would have been killed by that time, Debi-dayal wondered, how many women abducted?

Yet what was the alternative? Would terrorism have won freedom at a cheaper price and somehow still kept the Hindus and Moslems together? Perhaps not. But at least it would have been an honest sacrifice, honest and manly—not something that had sneaked upon them in the garb of non-violence.

How had they come to this? After living as brothers over so many generations, how had they suddenly been infected by such virulent hatred for each other? Who had won, Gandhi or the British? For the British at least had foreseen such a development. Or had they both lost through not having allowed for structural flaws in the human material they were dealing with? Had Gandhi ever envisaged a freedom that would be accompanied by so much suffering and release so much hatred? Had he realized it might impose transfers of population unparalleled throughout history?

He and Mumtaz were now a part of that migration, squirming, microscopic creatures caught up in the flow of some insect movement.

For him there had been no other answer. He had to go, whatever the risks. But it was certainly not necessary for Mumtaz to accompany him. She could have stayed on in Kernal, even though it was difficult to think of a young Moslem woman living alone at a time like this in this part of India, where gangs of hooligans went patrolling the streets, making house-to-house searches for Moslems. Mumtaz would have been almost certainly discovered, dragged out.

But the risks of staying behind were nothing to the ordeal of the journey. He had been exasperated by her stubbornness. He had fumed at her, entreated her, tried to reason with her, spoken harsh words. And as a last resort he had even tried to sneak away in the middle of the night, when he thought she was asleep. But she had not been sleeping. She had come after him, carrying a ready-packed tiffin basket and a couple of blankets rolled up in a bundle, shouting, "Debi, I am coming with you. I shall never be able to live without you!"

He had not even looked back or slowed his pace, but she had caught up with him. "Please don't leave me," she said in a trembling voice.

He did not reply.

"I came not because I was frightened to be alone, but because I cannot bear to live without you," she told him.

"You lived without me all those years," he reminded her.

"That is the very reason why I cannot bear the thought of your going away without me, don't you see? What were those years to me but a time of waiting—hoping that it would be someone old and kind who would take me away, praying that it would not be someone ugly and deformed, or perverted; not even daring to dream of someone like you. And then that evening I looked up and saw you—a god! For a moment I could not believe my eyes, for that was the greatest moment of my life. It was like a revelation, a sudden madness of joy. You have come to mean everything to me—the world itself."

A tiger cub he had saved, he kept telling himself, a very pretty tiger cub; now it was up to him to look after it. And yet, was that all there was to it—the blind devotion of an animal to its

master? Or was it something else, an emotion deeper and richer
—love?

That had been three days ago. And now they were perched on
the flatcar, waiting for the train to begin moving again.

He had become resigned to her accompanying him. Realizing
this, she now lay curled up against his body, fast asleep in a
sitting position.

A lump came into his throat. This was what he was giving his
bride: a ride in a packed flatcar on which they normally trans-
ported logs and steel girders. Barely a couple of weeks earlier he
had visualized that, now that he was going back into the family
fold, he would be able to give his wife all that a woman's heart
craved for: a car, clothes, jewellery, a house of her own, servants.
And now that the British were going, there was no question of
his having to remain in hiding.

In one short fortnight, gone unnoticed in the preparations for
the festivities to welcome the country's freedom, the whole of
India had been torn by a gigantic convulsion. Overnight the ordered discripline of British rule had been replaced by unimagin-
able chaos.

They had already been on the train for a whole day, and they
had barely covered sixty miles. They had another two hundred
miles to go. When would they get to Duriabad? Would they ever
get there?

Normally it was an overnight journey. You got into the Frontier Mail at night, and in the morning you were there. Only ten
days earlier Sundari had made the journey all by herself; now a
woman travelling alone was difficult to imagine. She had got into
an air-conditioned carriage, and the conductor had even agreed
to let her take her dog with her in the carriage. "Mumtaz and I
will follow you in four days," he had told Sundari. "You do the
groundwork."

"The groundwork" was breaking the news of his marriage to
their parents. He knew that they would be hurt. Men from their
kind of family did not marry Moslem girls, and still less did they
marry a girl picked up from a brothel. And yet he had felt convinced that Sundari would make them understand, prepare their
minds to receive Mumtaz as their daughter-in-law. He had always
depended on Sundari.

Two days after Sundari's departure, when he went to buy the
tickets, he was told that all train services had been cancelled.

After that, he waited another two days in the hope that the services would be resumed. But by then the uprooting of large masses of people was in full swing. All the Moslem railway servants had fled from their posts as the Hindus had fled from their posts on the other side: the stationmasters, signalmen, engine drivers, firemen, ticket-punchers, clerks, guards—everyone had gone. The majority of the Hindu staff too had panicked and run away. The authorities had brought over a skeleton staff from the south, unfamiliar with the line or its working, men who could not even understand the local languages. With their help, they managed to keep a trickle of traffic moving. But the only movement between East Punjab and West Punjab was that of refugees—ticketless travellers all.

He and Mumtaz went to the station dozens of times, trying to find out the timing of the refugee trains, but no one seemed to know anything. In the end they camped at the station itself, squatting on the platform in the midst of the throng of refugees. The train arrived at last, in the middle of the night and already packed to capacity. They all made a concerted rush at it in the darkness, for the lights of the station had long ceased to function. He had to force his way through the yelling, cursing throng, Mumtaz clutching tightly to his arm. He heaved himself on to the flatcar and pulled Mumtaz after him. And then he was one of the passengers, fighting off those who were still trying to get on. The train began to move. If there was a whistle or a warning bell, no one could have heard it over the wail of protest from those who were left behind. Many of them made a last, desperate onslaught on the moving train. A few managed to clamber up, holding grimly on to other men and women clinging to parts of the carriages. Many others were repelled. At least a dozen men and women must have been caught in the wheels and crushed. Their screams were Debi-dayal's last memory of the departure.

They crawled into the night jerkily, making frequent halts. Someone told them that the rails had been displaced by the mobs waiting to attack the trains; that the previous night a whole trainload of refugees had been massacred.

Morning came, the incredible violet mist of the Punjab summer. The plain stretched away on both sides. They passed scene after scene of carnage. At one place there was a scatter of pitiful human belongings: bed-rolls, bundles, tin trunks, chickens in bamboo baskets, brass utensils gleaming in the sunlight, perambulators, boxes, tiffin-carriers, earthen surais, bewildered dogs still chained to stakes in the ground—but not a single human being. It must have been a camp where a thousand or so refugees had been assembled for evacuation. What could have happened to them? Had they made a rush for a train, leaving everything behind, or had they just fled in panic, chased by some howling mob? A few miles farther, they saw in the distance a field covered in red cloth, as though left for drying. It was only when they came closer that they discovered that they were not passing some factory for dyeing bolts of cloth but a scene of massacre, transformed by some trick of the morning light into a mirage. The large patches of red, which had resembled saris left out to dry, shrank and shrivelled and faded before their eyes, leaving only pools of dried blood. The vultures, the dogs, and the jackals emerged, strutting disdainfully. They had pulled and torn the flesh of the bodies of the men and women strewn over the field to such an extent that there was now no way of telling how much mutilation had been inflicted by those who had attacked them. That must be the place where they had attacked the train the previous night.

The man with the black beard sitting next to them kneeled down and began to say his prayers. Debi-dayal was conscious only of a sick feeling in his throat. This was his land, the Punjab, the land of the five rivers. He had always loved it, in all its moods, through the rage of the summer and the healing hand of autumn. But no one could have seen it in this particular mood: unrolling a scene of devastation on both sides as though denuded by swarms of locusts or by invading armies. The trees were picked bare of branch and leaf by the passing hordes of refugees, the roadside villages lay empty and smouldering, overturned and burned-out cars and lorries and bullock carts and tongas littered the roads, and everywhere there were cattle, made suddenly ownerless, wandering about in groups, looking for food.

The land of the five rivers had become the land of carrion. The vultures and jackals and crows and rats wandered about, pecking, gnawing, tearing, glutted, staring boldly at their train.

"A million shall die!" Debi-dayal kept remembering. "A million!" Had that number not already been exhausted?

Now it was night again, and the train had come to another halt. This time they were at a covered platform. He was struck by the total absence of bustle and realized that the station was absolutely empty. Even the familiar, bored-looking Madrassi sentries had been removed. The train had been waiting there hour after hour. No one seemed to know why they were waiting or when they would go on. They had passed Amritsar and must now be very close to the border, Debi-dayal reflected. Then it dawned on him that they were waiting for the train from the opposite side to come through before they would be free to proceed. He had heard someone say that the refugee exchange was being done strictly on a reciprocal basis, a trainload for a trainload, with drivers and military guards being exchanged at the frontier.

The emptiness of the station and the silence made his nerves tingle. So far, they had been in no real danger. The mobs on this side were Hindus; they would never have molested him if he could prove that he was one of themselves and that Mumtaz was his wife. But this was the crucial moment. He had got himself up as a Moslem, complete with a dark brown fez and a long knee-length shirt worn over voluminous pyjamas gathered up at the ankles, and Mumtaz was careful to address him as Karim, a common enough Moslem name. But of course the mobs never respected the way you were turned out; you had to establish incontrovertible proof of your religion. That meant that they made you take off your trousers to make sure you were circumcised.

But in a motley crowd like this, men and women from all parts of India with their different modes of dress and divers casts of faces and shades of colour, they would never suspect that he was a Hindu, he told himself; no one would subject him to that particular indignity. Why, many of the Moslems on their own flatcar could not even speak the language of the Punjab. He would slip away, just an insect wriggling amongst thousands of others in a swarm.

The swarm? It suddenly occurred to him that the moment they crossed the border his fellow passengers would no longer remain the pathetic dregs of humanity that had shared the journey with him with the apathy of cattle being transported to the slaughterhouse. The mere fact of crossing the line would transform them into the ruling race, themselves eager to plunge into the sort of excesses they had been subjected to in the land they had left behind.

He turned to look at them. In the darkness only the nearest were clearly visible, the ones behind were like ghosts, their heads only faintly outlined, receding into infinity. He realized with a start that the man with the sleek oiled beard and the black achkan was staring directly at him. Did he already suspect him? He looked a religious fanatic if ever there was one. He had devoutly turned to the west five times every day and prayed, and he seemed to be mumbling holy words from the Quran all day. Debi-dayal shifted his gaze, trying to hide his nervousness. He must remember to keep away from him, avoid those searching, penetrating eyes of the religious zealot.

Who else? There was the woman draped in the black burkha squatting next to him, who must be the bearded man's wife. She too had seemed to stare at him with bold eyes through the net peepholes in her burkha. She had never once removed her veil, not even when she had squatted down to urinate, hitching up her skirts high over her waist, exposing her thighs and buttocks to their gaze but never her face.

He gave a sudden start. Mumtaz was nudging his shoulder, whispering something into his ear. He nodded and straightened his legs so that she could crawl over him and scramble down the side of the flatcar. Luckily, it was now almost pitch dark. For a minute or two, she squatted between the two sets of rails, keeping her head low, and then climbed back into her place.

Micturition was a purely physical need, and it was wrong to feel squeamish about its demands, but he still had not got used to that particular humiliation. The others on the train did not seem to mind where and how they relieved themselves. He and Mumtaz had always waited for the darkness. And he had to be particularly careful, go as far away from the track as he dared to, not knowing who was looking, trying to check, from whether he was circumcised or not, if this man with the typical Punjabi-Hindu features who called himself Karim was really the Moslem he pretended to be.

Was his face really that of a Hindu? Had the mullah with the black beard which was so obviously dyed and his young wife whose bold, lecherous eyes peeped through the burkha already marked him down?

Many people claimed that just by looking at a man they could tell a Hindu from a Moslem; he himself could never have told the difference. He fingered the typical, down-curving Moslem moustache that he had acquired, and felt thankful for the three-day growth of beard on his face.

There was a rumble of wheels coming from the opposite direction, and then it was drowned by the tumultuous yells of the passengers of the oncoming train which had now come into the zone of safety for the Hindus. Soon a train crawled past, just as crowded as the others, even in the darkness, they could see the snake with the ants clinging tightly to its body joggle past, its passengers yelling with joy:

"Jai Hind! Jai Hind! Mahatma Gandhi-ki jai! Jai Hind!" The night air shook with their yells.

The roar could be heard long after the train had gone. The passengers in Debi-dayal's train, who had watched them in a sullen silence, now buzzed with a new eagerness, knowing that they would soon be on their way. They had seen the southbound train that had come from West Punjab: the price for their own release had been paid.

There was a sound of footsteps in unison. Soldiers with torch-lights came and climbed into the guard's van. The engine hissed for a time and then gave a stifled whistle. The wheels began to move. Another hour, and they themselves would be out of danger. Then they too would be in a position to yell for joy, spend themselves in a sudden shudder of release.

"Pakistan Zindabad! Pakistan Zindabad!"

They had yelled themselves hoarse when they crossed the border of silence. Now they were in West Punjab. Debi-dayal had shouted just as lustily as the others. The train now crawled through the night at walking speed. The men and women around them stirred like a swarm of bees preparing for flight. The great fear was now behind them. Even at the rate they were going, they would arrive in Duriabad before noon, Debi-dayal calculated. Noon on August the fifteenth.

August the fifteenth!

He suddenly realized that for the past few hours they had already been a free people, both Indians and Pakistanis; that the sun that was about to rise would be the dawn of their freedom.

Then the train came to a halt, the first halt since they entered Pakistan territory. It was four in the morning, and the false dawn was already showing in the east. Soon it would be daylight. He felt elated, ready to greet the sun. He shifted his shoulder slightly, but Mumtaz, who was leaning against it, did not wake.

Suddenly his heart stood still. The sound in the far distance was only too familiar. It was the war-cry of a mob on the prowl, something like the roar of a distant sea. It was always the same, whether Hindu or Moslem; from a distance no one could have told the difference.

Mumtaz stirred against his shoulder. She was now awake, listening.

The sound came nearer, became less indistinct. In the misty darkness around them they could see nothing, but they could hear that some sort of commotion was going on farther along the line. They heard the bark of rifle fire and then suddenly the ra-tat-tat-tat burst of a machine-gun.

"Hai-allah!" Mumtaz whispered. She gave Debi-dayal's hand a gentle squeeze.

"No need for us to worry," someone was saying at the other end of their car. "They are our brothers; they can do nothing to us."

The roar of the crowd then suddenly ceased, but for a long time no one knew what had happened. Then they heard footsteps coming along the track. They peered into the darkness: a straggly line of soldiers marching, taking positions on both sides of the train, facing outwards. Then someone came behind them, shouting orders.

"It must be their captain," someone suggested.

"What is it? What is he saying?" everyone was asking everyone else.

"They say they are expecting an attack," someone said. "The troops are here to protect our train."

"Attack! Attack from whom? Not from our own brothers! After all we have been through!"

The darkness faded and a faint light came up in the east. Now they could see the soldiers clearly, waiting with bayonets fixed to their rifles, facing a vast, treeless waste. The babble in the flatcar rose, as in the other cars of the train. "What are they holding us here for?" they began to complain. "Who is going to attack us?" they kept asking the soldiers. "Who can attack us when we are in our own land?" The man with the oiled beard drywashed his hands and knelt down to pray.

"They always expect an attack at night," someone said. "They attack any trains—they are looters; they don't worry about whether their victims are Hindus or Moslems."

"Allah be praised! The day is coming."

"Yes, they dare not attack us during the day; not when our soldiers can see to shoot."

"Long live our soldiers! Shabash to our jawans!"

"Long live Pakistan!"

"Pakistan Zindabad!"

"Zindabad! Zindabad! Zindabad!"

"Khamosh! Silence! SILENCE!"

"Listen, someone is trying to say something!"

"I think it is the captain."

"Silence! Silence! Khamosh!"

"What are they saying?"

Suddenly there was silence. They could hear a voice in the background, saying again and again, "Listen! Pay attention here! Listen!"

They turned their heads in the direction of the sound and waited for what the speaker had to tell them.

"Listen! There has been trouble on the line a mile farther on. The mob dismantled the line, but now they have been dispersed. We feared they were going to attack the train, taking advantage of the dark. So we posted the sentries. Now the train can go no farther. It will be taken back from here. You will have to get out and walk. Another two miles, they will make arrangements to transfer you into another train. Is that clear?"

Yes, it was very clear. They began to curse and grumble. Now, after arriving in their own land, they were being told to get out and walk. The promise of another train two miles farther down the line did not ring at all true. Trains were not easy to come by these days; they all knew that.

"Listen!" the same voice yelled. "Khamosh!"

It was as if a switch had been turned off. The crowd's babble stopped.

"Now that it's getting light, I am withdrawing the sentries. They have been on duty all night and have to be relieved. Now get going. You haven't all day to wait here! Come on! Come on! Juldi!"

"Janabe-ali, please don't take away the soldiers! Don't abandon us—protector of the poor!" The clamour of protest rose from their midst. "What will we do without protection, here, in the midst of nowhere?"

"The sun will be up in half an hour. They do not attack in the daytime. You have nothing to fear."

He began to bark orders at his soldiers and they shuffled off after him, unfixing their bayonets as they marched and slinging their rifles on their shoulders. Meekly the passengers began to scramble out of the train, moaning and sighing as they stretched their cramped limbs.

The light was enough to see the distant hills now, the hills beyond which lay Duriabad. How many miles was it? The south-western breeze was on their backs, making them shiver.

And then they saw the men gathering in ones and twos on both sides of the track, and in the middle distance there were more and more figures, indistinct in the half-darkness. There was nothing familiar about the landscape now; this was part of the country that the trains always covered at night. The train stood forlornly in the middle of nowhere.

The sky acquired a blue tinge and the stars disappeared; the figures were now more distinct. And as they gathered strength they came nearer and nearer to the track, not saying anything, not even speaking amongst themselves. Their faces were grim and they walked with a strutting awareness of power. Most of them carried lathis or axes, and a dozen or so carried great curved swords or shotguns slung on leather holsters.

Even when they were within hailing distance, there was no exchange of words between the passengers who had alighted from the abandoned train and these onlookers. Then the passengers began asking questions.

"How far is the water from here?"

"Is there a grain shop? Can we buy some flour, or rice?"

"What is the name of this place?"

The onlookers did not answer a single question. They peered at their faces, hungry hawks selecting their prey, talking amongst themselves in whispers.

Then a thin-faced man with a hooked nose came forward. He carried a shotgun and a bandolier of cartridges slung across his chest.

"Which are the Hindus amongst you?" he barked. "Come on, tell us quickly. You will be saving your own time."

"There are no Hindus. We are all Moslems—Allah be praised!" said the man with the black beard.

The man with the gun frowned. "Nonsense! There are always Hindus, in every train—hiding, pretending to be Moslems. We found at least fifty in the last train."

"Fifty! More like a hundred!" someone said behind him.

More and more people were joining their leader now, asking questions.

"Come on, juldi!"

"We shall find out in any case. The sooner you tell us, the better."

"Last time there were even women—show us the women!"

"No, no; there are no Hindus. We are all Moslems."

"All Moslems. Pakistan Zindabad!"

"Pakistan Zindabad!" Debi-dayal said.

"Zindabad! Zindabad!"

And then someone shrieked. "There's a Hindu!—a kaffir! I used to know him, in Ludhiana!"

"Where! Where?"

They saw a scuffle, half a dozen men falling upon the man with the black beard and the achkan. "Pull him down!" the people yelled. "A kaffir! A shaitan! A spy!"

"I am a Moslem—of the faith! I swear, a Moslem!"

"We will see soon enough. Come on, bring him over!"

"No-o!" he began to scream. "Oh, no-ooo!"

A dozen eager hands held him down, tore away his clothes. "A kaffir!" they pronounced. "Yaaah! a Hindu!"

"Oh, spare me—please save me! I was only going to see my daughter, my only—hia—yaah!" He let off an ear-splitting scream as someone brought down a lathi on his head.

"Kill him!" the crowd yelled. "Kill the spy!"

"The impostor! A spy travelling in our midst as a Moslem!"

"But make him a Moslem first—cut off his penis!"

"You should have seen how they treated our men!"

"And the things they did to our mosque in Raniwada!"

"Yes, do his sunta—circumcise him!"

A man with a sword bent over the fallen man while the others held him down. His screams rose high above the frenzied yells of the crowd. Others led the woman in the burkha away; she was howling and beating her breast. Someone reached out and tore away her veil and then the others joined in eagerly and stripped off all her clothes. There was a short scuffle, an argument about who should take her away. Two of them lifted her and carried her away while the others hurled obscenities at them. Then the others came and stood flanking the man with the hooked nose.

"There's another of them! Look!"

"A kaffir! a Hindu! An enemy daring to come in our midst!"

"And here! Pretending to be a woman! In a burkha too. I was suspicious right from the start!"

"Shabash! Shabash! Well done!"

It was amazing how many Hindus had been travelling with them, in elaborate disguises. They were denounced by their fellow passengers and the men were ceremoniously emasculated before being abandoned to the vengeance of the crowd, and the women carried away. So the man with the dyed beard whom he had taken to be a mullah was an impostor—his woman too, in the burkha, who had kept her face hidden all that time.

Men, women, and children from the train fell on the victims, eager to show their zeal, spending themselves in ghoulish excesses, while the onlookers roared approval and encouragement. The screams of the victims rent the morning air. Someone threw a small child high in the air, and before it fell down, a man with a sword ran forward and caught it on the point of his sword.

Mumtaz and Debi-dayal stood hand in hand, not daring to move, just a couple in a crowd that had scented blood—the joys of revenge.

At least twenty men had been denounced, their wives and children given the punishment the crowd demanded. It was amazing how correctly they had guessed. Every one of them had sworn that he was a Moslem; not one had proved to be. No one was shown any mercy. Many were already dead even though their tormentors were still hurling stones at their bodies, bringing down lathis with loud whipping sounds, cursing. . . .

"There's another of them!" someone shrieked. "I am sure he is a Hindu!" He was pointing at Debi-dayal.

"Yes, he has been behaving most suspiciously; he has not even shouted encouragement at those who are bringing them to justice!"

"A kaffir! A spy! A Hindu!" the chant began.

"He is my husband!" Mumtaz said defiantly. "Karim Khan!"

The crowd was already forming around him, making a circle.

"Then can he prove that he is a Moslem?"

"Of course he can! But how can you inflict such an indignity on one of your own faith!"

"We shall see . . . we shall see."

The grabbing, coarse, knotted hands were already upon them, tearing them apart. Debi-dayal found himself dragged away, felled; felt the horny fingers tearing at his clothes, like the beaks of birds, the claws of animals.

"A Hindu!" they announced in triumph. "A kaffir!"

Above the clamour that rose all around them, he could hear Mumtaz's shrieks distinctly. "No! No-oo! No-ooo!" And then he saw her struggle and leap through the packed rows of men and boys around him. She hurled herself on his prone body, still shrieking.

He felt her arms tighten around him as they tried to force her away, felt her clothes being torn off her, heard the obscenities and the catcalls of the crowd. And then suddenly they were wrenched apart, and he could see her being carried away, naked and struggling, screaming at the top of her voice.

And as they forced their way through the crowd, through the gap, he saw the sun that had just risen.

That was the last thing he ever saw: the rising sun in the land of the five rivers on the day of their freedom. The next second his eyes were blinded by a great flash of pain that seemed to shoot up from the centre of him, as though a bomb had exploded between his loins.

And the last thing he ever heard was his name being shouted by his wife with all her might.

"Debi! Debi, my darling! I shall never live without you! I am coming with you too. . . . I am coming. . . ."

He surrendered himself to the pain, not knowing what she was trying to tell him, but taking a childish, pathetic consolation in the fact that she wanted to be with him wherever he was now going—go with him as she had always wanted to go wherever he went.

[36]

The Land They Were Leaving

THE morning dragged on, interminably slow. They all sat in the sitting room that had become their camping ground, looking at magazines, trying to hide their anxiety. The telephone was still not working. Towards one o'clock Gian got up and said that he would go and find out the latest information about the convoy.

"But you can't," Sundari's mother protested. "Is it really necessary?"

"Of course it is; otherwise we shall never know when they are ready to start," Gian told her.

"But it is not safe for a Hindu to go into the centre of the town, on a bicycle too."

"I think I shall be able to manage," Gian assured her. "Will you come and bolt the door after me?" he said to Sundari. She got up and followed him, without saying anything. In fact, she had not spoken a single word to him since he came upstairs.

Gian was gone for nearly two hours. Tekchand spent most of the time pacing up and down the passage, glancing alternately at his watch and at the road. Sundari sat in a chair in the passage, but with her back turned to the road. When her father saw the bicycle in the distance, he gave an audible sigh of relief. "There he is!" he said brightly. "You had better go down and open the door."

Sundari herself felt a curious sense of relief at Gian's return, but she did not speak to him. He parked his bicycle in the waiting room and ran upstairs.

"They still have no idea," he told Tekchand. "They are still waiting for information from the other side. I shall go again, later in the evening. I found out about the telephone too. There's no chance of the service being restored for days. The

356

wires have been cut in many places, and the poles felled. It seems that the Hindu employees of the company have either run away or are keeping in hiding. The Moslems are busy—busy with what everyone else seems to be doing."

"Is no one's telephone working?" Tekchand asked.

"Not one; the whole system's broken down. I'll just have to make another trip on my bicycle. They said something about starting the convoy tonight—but the inspector wouldn't tell me a thing. I shall go again in the evening."

"Why do they have to be so secretive about it?" Tekchand complained. "How are we to know anything about it, three miles from the town, if they don't let us know in advance?"

"I suppose they have to be secretive for our own safety," his wife pointed out. "To ensure that there is no attack just when the convoy is being assembled, with everyone neatly gathered in one place."

"How can we trust anyone, when the police themselves take sides?" Tekchand said in a resigned voice.

"The servants were saying that in Bhawalpur a whole convoy was taken into the desert and attacked by its military escort. No one escaped."

"Nonsense!" her husband snapped. "Servants' gossip, all built up on rumour and fear."

"But don't you think it's just as well to realize what we're in for?" his wife said very gently. "Why pretend things are better than they really are?"

"I managed to get two tins of condensed milk," Gian announced. He fished them out of his pockets.

"It certainly is good having you here," Tekchand said with feeling. "So comforting. That two hours you were away weren't so good, I can tell you. I felt quite lonely. It's good to have a resourceful young man in the house."

"I think that both you and Mrs. Tekchand should go and get some rest," Gian suggested. "There's no point in all of us waiting here, particularly if we are to start tonight."

"When did you say you were going back into town?" Tekchand asked.

"At seven in the evening. They should know by then."

"I certainly hope we are able to get away tonight," Tekchand said. "Every day that they delay, our chances of getting away become more difficult."

Sundari gave a nervous laugh. "Since everyone's doing all this plain speaking, what are they like just now?"

"Very good indeed!" Gian told her. "Only a few hours more, and we should be on our way—at least fifty cars, escorted by police jeeps and a few military trucks of the boundary force. Just a day's journey, and then we'll be across the border."

"A day's journey in one's own car," Tekchand pointed out. "Not in one of those convoys; not with the roads jammed as they are. Some of them take a whole week."

In the dark, Sundari first heard the urgent clanging of the bicycle bell. Then Gian came into the circle of light cast by the porch lamp. He was panting hard. Even as she opened the door, she knew that something had gone wrong.

He jumped off and ran up the steps, carrying his bicycle. "Something awful has happened," he told her. "The convoy was formed quite early this evening. It left nearly an hour ago."

For a moment they were both speechless, staring at each other as animals do when a shot rings out in the jungle. And then she gasped. "How are we going to break this to Abaji?"

"I have been thinking of that all the while I was coming back. I don't even know what to suggest. I don't think there are going to be any more organized convoys from this place—I mean properly escorted ones, the way things are shaping. To go on sitting here, waiting, would be suicidal."

"Do you think they were deliberately misleading us?" Sundari asked.

"It looks very much like it. When I was there at three, the man outside said they'd be starting in the evening. But the inspector was quite emphatic that they would not—told me to call at seven again. He must have known all the time."

"What is the alternative now?"

"I would suggest that we dash after the convoy and catch up. They couldn't be more than ten miles away, at convoy speed."

"Do you really think that is the answer?"

"How can one tell? That seems to be the most sensible thing to do. And yet, who knows, if we are caught before we reach the convoy . . ." He stopped in mid-sentence.

"Can't we pretend to be Moslems—give Moslem names, wear achkans and odhnis and salwars?"

He shook his head in despair. "They—they invariably make

the men undress, to see if they are circumcised. But they would spot us as impostors even without that. We would be driving in the opposite direction. And in your father's case—my own too— even that would not be necessary. Our ears are pierced for earrings. Anyone can tell that we are Hindus."

"Then you think we should chance it?"

"I would be all for it. There is danger in that too, but sitting here is just asking for trouble."

"Come on, then, that's what we'll do." She grabbed his hand and led him up the stairs. "Pretend there is no danger. Abaji will do whatever you tell him to do— What is it?"

He had halted on the stairs and motioned her to stop.

"Just a moment," he whispered. "What's that noise?"

They could hear the sound of a car coming up the road. "My God!" She gasped. "Does that mean it is already too late?"

He shook his head. "They don't come in motor cars. They come marching. It may even be your brother."

"I don't think so," she said. "Somehow I have a feeling that this is what we've all been waiting for. No, Debi has no car."

"But he could have got one. It's here! Switch off the lights, quick! And don't worry. I am sure it's nothing to worry about."

Sundari found the switch and turned off the lights. They stood in the darkness at the foot of the stairs, Sundari clutching Gian's wrist. He could feel the trembling of her body, and her fingers were like ice.

The dog came scampering down the stairs and began to bark. There was a sound of footsteps on the other side of the front door, followed by a knock.

"Ask him who it is," Gian said to her in a whisper.

"Who is it?" Sundari asked.

"Open the door, please. We are friends. We have come to escort you to the convoy."

"Name?" Gian whispered. "Ask him his name."

"What is your name?"

"Open the door and we will tell you," the voice said, and there was a loud and prolonged thumping on the door.

Gian leaned closer to her. "I'll go and hide," he told her. "Just in case. Let them think you are alone in the house. Just check up on some particulars—they may be telling the truth. But be tactful, please—polite!"

"We are all by ourselves in the house, my father and mother

and I," Sundari said. "I am sure you will understand that we have to be careful. Who sent you? Where are we to join the convoy?"

"What is it, Sundari? Who has come in the jeep?" Tekchand called out from above. "What are you doing in the dark?"

They were both startled by his question. "I am finding out who they are, Abaji," Sundari told him, hoping that her tone of urgency would communicate itself to him. "Please go and sit with Mother and—and don't say another word; it might not be safe!"

The banging on the door had suddenly stopped. In the silence, they could hear the whispered conversation in the porch, punctuated by a sibilant oath and a nervous giggle. "I'll put on the porch light," Gian told Sundari. "You peep out of the window and see if it's anyone you know. Where is the switch?"

She guided him to the switch and placed his hand on it. Then she went up to the window on the right of the door and pulled the blind aside. He flicked the switch on and off, and the porch lights came on and went out again. He went and stood close to her near the window and felt her body quiver at his touch.

"Who?"

She turned to him and held both his hands. "Shafi!" She gasped.

They ran up the stairs, still holding each other by the hand. Both Tekchand and Sundari's mother were standing at the head of the stairs, their faces beset with fear.

"Don't let them find out there's an extra man in the house," Gian warned. "I'll hide myself downstairs and come out only— only if it becomes necessary. For all you know, they may not—I mean, you may be able to buy them off."

They were breaking open the main door, hammering at it with some heavy instrument. "How many are there?" Gian asked Sundari.

"There were three outside the jeep, one at the wheel—oh, God! Four!"

The blows came louder now. Sundari's mother folded her hands in prayer and closed her eyes. "Jagadamba, mother of the world," she prayed. "Save us from this ordeal."

"Don't attempt to resist," Shafi yelled from below. "We have got revolvers. Here!" There was the report of a shot being fired. "See? The first person who comes against us will be shot."

"Go and lock yourself in the room with the statues," Gian whispered. "That will take them another few minutes to open—give you a little more time. Me too, I have to hide that bicycle."

He ran down the stairs and they saw him disappear in the darkness of the waiting room. The others had barely gone into the museum and locked the door behind them when they heard the front door splinter. After that one of them must have put a hand through the crack and released the catch, and suddenly the voices and the footsteps were in the house.

They could hear their progress in the hall below and up the stairs and then along the long passage that led past the upstairs rooms to the museum at the end. Spindle cowered at Sundari's feet, giving out low whimpers.

There was a loud crack on the door, as though it had been hit with some steel instrument, followed by a peremptory voice saying, "Open the door!"

They stared at the door in silence, heard the blows fall harder, saw the trembling of the door against each blow. "What do you want?" Sundari said fiercely.

For a second the blows stopped. "I want to ——— you!" a voice answered from outside. It was followed by the laughter of the others.

"The bloody swine!" Tekchand muttered in sudden anger. "That's no way to talk! And stop breaking up that door!" he yelled. He rushed up to the door and slid the bolt open. "Stop that, now!" he shouted, flinging the door open.

Shafi Usman and two men stood outside. Shafi had a revolver in his right hand and a leather holster slung across his chest. The other two held the tire-levers which they had been using to break down the doors.

"I'll give you a thousand rupees," Tekchand began, "if you leave the house—"

Shafi did not even look at him. He shoved him out of the way and marched into the room, his eyes fixed on Sundari. "Put on the lights, Hamid!" he ordered, still staring at Sundari. "You guard the door, Inoos!"

"Stop! Stop this outrage at once!" Tekchand said in a shaking voice. "How dare you break into—"

At this stage the man who was guarding the door came up to him and crashed his fist into his face.

Sundari's mother screamed. "Don't touch my husband!" she pleaded. "Please! You can have my ring, necklace, everything, but—"

Shafi laughed. His laughter was like a gorilla's coughing. "Stop the woman whining!" he ordered.

Hamid must have found the switch. The two chandeliers flooded the room with light, covering the bronze figures and the men and women with a harsh glare. Shafi advanced close to Sundari, screwing up his eyes.

"I will kill you!" Sundari spluttered. "Don't touch me, don't touch me—and leave the dog alone!" she shrieked. "Stop! Spindle! . . . Oh, no-oo!"

Spindle had made a dart at Hamid, the man who had put on the lights, and Hamid had brought the tire-lever crashing down on its head, splitting the skull open. For a few moments the dog lay twitching at their feet and then became still.

"You brute!" Sundari shrieked and made a rush at Hamid, but Shafi lunged forward and caught her. He pinned her to his chest for a moment and then pushed her away with force. She staggered and fell against the side of the carved sofa and then sank down on the carpet. But she got to her feet again and stood holding the side of the sofa, panting, her face a mask of hatred.

"Yaah!—look at those kaffir gods!" the man at the door was saying. "Just look at them! There's a pair actually . . ."

"I'll kill you for this!" Sundari was saying, glaring at Hamid. But as Hamid advanced towards her as if to hit her, Shafi stopped him.

"Don't touch the girl! You take the other woman!"

Sundari's mother gave a low moan. "The god will punish you for this," she said. "Your own god."

Shafi turned to Tekchand. "Your son took away my girl. You know what I did to her? I threw acid on her face—disfigured her for life. But that's not enough for me. I have to get a girl in exchange." He pointed his revolver at Sundari. "There!"

"Don't boast!" Sundari retorted. "She was not disfigured—and you haven't got me."

Shafi gave a short guffaw. He tossed his revolver in the air and caught it again. Then he put it away in the holster.

"Look, I shall give you a lakh of rupees," Tekchand said. There was a streak of blood running down his lower lip. "A lakh, if only—"

"Only a lakh!" Shafi taunted. "Did you hear that, Hamid? That's what they are worth to him, his wife and daughter—a lakh."

"Don't even talk to that animal, Abaji," Sundari said to him.

"Animal!" Shafi grimaced. "You'll see, soon enough, what kind of animal."

"Oh, Shafi, Hamid, look at these obscene gods!" Inoos said.

Shafi began to stare at the images, almost as though he had just become aware of them. He strode over, seized one of the statues in his hand, and crashed it on another. Then, as though seized with a frenzy, he went about the room, raining blows on the figures, toppling them down.

"Stop it! Stop it!" Tekchand shouted. "They are sacred to us!" The blood was still running from his lip. "Sacred, don't you see, just as your own god is sacred to you. And these women are my wife and daughter. They should be like sisters to you. I implore you, in the name of all that is sacred to you, your prophet Mohammed himself, not to touch them, your sisters—"

"Sisters!" Shafi turned on him viciously. "Is that how you Hindus treated our women? Like sisters and mothers! They were raped in front of their own men; in Nabha, Patiala; in Delhi itself. Raped, mutilated—they weren't sisters then!"

"Oh!" Sundari's mother uttered a stifled moan. She put her hands against her eyes and crumpled down and lay hunched up on the carpet. Tekchand darted forward to rush to her side, but Hamid intervened and pushed him back.

"Don't move, anyone!" Shafi barked. "Hit them if they make a move!" he ordered.

"Yaah!—look at those breasts!" Inoos waved from his post at the door. "Like mangoes. Look at— Toba! What was that?"

They turned their heads to the door, where Inoos stood framed, clutching the tire-lever in his hand and listening to the sounds of the scuffle that came from downstairs. And they heard the stifled half-moan, half-shriek followed by a thud. Shafi whipped out his revolver. "Go and see what is happening, Inoos!" he snapped.

They saw Inoos turn and go running down the passage, and then they heard the sound of other footsteps running up the stairs. They heard Inoos's yell at the end of the passage: "Hai-to-baa! There's another of them in the house, the—" And then a crash and a sudden silence followed by a series of bumps.

Gian had sprung out of the darkness, carrying the Shiva in his hands, and brought it down on Inoos' upraised arm which held the tire-lever; then, as Inoos staggered under the blow, he had swung again at his shoulder. Inoos crumpled where he stood, at the head of the stairs, and then went rolling down a few steps in slow, thudding bumps.

"The lying bitch—telling us there was no one else in the house!" Shafi cursed. He held the revolver at the ready, its hammer cocked, aimed at the doorway.

"Gian! Don't show yourself in the door!" Sundari shouted. "He's got a pistol aimed at the door!"

But even as she was saying it, Gian was in the doorway, in full view, wielding the metal image of an unshapely god. He was clutching it to his chest like a shield when Shafi pulled the trigger.

The bullet crashed against the metal and glanced off, making a distinct, bell-like sound which hung in the air long after its report had died out. Gian still crouched in the doorway, his face grim. "If you get the chance, make a dash for it and hide in the trees," he told them, without taking his eyes away from Shafi's gun. "It's quite safe below. I have laid out—"

"Stop the girl moving! Stop anyone moving!" Shafi yelled at Hamid, still holding the revolver rigidly aimed at Gian. "I'll look after this— Watch out! The woman! Watch out! Damn it, the old bitch!"

Sundari's mother had picked up one of the figures lying close to her and come to a sitting position. As Hamid turned, she swung with it at his legs from hardly five feet away. Hamid uttered a groan of pain and reeled against the sofa, throwing out his hands to balance himself.

Then everything happened in a split second, almost simultaneously, too quickly for their powers of reasoning to make any difference to the result.

"Chinal!" Shafi cursed in his rage and leaped to where Sundari's mother sat crouching. He thrust the muzzle of the revolver into her chest and fired.

Even as he was turning, Gian hurled the Shiva at him from where he stood. It caught him squarely on the side and made him stagger at its impact. And then Gian made a dive for Hamid, who had struggled to his feet, but he eluded him and made a bolt for the door. As Gian went racing after him, he saw Sundari pick up the Shiva he had flung at Shafi. At the head of the stairs he gave up the chase and turned back.

The sight that met his eyes made him stand still for a moment, feeling numb, his knees wobbly. Shafi was wriggling on the floor, shielding his head with his hands, and Sundari stood above him, the Shiva from the Little House in her hands. He saw her bring it down on Shafi's head, and then, when the man rolled forward and lay limp on the carpet, he saw her bring it down again and again, as though killing a scorpion or a spider, crashing in the dead man's skull until it cracked open and blood and brains spurted out in a red and white mess.

He ran up to her and put a hand on her shoulder. She whirled around, still holding the bloodied Shiva in her hands. "Your mother." He pointed. "Go to her."

For a second or two she stood glaring at him uncomprehendingly; then she dropped the Shiva and ran to where her father was bending over her mother, cradling her head in his lap.

She was still alive, but it was clear that she would not live more than a few minutes. There was a bubble of pink blood on her mouth, and her moans were getting less and less audible.

"What is it, dear? Yes, yes, I am here. Sundari is here too," Tekchand was saying to his wife. "What is it, Radha?"

"Please don't leave me here, darling, please take me with you," she was saying.

Her husband wiped the froth from her lips with his hand and then brushed her lips with his. "No, I shall never leave you," he promised. "Now rest."

Gian turned his eyes away, aware that this was something too private for his eyes and ears. For a moment he thought of going to look for Hamid again, but even as he was turning, he heard the jeep drive off with a roar and a crash of gears and saw its lights flooding the long tree-lined driveway of Kerwad House.

The pale light of dawn was just beginning to make their headlights unnecessary when they saw the long black snake of dimmed lights crawling ahead of them in the desert—hundreds of vehicles crammed with fleeing Hindus: the convoy.

Another ten minutes and they were a part of it, moving with antlike precision towards the part of India that was to remain India.

"They killed her," Tekchand kept saying every now and then.

"They killed her, my Lakshmi—and I have left her behind. Not even cremated. All alone! I promised I wouldn't. She would never have left me."

For Sundari it was heartbreaking to hear him. Strangely, he was not crying. He looked dazed, and the way in which he kept talking about his wife was curiously matter-of-fact.

"I have left your mother all alone. She would never have left me."

It was like a refrain, a background sound-track to a movie; it was in some way a cry in the wilderness too, heeded by no one. They concentrated on the drive, trying to blunt their minds to the dangers and hardships of the journey, saying nothing to him, aware that there was nothing to say.

About nine o'clock the convoy ground to a halt. A military jeep with a loudspeaker drove past them and told them that they were being made to halt because they were due to pass a convoy going in the opposite direction. They were ordered to pull their vehicles to one side of the road so that the other convoy could pass. It would take about an hour, they were told, and during that time they were allowed to get out of their vehicles if they wished.

Tekchand was listening to the announcement, his head cocked to one side. "They are going to my land," he mumbled. "I am running away from it. Leaving my wife alone—just lying in that room."

Men, women, and children got out of their vehicles, each trying to find a place to relieve himself, sheer physical compulsion heaping another humiliation upon them. They squatted wherever they could, urinating, defecating, washing themselves with their precious stocks of water, each trying to avoid looking at the welter of shamed humanity around him.

Sundari brewed a pot of tea on the primus stove and opened a tin of condensed milk. As she handed Gian his cup, he asked, "Where is your father?"

"He has just gone to stretch his legs," she told him. "He'll be back any minute."

"We have been here for half an hour already," Gian pointed out.

"Half an hour!" Sundari gasped. "Oh, my God! You don't think . . ."

That was exactly what Gian had been thinking. But he tried

to calm her fears. "I shouldn't worry. There are still another thirty minutes to go."

They waited without saying anything. All around them people were getting back into their vehicles. The convoy in the opposite direction went rumbling past. And then the jeep with the loud-speaker was back, ordering them to get back into line and move off. Their brief halt was over.

Meekly they got into the car and waited. The station wagon ahead of them lurched off, the men riding on its roof holding precariously to the carrier railing. The car behind them began to honk impatiently, and then the long lines of trucks and cars and jeeps took up the refrain. The military jeep with the loudspeaker came rushing up to them.

"What wrong?" a foghorn voice bawled at them. "Get a bloody move on! You there! You! Gian Talwar!"

Gian blinked. He found himself sweating. It couldn't be. He was staring into the face of Patrick Mulligan; the Teddy-bear shape wedged into the front seat of the jeep, crowned by the round red face, the pale grey eyes unblinking, the voice of authority hoarser than ever, more commanding.

"My father is missing," Sundari told him.

"What's that? Hell, miss, we can't wait all day for him! Move on, will you!" he ordered Gian. "We can't hold up the convoy for someone's old man!"

For a second or two Gian hesitated. Then he started the engine and threw the car into gear while Mulligan kept motioning him forward with his arm. Then, without looking at Sundari, he released the clutch. The Ford leaped forward.

Glossary

A

Aap: you, as in addressing elders.
Achar: pickle.
Ahimsa: non-violence.
Akhada: wrestling pit.
Arre: a mode of address, rather like "look here."
Avatar: incarnation.
Ayah: nursemaid.

B

Babu: clerk, white-collar worker.
Bachha: child.
Badmash: rogue.
Baksheesh: reward, tip.
Bania, or baniya: trader.
Begoon Bhaja: fried egg-plant.
Beta: child.
Bhai: brother.
Bhajan: devotional song.
Bharat-mata-ki-jai: victory to Mother India.
Brahmin: high-caste Hindu.
Bramha: god of creation.
Bud-tamiz: ill-mannered.
Bund: embankment.

Burkha: veil.
Bustee: slum.

C

Chalan: draft.
Chalo-Delhi: on to Delhi.
Champak: a kind of flower.
Chapatti: unleavened bread.
Chaplis: sandals.
Charpoy: string bed.
Chawl: tenement building.
Chinal: whore.
Chiraita: bitter extract of herbs
Choli: short blouse.
Chote-baba: little boy.
Churail: evil spirit.
Conna, or khana: a meal.

D

Dal: split pulses, usually curried.
Dand: push-up, an exercise.
Darogah: police inspector.
Dewan-bahadur: British-Indian title.
Dhoti: loin cloth worn by male Hindus.
Durwan: watchman.

F

Feri: paroled convict.

G

Godown: store-room.
Go-mata: holy cow, universal mother.
Gowala: cowherd.

H

Hai-allah: Oh, God! an exclamation.
Hai-hai: expression of regret.
Hai-toba: alas.
Halwai: sweetmeat vendor.
Handa: large vessel, usually copper.
Hapta: instalment.
Haram-zada: ungrateful one.
Hare-ram: Oh, God!

J

Jagadamba: universal mother, one of the Hindu goddesses.
Jagirdar: landlord.
Jai: victory.
Janabe-ali: sir.
Janwa: sacred thread worn by high-caste Hindus.
Jee, or Ji: yes, also polite suffix.
Jehad: a religious war.
Jellebi: a sweet.
Juldi-karo: be quick.

K

Kada: steel bangle worn by the Sikhs.
Kaffir: infidel.
Kajal: kohl.
Kamis: shirt.
Kangi: comb.
Kanji: rice gruel.

Kanungo: minor revenue official.
Karta: head of the household.
Katori: metal bowl.
Kaul: sanction.
Kebab: spiced meat-balls.
Kirpan: sword.
Khadav: wooden sandals.
Khaddar: handspun and hand-woven cloth.
Khamosh: silence.
Khes: counterpane.
Khobri: artificial cavity in the throat.
Koel: summer bird.
Koyta: curved knife.
Kshama: forgiveness.
Kukri: Gurkha knife.
Kurnisat: obeisance, a mode of greeting.
Kurta: a muslin shirt.

L

Lakshmi: goddess of wealth.
Lathi: bludgeon.
Lathial: official wielder of the flogging cane.
Loochi: fried wheatcake.

M

Macher-jhol: curried fish.
Mahapooja: elaborate religious performance.
Mahatma: great one.
Mali: gardener.
Malish: message.
Malkhamb: greased climbing pole.
Maloom: understand, know.
Mardan: portion of house set aside for its male members.

Marwari: rich trader caste.
Masala-paan: spiced chewing leaf.
Mohur: coin.
Muharram: Moslem festival.
Murdabad: death to.

N

Nahi: no, never.
Namaskar: a folding of hands, Hindu mode of greeting.
Nanda-deep: eternal lamp.

O

Odhni: scarf.

P

Paan: chewing leaf.
Pagri, also pugri: turban.
Pakoras: fried snacks.
Palla: end of sari worn over shoulder.
Panchas: independent witnesses.
Pandit, also pundit: priest.
Pooja: prayer.
Pungi: reed instrument.
Purdah: system of secluding women, literally screen.

R

Raaj: rule, kingdom.
Roti: bread.

S

Sahib: sir or mister, honorific suffix.
Salaam: salute, greeting.
Salaam-karo: salute (an order).

Salwar: loose trousers.
Sansar: worldly life.
Sanyas: renunciation of worldly ties.
Saraswati: goddess of learning.
Sayonara: good-bye.
Seer: (Indian weight) two lbs.
Shabash: well-done.
Shaitan: devil.
Shikari: hunter.
Sigri: stove.
Sitar: string instrument.
Sondesh: a Bengali sweet.
Soowar: pig.
Sunta: circumcision.
Surai: earthenware vessel.

T

Tabla: drum.
Takli: small spinning wheel.
Tandav: the dance of death.
Tehsildar: revenue officer.
Thali: metal platter.
Thana: station, usually police station.
Til: a variety of pulses.
Tonga: a one-horse carriage.
Tu, also tum: mode of addressing an equal or a junior.

V

Vetal: devil, deity of the criminal tribes.

Y

Yogi: holy man.

Z

Zindabad: long live.